THE LIVING MUST DIE

A novel by

Bill Davidson

BLACK BED
SHEET

The Living Must Die
A Black Bed Sheet/Diverse Media Book
December 2022

ISBN-10: 0-9979276-4-X
ISBN-13: 978-0-9979276-4-1

The Living Must Die

A Black Bed Sheet/Diverse Media Book
Antelope, CA

☼
Dedication

To Alan, Caleb, Lily and Ruby. Acknowledgement – Thanks as always to Nicola for her advice and encouragement and to Nicholas Grabowsky for believing in this book, along with some great guidance.

Chapter

1

Nina

Nina Simeon walked into the apartment she shared with Marcus to find him sitting on the floor, dazed and lazy-eyed. The room, a large one with high ceilings and tall windows, stunk of hash and the speakers were pumping out Burna Boy, loud enough to get another complaint. Blue smoke hazed the air.

He was lounging on cushions set against the bulky leather couch, his usual spot lately. His guitar, she noticed, was leaning against a nearby chair, along with a pen and a pad of paper. Nothing written on it, beyond a couple of aimless looking scribbles.

Nina had hurried across town, anxious with news that ought to have been bad, but was actually good — she was thinking of it as good — wanting to talk to him.

He raised a hand, hey, but she ignored it and crossed instead to the window, throwing it up and looking down for a moment on the bustle of 6th Avenue. When the window was open, like this, it was too noisy, but she didn't close it.

She'd bought this Lower Manhattan apartment when the cash was good, and was wondering how much of a wrench it would be if she had to sell up.

She didn't ponder for long. She snapped the music off and came to stand immediately in front of Marcus, hands on hips, so he had to tip his head, squinting up her unusual length.

"I'm done with it."

He wiped his hand across his face, bringing himself to some sort of awareness.

"Done with what?"

"Modelling. That's it. No more."

All he did was blink. "Yea, you don't need that shit."

Nina sat abruptly and started rolling her own joint, not sure if she really wanted to take the edge of the jagged excitement that was running through her. But it was hard to be high-wired when Marcus was drifting the lower edge of mellow.

"Damn straight I don't. What you got to understand, is this. I've got my life back."

He looked at her, no sign of comprehension there, so she lit up and told him, "SimeonStyle. SimeonStyle is what I'm talking about. Was half-way through college, making my own designs. Only eighteen and I'm putting on my own fucking show, all the stuff I'd designed. Cut and sewed most of it my own self. I ever tell you this?"

He grinned a slow grin. "A hundred times, probably. I guess you're going to tell me again." He waved a languid hand. "It's what you do."

"Sewed it up my*self*. Even hired the hall. Friends from college modelling. Thought it was goin' great and that fuckin Hayley comes up and says…"

He pointed, doing a surprisingly good impression of her agent, getting the smoky Brooklyn pretty much spot on.

2

"You can make a whole lot more as a model, the look you got going."

She pointed right back, determined to make her point. "*You can make a whole lot more as a model, the way you look, girl.* Wrinkly little shit. Well, get this. I'm not stepping on another catwalk, showing most my tits off to those skinny bitches. I'm focussing on my own stuff. Finally making a go of Simeon fuckin' Style. That's all there is to it."

She took a deep drag, passing it to Marcus when he reached out, as she knew he would. What she didn't tell him was how the meeting with her agent, ex-agent, had gone.

Hayley, stick-thin, stick-dry and cigar-voiced, had put her hands flat on the table, never a good sign, and explained the situation like this: "You're still a stunningly beautiful woman, Nina. But, now you're no longer a girl, your features are just too damn strong. Twenty-three and you've filled right out, gotten too wide in the shoulder. Jesus, I told you and told you, didn't I? You're like a goddamn quarterback. You lift weights, or what?"

Nina crossed her arms. "Not hardly."

"You gotta face reality, darlin'. Designers are looking for *ephemeral* just now. They want waifs. Not somebody who looks like they might get down off the catwalk and punch their lights out."

Nina's response, "Yea, well fuck them, then." And, as an afterthought, "Fuck you too."

She had wanted to tell the scrawny, dried-up little fucker to fuck off almost since the first day she met her. Definitely since the first time she'd complained about her weight. Since the day the woman convinced her to change her name from Simms to Simeon, on no better grounds than she looked a lot like the old-timey singer, Nina Simone. She told her that too, all of it. The last words she ever spoke to Hayley Bennet-Tindall.

Now she watched as Marcus closed his eyes and pulled in another lungful of smoke, holding on to it. Not fazed by the fact that her income, their income, was about to take a high-dive. Maybe he'd think about that later.

"Get anything done today?"

She tried to avoid any kind of edge to her voice, making it sound like she was just curious, even though she'd seen the empty pad. Him sitting there like he was barely hanging onto consciousness.

He blew out a long, smoky breath and found something to look at on the skirting board. "Don't nag me."

"Was just askin'."

She could have said a lot more, but held her tongue.

Nina had met Marcus Cole at a show in Paris not quite two years back, in the days when she was still sometimes referred to as a supermodel, and he was described as the coming thing in Afrobeat.

Looking back, she could see that she'd hated modelling for a long time. Maybe since the start. She kept finding herself viewing the whole scene, not like she was part of it, more like a watcher from afar. None of it seemed real and, if it was, it damn well shouldn't be.

That's pretty much what she was thinking that day in Paris when she was pushed and prodded and primped into another *creation* and got her big old pout in place to sashay down the catwalk. But not when she caught sight of Marcus. In the front row, and longer-limbed than anybody else in the room, he drew the

4

eye, making her look at him even when she told herself not to. An unfeasibly tall black guy with blacker tats crawling over his neck. A little beard, but not teased and trimmed tight. He probably just hadn't shaved in a while. Dressed in faded jeans and a plain grey tee. Not a logo in sight.

She made her eyes sweep over the heads of the audience, cool and heavy lidded, coming to the end of the walk and her final pose, bare hip and most of her ass showing.

A lot of nods out there. A few oohs and aahs. One consciously audible 'Stunningly crafted'. Her eyes slid back to Marcus Cole all by themselves, stalling at his feet, which were longer than feet should naturally be, bare, and none too clean.

He saw her looking and smiled his lazy smile. She didn't even know who he was, this rangy guy, but she smiled right back. She told the designer, who was royally pissed, that she just couldn't help herself.

Later, in his Paris loft, when they finally had to stop screwing, he picked up his guitar. Sitting there, naked and cross-legged, the soulful sound he made was just about the opposite of what she expected. Vulnerable and sad, rather than arrogant and in your face. She told him, "You just made me cry."

***

After the show in Paris, the one where Nina pissed off her too-hot-to-talk designer by stopping dead at the end of the catwalk with a big goofy grin plastered on her face, she pretty much went into hiding for a month. She didn't go alone.

That first morning with Marcus, which started sometime mid-afternoon, they went to a little café in Saint-Germain and ate a huge and delicious meal. All Nina had wanted was a snack, *une petite snack*, she told

5

the waiter. But such a thing didn't seem to be available, or even comprehendible.

So, with platters of seafood and salad and glasses of wine before them, Nina asked him, "What you doing in Paris anyway?"

"I'm in hiding."

He said it straightforwardly, popping a piece of baguette into his mouth and savouring it. "Isn't this just the best?"

For some reason, she'd expected him to be African, or maybe Jamaican, from the Caribbean someplace. His accent was Queens, with something very different in there that she was only minutes away from pinning down.

"It's going to make me fat."

He grinned, like he was imagining that and thought it was a good idea. She couldn't help but return the smile, just like that first time.

"What you hiding from?"

"Everything."

She sipped her wine. It was irritating, in a way, the way the French were so self-righteous about the quality of their food and drink, and even worse that they lived up to their own hype. The bastards.

"You're making a crap job of it, then. Turning up to the fashion event of the season. Sitting right in the front row."

He shrugged. "I knew you'd be there."

She barked out a laugh, but his eyes were on hers and they were serious.

"Nah."

"Honestly. That's the only reason I went. In the hope I would see you in the flesh."

She fluttered her eyelids. It couldn't be helped. "Well, you did plenty of that."

He nodded and almost smiled, but then shook his head. His expression saying it was all too much, and that his belief in what just happened might be coming along in a little while.

"Yea. I turn up, not knowing if I'll even get inside and, before I know it, somebody recognises me. This is brand new by the way, wouldn't have happened even two months ago. He made a real fuss about it. Slotted me right in at the front."

He looked embarrassed and baffled; at a loss. She smiled. "Did you enjoy it?"

"The special treatment? Nah."

He shivered at the memory of it. Pulled a face.

"No, I mean the show."

He took a moment over that, and she found she liked the look of him thinking.

"Kind of. But there was something about the whole thing that…sorry if this offends you, but I can't stand the whole fashion thing."

She bridled, but only slightly. "Let me guess. You figure it's vacuous? Pointless? Self-obsessed?"

"All of the above. Plus it hurts the climate."

"What doesn't? It's art, Marcus, same as yours. Maybe more important. More fundamental. Most folks first step towards creating their own identity."

He shrugged, not interested, and attended to some prawns.

"So, you're in hiding, but accidentally attended a global press event in order to cop off with a model you caught showing her air-brushed ass off in Vogue."

"Nobody would dare air-brush your ass."

"It's happened. They don't even ask. Can I come too?"

"What?"

7

"Into hiding."

"What have you got to hide from?"

"You tell first."

"Ok."

But he wasn't telling. He was frowning at his plate. She let that go on for several seconds, might have even reached a minute before her patience ran out.

"Well?"

He looked up at her, his expression calculating. She thought, he's trying to work out how much he can tell me, the stranger he's just spent the night with.

"I've been weak. Stupid."

She speared a piece of lettuce and used it to do a double tap in the air. "Stupid. Weak. Got it."

"Was in a band. We were pretty damn good. Together for five, six years plugging away. Got signed and thought, this is it. We were on our way."

"Like hundreds of others."

"Yup. Bounced from manager to agent to record company. Went on tour after tour. Always one step away."

"Uh-huh."

"Then, I know this is an old story, I got offered a deal. Not we, just me. Playing different music. Looking different. Packaged up, you know?"

"I know. You take it?"

"Both hands."

"But your album is…you've made it big, right?"

"Label thinks I could be huge."

"So, shit, man. Go for it!"

He switched to a posh old English gent accent, the change in voice and demeanour so sudden it took her by surprise.

8

"I've already been for it, old girl." He frowned, raising his chin high, his expression one of high-camp distaste. "And I didn't *like* it."

She guffawed. "You can do accents."

He dropped the act, wincing, making her think he was embarrassed. "Just that one. My dad, actually."

"You're going to have to explain that one. You look…" she waved her fork in his direction.

"Dad was black, and posh, and English. Dorset, actually." He switched back into the accent. "A thoroughly decent chap, old school, but had to work his socks off for every penny. Eton and Cambridge, don't you know."

"Eton. Where those rich boys wear top hats?"

"Yea, I've got a photo of him dressed like that, and don't think that was easy for him. Not at all." A grimace made its way up his shoulders but didn't quite reach his face.

"He'd be embarrassed of me, if he could see me now. The point I'm making, though, was that I got the exact thing I'd been fighting for. What I thought I wanted most in all the world. Like an obsession, you know?"

"Yea. I know."

"And now…"

He leaned in, making her think that this was the first time he'd ever said this out loud. "Now I don't want it anymore. I don't."

He was talking about his career, being handed the chalice of fame and finding it undrinkable. Old news for Nina, who was suddenly more interested in his father, the black guy who went to Eton, walking about wearing tail coats and high collared shirts, surrounded by all those privileged white boys.

"He's not around now? Your dad."

9

"Him and Mom both. An accident."

She didn't attempt a sympathetic expression. "Auto-wreck?"

He shook his head and rolled his eyes, the thing you did when talking about how dumb your parents were.

"That'd be way too mundane. Their car went off a cliff. Tried to drive up to our holiday home, a middle of nowhere place we have at Bourget Lake, up in the White Mountains, in their Merc convertible."

Then, catching himself, apparently feeling the need to explain. "This was after years of warning me not to attempt that road in anything other than a serious off-road vehicle."

Nina sat back, looking at him.

He put his head on one side, neither of them eating now. "You're beginning to form a picture. Thinking, wait now. This guy ain't from the streets."

"Something like that."

"I'm from the streets. Ones with scrollwork gates and their own security patrols. Doesn't mean I have to look like that. Or act like it. Your turn."

"I didn't set out to be a model."

"No?"

She shook her head. "Nu-uh. No way. Was half-way through college, making my own designs. Only eighteen and I'm putting on my own show, all the stuff I'd designed, cut and sewed most of it myself. I got my own label, still. SimeonStyle, but you won't have heard of it, it's not exactly thriving. Too busy being somebody else's model."

"So, how come you are one?"

She forked another mouthful of salad into her mouth, and sipped some wine.

"I'll tell you sometime, it's not that interesting really. There's one thing I don't get, though."

"What's that?"

"If we're hiding out, and you've got some lakeside house in the middle of nowhere, what are we doing in Paris?"

Chapter

2

Alice

Alice Simeon was four years old when Nina woke her from sleep, gripping her arms hard enough to hurt and hushing her. Bending over in the dark to whisper, "Got to be *quiet*, baby. Be quiet for mommy."

Alice wasn't quiet. She had been fast asleep in the damp mess of blankets that counted for their bed, the last thing she remembered was watching her mother sewing by the light of a candle, and now here she was, wide-eyed and holding her too tight, her voice whispery and scared. It scared her too, so she squealed, "Mommy!"

Then Nina's hand was over her mouth, clamping down, and Alice panicked.

They were living in the rear of the ruined shop at this time. A tiny, burned-out wreck of a place that leaked when it rained and smelled of damp and old smoke. The front shop was where her mom measured her ladies and sewed and sewed all day, till she was cranky and her cut-off fingers hurt so it brought her to tears. The tiny back room was where they slept and ate, when they had something to eat.

Alice bucked and screamed, "Mommy!"

Then there were other noises, urgent and heavy thumps from the front shop and her mom let go, no longer trying to hush her.

Instead, she stood, shouting, bellowing at the top of her voice. "Fuck it, then."

As loud as that was, it was nothing compared to the gun that was suddenly in her hand, sparking and banging in the dim light. Her mother roared as she fired, huge and terrifying as the gun exploded in hot sparks, the noise so great it hurt. Alice rolled into a ball as something smacked hard into the wall behind her, scattering wood chips and plaster. The room filled with smoke and the smell of burning.

She put her hands over her ears, closed her eyes, and screamed. Opened them again and her mother was gone. The gun banged from the front room and Alice rolled over to see, as more shots were fired, wanting her mother by her. A man shouted, an ugly voice yelling ugly words, and the wall between them shuddered under a massive blow, as if it might fall over.

"Mommy!"

Another huge crash, and then grunting and panting, a sound like animals fighting. She ran to the strips of plastic that acted as a barrier in the doorway but paused, not sure what to make of the noises. They weren't like anything she'd ever heard before.

When her mother cried out in pain, though, she burst through. Her mom was on the floor, wriggling underneath a heavy man. Another man lay nearby, but he wasn't moving. The heavy man hit her mother, punching her head, making her cry out. Alice ran across the messy floor and launched herself onto his back, shouting.

A second later, something slammed into her, so that she flew across the shop and struck the wooden counter. She yelled in pain, tasting blood, and the man atop her mom bared his teeth at her.

He was terrifying, dark and dirty and massive. Even his smell was dangerous. He growled, angry but grinning, like a huge crazy dog, enjoying himself. He grinned even wider, but then stopped. His expression changed, sliding from fierce to something else she had no name for. The closest she got was sad. He looked about himself as though he didn't know where he was. Then he lurched, like he couldn't bear his own weight, lurched again and fell away as her mom struggled to her feet. In her hand was the knife she used to gut deer, bloody up to her elbow. The side of her face shone with blood.

She glared at her daughter. "Tol' you to be quiet! I tell you quiet, you…"

The end of that sentence died. She shook her head and grimaced hard. Then her eyes turned upwards into her head, and she slid sideways to the floor.

"Mommy! Mommy, wake up!"

The man was groaning, holding his stomach in both hands as blood poured between his fingers, trying again to stand. He got to his knees, and dragged a foot under him, readying to get up. Alice screamed one last time, screamed for her mother, but Nina didn't move.

<u>Chapter</u>

3

James

James Spears had no memory of his mother, or his father. He knew that he must have had one of each, but it didn't feel like that was something that had anything to do with him. He never felt he'd lost a thing by not knowing his parents, although some seemed to believe that loss should be the aching void in the centre of his life. They also seemed to believe he should be desperate to replace them.

No. His first clear memory was of Ana-Maria, playing catch in the corridor of Bertillon's Home for Foundlings. The sun was streaming through the tall windows, making the waxed pine floor glow wherever it touched. The ball was blue. The sound it made when it smacked the floor was hard and sharp, almost like it could shatter.

Bertillon's was set in a big old house, a bona-fide early Victorian mansion, and one of the oldest houses still standing in Manchester. All the rooms had high ceilings and cornices, except for the attic dormitory, which was set aside for the youngest boys. The windows were tall, timber framed and mostly single glazed, the rooms even taller, which meant that it was draughty and often bitterly cold in winter. James could recall leaning over the headboard of his cot-like bed, so he could use his finger to draw in the ice on the inside of a window pane. But perversely, he could never recall actually being cold. Not in the worst New Hampshire winter.

The place smelled of wax polish, boiled potatoes and meat loaf. It was home to something like twenty to thirty kids at any one time, ranging from less than a year old, to fifteen. At fifteen it was time to take your leave, and make your way in the world.

Every so often, maybe as much as two or three times in any year, a man and woman, invariably alive – because only the living could adopt, that was only natural – would arrive and there would be a buzz of excitement. The children learned to tell when these couples were going to visit. The day before there would be a purge on dust and dirt and everything that was already polished to a sheen would be polished further.

The children would be asked to wear their best, even though the girls' smocks and boys' uniforms were patched and worn down. There would be baths, there would be haircuts.

Doctor Bertillon invariably greeted the couple at the big double doors and walked the grounds, if the weather permitted. Smiling and using his hands to show this and that, the monkey bars and the swings. The sandpit and the little sports field. They would walk and talk and all the watching kids knew what they were there for.

James had sat in many classes, knowing they were at the back – it was forbidden to turn to stare at them. He had played soccer and table tennis with them watching. He'd sang in the choir and played the piano.

He had also been called to sit across the table from those couples, several times before he was even five years old. He'd surely been chosen because he was such a cute little boy – that very word used more than once. A neat and tidy boy, with white-blonde hair and pale blue eyes, exceptionally small for his age.

It never led anywhere.

After the latest of many interviews over a period of years, James at this point eleven, Bertillon took him aside. The doctor was a short, dark-haired man, with a tight trimmed face and a tight trimmed beard and rimless glasses. No matter the weather, he wore a suit and a pressed cotton shirt with pearl cufflinks. Bizarrely, he had several suits. He probably had a dozen, every dark colour but black and all of weave so fine you couldn't see the yarn. Also brightly patterned bow ties, often in fabric that gleamed as much as his shoes.

"Mr and Mrs Fabreguettes were really nice people didn't you think so, James?"

James met the man's gaze calmly. "I guess."

"A lovely couple. But you weren't nice to them, were you?"

"I was nice."

Bertillon sighed. "I know what you're doing."

"I'm not doing anything."

"Why do you think there are none of The Returned here? I mean children."

The question came as a surprise, and James had to work hard to keep his face blank. The surprise being that he simply hadn't noticed.

"I don't know."

"Give it a go, though." He patted James's knee, as though encouraging him in a game, but not fooling anybody. "Try to think it through."

"Perhaps there are no Returned children who are orphans."

Bertillon shook his head. "You know that isn't so. Here's something to chew on. Why did George leave, after his accident?"

James hadn't given that any thought at the time – it was just something that happened – but had to now. George had been two years older than him, a quiet boy who kept himself to himself but nonetheless could be counted as one of his few friends. One morning, around a year back, James had heard Karen Gill, a girl of about his own age with curly red hair and redder cheeks, beginning to scream. It didn't build up from a shout or a wail, one moment he was in the silence of the classroom, working on a trigonometry problem, the next the screaming started.

She was at the rear of the house, and the entire class ran to the window to see her standing on the slabbed patio, set out with picnic tables and benches.

She stood wide-eyed and rigid, hands to her face as she screamed and screamed. In front of her was a bundle of clothes.

Then Bertillon was running, shouting something as he went. James was just one of many that spilled out to ring the patio, where George lay in a pool of blood that spread as they watched, his limbs weirdly twisted. His eyes were fluttering, going from confused to rolling into the back of his head, to confused again. He opened his mouth to speak but choked instead on a gout of blood.

Bertillon knelt beside him with his doctor's bag, hands moving quickly to find the damage and stem the bleeding. He was saying, "George! George, stay with us. Stay awake."

The carers stood impassively by, their arms at their sides, and so did most of the children. This was certainly horrible, but James found that he could quieten his face, just like Ana-Maria, and so his mind.

Still, he had to ask her, "What happened?"

Ana-Maria pointed to the open attic window, some fifty feet above where George now lay. "He fell."

Bertillon, looking desperate, his hands and shirt bloody, glared around him. "For God's sake, ladies! Take these children out of here."

Ana-Maria said, "His skull is crushed, he cannot live."

"He might yet! If I can…"

George shuddered, and convulsed, arching his back so that Bertillon had to take his hands away. When he relaxed, even a child could see he was dead.

Bertillon's face crumpled as a sob went through him. He closed his eyes for a long moment and then looked around, and now his expression was angry. It was as though he was angry with Ana-Maria.

He shook a bloodied finger at her. "Take. The Children. Away."

That wasn't the last time James saw George. The last time was later that day, when he happened to glance out of the window and caught sight of him walking out of the grounds. There had been nobody with him.

That was his last sight of George but, from time to time, he would see Returned children in town, going about their business. Sometimes just standing. Some as young as four or five and never with an adult.

James finally answered Bertillon's question. "They don't need adults."

The doctor sat back in his chair, apparently delighted with this. "That's it! That's it, exactly. So!"

He leaned forward again, the chair squeaking under him, his eyes fixed on James.

"So, what does that tell you?"

When James couldn't answer, he answered for him. "It tells you, no matter what they claim, The Returned are not the same as they were before they died. The living George *needed* adult supervision."

He raised a finger. "We are offered a very, very particular view of things, in this establishment, different from most folks. Maybe we get to see things just that bit clearer, what with all the carers being dead. Do you know what they said?"

The last question was rushed in at the end, like he was trying to trip him up.

"What who said?"

"The Fabreguettes. They said talking to you was like talking to one of The Returned. Not the first people to say that, actually. You're struggling to keep your face blank."

James was surprised to realise that was true. Bertillon had surprised him into looking surprised. He calmed his features.

"Don't you want to have parents, James? Be adopted by a loving family?"

"No."

"What do you want?"

"To stay here."

Bertillon looked off, gazing into the garden now, a scene of children playing.

"George wasn't the first to have an *accident*. I'm sure he won't be the last."

He turned again to James. "Have you been thinking about that? Having an accident?"

"No."

"There's no point in lying. If you want to die, you'll find a way."

The man had a point. "Yes."

"You would be the third, from this orphanage. You love Ana-Maria, don't you?"

No point in denying that either. It was more than endless games of soccer and hide and seek with Ana-Maria. It was more than the fact that she had once held him in her arms for the entire night after he had removed most of the skin from his shin in a fall from the Sugar Maple behind the sandpit.

"Yes."

Bertillon was suddenly intense. "The Returned don't love like we do. She doesn't love you."

"She does."

"She'll say that. Think about this, though. You have only a tiny amount of time as a first lifer. A tiny amount of time when you can feel the way you do, get enthusiastic, find things funny. Laugh. Nobody knows when that time is up and, when it is, why…"

He spread his hands wide, smiling. "Why, then you can Return. We all will."

"Ok."

He pointed at James's face. "A lot of the kids here do what you're doing now, keep their expressions blank. It's only natural, as the only carers I can afford and still keep the home going are dead ones. What I mean is, that the children here act more like The Returned than normal folks. And you, you do it more than most."

Bertillon leaned right in and took his hand. "I'm begging you not to have an accident, son. You have your whole life ahead of you. For God's sake, live it."

21

James wouldn't have lived it, that was a racing certainty, if it hadn't been for a girl called Alice Simeon.

Chapter
4
Nina

Less than a week after their conversation in Paris, Nina sat in the passenger seat of an elderly Land Rover, the rattling, noisy sort that looked and felt like some kind of early jeep. She could see what Marcus' father had been talking about, when he said this road needed a serious off-road vehicle. Some of the inclines were so steep that they were looking into the sky, leaning right back into the seats, then they were over the other side, heading downhill, and the brakes were squealing, working overtime.

They'd flown into New York two days before, staying in Nina's Manhattan apartment before heading north on 91, a drive of about four hours in a rented Ford. They stopped in Manchester, a small industrial-looking city that Nina had never been to, ate pizza in a town-centre restaurant Marcus liked, and picked up some provisions. Another hour and a half on 93 brought them into a tiny town called Dorchester.

Marcus told her, "This is exactly what brought Dad here in the first place. He was brought up in Dorchester, the one in Dorset, England. There's places all around here with Dorset names."

"What, he was just curious?"

"That's pretty much it. On nothing more than a whim we ended up living out here half the year. The warm half."

Marcus steered the Land Rover through the little town, waving to one or two people, who waved back, and got onto 118 heading South again, Dorchester Road.

"We take a left just after Buck's Corner, onto Tilly Whim Trail."

"Tilly Whim? That's what it's called?"

"Another name outta Dorset. You'll see."

118 was a standard two lane blacktop, but Tilly Whim Trail was Nina's idea of a farm road, little more than a single-track of dusty white stone, packed hard. They hadn't gone a hundred yards before Marcus pulled into a wide cement lot and stopped in front of a modern warehouse building. Off to the side was a small ranch-style house and a woman, middle-aged, Asian, stepped out from it, holding her hand up in a wave. Marcus waved back, climbing out, motioning Nina to do the same.

The woman called out, "You staying for a bite, Marky?"

"Just picking up the Rover and pressing on, thanks, Mei-Ling. Andy about?"

In answer, she simply pointed to where a short, stocky man of about thirty was walking out of the warehouse. He was wearing double denim and boots, like Marcus himself, but also heavy work-gloves, which he pulled off as he approached, smiling wide.

"Marky"

"Hey, man."

As they shook, he turned to include Nina.

"Andy Lee, Nina Simeon."

The man had a very wide smile. "Well, I can see that. You two staying for dinner?"

The woman from the porch answered, sounding pissed off. "No, they rather eat crap out of tins than a proper cooked meal."

She waved her hand in dismissal and disappeared into the house.

Neither Marcus nor Andy, surely her son, seemed to take it seriously.

Andy said, "The Rover's all charged and ready to go. Changed over your gas bottle up there, fixed those shingles. Everything looking good."

Marcus left the Ford where it was and they followed Andy into the warehouse. It was packed with everything from house doors to ride-on mowers and rototillers. Off to one side was an ancient green Land Rover, which Marcus patted, like an old friend.

Andy helped them load their stuff, chatting all the while, calling Marcus Marky.

When they pulled away, Nina said, "Marky?"

"What I was called when I was a kid. My Dad and old Mr Lee worked so hard on Tilly Whim, getting it habitable, because it absolutely wasn't, they got to be buddies. I've known Andy since before I started grade school."

Pebbles popped under the tyres and pinged off the underside of the car.

"I see why you wanted the Land Rover."

He laughed at that. Even whacked the wheel a couple of times with the heel of his hand. "No, you really don't. Not yet."

As they climbed, Nina noticed the occasional house or farm, but soon there was nothing to see but trees, mainly Spruce and Fir, mixed in with Birch and Pine. It grew cooler, and smelled greener, the trees closer, sunlight still strong but no longer constant, flickering at them through overhanging branches. The tyres crunched on, everything rattled, and behind that, nothing but birdsong. Nina didn't want to complain, but she was tired and hungry and this car was the most uncomfortable damn thing she'd ever been in.

It seemed that the climb was never ending. She was just about to mention that, when the road flattened and opened up. Marcus pulled off to the left and stopped, grinning at her.

"We here?"

She asked that even though she could see they weren't anywhere. They were sitting before an ugly gate of rusty steel and weld mesh, ten feet tall and heavily chained. It looked industrial and out of place here, amongst the trees and goldenrod. Beside it there was a peeling sign, bullet holed and barely legible. It read, **Tilly Whim Only. Private Road- No Trespassers.**

Marcus was already out and removing the padlock, unwinding the chain so he could push the gates open. Beyond, an even rougher road led through the trees.

"Not far now. This is where we really need the Land Rover."

He waggled his eyebrows at her, climbing back in and looking suddenly like a delighted ten-year-old. "From here on it gets really rather hairy."

Nina didn't tell him that he looked like a kid. Nor did she tell him he had just sounded all the way English, not Queens at all. She would bet this was a line his Dorchester, Dorset father had used every time they came here, and he didn't even know he was doing it. She'd been picking up on that more and more. Every so often the Queens accent would slip, like a curtain being pulled aside, and he sounded like a completely different person.

His father hadn't been exaggerating. Branches on either side overtopped the road and scraped and thumped the already well scraped and thumped paintwork. Tiny stones and sometimes good-sized rocks clattered the floor pan almost constantly. They rounded a bend and had to roll to a stop, finding themselves face to ugly face with a full-grown moose.

The moose regarded them steadily for a second, before turning and blundering into the forest. It occurred to Nina that there was hardly any room for it inside there. That was thick forest and it was a bulky item.

It seemed that there was nothing flat around here, and they were either going steeply up, or steeply down. There was a long handle bolted to the metal dashboard, and she found she had to keep gripping it, often while she was stamping hard on a brake pedal that wasn't there.

She had noticed a chainsaw in the rear of the car. They only needed it once on the drive, to cut up a tree that had fallen over onto the road, but they had to stop twice more, so that Marcus could drag branches away.

The first sight of Lake Bourget was breathtaking, partly because it was a breathtaking sight, and partly because the trees on their left suddenly disappeared, replaced by nothing but fresh air, and a dizzying hundred-foot drop to the water below. There was no barrier, and the edge of the road didn't look too solid. It looked *crumbly*. Marcus rolled to a stop, maybe giving her a chance to appreciate the view, the sudden freshness of the air, maybe just enjoying the moment and its effect on her.

She grabbed the dashboard handle. "Surely this can't be safe."

He shot her a slightly crazy grin. "You'll get used to it."

Nina thought, *no. I won't.* She tightened her grip and considered climbing out, telling him, turn around first chance you get. I don't care how nice this place is, take me home. But he was already moving again, and the moment was past.

Soon, they were struggling up the steepest grade so far, then it eased and widened into a flat space before a long slow drop, all the way to the lakeside.

James let the car ground to a halt. "Tilly Whim."

If her first sight of the lake had been breathtaking, Tilly Whim was simply a shock. Despite the fact that he had been unusually closed mouthed about it, she had made it up in her own mind, and come to imagine a tall white Victorian house, with steep roof and fancy gables.

She frowned, trying to make sense of what she was looking at.

Bourget Lake stretched away to their left and into the bruised distance beyond, layers of snow-capped mountains, all the way to Canada for all she knew. In the late afternoon sun, the water glimmered, near-blinding sparks of silver over blue, fading towards a deeper green in the distance.

Facing the lake was what looked like an abandoned frontier town, a cluster of dusty clapboard houses, some nothing more than ruins. The building nearest the water was the only one with two levels. It had the look of a school-house from television Westerns, something like *Little House on the Prairie*. There was one very large barn-like building and, stretching away towards the mountains and the trees,

28

a wide pool of black-mirrored water, with rusting iron gantries hanging above it.

The whole village, if that's what it was, was set in a flat, cleared area the size of two or three football fields. It looked as though the mountain had been dug and ground away to make the space, so that it ended in an ugly wall of scarred granite, fifty feet high. Trees hung over the high edge of that sheer cliff, with some scrubby bushes clinging to its face. A few rough blocks of stone, the largest the size of a truck, lay amongst weeds.

She turned to James, who looked like he wanted to laugh at her expression.

"The fuck is this?"

"Tilly Whim."

Nina just shook her head.

"Tilly Whim isn't a house." He waggled his fingers in delighted hocus-pocus. "It's a town. A *ghost* town."

"You have your own ghost town?"

He shrugged. "There's a few of them about the mountains. Somebody has to own it. My dad couldn't resist."

She gave him a long flat look. "You've brought me to a ghost town?"

He put his hands up. "The schoolhouse is nice inside. You'll see. We've got our own dock, look."

Nina had noticed the dock, a rickety timber finger pointing towards a bobbing sailboat, but that wasn't what she was looking at. She was looking at Marcus.

"The schoolhouse. Seriously? Does it even have electric?"

"Sort of. We put solar panels on the roof. And it's got a generator, if you really think you need it."

They were staring at each other, Marcus looking disappointed and confused. "You don't think this is cool? We can get by without electricity."

Nina nodded slowly. "I see now why you were hiding out in Paris."

Marcus opened his mouth, and shook his head, but contented himself with a loud exhale through his nose before he put the car back in gear. The brakes squealed horribly for the whole journey down, making her wince, her grip tight again on the handle.

At the bottom of the slope, they had to stop at a wide area of gravel and Witchgrass, so that Marcus could unlock another ugly metal gate. He did that in silence, not looking at her, and that was just fine. He drove through and into the compound, if that's what it was, following a track to the building that she had thought was a schoolhouse, and turned out to be a schoolhouse.

There was nothing pretty about this building. It was weathered clapboard, two blocky grey stories of it. The windows were covered by steel shutters of rust-stained white.

The first thing Marcus did was walk around the property. Despite his claims of safety, he brought a nickel-plated Smith and Wesson out of a pack. Put it in the pocket on his jacket.

He saw her looking.

"In case of snakes."

"How would that work on a grizzly?"

"You don't get them this far East."

"What do you get?"

"Brown Bears."

"So?"

"Just annoy it, probably. Don't start freaking out. City girl."

"Yea, like you're Davy Crocket. Do you get bears here?"

"Not often. They don't bother you, if you don't bother them."

They didn't meet a bear, or see a snake, although Marcus said there were definitely snakes around, mostly nothing to worry about. They walked around the outside of the schoolhouse first. It was bigger than a standard family home in the 'burbs, and as grey as a building could possibly be. A wide porch ran all the way around.

Although it had seemed shabby at first sight, it was obviously in decent order. The satellite dish looked out of place on a high pole to the rear, but Nina was pleased to see it. Out back, a line of White Mountain Gas bottles stood inside a weldmesh cage.

Marcus unlocked the double doors of a lean-to shed, and she caught the smell of kerosene. She was relieved to see the modern, high-tech generator in there too.

Nina's eye kept being drawn towards the other houses, most of which had collapsed in on themselves. There was what looked like an old-style store of some kind, like Ike Godsey's from *The Waltons*, and what was maybe once a stable.

Apparently satisfied all was in order, Marcus took her up the steps to the house itself, thumping his feet hard on the rough pine boards of the porch.

The main doors, which faced the lake, were tall and double-wide. Marcus unclipped the steel shutters, setting them aside to reveal modern French doors, almost floor to ceiling. Light poured into the place now. They walked into a room, so large it had to take up most of the ground floor, and she could see that inside of the house looked comfortable, if a mismatch of old and new. Two bulky and saggy leather couches, covered in rugs. A modern flat screen. A turntable with the biggest speakers she had ever seen inside a house, Wharfedale, alongside a long line of vinyl.

The floor was pine, but scattered liberally with patterned rugs that favoured deep red. Indian and Chinese, she thought. White laminate drawer sets and bookcases, from Ikea by their looks. Three different guitars, including a cherry Gibson Les Paul leaning against an elderly Fender amplifier.

She walked into the middle and did a slow spin. "This was the classroom, right?"

"Right."

She had expected the walls to be wood lined, just like the outside, but they were standard board. Now she could see it properly, those walls had to be more than two feet thick.

Marcus, following her eyes, said, "It was kind of a hobby for my dad, bordering on obsession. Working on this place, I mean, him and old Mr Lee. Always doing something, bringing stuff in, sawing and nailing and digging."

Marcus patted a wall. "He insulated the hell out of it."

"I guess it must be cold here in winter."

He grinned at that, beginning to relax again, maybe seeing that she wasn't so tense. "You wouldn't want to be here in winter, Jesus. Couldn't even get here, once the first snow hits. Couldn't get out if you did."

"So, purely a summer place?"

"Well, Spring is kind of beautiful, and Fall." He shook his head. "All the trees, the colour they get on them. It's kind of mind-blowing. But you got to watch it, make sure you don't get caught out. Any snow at all, you're in a jam."

She pointed at the log burner, a black behemoth with double glass doors, clearly a recent addition. "Use this much?"

"Any excuse. At this altitude it can get chilly at night, even after a long day of hot sun. And I love a fire."

She stood for a moment, staring out at the long line of the lake, then turned and smiled, pulling him in for a long kiss. "Maybe we'll sit in front of it tonight."

She pressed her finger into his chest. "But, right now, I'm starving. I'm a different person when I'm hungry."

He nodded, like he was agreeing with her, hugged once and let go. "I'll rustle us up some pasta. You go explore. I won't be twenty minutes."

The house was gloomy, with most of the shutters still blocking the sunlight. The kitchen was basic, but functional and, when she hit the overhead light switch, it lit up brightly. There was a four-ring burner, sitting atop a worksurface, with a rubber hose leading through the wall, probably to the White Mountain gas bottles she saw earlier. Also, an ancient triple ring electric stove, a monster from another age in cream enamelled iron. Everything was clean, except for a layer of dust.

Marcus came in, carrying the box of provisions they had bought in Manchester, and saw her looking at the two stoves.

"Sometimes we have gas but no electric. Sometimes we have electric but no gas. There ought to be enough power to run the lights, and I'll have the shutters off in no time."

The next downstairs room was, and this was a relief, a big bathroom with a flushing toilet, which she used. The water that came through the tap was muddy at first, but she waited and, after a while, it ran clear. So cold it stung her fingers.

She opened another room, finding it set out like a study, with a big desk and stuffed leather captain's chair. As well as getting the food going, Marcus was hurrying around the outside, unclipping the shutters, letting light in. She sat at the desk and watched him working as he removed the shutters from this room. He didn't see her in there, even when she waved, which was a strange feeling.

There were two other ground floor rooms; a store and something that seemed to be used as a recording studio, including a very high-tech mixing desk. So much for The King of the Wild Frontier.

The place smelled dusty, but not damp. She took her time going into each room, not quite trusting there would be no snakes around, or maybe some kind of outsized mountain spider.

Upstairs, there was one big bedroom, with a King size and built-in wardrobes, and two smaller bedrooms with double beds. None of them were made up, but everything seemed clean enough. Light streamed through slits in the shutters, striping the place.

There were two other rooms, but they were either empty or had storage boxes and odds and ends of furniture in them. Returning to the master, she turned slowly around, taking it in. Nice enough, she supposed.

Downstairs again, she poked around the living room, smiling to hear Marcus singing to himself as he cooked. It smelled great, making her stomach grumble noisily.

There were lumpy oil paintings on the walls, and blow-ups of some old photographs. One she recognised as this same room, a very old photo taken from the exact place she was standing now, which was no doubt the idea of whoever put it here. Marcus' father, she guessed. It showed lines of desks, with unsmiling boys and girls in smocks and short trousers sitting behind them. An austere woman stood in the aisle, the teacher in front of her blackboard, which still bore the sums the children had to calculate on that long-ago day. Nina amused herself for a few minutes, matching up features of the room, then moved on. The next photograph was another old black and white, this of a working quarry. It was, she realised the pool she had noticed earlier, but before it had water in it, easily recognisable because of the cranes lifting slices of stone from the hole. It was deep, and busy with spectacularly moustachioed men in trousers and shirt sleeves, a couple of sad-looking ponies in there too.

She wandered into the kitchen to find Marcus standing over a boiling pot of pasta. Another pot with sauce was warming next to it, and the little table already held an opened container of mascarpone and a jar of olives.

He handed her a glass of red wine. "Five minutes."

***

They ate overlooking the lake and, even though it was just dried penne and shop-bought sauce, it hit the spot better than that fancy meal in Paris.

Wiping her plate with a hunk of bread, she said, "See, I'll be better company now."

35

He leaned back and sipped his wine. "Want to take a little wander around the town? Or is it too creepy?"

She pointed her glass at him. "You have your very own ghost town."

"Pretty cool, huh?"

She had to smile. "It's cool."

The town was really one street of eight houses, plus Ike Godsey's store and the stable, backed by a big mill building. Marcus told her. "It's named after a quarry in Dorset, Tilly Whim."

"Weird name."

"Even across there it's weird. The locals figure the guy first had it, the one in Dorset I mean, was called Tilly. And the old derrick's for pulling out the stone were called whims."

"So, this place?"

"Opened first as a quarry. This is the Granite State, and the redstone granite out there is meant to be something special. They faced buildings as far away as Washington with the stone brought out of here."

"They took it out that road?"

He pointed to the water. "Floated it out on barges. But it was always too remote to be viable, even with the fancy granite, so it went bust. Then the logging started and that's when the town got built."

"So, what happened?"

"Smallpox. There's a sad little graveyard near the forest edge. Bad business decisions, according to my dad. Whatever. It just didn't work out."

The first house they came to was in decent enough shape, and had a name carved into the wood above the door. *Old Joe's Cottage.*

Nina wiped the glass and looked inside. "Jesus. It's still got furniture."

"Want to go in?"

She shook her head. "Maybe later. Looks like it's full of spiders, and snakes."

Marcus nodded, serious. "Might be a few bears in there as well."

They wandered around the store, which still had a few ancient cans with faded labels on its dusty shelves, Shaker's String Beans and Dogwood Brand Tomatoes. She picked one or two of them up, sniffed them.

"Wonder what's in here now."

"I opened one when I was a kid. Corned beef. It was just a stinking lump of black stuff."

She put them back, looking around. "Ok, I admit it. This place is something else. In a creepy kind of way."

She poked around the dusty shelves, finding boxes of corroded nails and even a few rusty tools, still with sale labels attached. "It's Godsey's."

"Godsey's?"

"From *The Waltons*. You never watched *The Waltons*?"

He shook his head and performed a shrug that involved his whole face, making her shake her head and turn away, but smiling.

The stable, amazingly, still smelled like a stable. She swept her hand across the ancient leather of a worn-out saddle and bits and pieces of tack hanging from pegs. Brooms and zinc buckets sat, still waiting to go to work.

Most of the other houses were in worse shape than Old Joe's, so they walked slowly out of town and into the huge, barn-like building that still smelled strongly of pine. Sawdust and woodchips drifted a foot deep against the walls and the massive cutting bench, the huge toothed wheel of which had rusted solid.

Marcus pointed out a wide, meadow-like area of goldenrod and weeds. The remains of a rotted, collapsed fence. "They had their own little farm here, look. So they had fresh vegetables. You can still pick apples, from those trees."

Finally, they came to the pool, fifty yards across and tucked under the hollowed-out face of the mountain. When she had seen it from the road, it had looked black. Now, standing beside it, it was blue and, standing at the edge, it became obvious that the sides were sheer. She thought about the photograph of the quarry, how deep it looked. The upper layer of water, maybe six feet of it, were clear, and she could see fish finning lazily in shoals. Under that, it grew murkier, but not so she couldn't make out the blurry shapes of something large and mechanical.

"Can you swim here?"

He made a face. "You could. It's freezing, though. Colder than the lake. You can fish it, though. Brown trout, mainly."

Nina turned away. "I don't fish."

***

Back at the schoolhouse, Nina held the ladder to help him take the shutters off the upper floor. Helped him wash up the dishes and then read her Kindle while he busied around, doing stuff he didn't explain and she wasn't interested in.

After a while, bored, she wandered upstairs and into the master room, finding the bed had been made with beautiful white linen. She walked to the big window to look out over the lake. Marcus was right, this place was stunning.

He was there then, leaning in the doorway, watching her. She turned so that her back was to the window and the bed was between them.

"You bring a lot of people here?"

"You mean girls?"

Not waiting for her to answer, he went on. "I used to come here with my band, back when we were together. You can imagine, we could crank it right up. The only other people living on the lake are the De Beauvoir's, about a mile North from here."

"But?"

"But you're the first…I'm not sure what we are to each other. This is the first time I've brought a girl here."

She dropped her eyes to the bed. "This your parents?"

"Yea. Their bed."

"Ever slept in it?"

"Nope. But don't worry, I don't feel weird about it."

"No?"

He looked around the room. "Ok, I do. But it's time to get over it."

He walked towards her, and she could see the look in his eye. He was clearly thinking about getting over it right here and now.

***

It got dark quickly at Tilly Whim. And it got *dark*.

She and Marcus sat on the porch overlooking the lake, the only light the yellow spilling from the yellow hurricane lamp in the main room, and the stars. Marcus was sitting on a long cushion, his back to the wall of the house. Nina lay inside his arms, naked, with only a loose rug about them.

The rest of the day had gone by in a haze of screwing, wine and weed. They had snacked some more and were now lying, staring into the astonishing spray of light that revolved slowly about them.

Marcus handed her the wine glass they were sharing. "You're supposed to say, I didn't know there were so many stars. It's a traditional thing to say."

"I didn't know there were so many stars."

She sipped the wine. "Nah, that's not so. I knew. I just never experienced it. It's an experience."

For a while, they were quiet. Nina thought that, if she stroked him, anywhere really, pretty soon they would be fucking again. So, she stayed still, because she was beginning to get a bit tender.

She pointed to the sail boat, surprisingly visible in starlight.

"Can you drive one of those?"

"I'm a great sailboat driver. We could catch a lake trout for dinner tomorrow."

"You can, if you want. Is it deep?"

"It's deep. Cold, too."

He pointed. "The only way to get to the sailboat from the dock is with the canoe, or an inflatable. Something with no draught, because of submerged rocks."

"I thought they took stone out of here on barges."

"They did, but something must've happened. Maybe a barge sunk, or was sunk. Maybe some stone got dumped in there deliberately. Who knows, now? The point is, it's rocky as hell, which isn't brilliant for a lakeside place, to be honest."

Nina snuggled in, feeling warm and happy and satiated. Not caring about rocks in the water. Marcus felt the need to tell her more about it.

"I guess that's another reason why the house hasn't been broken into but once. Try approaching from the lake, unless you know where the rocks are, you're sunk."

Then, sounding sleepy, he said, "We're looking straight north right now, right up the valley there. Even in summer, we get a norther blowing, Jeez. That's Arctic air, the Canadians don't warm it up much before it gets here."

He yawned, sounding like he was falling asleep. Nina leaned back against him, listening to his breathing changing, and smiled to herself in the darkness. She shifted slightly, then shifted again, sliding against him, trickling her fingers down his thigh and he wasn't sleeping anymore.

***

After a fortnight of hiding out at Tilly Whim, eating freshly caught fish and jars of pasta sauce, she told him, "I like living way out here, away from the City."

"Me too."

"Do you know what else I like?"

"I guess you're about to tell me."

"I like living *in* the City."

They were on the sailboat as she said this. It was a hot day and she was lying on the deck, sunning her bare butt. Marcus feathered the tiller, apparently mesmerised by her backside.

"You're a contradictory woman."

"You mean contrary."

"Well, you just contradicted me, so I'm not sure what I mean. I guess you'll tell me that as well."

"I like it here, but I'm coming to the end of hiding out. I need to get back to work. Got a show in Milan week after next."

"Why don't you quit with the modelling, you hate it so much? Put all your energy into your design. What's it, SimeonStyle?"

"What I'm saying, I want both. City and not city."

"Yea, we're way out in the not city."

She got up on her elbows, so that she could look directly into his face. "I'm goin' to say something now."

"Ok."

"I want to live in the City, and sometimes I want to live as far away as a person can go."

"Ok."

"I'd like to do that with you."

When he didn't answer straight away, she added. "You big lummox."

***

Two years later, she came back from telling her agent to fuck off and found Marcus wasted on the floor, and told him she was never going on the catwalk again. Instead, just like he had said that day on the boat, she was going to throw everything into the label, SimeonStyle.

He struggled to focus on her. "About time too."

Marcus was no longer the coming thing in Afrobeat, and that was fine by her. What was less fine was his inability to replace it with anything. Anything at all. He called it lack of motivation. She called it by another name.

The other thing that wasn't fine was what social media, and those fucking nasty magazines, had to say about it. You read any of that stuff, he had been a rare talent burning bright, ready to set the world alight till he met that damn woman Simeon.

Always a problem to work with, that one, coming to the bitter end of her own career and not wanting to do it alone, she dragged the great Marcus Cole down with her.

She gave the great Marcus Cole a cool look and left him lying on the floor with the joint she had rolled but didn't really want. Hurried into her workroom to start making phone calls.

Chapter

5

James

Doctor Bertillon, with his three-piece suits and bow ties, was a dandy, rumoured to be privately rich, even though he spoke of a struggle to keep the Foundling Home from closing. The term 'old money' was used about him. A man from an old and rather grand New Hampshire family.

The ragged condition of the children in his care was a constant upset to him, and the mending of clothes a daily task for kids and carers alike. Before James was ten, he could sew and darn.

There were seamstresses in Manchester, and even a few who called themselves dressmakers or tailors, but Bertillon had his own clothes made by a woman called Nina Simeon. James had noticed the fancy double S on the labels inside his jacket.

SimeonStyle was a downtown landmark. Although the shop wasn't large, the window was one of the brightest and certainly the most unusual. The clothes on the unsettling mannequins, old ones from Before that struck bizarre poses, almost as though they were challenging a person to a fight, were considered by some to be the best in town. Clearly, that was Bertillon's own view.

One bright morning in May, James raised his head from his studies to see two of the most extraordinary people he had ever set eyes on walking up the path towards the house. Both were black, which was very different to the dull grey of The Returned. There were some black people in town, but not many. Most were white, if they were alive, with a fair number of Hispanics in there. Ana-Maria had already taught them what that meant, having been one herself, during her breathing years.

It was not, however, their colour that made them extraordinary. They were both strikingly tall and, whilst the old lady walked with a step that demanded attention, the girl walked head down, and shoulders up. As though she was avoiding attention. Fat chance of that, thought James.

Beside him, Martin Klopp whispered, but still his voice carried something like awe. "That's Alice Simeon."

He leaned in closer. "See the way her boobs move when she walks."

James did indeed see the way her boobs moved when she walked. He glanced at the front of the class, where Ana-Maria was staring at him.

Ana-Maria turned to see what he had been looking at, helped by Martin who said, "James really fancies her, Ana-Maria. He was talking about her boobs!"

Ana-Maria wasn't upset, even with the kids laughing. Nothing upset her, but sometimes she struggled to understand things that should be completely obvious. Like now, when she asked, "Which one are you talking about?"

James had coloured, but now he frowned, catching the last glimpse of the old lady and the stunning girl before coming back to check that Ana-

Maria was serious. Of course she was serious. The Returned never joked.

That was the first time he caught sight of Alice. It lasted seconds, ten and most, but it seared. It felt like someone had run a current of excitement through his testicles, one that travelled all the way up into his chest and into his brain.

Ana-Maria often irritated him, but that day when she asked *which one*, he had seen her for the first time in a light that was…he struggled to put it into words, and he felt kind of ashamed.

Less than impressive, that's what. Kinda dumb, in fact, thinking a twelve-year-old boy could go for an old lady of forty or something. That night in bed, in one of the brief moments when he wasn't replaying the walk of Alice Simeon, or fantasising about talking to her, he thought about what Dr Bertillon said about The Returned.

Maybe he was right. They surely couldn't even *understand* love, if she didn't know which of the Simeons had turned all the boys in the class to jelly. The girls too, probably.

In the next bed, Martin seemed to know something of what was going on in his head. He whispered, "You've no chance, squirt. You wouldn't even come up to her brassiere."

The boy didn't have to say that, it was painfully obvious. If ever there was a boy and a girl in different leagues, it was James Spears and Alice Simeon.

Chapter

Alice

If Alice's mother thought something was worth saying, she hardly ever said it once, that wasn't how she went about things at all. When Nina Simeon had a viewpoint, you could count on hearing it again, oftentimes the same words and even the exact same rhythm in those words. Alice found out early that you couldn't stop her if you tried. She might say, "Mom, you musta said this a hundred times. I'm sick hearing it."

That would be more or less heard as a call to double down. Most likely she would point as she repeated whatever it was, as if to say, I told you this before, but you didn't attend. Attend now, girl, because this here's important.

One of her favourites was, "Before the Change, you coulda made a damn fortune, girl. Woulda been rich and famous."

That was usually accompanied by a coolly appraising look, up and down the considerable length of her.

She would say that any time Alice came home crying or tried to shut herself away in her room.

"A girl like you, beautiful as you are, those long limbs of yours, they would be falling over themselves, beggin' you for the honour of dressin' you up in their clothes. Everybody would want to look like you. Everybody."

Her mother was prone to exaggeration, but this was way out into some strange place of her imagination, and an outright lie. Alice was certain of that.

Because everything about Alice Simeon was *wrong*.

It didn't start out wrong. Her first few years of school were very nearly as right as could be. In a city where there were few black faces to be seen, there were two in her class – her and the tiny, funny, twitching jitterbug Cassie Fanning.

It didn't seem to make much difference anyway. She and Cassie were best friends, but she had so many others, like skinny Miranda Crossways with her fizzy red hair. She loved that school, almost from the first day. She was the fastest runner, faster than most of the boys, the highest jumper, the best at skip-rope and catch. And she could sing. Everybody wanted to hear her sing, it felt like.

She liked her teachers and worked hard, wanting them to like her, which they seemed to, including sister Mary-Rose, who was dead. And a nun. She seldom thought about the gunfight in the old shop, the one that ended with two dead men and her mother lying in a pool of blood, and hardly ever woke up wet or crying.

They rented a house from Mayor Little in Oak Hill Drive, which was a safe neighbourhood, also a well-situated shop, right on the corner of Elm Street and Pearl.

So, Little was their landlord twice over, which explained why he often came around in the evenings, oftentimes bringing candy or liquorice for Alice, patting her head. Smiling at her as she was sent to bed. Smiling like he owned her as well as the house, and her mom just going along with it, even though she was tense and tight and angry inside herself.

Things began to change not long after she turned eleven. She was still doing fine in all her subjects, but something somewhere was beginning to slide off beam. Something inside. She went to school but found herself staring at the teacher, or her classmates, seeing them less and less as friends. They were too strange, too alien. One day Cassie had been talking ten to the dozen as usual, dancing in place in the school yard whilst Alice stared at her with something close to horror.

Finally, Cassie noticed.

"What's up? You look like you ate a bad egg."

Alice's response was to burst out crying, and run to the toilets, locking herself in.

If there was a moment when everything began to go wrong, that was it. She no longer felt right with her friends, or even in her own skin.

Cassie followed her around for a while, demanding to know what was wrong. "Alice, tell me what I done. Please!"

Alice couldn't tell her, because Alice didn't know.

Around this time, she had taken a ferocious growth spurt that put her a full head above anybody else in her class. She grew hair where no hair had been before, and started to bleed.

And she slid from being a popular girl with an easy relationship with her many friends, to being regarded as the school weirdo.

Cassie told her that. "You're weird Simeon. A real freak. I'm not your friend no more. And you know what?"

"What?"

"I'm so sick hearing you droning on, like you think you're the great singer. You think you're all that but everybody hates it. Hates hearing you."

Alice worked hard to try to be alone, staying in the library at breaks and avoiding all games. She wanted to be invisible, which was much harder, because, even though she ate as little as possible, she simply wouldn't stop growing.

She wore low shoes and flat-out ignored her mom when she told her to walk straight. "Walk with your head held high, girl, even if your ass is trailin' the ground."

It didn't matter how many times that line was repeated, the last thing she was going to do was hold that head any higher than it needed to be. Her mom, again, "Look at you. You're like a half-shut knife."

Weirdo and freak were words that began to follow her, she could almost feel them tattooed on her skin. Cassie Fanning was the worst. Once, Mrs Twining, her Music teacher, leaned in close to whisper, "Why don't you just haul off and punch that girl? Once should do it."

But Alice couldn't bring herself to hit back. Even though Fanning was about half her weight. It was Fanning who first called her Kong, Fanning who stole one of her shoes, pulling it right off her foot and then standing there, daring her to try to take it back. Then showing it around the school, so everybody could laugh at how huge it was, pretending to swoon over the stink from it.

Fanning who danced behind her chanting, "Skinny-malinky-long-legs. Umba-rella-feet. Went to the classroom, too big for the seat. Went to the park and chased the boys around. Skinny-malinky-long-legs, biggest girl in town."

That song was the background music to her schooldays. She could hear it in her sleep.

Back home, crying, her mother took her by the shoulders to tell her, "You're so damn beautiful, girl. Before everything went to shit you could've wrote your own cheque. You woulda been a supermodel."

Whatever *that* meant. Her mother was always using language that might have made sense when she was young, but found no purchase now.

Mayor Little seemed to notice a difference in her. The way he looked at her changed, his gaze no longer flitting over her, a quick grin and then dismissal. She might not have noticed it herself, not then, if she hadn't caught the expression on her mom's face. That tight, dangerous look she had, not suppressed quickly enough to hide from Alice, whose internal radar was tuned hard to her mother's moods.

Then the evening came when Little eased his languid way into the house, as if he had a right to just walk in there, put that big smile on her and left it there as he spoke.

"Why don't we let the girl stay a spell? What do you say, Alice? You ever had you a glass of…"

Nina's voice changed at that, dropping and hardening, and she got herself right in front of the mayor so his eyes widened and the words dried on his lips.

"You get on girl."

She didn't even turn to look at Alice, her eyes were on Little and his on hers, like he was suddenly afraid. Then, as quick as that, it was all change. The man seemed to give himself a shake and straighten, the grin gone now, as if it had never been.

Nina took a step back and away, her shoulders slumping as her head dropped. Alice didn't know what had just passed, but something had. Her mom looked beaten and that wasn't right, because nothing in the world could beat her.

Nina turned to her now and her voice was gentle. "Get on now. Get to bed."

She looked quickly from one adult to the other and did as she was told. She didn't understand the currents flowing in that room but she wanted out of it.

***

She forced herself, or was forced, to school every day, kept her head down, literally and as far as it would go, no doubt looking remarkably like a half-shut knife, and the years inched past.

Until one day in sixth grade – she had just turned twelve – when Pierre Bertillon, who was some kind of second cousin thrice removed from the guy who ran that creepy orphan place, asked her out. Pierre was two years older, a good-looking boy, popular, and as tall as she was.

He cornered her outside the hall, where she'd been struggling over her latest piano piece, going through it yet again for Mrs Twining. He said, "You're talented, aint'ya? Singing and playing instruments and all."

"You were listening?"

"Sure. You're a real pretty girl, Alice."

She searched his face to see what this was about, but he just smiled. "Prettiest girl in all the school, I'd say."

She managed not to stammer, or run away. She looked at the corners and stayed quiet.

"You think me and you could, you know, spend some time together. Out of school."

She bit her lip. "I guess."

He grinned, and pushed his hair out of his face. "Meet me down Derryfield Park at five o'clock Saturday? By the pavilion."

She looked around, thinking about it, suddenly not knowing what to do with her limbs.

"Okay."

She couldn't meet his eye, but he dropped in the knee until they were looking at each other. "You wouldn't stand me up, now? I'd hate to be stood up."

"I won't stand you up."

Nervous as she was, she didn't. She thought really hard about what to wear, trying on almost everything she owned until eventually going with sneakers, a short flared skirt and a top that she knew to be a little on the tight side. She normally wore her hair in a tight braid, but today she brushed it out over her shoulders, put on lipstick and her mother's perfume, sneaking out to avoid being spotted, and questioned.

She was so nervous walking into the park that her legs trembled, she was so sure he wouldn't be there.

He was there. Standing in the shadow of the pavilion, wearing jeans and a frayed tee that showed off the muscles in his arms, smoking.

When he caught sight of her, he raised a hand, the one with the cigarette in it. The other hand was pushed deep into his pocket and his shoulders were high. His hair, as usual, hung over his forehead, like he had to have combed it that way.

She stopped a few feet away and smiled, tentative. Unsure what he might be expecting, having heard some of the other girls talking about boys, sniggering about what they wanted to do. How some of them wanted you to go all the way.

He smiled back, lopsided, eyes narrowed romantically against the smoke. "You came. Wasn't sure you would."

"Wasn't sure I would either."

He held the cigarette out. "Smoke?"

He might be surprised to know that she did smoke, from time to time. Her mother was a heavy smoker, and it was a simple matter to filch cigarettes from her, and smoke them in her room. She didn't notice, or didn't seem to, and for sure would never catch the stink of it on her. The whole house and everything in it stunk of tobacco.

So, she took it from him and inhaled deeply, holding it and then blowing a stream out of her nose. He opened his eyes wide, then narrowed them again, nodding. Giving some serious appreciation to her competence. She handed the cigarette back, but he waved it away.

"You finish it. Seems like you're no stranger to a smoke."

Alice took another draw, but this time didn't inhale. Pulling it down into her lungs always made her light-headed, and not in a good way. She looked around, not knowing what to do with herself. It was a warm enough day, and there were a few people in the park, all at some distance. A couple of older men taking a brisk walk, a family letting their kids climb around in the play area, but nobody close enough to see her smoking.

"So, what do you want to do?"

He looked at her from under his lick of hair. "Just hang out. Get to know one another a bit better. I don't really know you."

"Why did you ask me out?"

He dropped his eyes from her face to her too-tight sweater, leaving them there as he put his hands out to the sides. "Are you shitting me?"

Now that his eyes were down there, they kept going, slowly. "Look at those legs, Jesus! You're a babe."

Alice squirmed and giggled, not sure what to make of this, putting a hand over her mouth. "I don't think you should be speaking like that."

"Come on. You love it. You're such a fucking ride, Simeon, honest to God."

He put his hand out, his eyes on hers again, smiling. She smiled back, uncertainly now, but still took it and squealed as he tugged, bringing her towards him.

She giggled again. A nervous snigger. "Where are we going?"

"Just inside the pavilion. We can sit down."

Derryfield Park pavilion was a wooden structure with a steeply peaked roof, but only three full sides to it. The fourth was open, looking down over the empty sports field. A rough bench ran the length of it and it was a favourite for romantic trysts, smokers and underage drinkers. Inside, there was a hectic mess of carved and written messages, many of which were x-rated.

"I don't like it in there. It stinks of piss."

But she wasn't fighting him. He grinned – a handsome, charming boy – then suddenly pulled her hard, right into his arms, which surprised but didn't exactly alarm her. That didn't happen until he twisted and pistoned his arms out again, shoving her into the gloomy interior.

"*You* stink of piss."

She almost fell but someone nearby, a boy, laughed and caught her. She squirmed in his grip, turning to see two older boys from school. Kier McCandless and Eddie Levant. She tried to shout but it was knocked out of her as Pierre drove forwards, forcing her to stumble backwards.

He had his hands on her breasts, and was laughing, shoving her further inside. "I've got her by the tits guys!"

Alice still had the cigarette in her hand and raked it across his face, causing him to yelp and cuss and turn away. McCandless gripped her arm and she tried to slap him, but he caught her wrist.

They were too strong. Levant was grabbing at her skirt, trying to push his hand up there, giggling hysterically, and suddenly Pierre was back in her face and he was furious. There was a red mark across his cheek, not far from his eye.

"You coulda blinded me you big freak. You bitch." He spat in her face, then slapped her.

"Hold her down."

Alice thrashed and bucked. She managed to kick out at Levant, who had bent down in front of her, maybe trying to haul her panties off, sending him momentarily sprawling. McCandless had his forearm across her face, dragging her back, and she bit him, putting everything she could into it and feeling the gristly sensation of skin and muscle breaking beneath her teeth.

He yelled. The thing she wanted to do. Yelled and cussed and yanked his arm away.

Pierre drove her hard against the back wall, smacking her head hard enough for her to see sparks, rattling her teeth together. His face was inches away, twisted and ugly. He and Levant tried to pin her arms, and they struggled, the only sound now feet scuffling against concrete and their panting and grunting. McCandless jigged around nearby, cussing and holding his bleeding wrist. She writhed and thrashed, managing to slap Levant and then push Pierre back, just for a moment.

A moment was what she needed to fill her lungs and scream. Unlike McCandless' yell, hers was full-throated and piercing, loud enough to make all three draw back, their expressions going from fierce to shocked in an instant.

Pierre skipped back and she squeezed her fists tight and screamed again, coming forwards to do it right in his face, screaming *at* him. They were all falling back, pulling at each other. Turning to run.

There was just a second, when Pierre grabbed the other two boys, his hands on their shoulders to push them out of there, hissing at them to git going. Just a split-second before they took off, when Alice took two long steps and kicked.

That kick landed square on his ass. It probably barely raised a bruise but it made Pierre Bertillon hop in the air, in the shameful second before he ran away. And, as he ran, Alice was no longer screaming. She was shouting, cussing them out, using words she'd never used before.

She very nearly chased them out of there.

Chapter

7

James

It was a week after he saw her walking towards the house that James found himself face to face with Alice Simeon, and he didn't have to do a thing. All the Bertillon Foundlings, as they were known, were called to line up in the assembly hall, three lines of ten, shortest in front, tallest at the rear.

Even though he was by now almost twelve, James's place was still firmly in the front row. He had no idea what this assembly was for, but it hardly mattered, he just trailed in and took his place.

Two boring minutes later, the door opened and Dr Bertillon walked in, looking over his shoulder and grinning inanely. An expression that sat poorly on his face. A second later, the person he was grinning at stepped into the room and it was Nina Simeon.

Ok, in the absence of her stellar daughter, this was an amazing looking woman, James had to admit that. A whole half head taller than the Doctor, straight backed, wide shouldered. She looked like she could put him under her arm and walk off. Also, despite her great age, she was still quite obviously beautiful.

As she turned her head, though, James caught sight of a puckered ridge of pink skin high up above her right cheek. A scar, disappearing into her hairline.

Her expression had been stern, concentrating hard on something the man was saying, but now she caught sight of the children and smiled, lighting her face up. Embarrassingly, James felt a little lift in his balls.

The woman twisted her head around, that same smile in place, and spoke to someone following her into the room. For a second, James permitted himself to hope that it would be Alice.

It was Alice.

Alice was even taller than her mother, well over six feet, had to be. Something rustled through the room, maybe a sigh or a groan or a shuffle of feet. James felt his face begin to heat up, and knew he had gone a deep shade of red, all the way to the stinging tips of his ears.

Bertillon smiled, "Children, this is Nina Simeon and, 'em, Alison. Alice?"

He did an embarrassed little dip as Nina said, "Alice."

Her voice was shockingly low for a woman, a huskiness in there that James felt in his lower belly.

Bertillon nodded and turned to the foundlings, his attention flickering back and forwards as though he didn't want to take his eyes off Nina.

"Our current uniform has been through a few wears, eh, children? Mostly, what you're wearing is third or fourth hand by now. So!"

He clapped his hands, still grinning like a pure fool.

"So Ms. Simeon has given the foundlings of this town the most incredibly generous offer. Believe it or not, she has offered to design and make new uniforms for both girls and boys. She wanted to have a look at you all, get some idea of the size of the problem, haha!"

James had never seen Bertillon like this. Nervous. Animated. Like he couldn't stay still. With his newfound balls-foremost view of the world, it was fairly obvious that the poor sap felt for Nina what he felt for her daughter.

Alice at this moment was frowning hard, concentrating. She had a hard-backed notebook out and was hastily writing in it. Sketching too, by the looks of things. James was only about three feet from her.

Nina smiled and nodded at the latest inane thing out of Bertillon's mouth and turned to the class. Her gaze grazed James, but he barely felt it because Alice was suddenly *looking right at him.*

She was looking at him and frowning, as if he were a math problem, and then bending again to her book, scribbling away, maybe sketching. As his ears heated to the point of pain, her eyes moved on to someone else.

Nina held up a hand and James, being so close, noticed with a shock that the tips of three of her fingers were missing. They quite simply ended a knuckle short. Along with the scar, it was obvious this was a woman who had seen some hard and dangerous living.

"Hi, y'all." Her voice was so deep, and her accent right out of the old world, sounding like someone in the films they watched on Friday nights, from those barely imaginable cities from Before, Chicago, or maybe even New York. For a dizzy moment, he thought about raising his hand to ask, "Have you ever seen the Empire State Building?"

Or the Liberty Statue. He couldn't bring himself to speak, instead forcing himself to attend.

"The Doc here is setting me and my girl loose on y'all. I don't know if I should say thanks, or sorry. But I can say you'll have new uniforms before winter. So, before Alice and I get carried away with ourselves, is there anything you want? This is your one and only chance to make a request."

It seemed that nobody would speak until Karen Gill piped up. "Can we have pleats in our skirts, Miss?"

"Pleats! Sure you can. Anything else?"

Alice nodded seriously at the girl before scribbling a note. James tried to come up with something to say, anything to have her eyes on him again. But he simply could not think of a single thing he wanted from a uniform.

In hindsight, he might have asked, can it be any other colour than mustard?

***

The next time James Spears saw Alice Simeon, she laid hands on him. She took the points of his shoulders in her long, long fingers and twisted and turned him, then walked all around, rearranging his limbs the way she wanted them. These clothes weren't made to measure, but there had to be a range of measurements and he was at one end of that.

This close up, the difference in their heights was all the more apparent. James at this stage in his growth was barely above four feet, so the gap was huge. As Martin said, he barely came up to her chest.

She was coolly professional, focussed on her job in hand, and appeared more than slightly irritated. They were on their own in Bertillon's office, and all he had to do was stand there and avoid getting an erection. There were tales circulating about what Nina Simeon would do to any boys who took a hard-on around her daughter, none of them particularly plausible, but frightening nonetheless.

He could smell her, and she smelled wonderful, soap and clean sweat. He could hear her, and she didn't sound wonderful. She seemed to force each breath noisily through her nose. It was unattractive and just plain weird, especially to someone who was so used to being close to adult women who did not breathe at all.

It was the flaw that made his heart shiver in his chest.

So, she fussed and tutted and measured. At one point she knelt down in front of him and, for a fraction of a second, he caught a glimpse of what was inside her blouse. This was when she was measuring his inside leg, which did not after all require her to fit the end of the tape into the tender space beside his ball sack, as Martin claimed. Martin saying she would have to sock it right in there, even take hold of his cock and shift it out of the way if it was hanging inconveniently. This, he warned, was the point of peak danger for taking a woody, when it couldn't be missed. In reality, the inside leg was measured from a point on the front of his thigh.

If she noticed any twitches down there, and she might have, she ignored them.

There was one moment, though, when she looked at him, right into his eyes, and him into hers. It was, he thought, the moment when she saw him as a person, a boy around her own age; the first time they really saw each other.

It wouldn't happen again for over a decade.

Chapter
8
Nina

Nina was in her workroom, and had been since six that morning, more than eight hours ago. She had been drinking Coke and coffee and eating cereal bars, and even then resented the seconds spent going to the fridge or the Espresso maker. She'd had the designs in her head, solid so she could see them, for some time now. They'd made it onto paper with no hitches, but the jump to the making stage was where it too often went awry. Sometimes things just didn't work at all. She'd tried working with another designer, and that turned into a time-wasting bust. She was employing a talented seamstress, but some things you just had to do yourself.

She was working on one of those more difficult designs right now, an almost utilitarian dress, off-set by one or two surprising details and in wildly printed linen. Her fingers were sore, her head ached and she was jittery with too much coffee and sugar and too little proper food, when Marcus walked in.

"You got to come see this."

She rounded on him, fists bunched at her sides "For fuck's sake! Didn't I make this clear enough? This goes right, SimeonStyle is in business, it goes wrong, I'm screwed."

She hesitated, letting him notice it. "*We're* screwed."

"Nina listen, you…"

She should be paying attention to his expression. She even told herself that, but she'd been in crisis mode, annoyed at him for not being in crisis mode, for so long that it wasn't easy to shift gears.

"Listen to what I'm saying. We're going to the absolute wire here. The end of the *week*. If I don't get this done by…"

"Nina."

That's all he said, but it was enough to stop her dead, and now she did take note of his expression. She stepped quickly forward and took his hand.

"Who's died?"

The last thing she expected was for him to laugh at that, and for the first time she got really worried, a scared feeling in her stomach. She searched his face for a clue, but all he did was squeeze her fingers and say, "Who's died? Jesus. Nobody! Everybody!"

That didn't help one bit. She snatched her hand back, but then held it out again and he grabbed it, leading her from the room. As she went by, she grabbed her phone, only now seeing all the missed calls.

"What's happening? You're scaring me."

"Sorry baby, but be scared, okay? This is the time to be scared."

Her heartbeat ticked up. "Another virus?"

He frowned and shook his head, then stopped, thinking about it. "Maybe, who knows?"

"Marcus!"

Coming into the lounge room, she could see *No Bull, No Surrender* on the screen, that damned Phil Raleigh ranting as usual.

"You're watching this crazy shit? *This*! Jesus Christ, you can't believe a word…"

"Just listen, ok?"

The bulked-up asshole was even more excitable than normal, jumping around, waving his hands about.

"You heard it right, folks, the dead are walking. They are walking. They are walking all over the world. All across the globe. For those with guns, lock, load and bolt your doors, friends. For those without, didn't I tell you this was coming? I told you and told you…"

She turned to Marcus. "What you been smoking, you moron? This fucking guy. This…"

Marcus put his hands on her shoulders and turned her back to the screen. "No, really, something weird is happening, it's not just…"

Nina pushed his hands away, but that wasn't enough for her, so she shoved him hard in the chest, making him take some stumbling steps backwards. Found the remote and snapped to CNN, seeing the worried faces there. The reporter was talking about some weird reports coming through.

"If you are just now tuning in, there are unconfirmed reports, not just from the US, but all over the world including Canada, the UK and Australia. I repeat that these reports are not confirmed by this network, however they seem to suggest that people who have been declared dead…" the presenter's face underwent a strange change, as though she didn't want to have anything to do with the rest of the sentence. "…are recovering."

She switched to Fox, NBC, then found BBC world news, a concerned newscaster saying, "These reports are as yet unconfirmed, I repeat, unconfirmed…"

65

She hit mute, watching the woman talk, the worry etched into her face.

Marcus turned to her. "It's happening. All over the world."

"What is?"

She hadn't seen him so wired for a long time. So awake. As though he was, in some place inside himself, enjoying this. Like it was what he'd been waiting for these past two years. "Isn't it obvious? It's the zombie apocalypse."

She sat down, her legs folding to dump her onto the couch.

"The zombie apocalypse. You just said that right out loud. Jesus. I need a drink."

He went to the sideboard and came back with a bourbon over ice. She took it, then looked around the room.

"You're not smoking."

"This is no time to be stoned. So no, I'm not smoking."

Marcus flicked the news back on, running through the same channels whilst Nina checked everything she could on the internet, Twitter, TikTok and Facebook, and everywhere seemed the same. Something monumental was happening, bigger than the virus, tales of the dead coming back to life. But it was all so outrageous, so unbelievable, that it could not be believed. None of the serious news channels were believing it, because there had to be another explanation.

After a while, she finished her drink and said, "Well. If it's the fuckin zombie apocalypse, I'm meeting it with my collection *complete*. Those brain munching fuckers might be more stylish than you'd expect."

And went back to her workroom. This time, though, her hands were stupid and her head was slow. Her response was to drink more coffee, turn her music up, and double down. If this was to be finished by the end of the week, she could not afford to stop.

***

It was only two hours before Marcus came for her again, this time simply snapping her music off and standing by the door. He stared at her for a few seconds and it occurred to her that she was looking at a stranger, and that he might be thinking the exact same thing.

He didn't say a word, and didn't wait for her, knowing that when he left the room she would have to follow. His face was grim, but his eyes were just so damned alive, and there wasn't a bit of smoke in the air.

No Bull, No Surrender was back on, she saw, now airing a clip of some kind. She accepted the drink he handed her and sat to watch footage of a family, heads bowed, praying around a hospital bed, where an emaciated man of about fifty lay, quite obviously dead. It looked more like a waxwork than something that had once been alive, lying there.

"What's this?"

In answer, he pointed at the screen, not taking his own eyes from it. "These are coming in thick and fast now. I've not seen this one."

Something about the scene, the whole set up suggested this was a group of serious weirdos. For some reason she thought they might also be Brits. That was borne out when the pretty young woman at the foot of the bed raised her head from prayer and turned to talk into the camera. Her accent was Irish.

"Hello. My name is Josephine Anfield. My beautiful Daddy, Peter Anfield, lost his long battle against cancer this morning at 6.13. That was almost an hour ago, and we, his family, are devastated. We just can't believe he's gone." She leaned over the bed to take another woman's hand, surely her sister, and they smiled bravely at each other.

"He's in the arms of Jesus now."

The family nodded and said, "Amen."

Nina leaned in to listen to the woman talk about her father, the dead man who lay behind her, things he had done in his life, and watch the rest of the family nod, and smile and weep quietly. An older woman, maybe his wife, sat closer to the head of the bed, her own head down and her hands clasped before her. She was the only one not looking at the camera and quite possibly didn't approve what was going on, the family's grief being recorded.

Josephine closed her eyes, clasped her hands and prayed hard to the camera.

"Dear Lord, your son Peter has closed his eyes one final time."

Although not known to Nina, this was clearly some call and response prayer, because the others closed their eyes also, chanting together. "He has closed his eyes."

"But with your good grace."

"With your good grace."

"He will open them in heaven."

"He will open them in heaven."

Nina turned to Marcus. "Can you imagine doing this? Is this for their Instagram…"

"Shh!"

He said it so sharply, shutting her up like that. Nina glared at him then turned back to the screen just

68

in time to see the dead man open his eyes. Not waiting for heaven.

The woman, Josphine, was talking again, no longer praying, the family nodding and trying to be brave in their grief, all of them looking at the camera, not at their dead father. Josephine was saying how courageous he had been. How he hadn't been able to so much as move his limbs in the last weeks, or even raise his poor head to take a sip of water. Saying it was a blessing, that God had finally taken his son back into his loving arms.

When Peter Anfield sat up, the woman who Nina had marked as his wife was first to notice. She leaned back and issued a little squeal. Nina did the same, grabbing Marcus' arm. Watched as the woman stared, eyes so wide she looked a little crazy.

Then she said, "Peter?"

She leaped to her feet then and grabbed his hands, shouting his name over and over, and the rest of the family turned to take note. Peter Anfield sat straight up in bed, staring at his wife, turning to look at the rest of his family.

Their expressions were shocked, their voices were shocked, somebody was shouting for a nurse. In the middle of the sudden confused melee, Anfield sat calmly, looking from one face to another. The image had been jerked around, and now it shifted and fell out of focus, maybe the phone or whatever had just been dumped on the bed.

The last thing on the clip was a voice, oddly dry and thin, saying, "Josephine."

Then Raleigh was back ranting and shouting, saying we got to kill 'em. Got to kill 'em all. But he was only on for a few seconds because another clip started playing, one of a terrified woman being filmed in some eastern country. This had to be Siryah or Afghanistan, Nina wasn't so up on all that stuff, but the woman was on her knees in the dirt, in front of bearded guys, one of them waving his forefinger at the camera, doing that lecturing thing.

Raleigh, not even on screen, was still ranting, but his voice was faded down, leaving them to watch the woman, screaming and pleading. The man beside her stepped to the side and put a pistol to her temple.

"Oh Jesus Christ! They're not going to show this on daytime?"

Marcus pointed. "This is the one I saw before."

"No!" Before she knew she was going to do it, she slapped Marcus, hard across the face. The first time either of them had raised a hand to the other. Turned back to the screen despite herself to see the woman shot through the temple, blood jetting out shockingly as she fell, a sack of dead meat.

"What the fuck is this…"

He grabbed her, stopping her from moving away. "Watch!"

The same three men, in their beards and turbans, seated now, lecturing the camera cross-legged and holding assault rifles. It was clearly later, the light going in the desert. Behind them, not one but three dead women, blood pooled and dried around their ruined heads.

One of the women jerked. Nina pulled herself free, but then grabbed Marcus' hand. The woman sat up.

Nina was all but running on the spot, like a little kid trying not to wee herself. "What's happening? What's…"

"Will you just for God's sake *watch*?"

70

First, one man turned, the one who had used the pistol. When he turned back to his fellows, his expression was simply bemused. Now they were all twisting to see. One of them laughed. Then another.

The woman got up, moving stiffly and so did the men, snatching up their guns. They were still laughing, but clearly no longer thinking this was all that funny. The executioner himself unloaded on her, a full clip tearing her open and throwing her back and down, like a doll.

Nina turned away, thinking she might be sick. When she turned back, the woman was getting up again. So was a second, the same one she had seen shot through the head earlier.

The screen went back to the *No Bull, No Surrender* Logo behind Raleigh, a riff on the Stars and Stripes.

Raleigh had his own weapon now, a pump action shotgun. Every sentence was a scream, his voice hoarse from yelling all day. "You know what this is, America! Fellow patriots this is it, this is exactly what we've been warning about. Them God-Damned Chinese. We ought to have dealt with them, but we were weak. Now we reap what we sow. God's own country, we got to deal with the Zombie Apocalypse. And as God is my witness, we will. No zombie gonna eat my brains, friends."

Despite showing a clip where someone got up after an entire magazine of automatic fire blew them down, he was waving his gun, shouting about America knows how to deal with these God-Damned Chinese zombie bastards.

The last thing he shouted, before Marcus changed to BBC, was "Lock and load, friends and neighbours. Lock and load."

71

On the BBC news desk, two reporters, a man and woman, looked pale and stunned. The woman was saying, "...because there are simply too many corroborated, eye-witness reports to think anything else. Our Paris correspondent, Martin Cleverly, was attending the funeral of Giles De La Croix, ambassador to..."

Marcus hit the power button, and then took her in his arms.

"It's really happening. This isn't just some conspiracy theory crazies out there. It's happening all over the world."

"What does it mean?"

"It means, survival. We got to survive, honey. It all boils down to nothing more than that."

She searched his face, seeing the light in there. Just as if he had been waiting for something like this.

"Do they infect people by biting?"

"Nobody knows. Yet."

"By killing?" She hurried to the window, looking out over a street that wasn't as rammed with traffic as usual, but was still rammed.

"Jesus, people are just going about their business."

"Not for long."

"Are they attacking?"

"Of course."

She looked away from the sight of people walking out there, driving in their cars. "You seen them do that? Eating brains?"

"That's what zombies do."

"But have you seen it?"

"Not yet."

Outside, not far away, there was a gunshot, followed by the pop-pop-pop of a semi-automatic, causing her to turn again to look. People were pausing, then some were running, or diving into stores. But not all.

Directly across the street, a bearded man wearing the Stars and Stripes over a flak jacket was raising his assault rifle high above his head and shouting something. She watched for a while, but that's all he seemed to be doing. Holding his gun high and shouting.

When Marcus joined her, putting his arm about her shoulders, she asked him, "How much food do we have?"

Chapter

9

Nina

On the evening of Day One, the day the dead rose, Marcus and Nina had taken a drive to Walmart. They tried to. The roads were gridlocked and, if there was any chance of them becoming anything else, there was no sign of that happening anytime soon. In the end they did the same as almost everybody else and abandoned the idea, along with their car, leaving it jamming up the street with all the others. Ten minutes later they were hemmed in and running as best they could, swept along in a panicked flow of people, because somewhere nearby there was some kind of shoot-out going on.

They didn't see who was doing the shooting, not that first day, and they didn't see anybody get shot. The street was too full of people, jam packed and rushing headlong in their terror. Fall, and you would be trampled, probably to death.

They got to their apartment block but found the door locked and closed, their electronic fobs beeping but not unlocking. Just as Marcus was stepping back to kick the door, Thiago, the concierge, hauled it open.

Even as they both fell inside, Nina noticed he had a pistol in a holster by his side. A short, muscular guy in his early forties, he invariably wore a smart grey suit with collar and tie. He was wearing it now, looking much the same as always apart from the gun and a sheen of sweat across his face.

He saw her looking.

"Sorry folks, everything's going crazy. Somebody tried to bust the door in earlier. Pointed a shotgun at me."

"Shit! You ok?"

"A bit shook up, is all. Think I best be armed, though, till this settles down."

"That why you changed the code?"

He shook his head. "I didn't. There was a black out, about ten minutes ago. I've not managed to reset yet."

"City wide?"

He opened his hands, threw them in the air. "I don't know how to even find that out. Everything's gone to…it's gone crazy."

Marcus barked out a laugh. "You were right the first time. Everything's gone to shit, man."

"Were you trying to get out of the city?"

"Walmart. Not possible."

"I hear people are leaving, or trying to, trails of cars blocking the highways."

Marcus and Nina exchanged a look, both seeing how that might happen.

***

In the apartment, Marcus spent an hour on his cell, most of that just trying to get through. Knelt in front of Nina and pulled a face. "I just transferred five grand for a couple of hundred bucks worth of food."

He looked like he expected to be scolded. Instead, she hugged him tight. "At least you managed to get some, what did you get?"

"What they're going to bring. It wasn't like putting in an order at Trader Joe's."

Then he said, "If they bring it."

"I'm scared."

The light was still there in his face, but there was something else in there as well. He compressed his lips for a moment, maybe to stop the tremble. "Me too."

Guns crackled throughout the night, and the news had back to back shots of looted stores, sold out gun shops and guys with assault rifles massing on the streets. Camping out in cemeteries, waiting for the dead to rise.

The food delivery didn't come that night, or the next, but on the third morning Marcus got a call, saying come to the rear of the building. He wanted to go alone, but she wouldn't hear of it. In the end, they both went. Marcus pushed his Smith and Wesson down the back of his jeans.

In the hallway, they met Thiago, his expression wary.

"Those guys in loading anything to do with you?"

"Yea, we got a delivery."

"Listen, I don't want to tell you your business, but…"

He shrugged. Nina and Marcus exchanged looks and she asked, "But what? It's a food delivery."

"They don't look like Safeway employees to me, Ma'am."

They followed him to a narrow window overlooking the loading bay, where there was a seriously beat-up truck waiting, a Nissan pickup with a guy standing on the bed beside some boxes and another leaning against the hood, both of them smoking. They looked like Nina's idea of bikers, but

76

not on bikes. Studded denim, muscle tees, tats and bandanas. Hair pulled tight into pony tails.

Thiago pointed, his voice low. "Guy in back has an AK. Don't know about the other, but those are tasty looking fuckers. Pardon my French."

Nina pointed to the pistol, still strapped to his hip. "How would you feel about coming with? Just standing in the background."

"Listen, Ms Simeon, no offence but I didn't sign on for…"

Marcus asked, "You got food, Thiago? Enough to last."

The man sounded annoyed, talking to his wealthy resident. "Got about two packs of pasta and a bag of rice left. Some stuff in tins I don't even know what. So no, I don't have much food."

Marcus pulled out his own revolver, showing it before pushing it back in his belt.

"Ok, then. We do this together, man, and we share. Not 50/50, but we give you enough for maybe a week."

In the end, the guys just delivered the groceries. The driver did ask, though, "You need anything else man?"

Marcus shook his head to weed and crystal meth, surprising Nina. He surprised her more when they asked about guns, or ammunition.

"What you got?"

"What you need?"

"A hunting rifle." He glanced at her. "Two. And ammunition to go. Scopes."

The guys looked at each other and their demeanour changed, becoming more business-like. "We got a Weatherby Vanguard .375. That's a serious fucking firearm, man. Meant for dangerous game, if you get my drift. Top end, big gun. Big money. That the sort of thing?"

"Give me a number and I'll tell you."

A price was mentioned that caused Nina to gasp, but Marcus didn't even haggle.

"We got a Ruger, nice gun, more lightweight, takes your 6.5 mil Creedmoor. You don't want a pump action? And a Glock?"

The other guy, who hadn't been part of the conversation and looked like he was on something, turned his hazy gaze on them. "Marcus fuckin Cole, yea?"

Marcus took a moment, looked back at where Thiago was standing. "Yea, that's right."

The man nodded. "Marcus Cole. Man, that track, Takin' it Down. Musta listened to it a million times. Marcus Cole, shit."

"Glad you liked it."

"Nothing's coming out of the cemeteries, man, tell you that for nothin'."

"No?"

"Me an' my crew staked out St John's, where my Uncle Tommy's planted. Wasn't the only ones neither, looking to shoot us some of the fuckin' undead, man. Woulda shot Tommy if he rose."

Thiago asked, sounding like he really wanted to know. "But nothing did?"

He shook his head, bewildered. Which was maybe his natural state. "Nothin'. Nothing climbin' outta there. What does that tell you?"

Marcus shrugged. "Fucked if I know."

"Damn straight. Fucked if anybody knows. And I mean anything."

When they left, with an order for four guns and enough ammo to start a small war, and Thiago walked

78

off with a grateful bag of supplies, she said, "You're thinking about Tilly Whim."

"Aren't you?"

"Yea, actually I am."

"We can't go yet, though."

She threw her arms up. "Why not? Jesus, the world is going fucking crazy. Let's get out of it."

He shook his head. "Winter will be setting in, soon enough."

"Not yet it hasn't…"

He shook his head. "Think about it, honey. It's already too late, this year. We need to plan this out. Need rifles to hunt and provisions and a serious store of logs."

Somewhere, somebody was screaming. Somebody shooting. It was just the two of them now, standing in the empty car park and the first they knew about the zombie was when it came out of the alley at the other side. It looked like it had been an overweight young woman. Now it was burning, like a torch, but still walking, trailing smoke.

Behind it came a man with a pistol, he was walking unsteadily, like something was wrong with his limbs. An old guy wearing a pair of saggy joggers and a Nirvana tee-shirt. He pointed the pistol and shot at the burning zombie.

Nina saw how the slug hit the thing's back, slapping it forward a half-step, but it just kept moving. There was a woman there as well, the same age as the guy, wearing a torn-open house coat. She ran after him and grabbed his gun arm, screaming, "Leave her alone. Leave her be."

She was crying and so was the man, they looked like two people in the most terrible pain, but he threw her off. "That ain't her! It ain't her! It's a fuckin zombie is what…"

He aimed again but the woman grabbed at his arm and the shot went wild. The burning zombie kept walking, until it fell to its knees and then onto its face on the hard cement.

It rolled over, rolled again and the fire started to dwindle. Even before the flames were properly out, it got stiffly to its feet again and turned back to where the couple were still struggling over the gun.

Nina hid behind Marcus, not wanting to see this horror. Most of the woman's clothes had burned away, taking skin and hair along with it.

And eyelids. What was left was charred and bloody. She didn't want to see it, not for a second more, but couldn't help but hear it say, "Mom, Dad. It is me."

***

Two weeks in, Marcus was still tuning in to watch Phil Raleigh, even though he hated the guy. Raleigh's long running show, *No Bull, No Surrender*, had gone, though, replaced by the more focussed *Burn 'Em!* He was on nightly, with one message, the only one that mattered now, he said. Shouted. The man no longer spoke.

"Folks, we've all got nearest and dearest. Some of us still have living parents, or are blessed with kids, and God willing they will live a goodly sum of years. But one day we will all of us die. Jesus raised Lazarus, he rose his own self, but he told us straight that everybody got to die, if they got any chance of making it to the blessed gates of heaven.

"My lovin' wife Arlene knows what to do, the day that I pass. And I'll do the same for her."

He put his hand on his heart and stared high and away, into the distance.

"It's what any good, God-fearin American must pledge to do."

The thing he raised these days, was no gun, it was a five-gallon gas can, emblazoned with the Stars and Stripes and his logo. The logo featured a scrawled '*Burn Em!*' backed by the silhouette of a flaming cross, complete with crucified figure.

He looked high above himself, as though praying. "Take me out and cremate me, Arlene. If ever you loved me, burn me right up, and I'll do the same for you, out of love. Out of love, will I burn you to charcoal and cinders, so you cannot rise as abomination.

"But." He pointed at the camera, his expression hardening. "But if you die and I'm not around. If a vile, godless abomination rises in place of my beloved Arlene. I will nail it. I will nail it hard unto a cross. Nail and chain its evil ass so it can't wriggle free. I will…"

Nina jabbed her thumb on the remote, wishing there was something else more emphatic she could do to kill the screen.

Chapter
10
Alice

It was obvious that Nina knew something had happened, maybe even suspected a boy had been involved but Alice wasn't about to tell her anything. What she did say, she was done with school. There was some trouble and shouting over that, but they both knew it made sense. Most kids, with a job waiting for them, didn't make it past fifth grade.

"I just don't see the point, Mom. I can read. Can count better than you. What more do I need?"

Of course, she argued, but in spite of all the high volume cussing and arm waving, Alice could see she her heart wasn't in it. Her foreshortened fingers were beginning to ache, more every year, the blunted tips needing to be dipped in balm nightly. New orders kept picking up and Alice was already working weekends, and sometimes an hour or so in the evenings. Her mom needed her in the shop, and they both knew it.

It was settled like this; Nina had somehow found herself in possession of a massive bolt of the ugliest cloth you ever saw, given it for free. This was a heavy twill cotton, on the yellow side of mustard. She said, "Ok, then. You want to work full time, I got a project for you. You know the fella Bertillon?"

Alice froze, eyes wide. Her mom held up a placating hand.

"Yea, I know. That big old place is run by zombies, 'cept for Bertillon hisself."

She shook her head at the mystery of it. "Poor kids, can you imagine what that must be like? What it would do to their heads? But you won't have to have anything much to do with the deaders. Those orphan kids are dragging about in rags, and we're going to do a good thing for them. We're going to make them new uniforms. Doing it gratis, for free."

Alice was confused as to why her mom would think being around The Returned would upset her. Sister Mary Rose was Returned. She said, "Wish you wouldn't call them zombies, Mom. It's not nice."

When her mother just rolled her eyes, she turned to look at the bolt of horrible mustard cloth. "You think we're doing a good thing?"

"Beggars can't be choosers. So, yea. I do. Plus, we get to tell everybody we done it."

She pointed. "And I'll call the deaders zombies if I want. I got more *experience* of 'em than you."

***

Monday came around, the day when she should be going to school. Nina wrote a letter and hand delivered it, insisting that Alice come with. Before they left the house, she picked up a leather handbag and held it out.

"Here. Take this."

Even before Alice took it, she could see there was something heavy in there, but it was still a surprise to look inside and see her mother's old nickel-plated revolver.

"What's this?"

"You can see what it is. You won't tell what happened, but from here on, you go outside, you go armed."

Alice tried to give it back. "They don't allow handguns in school."

"You're not at school. We're just going to hand in a letter. Now, I'm guessin' a boy tried something with you. You won't tell me, so I've got to make things up for myself. I'm guessin' it's a boy, and I'm guessin' he's at the damn school. You see him, do *not* shoot him."

Then she said, "You see that little shit Cassie Fanning, shoot her all you want."

Chapter
11
Nina

When Nina and Marcus left the apartment, they went armed. Nina felt ridiculous wearing her cowboy-style holster, grumbling about looking like Calamity fucking Jane, but didn't refuse. Covered with a long coat, it was barely visible. Marcus had no such qualms about the new Glock, hanging under his armpit. She even caught him practicing, pulling it from the holster and pointing at his reflection.

In some ways, life had simplified, distilled right down until it was all about food. There were less people on the streets, and most of those who were looked scared or had a dangerous, predatory look to them, like they'd gone feral. Others begged for pity, holding cards saying their children were starving.

It seemed that there was always the smell of burning in the air, and palls of choking smoke often hazed the skyline. The roads remained clogged with abandoned cars, and nobody but the cops, the military and biker gangs attempted to drive anymore.

If gunfire crackled or banged in the air, a lot of guns were pulled and the street emptied fast. One morning, after an unsuccessful foray to Grace's Marketplace, which was rumoured to have a delivery, they found themselves in an unusually focussed stream in East 66th Street. A real press of people,

85

many chanting and all in a hurry. There was an uneasy feeling of excitement in the air, a sense of something about to happen.

Nina and Marcus went with the flow, coming eventually to what was left of the 7-Eleven on the corner of 2nd Avenue.

This had nothing to do with food. Being tall, Nina managed to see over the heads of those massed before her. Some heavy-looking guys had hold of an woman who wasn't just elderly, she was plainly dead. She was smaller and lighter than them, but still they struggled to hold her.

It took five of them to wrestle her down, dropping out of sight. Beside her, Marcus hissed, "They're going to burn her."

Nina couldn't see the cross, but she could see a heavily muscled arm raised again and again, the sound of the hammer almost lost in all the yelling.

Then they were hauling the cross upright, lashing it to a lamp post. It had to be ten feet tall or more. The woman, who had been a slight, white lady in her sixties, was nailed to it, with chains binding her limbs and body tight. She spoke loud enough for Nina to hear.

"My name is Gillian Deeney."

What she said next was drowned in all the shouting, people screaming, "Burn her! Burn her!"

She kept speaking, and Nina caught some of it. She was saying that she was still Gillian Deeney. That she had children and grandchildren. Nina clearly heard her say, "I'm a mom."

All the while, scrap wood was being piled around the bottom. The woman didn't stop talking, even when it was lit and the voices of the crowd dropped. She talked about who she was – an office manager and mother, grandmother to four. She reeled off their names, talked of her late husband and her love for him. How she liked to bowl and sang in a church choir.

All the while, the fire was getting hotter, beginning to scorch her clothes. The fabric caught, sheeting her in flame and still she talked. She didn't writhe or scream, but did manage to pull one arm free, and then tried to undo the chains.

She was burning, a human torch, her flesh crisping and turning black. It stunk. Nina turned and pushed blindly through the crowd, many of whom were hurrying to get away, just like her.

***

A week after Nina witnessed that fiery crucifixion, Thiago called from the lobby, asking would they want to take part in a meeting of residents. Those who hadn't already high-tailed it out of the city. That night, they joined a group of only about forty people in the basement. Nina nodded to one or two people she knew vaguely, getting wary nods in return. This was a wary time and she and Marcus were the only two black residents.

They were all white, these people, all wealthy, and mostly over sixty. No children, except for one young mother holding a baby. A large, puffy-featured guy stood with his hand on the shoulder of a blonde woman who was only about a third his age and beautiful – she could've been a model if she was taller. As Nina watched, he glanced her way, then came back to run his eyes candidly up and down before looking away again. She barely knew the name of a single person here, even this guy and his surely trophy wife, both of whom lived in the next apartment. These were her immediate neighbours.

The woman, the trophy wife, glanced across a second later, and smiled, but tightly. A tall, slim guy in his thirties was last to arrive, looking irritated, and pushed through to the front of the loose semi-circle. She'd seen this guy around a few times, even passed a few words with him in the elevator. He was a good looking, floppy-haired guy. A sharp dresser and a guy who clearly worked out.

She'd hated him on sight.

Thiago, looking nervous, stood facing the residents. "I think that's everybody. Thanks for coming, folks."

He shifted foot to foot, licked his lips and opened his mouth to speak again, but Mr Sharp Dressed Man spoke over the top of him.

"For God's sake. You haven't even been clear why you called this meeting, if I can even call it that."

He looked around at the other residents. "I'm sure none of us know why we're here. You haven't been clear as to the *purpose*."

Thiago wiped his face. "A couple of residents suggested I do this. Thinking we needed to talk about, you know…"

"No. I don't know."

The tall guy with the trophy wife agreed. "Neither do I." He clicked his fingers in front of his face, twice. "Spit it out, man."

It was obvious that spit was in short supply, as far as Thiago was concerned. He held up his hands and looked at Mr Sharp Dresser. "Look, Mr Collier, everything's going crazy, right?"

Collier barked out a sarcastic little laugh. "I'll tell you what's crazy. I couldn't get into my own building with my fob. The amount this place cost…"

Marcus turned. "Hey."

Collier lifted his eyebrows, seemingly surprised that someone had the temerity to interrupt him, but Marcus wasn't finished. "Shut the fuck up. Let the man speak."

A ripple went through the little group, but nobody said anything for a moment. Thiago nodded. "Ok. Things have gone to hell, right? Looks like Government has nearly broken down. Feds on the street. Militia."

Collier threw up his hands, looking around the room but pointedly ignoring Marcus and Nina. "Why do we need to hear this from the *janitor*?"

Thiago pressed on, as well as he could. "The electric keeps going out. Water pressure has dropped. Internet keeps dropping out."

The elderly lady at Nina's elbow nodded. "Tell me about it."

"Police won't come if you call. Lucky to get a medic if you're sick."

Some murmurs of agreement now. Other heads nodding.

"And…" Thiago took a deep breath, getting to it. "Anybody standing here now dies, they ain't gonna stay dead."

That stopped the noise, but only for a moment, then everyone was talking at once. The husband of the trophy wife, some financier guy, Nina recalled, almost getting to his name, was trying to dominate. So was Collier, but there were too many people trying to have their say. Thiago called for quiet a couple of times without success and, after a few seconds, Nina pushed to the front to stand beside him.

She held her hands up for quiet, glaring hard around the room, and eventually the talking stuttered to a close.

"Ok. There's really only one question, that I can see."

The finance guy drew himself to his full height. "Who made *you* spokesperson?"

Nina ignored him. "Anybody dies, do we want them coming back?"

Mostly, people were shaking their head vehemently. One or two looked uncertain.

"If that's what we want, we got to burn anybody who dies. Do it our*selves*."

She left it a moment to let that sink in, before adding, "And do it right smart, before they come back."

Collier blew out an exasperated sigh, "And how do you propose we do that?"

Thiago made a face. "Build a pyre, like you see all around the city. In our parking lot."

"There's precious few parking spaces as it is! I've paid…"

Nina had had enough. "You!"

She pointed a finger. "Nobody gives a shit how much you paid. We've all paid, but now we need to build us a pyre."

"If you think for one minute I'm getting involved in dragging some loser's carcass down…"

The old lady spoke over him, shouted really. "We need a cross. In case somebody dies and we don't get there fast enough."

In the end, there was no real agreement. As the meeting broke up, Marcus put a hand on Thiago's shoulder. "I say we just do it, man, you and me. You got timber?"

Thiago thought about it. "I got some, a few heavy members. No light stuff I can think of, and probably not enough."

"So…?"

Thiago nodded to himself, like he was coming to a decision. "But I got an axe. And the keys to all the empty apartments in here."

"What you thinkin'?"

"I'm thinkin' about dining tables, sideboards. Some of the pieces in this place, Jesus, took four big guys to carry it in."

He looked from Nina to Marcus and shrugged. "We got a building full of wood."

Chapter
12
Alice

In the main part, Alice was more than a little relieved to have left school and her classmates behind, but there was one regret, and it was a big one. Mrs Twining, the music teacher.

The day after she and her mom delivered her leaving letter, she unpacked her schoolbag and burned all her exercise books in the yard behind the house. She searched out and burned every little thing related to the school, even taking the sports certificates down from her bedroom wall.

The only things to escape immolation were her two commendations for singing, and the photograph of her and Mrs Twining, standing on stage after her rendition of *Amazing Grace*. Kirstin Twining was tiny, and white with a thin fizz of white-blonde hair, so they were a striking mismatch, but both of them were grinning fit to bust.

She put them into a drawer, safe inside a stiff buff folder.

And she kept practicing on her mom's battered Martin guitar. A quality guitar, Mrs Twining had said, when she saw it, guard that with your life. They won't be making another like it anytime soon.

That was on the one and only time she ever took the guitar into school, unsure of her ability to prevent it getting smashed up or stolen.

She said, "I don't know what my mom's doing with a guitar anyway. She isn't remotely interested in music. Seriously. Gets irritable if I practice too much."

At this moment, she was sitting before the school piano, having her regular lesson from Mrs Twining. The woman had picked her out specially to teach one on one.

Twining tutted at that, and shook her head, but didn't comment. Alice was wont to complain about her mother's philistine nature, and her disdain for music, and it was clearly a struggle for the woman not to commiserate, but she mainly kept her counsel.

Instead, she said, "Maybe it was a gift from her husband."

"What?"

"The guitar. Maybe she got it from him."

"Her husband?"

Mrs Twining blinked as Alice stared at her. She held her hands over her mouth.

"I spoke out of turn there, please don't tell your mom."

When Alice just kept staring, she tried again, speaking carefully.

"It's just that I recall, seem to recall, way back Before, reading about your mom in a magazine. I think she had a relationship with…"

She frowned and looked away. Shook her head. "I forget his name. A singer though. Not the sort of music I ever went for. I think they might have married, but maybe not. They were different times, Alice."

"How long ago was this?"

"A long, long time ago. Thirty years, something like that."

"I wonder if she wanted to stop him singing as well."

Mrs Twining's eyes flickered, as though recalling something, but all she did was say, "Ok. Back to Chopin."

Alice wasn't ready to go back to Chopin. "So, people knew about her then? She said they did, all around the country, but I was never sure."

"Yea, she was famous, you could say. Not like Mayor Little either, much more than that. Fame was more of a thing back then."

Alice heard the disbelief in her own voice. "For wearing clothes?"

"It's hard to explain celebrity now, in terms you'd understand. But, yea."

A month after she left school, her mom was talking to someone at the front door, someone who had rang the bell. Alice recognised the voice and hurried into the hallway.

Nina was standing, hand on her hip, staring down at the woman, nothing friendly or welcoming in that stance. Mrs Twining looked tinier and whiter than ever, standing one step down, holding a leather music satchel, clutching it tight with both hands and struggling to maintain a smile.

Her eyes flicked beyond the woman no doubt glaring at her from the doorway, and caught sight of Alice. She began to say hello before squealing because Alice was barging past her mom and out there, throwing her arms around her and lifting her bodily from the floor.

"Alice!"

She put the woman down and did a double-hop backwards, shocked at herself for what she just did, to a teacher no less. But Mrs Twining was laughing.

"I'm pleased to see you too."

"Sorry about that."

Alice glanced at her mother, who stood now arms folded, eyelids heavy. "Well, I guess you better come in, Mrs Teacher." She raised a finger. "But mind…"

"Oh, Mom! Please, come on in, Mrs T."

Nina turned on her heel and marched away, making herself scarce as Alice fixed them both lemonade, which they drank in the living room. The teacher looked around her. "You have a lovely home, Alice."

"Thanks. Lived here as long as I can remember." She made a face. "Pretty much."

"I was sorry to hear you were leaving, though I can't blame you. I know it was tough."

Alice shrugged, and dropped her eyes to her drink.

"But, look. I'd like to keep up our lessons, if that's ok?"

"I don't think we could…"

"I'm not asking for money!" She leaned forward. "You're a natural musician, Alice. Most natural I ever taught."

Alice pulled back. "Naw."

"Yea. To be honest, I'm not a natural. What ability I have I've worked like hell for. It just seemed to fall under your fingers. And your voice!"

"What about it?"

"I figure, by the time you've matured, you'll be a contralto."

"You mean, like a man."

"No."

"I get told that all the time. You sound like a man, Simeon."

"No! Some of the best ever female singers ever were contralto. Nina Simone, for God's sake."

"What?"

"I heard your Mom used Nina Simone's name, because she looked a helluva lot like her. She hasn't talked to you about this?"

When Alice just shook her head, she waved a hand. "Never mind. The point is that your voice is already rich, like honey, and is well on its way to being contralto. Be proud of it."

"Maybe. I guess."

"But, for now. How about you come to my house on Friday evening's, after work? We'll just pick up where we left off."

Alice tried not to cry. "You would do that for me?"

"Sure I would."

"I don't have a piano, here. I can't practice, now I'm not at school."

"I have three pianos. I'll let you have one."

"Three?"

"When everything went to hell, nobody was thinking about musical instruments. I kept my own and saved two others. Could've had a dozen, if I wanted."

"Wow."

"And I know somebody could give you guitar lessons, but he wouldn't do it for free."

"I doubt I could afford it."

"You want, I'll speak to him. See what we can work out."

Alice compressed her lips, then nodded.

Chapter
13
James

Every Sunday morning, Doctor Bertillon led the inhabitants of the home that bore his name on a twenty-minute walk to attend mass at the Church of the Risen Flock. They made that walk, more often than not, in the dark. The chapel was a small one, and six o'clock mass was set aside for *The Foundlings*, as they were invariably referred to by Father Michaels.

Getting out of bed at four-thirty on a freezing Sunday morning was never James' idea of a good time but, once he was up, there was something special about the day. As a younger kid, the downhill walk to the old stone church was one of the few times he got to see what the world looked like outside of the grounds of the home. There would also be very occasional, carefully managed, outings to Derryfield or Veterans Park, and one notable time a visit to the theatre.

It was only later, once he hit thirteen and was allowed to accompany Ana-Maria into the centre of town, that he understood how carefully he had been protected, and the reasons behind it.

Most Sundays merged into one another but, one day, months after Alice Simeon delivered their new uniforms, he walked close to the front of the double line, holding Karen Gill's hand. All the children went hand-in-hand. That was just how it was. Bertillon strode in front, behind him two carers, Ana-Maria and Frieda, then the snake of newly mustard-clad children and, bringing up the tail, the last carer, Nicolette.

Until recently, it had been nothing to James whether he held a boy's hand or a girl's. He barely noticed that Karen *was* a girl. But something had been started in him, kicked rudely into life by that first sight of Alice walking long legged and head down across the yard.

Now, he was painfully conscious that the hand in his belonged to a girl of his own age. She was taller than him, of course she was, and not as pretty as Alice Simeon, but then, nobody was.

The new skirts were shorter than the old smocks, stopping mid-knee. He had spent a lot of time in the last week surreptitiously looking at Karen's legs, and noticing that she was developing breasts.

Her hair, which he had pulled often in the last few years, was deep red and shone. He wondered if it was a sin to get a boner in the church and tried to make himself stop thinking about it.

Karen whispered. "Why are you jiggling about like that?"

"I'm not."

"You are. And you keep pressing on my thumb."

He turned to look at her, and found her eyes looking into his. Had to look away.

They were just reaching the church now and it was beginning to get light, enough to see the spoilers had been at work. Painting the Z-word on the doors of the church and shooting up the sign.

Bertillon tutted and shook his head, but the carers didn't react and neither did James.

Karen leaned in. "Again! What's wrong with those people?"

Everybody knew the answer to that, because it had been repeated so often. James trotted out the usual line.

"They're ignorant. Don't know any better."

Karen gave the normal response. "They will though. Eventually. Nothing is surer."

Father Michaels stood as usual in the doorway of the chapel, nodding to them as they arrived, beaming. "Ah, Dr Bertillon. Good to see you. Ana-Maria, Frieda."

The man's memory was excellent. "Martin, Karen. Ah, James, the math wizard! And there's Serena, our little artist…"

They passed the door with the messily painted Z, and James caught a distinctive acrid odour. This time, when Karen leaned in to whisper, she was close enough that he felt her breath on his face.

"They even pissed on the door. Gross!"

The children filed into the chilly church and sat, the cold from the pews eating into their bones. James followed Karen and, when he settled himself, she shifted, so that her thigh lay alongside his. He held his breath, staring at her leg, her bony knee just visible, most definitely pressed against his.

Was she doing this because it was so cold? He glanced quickly at her, but she wasn't looking at him, her eyes were on the altar. Do not, he told himself sternly, get a hard on.

Father Michaels wasted no time getting started. He wore his usual faded black robe, with only a satin stole in green and gold for colour. He held up his hand, and began. So modest and quiet in normal life, at the pulpit he was a firebrand, every word spoken with meaning, and even more volume.

"In the name of the Father, and of the Son and of the Holy Spirit."

"Amen."

"May the Lord be with you."

"And also with you."

He paused for effect, as he always did.

"Jesus said, unto Mary and Martha, I am the resurrection and the life. Whoever believes in me, they may *die*."

"They may die."

He raised both hands, high above his head. "Yet shall they live!"

"They may die, yet shall they live."

"John, ah-3.16!"

He pointed at his little congregation. "John 3.16. God so loved the world that he gave his only begotten son."

He threw his hands in the air, keeping them there. "That every person who believes in him *shall not perish*."

"They shall not perish."

"But shall have eternal life!"

"They shall have eternal life."

Karen's leg left his, and he felt the loss of it. He glanced at her, but she was busy, answering the priest. When he moved his own leg to touch hers, she didn't move away.

"Isiah 26.19!"

Again, he pointed, his finger picking out James and Karen as he briefly dropped his voice to a near normal register.

"Isiah 26.19, children. Thy dead men shall live. Together with my own dead body shall they arise."

Then, all but shouting. "Awake and sing. Sing ye that dwell in dust, for thy dew is as the dew of herbs, and the earth shall cast *out* the dead."

"The earth shall cast out the dead."

They made the sign of the cross and, when Karen dropped her hand, it fell onto his knee, and stayed there.

***

Only a few months later, James and Karen were chosen to accompany Ana-Maria and Frieda to town, ostensibly to help them pick up supplies. It didn't go as he had expected it to. The whole-school expeditions to town before then had always taken place in the early part of the morning. As Martin put it, getting it done before the assholes haul their asses out of bed. Even then, James had seen some sights and caught the strange looks the line of foundlings received. He knew the route across Notre-Dame bridge, and had seen the Merimack in full flow. He had canoed the pool in Livingston Park, and visited the shops around City Hall Plaza. Walked Elm Street and goggled at the other worldly mannequins in SimeonStyle.

He'd sat a high stool at the soda bar in Amherst, and drank a chocolate ice float, the best thing he'd ever tasted. The children had even gone by bus to The Palace one unforgettable evening, to scream and laugh with the rest of the audience at a performance of The Wizard of Oz.

There were no Returned in the audience that evening, James didn't even notice that until Karen pointed it out to him, leaning so close her lips tickled

101

his skin. She was right. The Returned were on duty, sweeping up popcorn and doing similar chores, but even the carers didn't join them in the audience. Only Bertillon himself did that.

He didn't think about that for long. He was too busy thinking about Karen, and staring wide-eyed at the story of Dorothy and the witches.

So, when the afternoon came that they would accompany Ana-Maria and Frieda, he was mostly simply excited, hoping that he and Karen might even find a way to spend some time alone. Even if they didn't, it was a huge adventure, and they were in it together. He also had some responses ready for the ones who might be rude. Saw himself putting those spoilers in their place. Showing them the error of their ways, doing that right in front of Karen.

The walk to Notre-Dame bridge was the same as it had been before, more trucks and cars certainly, and more folks hurrying about their business. The carers marched ahead, with the children behind, so they held hands and pressed close together. Once or twice, he went on tiptoe and stole a brief kiss.

Things changed on the other side of the Merrimack. Bridge Street was so much busier, more folk milling around than any place he had ever seen. So many people, and so many cars. The workshops on either side of the road were busy too, and noisy. A garage, advertising professional automobile computer removal, was the noisiest – with exhaust noise sounding like automatic gunfire. Karen, looking shocked, dropped his hand so she could cover her ears. Godley's Shoes was noisy too, and huge. The smell of cured leather was strangely pleasant and sickly at the same time.

It only got even busier as they turned into Elm Street, holding hands again, ever more tightly. So many people, and every one a stranger, some with pistols at their hips and cigarettes in their mouths. There were so many trucks that a person would have to wait for a gap, just to cross the road. The noise was so great it threatened to overwhelm him.

Some stared openly at the little group, none friendly, but not exactly unfriendly, so far. Ahead, James could see stores, bars and cafés crowding the street. Their signs hung over the sidewalk, so many it was hard to focus on any one. The smells were different now, tacos and pizzas and beer. Despite his nervousness, James's stomach rumbled.

As they approached the junction with Lowell, a group of a half dozen men were standing just beyond the corner, outside something that described itself as Maynard's Liquor and Tobacco.

Coming closer, James realised that every one of those men had a gun of some sort. Two had assault rifles slung across their chests, one had a shotgun, which was tipped casually over his shoulder. The others had pistols at their belts.

He looked from Frieda to Ana-Maria, but neither of them paid any attention, or reacted in any way. They just kept walking, getting closer to the men, who were now taking notice, turning to see. Karen and James pulled together, her grip on his hand so tight it hurt.

Rough-looking men, James thought, hard-cases. Home rolled cigarettes in their mouths or cupped in hands, beards or stubble faces, skin red from the sun. They were turning to each other, one pushed himself off against the wall he had been leaning against, and flicked his still smoking butt onto the sidewalk. Another hawked loudly and spat in the road.

One, a big guy with a dirty cowboy style hat, an assault rifle hanging above his impressive gut, stood square in front of them as they crossed the intersection.

"Well, lookee here. Jesus H Christ, boys."

Frieda and Ana-Maria simply continued, trailing James in their wake.

"Two of them kids from the zombie school. Fuckin yeller jackets. And their zombies, bold as you like."

They crossed the intersection and reached the sidewalk, coming right up on the men. Neither of the carers broke stride, or gave any indication that they had even noticed them, passing with only inches to spare. James, his words of rebuke forgotten, followed close, having to hold Karen back as she threatened to break into a run.

The big man laughed and shouted after him, "Yea, you better run, you yeller-jacket little shits. What you doin' with them deaders anyways?"

Safely past and on their way, James looked from one of his carers to the other, but they didn't glance his way. Clearly, as far as they were concerned, nothing had happened. Karen leaned in to whisper to him, "Weren't you scared? How could you not be scared?"

He turned to her, trying to slow his heartbeat and keep his expression calm, hoping his voice would be ok. It seemed fine. "There was nothing to be scared of."

"Those were scary men, James."

Elm Street was now a bustling and bewildering confusion of people and shops and smells. Stalls selling hot roasted peanuts and sugared popcorn, open-fronted shops where men sat in chairs having their hair cut. Beery, smoky bars, eateries smelling of bacon and fried onions. A yard and workshop where men in oily overalls worked noisily on cars. A house where women hung out of the upper windows, almost nothing covering their boobies. Karen gasped when she saw them and covered James's eyes, taking hold of his head and turning it so he couldn't see.

City Hall was on their right now, a grand old building with a tall tower, and a fancy clock. It was surrounded by stalls.

People called and laughed and shouted out their wares. They reached SimeonStyle and James stared to see the mannequins. They looked a bit crazy in the head, like they were spoiling for a fight, but none of them were wearing mustard twill.

Nina Simeon herself was in the doorway, smoking a leisurely cigarette. James tried to see past her, hoping to catch sight of Alice, but she didn't seem to be around. Beside him, Karen gave him a little tug on the hand, maybe knowing what was in his mind.

Nina smiled at him, and winked. But didn't say anything.

They entered one of the larger stores, Baldwin's Dry Goods, and James stopped to look at all the stuff on the shelves. It seemed like they had everything in the world in here. It smelled exotic, with a haze of tobacco smoke in a flat layer just above his head. He turned to Karen who stared at him wide-eyed, her jaw dropped right open. She even did a little dance, like she couldn't keep her feet still.

"Look at all this stuff! Did you ever imagine such a thing?"

James nodded, serious. "It is impressive."

Frieda handed over the order and the tall man behind the counter took it without a word and went off to fill it. After a while, though, he seemed to notice them, wandering around the shop, Karen goggling openly at the wonders on display.

"Hey, you."

Karen issued a little squeak, but James simply turned, hands behind his back, keeping his face blank. The man frowned and pointed at them.

"You two have the look of kids who enjoy a liquorice whip? Am I wrong?"

James answered. "No, Sir."

The man's finger moved to a jar on the counter. "Help yourself. No more than two mind. I'll be watching."

James followed Karen to the jar and accepted a red whip of liquorice without comment. Turned to find Frieda watching him.

Ana-Maria was looking the other way.

Chapter
14
Nina

Nina heard the knocking on her door, the sound frantic, and grabbed the nickel-plated Smith and Wesson. Had that down by her side as she checked the spy-hole to see her neighbour, the blonde one she thought of as a trophy wife but didn't know her name.

She was pretty much hopping on the spot, looking scared.

Nina cracked the door, so she wouldn't see the gun.

"What is it?"

"You gotta help! Mason's taken pills!"

That was the guy's name, she recalled. Mason Franke, the financier. She shook her head, still not opening up. "Call Thiago."

"Too late! He's dead. I don't even know how long. I got to get him out back, burn him quick. Is Marcus there?"

Nina shook her head. "Out trying to get some food."

The woman, the trophy wife who was a real person after all, looked terrified. "I can't carry him on my own. I might have to burn him where he lays."

Nina closed her eyes. "Shit!"

She dumped the gun, a fat lot of good those things turned out to be, and hurried after her, the

107

woman wearing some kind of baby doll thing, but with a man's robe pulled over, bare feet.

They ran into the apartment and the guy was sprawled over an easy chair, two empty pill bottles on the floor beside him. He'd been sick, and pissed himself, and the tastefully, or at least expensively, decorated room stunk.

Franke was, Nina thought, in his early sixties. Hard to tell as he'd had so much work done. Now, fancy hairstyle sticking up, unshaven face slack and big belly hanging out of his pyjamas, he looked older.

The first thing that Nina did was to walk over there and put her hand to his forehead.

"He's still warm. Can't be dead long."

"Shit! I never thought to do that. I'm kinda…"

To show what she was kinda, she shook her hands out before her, like electricity was running through her.

Nina made herself take a long breath, and put her hand on the woman's arm. She was no use to anyone like this. "What's your name?"

"Shit. Fuck. We've not even been introduced. I'm Ashleigh. Friends call me Ash."

"Ok. I'm gonna call downstairs, Ash. Tell Thiago we're coming down in the elevator with Mason, and we got to burn him right quick. Ok?"

Ash was twittering in her ear as she picked up the phone by the door, asking how can we get him there? He's a big guy. A big fat guy.

Nina ignored her, getting through on the second ring, explaining the situation in as few words as possible. Thiago got it straight away.

"I'll start the burn, Ms Simeon, be back to help before you know it."

"Meet us in the basement?"

"You got it."

She turned to Ashleigh, put both hands on her upper arms. Jesus, the woman was thrumming like a tuning fork. "Listen to me. You listening?"

The woman nodded. Then said, "I'm listening."

"There's a clock ticking, right now. You feel it?"

A wide-eyed, terrified nod. Of course she did, she was feeling nothing else.

"You work out, don't you? Probably every day." It was a guess, but not much of one. "You're strong, not weak. Together we're going to drag this body along the passage, get it to the lift. We're going to do that, ok?"

The woman nodded, maybe believing, maybe not. Definitely wanting to.

Nina stepped over and picked up one of the man's sprawling legs. The woman had been telling the truth about her husband, he was a big guy, and seriously overweight. Must go way over two hundred pounds.

"Grab his other leg. We've not got time for anything fancy. Going to drag him, simple as."

Ash took hold, tucked the guy's foot under her armpit and Nina took a big breath, readying herself. "One, two three, *pull!*"

The guy came off the chair easily enough, bones and flesh hitting the floor in a rippling series of uncomfortable thuds, but the thick-pile carpet seemed to stick to his back, and they were only able to move forward in snatches, inches at a time. It was harder than Nina expected and, by the time they reached the front door, she was already gasping for breath.

The passage would have been a lot easier if it had been tiled, but it was carpeted. Still, it wasn't so luxurious, and the guy didn't seem to stick so much, so they got some momentum going. Nina could see the elevator doors ahead, and kept shouting to Ash, swearing at her, telling her to fucking pull.

At her own door, which she'd left ajar, she paused and hopped inside, picking up the Smith and Wesson after all, and sticking it down the back of her waistband.

Ash watched her do it, and dropped her eyes to her husband's face. Compressed her lips, but didn't say anything. They were both seriously winded by the time they reached the elevator. It was right there, when Nina pressed the button. Probably Thiago's doing.

Something on the man's clothing seemed to catch, half way into the cab. Pull as they might, they couldn't drag him in. The doors kept trying to close, dinging, and opening again. Nina hopped out of the elevator, having to stand on his chest, then bent to grab him under the arms. The gun fell onto the floor with a loud clunk. She ignored it, getting her hands under him and putting everything into a lift, snarling at Ash to for fuck's sake *pull*.

Somehow, they scrambled and rolled the body in. Nina grabbed her pistol and the two women leaned against the walls, breathing in big whoops and staring at each other as the elevator descended.

At the basement, Nina could have wept when the doors slid open and Thiago was there. He took in the situation in a second and didn't waste any time, grabbing Mason's right foot. With both women pulling the other and the floor slick-painted concrete, they were moving now.

Thiago, through gritted teeth, asked, "How long?"

"We don't know. He's a suicide. Pills."

"Shit."

Nina could smell the pyre before she saw it, a criss-cross of construction timbers piled atop a heavy mahogany dining table, with broken up chairs as kindling, the whole thing stinking now of burning gasoline. The flames were high already. Some fool had parked their Jaguar SUV right nearby, too close for comfort.

As they got nearer, the heat increased. Thiago turned to the women.

'Ok, we got to pick him up."

Ash shook her head, but he said, "Mrs. Franke. We got to. I should have waited to set this alight, but there's nothing for it now. We got to pick him up. Throw him in."

He got down and grabbed Mason under the armpits. Nina got herself under his ass at one side and, after a hesitation, Ash got the other. On the count of three, they lifted.

Nina was surprised when the smaller woman bared her teeth and roared, everything in now. They ran at the pyre even as Nina felt the guy slipping from her hands. She clapped on tighter and roared herself because she couldn't let him slip.

The fire burned them all as they tumbled him on, so that they stumbled backwards yelling and crying and wiping at their scorched skin and smouldering clothes.

A second passed. Another. Then, Mason Franke sat up and screamed.

Thiago jumped back. "He ain't dead!"

Franke writhed in the flames, screaming, trying to crawl out. Nina pulled the gun and yanked on the trigger, missing with her first shot, hitting him in the belly with the second, then in the head. That third shot knocked him back and down.

They stood there for several seconds in silence, apart from the crackling of the fire, the popping of burning flesh, and their own breathing.

Nina glanced around at the many windows overlooking this lot, faces at many of them now. She looked across at Ash, who was staring at her husband burning. Her robe had fallen open to show her ridiculous, barely there at all nightwear, scorched and holed now, but she wasn't thinking about that.

As the heat built, they had to shuffle back. The paintwork on the Jag was blistering, and Nina wondered if there was any risk it might catch fire, or the tank explode.

Thiago put a hand on Ash's arm. "I'm sorry for your loss, Mrs. Franke."

Then, looking hard at Nina, not Ash, he said, "You two don't have to stay and watch this."

Nina put her own hand out, thinking to steer the woman away, but she shook it off.

"No. I should stay. I should do that."

Nina caught the concierge's eye again, or maybe the other way around. He widened his eyes pointedly at the gun, so heavy and yet forgotten in her hand.

"Okay, Mrs Franke. I'll call the cops. They'll want to know."

That got Ash turning from the fire, as Nina tucked her gun away. "They'll want to investigate?" She blinked. "Of course they will."

But Thiago was shaking his head. "Nah. Things have moved beyond that. I'm betting all they'll do is note it down, for records. If that. Everything's turning to shit, pardon my French. Might give you a call, is all."

Suddenly the door to the stairs burst open and a man came out at a dead run, sprinting towards them.

It was the guy from the meeting, Collier, but there was nothing smug about him now. He was furious, cursing as he came. Nina reached around for the Smith and Wesson.

But he wasn't coming for them. He was coming for his SUV.

They watched as he leaped in, continuing to cuss them out, pausing only a moment to check out Ash in her burned-up baby-doll before tearing away, tyres squealing and paintwork smoking.

Ashleigh wrapped her robe tight around herself and Thiago left, saying he'd make the call, leaving the two women with the fire. It was now so hot that they had to stand well back. Ash had been quiet, but now she said, "Mason was a hedge fund manager."

"What's that?"

"That's what I said. He told me, it means, no matter what, I'm going to be rich. Doesn't matter what the hell else is going on."

Nina nodded. "One of those guys."

"One of those. That's why he did it. Could cope with all the other shit going down, everything going to hell. He just couldn't cope with being wrong."

She looked up at Nina, searching her face. "You are…"

The pause was so long that Nina had to ask, "What?"

"Heroic. I never imagined myself saying that word, I mean about another person, but you are."

Nina looked away, embarrassed. "I'm big is all. Can you imagine two women your size pulling that guy?"

It was about as far to the side of the wrong thing to say as you could get, Nina knew that as it came out

113

of her mouth, but Ash blew out a bitter little laugh. "Yea, we'd still be up there. He'd still be alive."

They waited until the pyre burned down, then walked out of there.

Chapter

15

James

James' internal clock woke him with a feeling that something was wrong. He sat up in bed, feeling sleepy and confused and took a moment to check the time from the wall clock. Then he leaned over the gap and shook Martin's elbow.

"Hey."

Martin's head was still under the covers. "Wussup?"

"It's past twenty minutes to seven"

Martin looked up and blinked around the dormitory, with little sign he had understood what had just been said. "What?"

"It's Sunday." James pointed to the clock and watched as Martin came properly awake.

Others were pulling the covers off themselves and sitting up, frowning and muttering. The feeling that something was wrong was too strong now for James to stay in bed, take advantage of this unlooked-for lie in. His clothes were folded neatly on his stool, and he dressed quickly, making his bed up just as rapidly.

The door opened as he finished, and Bertillon stood there, his expression grim.

"I thought I'd let you sleep, boys."

"Is there no Mass today, Sir?"

"We'll celebrate Mass at ten this morning. In the assembly hall."

Martin and James exchanged looks. James turned back to the headmaster.

"Why not…"

Bertillon raised a hand. "I have some bad and shocking news. I'm afraid the chapel has been damaged in a fire, in the early hours of the morning."

Martin all but jumped from bed. "The Spoilers…"

Both hands up now, palms out. "Let's not jump to conclusions. All we know is that there was a fire last night. And that our chapel is badly damaged. Hopefully not beyond repair. The Police are investigating."

"The Police won't try to find who did it. They were probably in on it!"

"Martin Klopp! One more word out of you and there will be consequences. For all we know this was an accident. I won't have unfounded allegations being made in this school. Now, get ready, all of you. We have the honour of hosting Mass this morning, so we will have visitors and…"

He held up a warning finger. "And Father Michaels will be most terribly shaken up by this. Imagine what this has done to him. Our job is to support him, as he has supported us all these years. This is his time of need."

Once Bertillon closed the door, the boys turned to each other and Martin made a fist. "Those fuckin' spoilers. It's a wonder it took them this long."

James nodded. "Fuckin' spoilers."

Chapter
16
Nina

Nina kept the Land Rover as close behind Marcus' Silverado as she could. This was what they had agreed – he would drive the pickup and she would follow in the Land Rover. She had the revolver handy, and the hunting rifle was loaded and clipped behind her.

The journey had been long and there had been some close calls. Militias and real military were everywhere, roadblocks every fifty miles or so, and if there was any kind of law, it was a dangerous and capricious kind, with decisions made on the hoof. At one terrifying moment, they found themselves flying along at sixty but still hemmed in, Harley's roaring on either side, white guys with guns who peeled away only when a Humvee appeared in the distance, a marine manning the big gun. Nina had been used to the colour of her skin marking her out, but never felt that it put her life on the line before this, a black woman in convoy with a black man.

They got off the main road to camp in what felt like the middle of nowhere on their first night out of New York and took turns sleeping, got moving again before dawn broke. After two days hard travelling, a journey that used to take about seven hours, they were exhausted and strung out, but had reached the gate to

Tilly Whim. Up this high, crusts of iced-over snow still clung to the shadowed areas.

The gate was still there, still locked, but the sign was gone. When Marcus jumped out to unwind the chain, he stood on it. Picked it up to show her.

That sign had always been pocked with small calibre bullets. Now it looked like the army had unloaded on it. They stared at each other for a long moment before Marcus ran back to the Silverado and they drove through, stopping again just past the gates.

This time, after adding a new length of heavier chain, they donned work gloves and hauled a bale of razor wire from the Silverado, unrolling it behind and around the gate.

This was what they had agreed, but now Nina had to ask, "You sure we shouldn't see what's down there first? Maybe we need to make a quick getaway. Maybe your friend Mr Lee is there with his family, waiting to kill us."

Marcus shook his head, a quick motion like he didn't want to consider that. "Nah"

"Maybe just gangsters then."

"I been thinking about that."

"So?"

"I figure, there's somebody there, we're good as dead anyway. And if Andy Lee hasn't come through with our stuff, for whatever reason, we're in a lot of trouble."

"Okay."

"Let's get rolling. Andy should have cleared any recent windfall."

"If he's come through."

"Whatever. From here to the house, I'm not stopping. You see me stop, it's because somebody is forcing me."

118

His expression was grim. "Be clear on this. Somebody tries to stop me, there's going to be shooting." He held the Glock up. "We might have to fight, Nina."

It was less than a hundred yards from the gate when Marcus' lights flashed on, and he braked hard, coming to a dead stop.

Nina halted inches from his bumper, pistol already in her hand as she twisting about, trying to see what was happening, and look everywhere at once. This was, even she could see, a good place for an ambush, the way the trees loomed either side, hardly enough space for the Silverado.

Her heart was hammering so hard that it hurt her throat. Ahead, Marcus opened the driver door and got out, moving very, very slowly. The Glock was in his hand, but it was down at his side. She was still wondering should she get out too when he sank at the knee, still moving slow, till he squatted almost as low as he could go.

Got right down on his knees, his back to her.

"Shit!"

She was out in a second, using the door as protection, aiming and ducking and shifting to present a harder target. She took a big breath, then sprinted towards Marcus, slithering to a stop as a small brown animal hopped into sight.

Marcus glanced at her with a grin, then scooped it up and stood.

She waved her gun in the air. Hissed at him. "What the fuck?"

"A puppy! Look."

She put her hand on her throat, the place her heart was beating hardest. "Marcus!"

He blinked at her, suddenly embarrassed. "It was just there."

They stared at each other, then looked around, seeing nothing but trees pressed in close. Under the canopy, it would be hard to push through the underbrush, without something like a machete.

The puppy wriggled in his arms, trying to lick his face. A crackle in the woods, and they both pointed their guns in that direction.

She whispered, "A puppy. How can that be? Way out here."

"I don't know."

In the distance, maybe from the main road, a dog barked. Another answered.

"Let's get moving." She pointed at the puppy, still wriggling in his arm. "You taking that thing?"

He looked at it and nodded, pulled it to his face. "Might come in useful."

"Plus, you like it. Jesus Christ."

***

The area before the gate to the town itself was stacked; bales of razor-wire and fence posts, wooden crates full of seed stock. It looked like almost all of the stuff that had been ordered.

Marcus swept a hand across his brow in pantomime relief, climbing out of the Silverado with the puppy now jumping around his ankles. It ran to Nina, wagging its tail so hard its whole back end got wagged with it, pissing as it came.

It looked like a Labrador crossed with something else, a little tan pup, dark faced and blunt nosed, all excitement and tongue and claws.

For the moment, Nina ignored the damned thing. She strapped the pistol on, not minding the gunslinger look now, and used her Ruger to scan the trees each

120

side, coming around to search the schoolhouse for movement. This was maybe the most dangerous moment, because anybody would know they would have to stop at these gates and there was no chance of any kind of quick getaway.

Birds sang, the wind blew, and the car engines ticked quietly as they cooled. There was no other sound, that she could hear.

Marcus dropped the Weatherby from his face and blew out a shaky breath. He nodded to all the stuff piled around the entrance

"Andy did it! Jesus. Looks like everything's here, pretty much."

He walked to the gate, almost treading on the puppy more than once, and unlocked it whilst she continued to scan the woods. There were a lot of woods to scan.

Minutes later they pulled up outside the schoolhouse and again came out armed and ready. They searched every room, searched the houses and the mill, pushing doors open and hauling tarps aside with gun muzzles, taking their time before they started to feel they could relax. The fucking puppy scampered around, yipping and jumping on them, making a deadly serious business seem more than slightly ridiculous.

Inside the Land Rover again, Nina did a U-turn and drove them all the way back to the top of the steepest incline. On their right, the ground fell away to the rocks lining the lake. Below them, the road dropped steeply for better than a hundred yards. This, she knew, was the exact place where his parents had gone off, coming to their lakeside cottage in a fancy Mercedes.

Moving carefully, they slid out, shoving the puppy back inside when it tried to follow. Nina felt uncomfortable standing so close to the drop, so stepped around the front of the Land Rover first chance she got, joining Marcus with his chainsaw. She held the Ruger ready as they walked downhill, searching as they went. Stopping about halfway down, Marcus pointed to a particularly large tree.

"This one."

The chainsaw burst into horribly noisy life, she could imagine the sound echoing around the hills and across the lake. Heads coming up and taking notice, eyes squinting.

The Ruger wasn't as heavy as the Weatherby, but it was beginning to feel like a hundred pounds in her arms as she squatted and searched.

Finally, Marcus told her to scoot back, well up the slope. A few seconds more of clattering chainsaw work, and the tree fell with a squealing, crashing noise, blocking the road.

Marcus sought her hand and they stood together and stared at what they had done. The tree could be cleared, if somebody really wanted to get past, but it would be a serious task. It would be noisy.

Nina squeezed his hand harder. "It blocks us in too."

He nodded, but said nothing. She knew they could shift it, with a lot of time and effort, but it felt final. The actual, physical point of no return.

She pressed her stomach, pushing against an ache. "When was the last time we ate?"

***

Back in the house, Nina pulled together a hasty bean hot-pot whilst Marcus inventoried their supplies. She was relieved that the damned pup scampered off

122

behind him, leaving her in the first moment of peace she'd had in many days. She chewed a cereal bar as she watched them from the window, seeing him checking things off the list whilst trying not to tread on the thing, and felt a knot of irritation in her chest. The last thing they needed was the complication of an animal, a baby, one that depended on them.

That evening they sat on the veranda, drinking wine and staring down the lake. It was such a familiar scene, but now different. Partly because she was seeing it through the eyes of defenders, but mainly because the sky seemed so unutterably vast. It had always been vast, the sweep of the tree-lined mountains falling towards the water so massive it awed the mind, but she had never felt it so clearly.

For the moment, the puppy slept, whimpering in its dreams and curved into Marcus' long thigh. He grinned at it, and swept his hand along its sleek flank, pulled it closer in to his leg.

"You're a nice little doggie, aren't you?"

Now that they were finally here, the enormity of the task ahead was sinking in, for Nina. The pad that Marcus once wrote songs on was now a list of tasks, he'd set them out meticulously, in priority order. It was an overwhelmingly long list, covering two pages. At least, he said, holding up the inventory, against all the odds, most of what they needed was there.

Top priority was to make the place more secure, but it wasn't as simple as that. He tapped the pad with his pen.

"We can't spend our entire Spring putting up fences and razor wire. If we do, we miss the start of the planting season. Shit. There's so much work needed to turn this place into something that'll sustain us."

This wasn't new information, but now she could feel it, like a weight right inside her chest. The next six months would be a race against time, Marcus had been saying that a lot too. Now he said, "If all we needed to do was survive the first winter, just that one, we'd be ok. But it isn't just one. We got to plan to be here for years."

Nina watched him pet the sleeping dog and asked, "What do you really know about farming?"

He smiled, apparently pleased. "Nothing, but don't worry. I don't know about defence either so it all balances out."

***

The rototiller was a beast of a thing, inclined to buck and jump and constantly threatening to break shins or slither sideways. Marcus insisted on using it himself, until they had their first major bust up in Tilly Whim.

Nina had to make him see that there was so much seriously hard labour, and he couldn't possibly do it all. He looked so much like a little boy, about to cry, maybe he did cry when he turned away, but she couldn't just let this slide. For all his lists and finger counting, he couldn't bring himself to imagine not doing all the heavy lifting himself.

Nina ended it by just firing the tiller up and grabbing on. Man, the thing was an awkward bastard. She had to fight it every step of the way, Marcus watching. Every few seconds it felt like she was only just – just – strong enough to hold it, but she kept going, ignoring him. After one completed drill, the muscles of her arms were screaming.

She pushed and hefted and cussed the thing around, and started the return. She could, she thought, just about manage this. At least on the meadow, which, after all had once been farmed.

Luckily, the puppy – Marcus' puppy, that was clear to all three of them – hated the rototiller, so kept out of the way, whimpering and howling.

Marcus left reluctantly, and soon she saw him in the distance, putting a tall timber post into the ground, the first step in the huge job of circling the place with ugly, nasty razor wire. The guy who he bought them from told him not to worry, the first hundred posts would be the worst. Marcus telling the story like it was a joke. After her first day of rototilling, and his first day putting in posts, nobody was seeing the funny side. They collapsed into bed and had a groaning competition, which eventually turned into vaguely hysterical laughter.

She'd never been so sore, or so tired. Despite the heavy gloves, her hands were badly blistered, the skin shifted around in places like it was no longer properly connected to her flesh.

The damned pup scrambled and whined on the floor, too short to climb onto the bed. Marcus leaned over and crooned to it, "Aw doggie, you want to come up?"

Nina held up a hand, fingers splayed. "Do *not* bring that creature into our bed. Less you want to sleep on your own with it."

Marcus contented himself petted its floppy ears. "Settle down, doggie, settle down."

The aches were worse in the morning, so bad Nina could barely move. Marcus was in no better shape. Coffee and bacon pancakes didn't do much to set it to rights, but at least she had a little more energy. Enough to imagine starting again without crying.

Marcus, the dog on his lap fighting to get onto the table, shovelled his food in, then picked up the maple syrup bottle and gave it a shake. "Once this is gone…"

"I'm more worried about wine. And bourbon. We ought to have brought more bourbon."

"Maybe we can make our own."

"You think?"

He smoothed the dog's ears down, and shrugged. "We've got yeast."

"What do we do with it, though?"

"Google it."

She barked out a laugh at that. Their old world hadn't seemed fragile at the time they lived in it. It's precarious nature, teetering on a digital network so insubstantial that it barely existed, hadn't been made clear until those digits stopped flowing. It was no joke, but still she laughed.

After that, it was day after day of back-breaking work for Nina and Marcus. After she'd tilled the meadow, it was time to tackle the rougher ground, and that meant removing trees.

That first tree took a whole day, all by itself, and the damned dog – Doggie – seemed determined to get itself stomped or hit by a spade. Which, she thought, might not be a bad thing.

***

No, Nina didn't like the smelly, noisy and constantly demanding Doggie. Didn't like that it still sometimes pissed and even shat indoors. Was revolted by the noise and sheer wetness of his licking and chewing – he would like and chew anything, over and over, on the couch if she wasn't there to chase him away, leaving wet and slimy patches.

She didn't like the dog, but did like the Ruger. That was a surprise and one she didn't see coming. She'd always scoffed at those second amendment folks and their guns, but there was something about the lethal practicality of the thing, mixed with an odd kind of beauty.

She didn't practice every day, hitting bottles and cans at range, but got herself out there every few days. Marcus pretended it didn't bother him that she got more hits than him, but she could see that it did. Not seriously though, he could laugh about it.

The first time she shot and killed a deer she cried for about an hour.

That damn Weatherby, the size of the cartridges, most times he used the Ruger as well. She was thinking that he'd been a bit of an asshole buying this thing, a dangerous game rifle it was described as, until the day a bear ambled across the newly ploughed field.

They were at the side of the schoolhouse, Marcus chopping logs which Nina would then barrow to the old store, stacking them high She had just returned for another load when Doggie started acting weird, growling deep in his throat, barking and skipping around behind Marcus. Doggie had grown fast in the weeks they had been there, but was still very much a puppy, tan with a blunt, black nose and a long tail that thrashed around behind it, often needing chased, and bitten.

Nina turned in time to see a bear, dark brown and massively bulky, walk ponderously from her new-ploughed meadow and into Tilly Whim's one and only street, the place where she had been standing moments ago. They always kept their guns handy and snatched them up now, backing up, but hoping they wouldn't be using them. Doggie was making a huge racket and Marcus grabbed him, holding him under his arm as they retreated to the house. Once inside, they closed the door and watched through the window as the bear kept going until it got to Marcus' part-made fence, bound around with razor wire. Watched it stand on its hind legs to push.

It could have shoved the whole thing over, that much was clear. Instead, it turned and ambled, pretty much back the way it came, sniffing as it went. All the while, Doggie was barking and squealing, whimpering and yipping. Once the bear disappeared from sight, Nina said, "Maybe I should practice with the Weatherby."

Days rolled into each other, gathering into weeks and then months. Nina's hands grew so hard and calloused she would stare at them in fascination. The fingers had ridges of hard skin that she could stick with the point of a needle and feel nothing.

She had always thought herself physically strong, but pushing that damned machine or digging or splitting logs caused her arms to cord with new muscles, and her shoulders widened and filled out, like that's what they had wanted to do all along.

She thought, if that scrawny little Hayley could see me now, she'd shit herself. Not that she could talk to Hayley, or anybody else.

Marcus unbolted the old radio from the Land Rover and brought it inside, along with its battery. It was always exciting when they picked up a local or military radio signal, but it never lasted long, and it was never good news.

Marcus worked long, long hours and came back to the house most days bone tired and starving, Doggie at his heel. Sometimes, Doggie would follow Nina instead, even though she didn't have a kind word for it. She didn't chase it off anymore, though. Not since the bear.

Following an article on cold-weather survival farming, printed from the internet back when such things were possible, they planted potatoes, carrots, zucchini, beets and peas. They planted corn and, once it started to get some height, sowed beans around it. They planted kale and onions and Nina built a greenhouse of polythene sheeting against the old mill building, in which she grew tomatoes. She made a herb garden at the side of the house.

Everything was hard work and invariably took longer to complete than they estimated, but it was surprisingly satisfying.

They fell into a routine where she was doing most of the cooking and cleaning and she wasn't exactly happy about that, especially with all the heavy stuff she was putting in. But, she figured it was the way that suited their needs right now, what they were aiming at. There would be time enough to turn things around once winter set in.

There wasn't much to talk about, but they talked about it anyhow. And, despite being so damned tired, they made love almost every night that summer. Not the long, energetic sex of their early months, neither of them had the energy or interest for that. But it was better. Nicer.

Afterwards, she would put her head on his chest and he put his arms around her. He hadn't gotten bulkier, exactly, but his long, long limbs felt like they were made from steel wire. Doggie slept on the floor and only occasionally tried to creep up onto the bed, earning himself a scolding and maybe a whack from Nina.

For the first time since that first day when Marcus brought her out of her workroom to show her Raleigh screaming from the television screen, she felt safe.

The first inkling she got that that sense of security was false were shots in the distance. She'd been used to hearing her neighbours at the other end of the lake, the de Beauvoirs, people she'd never met, doing their own target practice. They even had an assault rifle.

But target practice had a rhythm to it, one she had come to recognise. The potato plants had grown well, as well they might all the attention they got, and she was hoeing between rows with sun hot on her back, when the shooting started. She straightened as Marcus came around the side of the house, Doggie at his heel as ever. He turned his head, questing, trying to pin down the direction of the sound. A real firefight.

"That's from the De Beauvoir's."

They fetched their rifles and tried to sight on the place, but there was nothing to see behind the distant curve of trees and it wasn't long before the shooting grew more sporadic, and eventually stopped altogether. The de Beauvoir house was just about in sight, but it was so far away and set back from the shore. If the fight was there, there was no evidence of anybody moving around.

She dropped her binoculars and squinted down the lake. "Should we go see?"

Marcus took a moment, then shook his head. "If they fought them off, they might just shoot anybody else comes close. Not like we can phone ahead. If they didn't fight them off…"

He shrugged. They kept their sights on the water for a while, but it stayed quiet.

Marcus said, "Maybe they had a disagreement amongst themselves."

He knelt down, so that he was nose to nose with Doggie. "You got to listen close, man. You're our early warning system, got it?"

Doggie's tail whacked against the wall with enthusiasm, and he looked exactly like he was smiling, which maybe he was.

Marcus was still grinning, saying clever boy, good boy. He was always telling Doggie he was a good boy, when all he was doing was going about being a dog. Just one of those things about Marcus that was beginning to get under her skin.

***

Summer slid by into an extraordinary Fall, the colours rapturous. Not that they had much time to notice because they were working to a deadline that was coming too fast for comfort, getting the harvests in and laying it up for storage. Making pickle and jelly and cutting more logs.

The days turned cooler until a morning came when the wind was bitterly cold, a knife against the skin, and they needed their heavy coats and gloves.

Lying in bed in the early hours, weeks later, Doggie's head came sharply up and pointed towards the lake. There was nothing unusual about this in itself – Doggie's head came up at everything from a squirrel to a high wind.

Marcus was still asleep, and Nina drowsing, when he issued a subdued *woof.* Then a low growl.

She glared at him. "Shut up."

He didn't shut up. He gave another woof and got to his feet, trotting to the window. After a moment's huffing, she pulled herself to follow. It was a clear night, with a yellowish moon, so everything was visible, including a little speed-boat, about two hundred yards out, ghosting towards the dock. What looked like four guys in there, two of them paddling with oars. Two with guns, one of whom was lying along the prow with a torch, leaning over to look down into the water.

Clearly, they already knew this wasn't a place you could just sail a boat into.

Doggie went from his subdued woof to a full out bark. If the guys in the boat heard it through the double-glaze, they didn't show anything. Marcus did, rolling out of bed, going from fully asleep to wide awake in an instant. Taking in the scene and snatching up his rifle in another.

The three of them ran down the stairs, Nina being left behind because Marcus was taking them three at a time. She gasped, "What do we do? What do we do?"

"Defend ourselves."

By the time he skittered out onto the frosted veranda, the boat had halved the distance. Nina was just coming out of the house, her legs like lengths of stove wood, when Marcus fired his warning shot.

It might have been a warning shot, she wasn't sure. It couldn't have been far away. The boat rocked, men shouting. They returned fire. Nina saw splinters fly from the deck, only feet from where Marcus crouched.

He sprinted right, away from the house, getting himself behind a pile of firewood before he shot again. It occurred to Nina in a weird moment of calm that it would be a disaster to have the windows shot out. It wasn't like you could just call up a glazier.

She cut left, sprinting away from the house and ducking behind the Silverado. A bullet smacked into the ground right in front of her, spraying dirt She put her eye to the scope and the four in the boat jumped into shaky focus.

132

All six of them shot at each other. She saw Marcus' slug blowing a chunk from the boat, its screen disappearing. A bullet hit the Silverado, inches from her face. Another shattered its windscreen, raining glass on her. Marcus was firing, not ducking. She dodged and loosed off another couple of shots. The boat's motor burst into life and it swung around in a steep curve. It sped away, picking up speed but listing badly.

The men, she could see, were concentrating on bailing now. Keeping their vessel afloat.

Nina's ears were singing from the gunfire, the nerves beneath her skin singing louder from the slugs that might have hit her, but didn't. The only noise now was Doggie barking, and the fading sound of the motor. As she watched, a gunshot flashed in the darkness, then another.

If they hit anywhere nearby, it wasn't obvious.

Marcus hurried to her, Doggie at his side. They looked, she thought, more excited than upset.

He pulled her in tight. "You ok?"

She had to untangle herself, step back and look down at her nightdress, feeling she needed to check. She was shivering so hard it was like a pantomime of shaking. Her jaws rattled as she spoke, making the words come out as a stutter.

"Fine. You?"

"Nothing. They didn't come close."

She closed her eyes and forced some calm into her limbs. "Neither did I. Come close, I mean. I can hit a beer bottle at that distance, nine times out of ten, but couldn't hit a person."

He blew out a laugh. It was definitely a laugh, not even a hysterical one, like he thought the whole thing was funny. "I only hit the *boat* three times. Jesus."

133

She grimaced hard, as the closeness of what had just happened hit her, and put her arms around Marcus, leaning against him as her legs went from shaking to a full-on wobble, making it difficult to stand.

He was shaking hard too, adrenalin still pumping around in there, she guessed. Or maybe just the cold.

"If we didn't have Doggie."

"We do, though. We have each other."

He managed a laugh of sorts. "And, when push comes to shove, we can't shoot for shit."

Chapter
17
James

James and Karen were in the games room and for once they were on their own. They were kissing, and had been for some time, when James heard the commotion in the hall. Bertillon's voice, raised and upset, hurrying feet.

The only other time he'd heard anything similar was when George had his accident.

Karen, the girl who found him lying in a spreading pool of blood, put her hands over her mouth and shook her head, willing it not to be. Forgetting all about being circumspect, they ran to where Bertillon stood, at the front door. He stood in a circle of anxious children, one hand on Martin's shoulder, but his eyes lit up when he spotted James and Karen. He pointed.

"You and you. Come. There's not a moment to lose. Literally."

"What…"

"Come!"

Bertillon had a car, one that he was extremely proud of but very seldom turned a wheel. It was a sleek BMW which had been fully de-puterised, so it ran, he said, like a dream. None of the children had been inside it, but they bundled in now.

It smelled expensive and technological. When Bertillon pressed the switch it roared into life. The speed it took off at was astonishing, making the children gasp, but there was no chance to enjoy this strange experience.

Bertillon was upset, that much was clear.

Martin, sitting in the front passenger seat, caught his breath enough to ask. "What's happening, Doctor?"

"Father Michael is in terrible trouble. Terrible. We're going to help. Try to."

Martin turned around to look at his friends, and the expression on his face was clear. How can we help?

"What's happening, though?"

"Ignorant, superstitious people, that's what's happening. They're going to burn him for a heretic, unless we can stop them."

He glanced over his shoulder. "I'm hoping that the mere presence of children will make them come to their senses. Who would perform such a heinous act before children?"

All this time Bertillon was driving, showing amazing skill in moving his vehicle from one street to another.

There was a crowd outside the chapel and, rising high above their heads, a wooden cross. Bertillon screeched to a halt and they bundled out, sprinting to the edge of the crowd, who were shouting, baying. Burn the false preacher. Burn the heretic.

Bertillon pushed people aside, forcing his way to the front, and the foundlings ducked behind and followed.

Father Michael, battered and bloodied, was already tied to the cross, brushwood at his feet. The air stunk of gasoline. A priest stood in front, holding up a large bible and shouting.

Bertillon bellowed, creating a moment of quiet. "Here now! Here now! What's this? Have we really come to this, Father Milligan?"

The priest, Father Milligan, turned. "Bertillon! You dare show your face on this day of reckoning? Shame on you."

All around, cries of shame. Bertillon was red in the face. Someone pushed him into a stumble, a punch landed on his shoulder, but he held his ground.

"The shame is on you. All of you, if you murder this man."

"He is a heretic! Bearing false witness, using the Bible itself."

"He is a good man."

"He preaches openly that the undead are God's work! Those monsters are no work of The Lord!"

Something other than a fist hit Bertillon on the side of the head, and he bent momentarily, holding himself. Then he straightened and yelled again.

"There are children here! Foundlings. Will you murder this man so horribly in front of innocent children?"

The priest shook his finger at Bertillon, shouting so that spittle flew from his mouth. "You brought these children from your den of sin."

"Den of…"

"Quiet, man. You and these children may survive today. You may not." He turned to point at Michaels.

"False prophet. Will you repent?"

Michaels raised his bloodied head. "I will not! I preach the true word of God."

"He is condemned from his own mouth. Set the torch."

Bertillon, seeing it beginning to happen, called out, "I'm sorry, Father. The children cannot witness this."

The gas-soaked brushwood was already alight as he laid hands on the children, beginning to lead them away. Michaels looked at Bertillon, then down at James and his friends. His face was white and shaking, his eyes pouring water.

"Stay. Please. Pray for me. And for the souls of these misguided fools."

Karen grabbed James's hand in both of hers, so tightly he thought his fingers might break. Bertillon looked around, for once lost. It was obvious that he wanted to take the children, but he had been asked. He bent and pulled them to him, so they formed a tight cluster of four.

"We must be brave and stay, for our friend Father Michaels. But don't look. Don't even peek. And stop up your ears, because he will scream. Now, pray!"

Karen curled into James, pushing her head against his neck, and tried to pray. He heard her do it, through her sobs. Martin clenched his fists and looked at his feet, his face white. Bertillon, his hand on both boys' shoulders, stared resolutely ahead.

James stared straight ahead too. He didn't close his eyes or stop up his ears. Father Michaels held himself tight and trembling as the flames caught around his feet, and lapped around his legs. He was praying, James saw, his face a trembling mask.

When his clothes caught, he opened his eyes and let out a full-throated scream, stretching his neck impossibly. He screamed as his robe burned and his flesh blackened. Behind him, James heard Bertillon sob. "I should have brought a gun."

Michaels stretched his scrawny neck even higher as his screams turned into a bubbling noise that sounded something other than human. Then, mercifully, he slumped down into the flames.

It no longer smelled like gasoline, and burning brushwood. It smelled like bacon frying on an over-hot griddle.

No one put a hand near them as they turned to go. Some of the crowd had already thinned, and many of those who remained seemed pale and shocked. The priest, Father Milligan, stood trembling before the dwindling fire and its charred corpse, his head high as he continued to watch. Bertillon raised his voice.

"I would pray for you, Father. If I thought it would do any good."

Karen sobbed uncontrollably on the slower journey back. James held her tight, and tried to find someplace in his mind to put the burning priest, so that he could no longer be seen.

Chapter
18
Alice

Alice enjoyed driving the ancient, rattling Land Rover, and simply tuned out her mom's complaints about the cold or what the hard ride did to her old bones. It still wasn't exactly safe, two women driving on these backwoods roads, but it was a lot safer than it once was. The new chief of Police, Gabriel Lamont, was taking a hard line with gangsters and bushwhackers, as he called them.

Still, they were careful, and ready. Her mom was a dead shot with that Ruger, and wasn't one to hesitate. Alice had to work harder to hit her target with a rifle, and that damn Weatherby was a beast.

The Land Rover still had two bullet holes from the only time they'd been ambushed, but that had been a long time ago, when she could neither drive nor shoot straight. In her memory, the car had shuddered to a halt as a gun fired somewhere nearby, slapping the Land Rover somewhere.

Her mom returned fire even as she braked, reaching over her to do it and briefly deafening her, then the car was flying backwards, jumping and jolting, the engine screaming. Her mom cussing.

Now, aged fifteen, she drove whilst her mom rode shotgun, holding her rifle ready, eyes squinting through her own cigarette smoke.

Today they were heading into Bear Brook Park, hoping for deer. Stevie, the butcher, would take as much deer as they could get. Deerfield road was almost empty once they got on it, which they expected but didn't much like. Alice hauled the old vehicle off the main route and onto Podunk Road, heading now into the forest itself.

They kept going, but dropping to little more than walking pace, because of fallen branches. Finally, they pushed off the road, turned the Land Rover around so it was pointing the right way to get out of there, and spent a few minutes hiding it with bracken.

They shared a last, relaxing cigarette, taking in the sounds of birds and sight of trees shifting in the slight breeze. Then, they shouldered their rifles and headed into the forest. After a while, they started climbing, and Alice noticed how easily her mom got out of breath now. She had always seemed so fit and strong. Indestructible. But she was getting old. Fifty-five.

An hour later, they were tired and hot and sweaty and hadn't seen a sign of a deer or even a bird of decent size.

They had blundered into a marsh and got their feet wet, but were now approaching a ridge. They approached slowly, careful of noise and showing themselves against the skyline, finally laying down behind a handily fallen tree trunk.

From here, a wide stretch of forest opened up below them, dropping right to left into a wide pool, the surface of the water such a mirror for the sun that Alice had to squint. She unslung the Ruger and searched carefully through the scope, inching along. Deer could be hard to spot in the forest. She shifted, shifted again, then stopped, feathering the focus. There was something between the trees, about a hundred yards away, but it wasn't a deer. It was almost like a shadow, but that couldn't be right. She frowned and clicked the focus again, and then gasped as she realised what she was looking at. It was one of The Returned, a middle-aged woman seen from the side. Naked. Just standing there.

Alice shivered involuntarily and moved on, stalling when her scope settled on another. It was like an optical illusion, she thought. There was a group of The Returned, standing naked amongst the trees and, until you figured out that's what you were looking at, their colour made them no more than shadows. All but invisible.

But, she had her eye in now and counted a dozen before moving on, and freezing in place.

She whispered, "Mom."

Nina was looking through binoculars, scanning the other side of the slope, but something in her daughter's voice brought her around fast. Keeping her voice low, she asked, "What's wrong?"

Moving slowly, keeping her head down, Alice pointed.

"What am I looking at?"

"Just there, between the trees. Keep looking, they're hard to spot."

"They?"

Alice could hear her mother, muttering low, a habit she'd picked up, so heard the change in her breathing as she grew still. "Jesus."

Even though this was said in a whisper, Alice leaned closer. "Keep your voice down. What are they doing?"

"Standing."

"You'd think they'd get tired of that."

Nina shook her head. "No. They won't. There has to be…God, I keep seeing more of them."

"I think there might be a hundred in there. What do we do?"

Nina looked at her like she was crazy. "Do? We get out of here. Quiet as we've ever done anything in our lives. I don't even feel comfortable looking at them. Like they could know, somehow."

After a few minutes of her constantly staring through the binoculars, Alice whispered, "Well, why you still doing it?"

"Hush."

As the minutes dragged uncomfortably by, it occurred to Alice that she wasn't just searching, she was searching for someone in particular. She stayed quiet, and was looking out over the lake when the sun went behind a cloud, and the water became suddenly clear, no longer reflecting the sky. Her hair began to rise, she felt it, starting at her forearms, all the way up the nape of her neck and scalp.

The dead in the forest was one thing, but seeing those dark shapes standing still and quiet underwater was another. Hundreds of them, stretching out into the deeper part of the lake.

She whispered. "They're in the water too. Just standing there. Mom, let's get out of here."

She stared at the dark underwater shapes for a while, then eased back to look at those in the trees, so was looking when heads snapped to turn their way. Dozens at once, like a switch had been flicked. In the second before she turned away to slither back from the log, she saw many beginning to move. One instant they were still and quiet, like they hadn't moved for years, the next they were in motion. Coming this way.

The two women slithered downhill, through mud and leaves, then gained their feet, and ran. Nina, who had been sluggish when they were climbing, was running so hard that Alice had to shout, "Slow down! Slow down, Mom. You'll fall."

Something came back over Nina's shoulder that might have been "Fuck that." But she did slow, slightly. Still, both women kept running, slipping and sliding down the slope until it flattened out, then Alice was behind her mother, pushing her butt as they struggled up a rise. Down again, hoping they were on the right track. Alice saw the marsh they had wandered into earlier, away to their left, and pointed. They angled that way.

Every so often she would glance behind her, but the Returned weren't in sight yet.

Nina was puffing now, no longer able to run, but they kept half-walking, half-running till the ground flattened again and they caught the road.

There was a horrible moment when they weren't sure where the Land Rover was, until Alice spotted a huge Douglas Fir she had taken note off. They ran the last hundred yards, Alice half-carrying Nina, helping her into the driver seat. She scrambled at the brush as her mother started the engine, leaped in and they got out of there.

Nina was gasping for breath, foot to the floor, crunching through the gears. Alice kept her eyes on the path behind them, but saw no movement.

After they gained the main route, Nina, still out of breath, said, "Maybe we overreacted there."

Alice had been wondering about that. "I'm not even sure what happened. I don't know if they came after us. You think we should tell Chief Lamont?"

Nina, getting her breath back, was still looking more at her mirror than the road ahead. "I just don't know what we would say."

Chapter

19

Nina

Nina woke and everything was different. It sounded different. The drapes were pulled aside and Marcus stood framed at the window, against a sky the colour of beaten tin. When he breathed, his breath plumed against the glass.

Doggie stood beside him, where else, wagging his stupid tail, and smiling wetly. Nina slid a foot from under the covers, then tucked it back, wrapped the whole duvet around herself before climbing to her feet and joining them.

He grinned to see her, a little boy again.

"All the years I've been coming here, this is my first snowfall."

They rearranged their covers for maximum warmth and stood in each other's arms, staring. Somehow Doggie got himself between them. Marcus, oblivious to how irritating this was, ruffled his head. She knew what he would say before he said it.

"Good dog. Such a good little Doggie."

Only a few inches had fallen in the night, but it was still snowing and the cover was solid. Everything was blindingly white, except the trees, some of which hadn't lost their fall leaves. The glimpses of gold and red against the white took her breath.

The other relief from white was the lake, which was so dark under the lowered sky it might as well be black.

He squeezed her waist. "We've done great, honey. We're going to be ok."

They were ok for now, she knew that to be so, but that didn't mean it would be easy. That first morning, they hurried downstairs still wrapped in blankets and Marcus got the log-burner going. Even an hour later, it wasn't warm in the room. Doggie kept whining at the door, going on and on, asking to get out. He scratched it with his claws, marking the wood, but when she finally opened it to the blast of cold, telling him to scat if he thought it was such a great idea, he slunk backwards. A minute later he was back, whining and scratching.

Marcus said, "Don't be so impatient with him. This is his first snow fall too, remember."

She glared one to the other, two boys in cahoots it felt like, then stomped off to cook up a breakfast of turkey, sliced thin and fried with pancakes and coffee. Once she'd eaten, she could ignore the damn dog and had to admit it was kind of exciting, like an adventure, that first day, as they sipped their coffee and stared out at the whiteness that would surround them for almost three months.

They hauled more firewood in during that day, with Doggie bounding around them through the snow, barking at it and even trying to bite it, making even Nina laugh. In the evening they banked the fire so it would still be hot in the morning. Their bed was so cold, they giggled like kids getting into it, and just let him when Doggie climbed on too. He was like a furry hot-water bottle.

The next morning, the water didn't run, and three days later, during a snow-storm, the gas froze in its rubber pipe and could not be thawed. After an hour of trying to heat it up with water warmed on the electric stove, Marcus put his thick clothes on and boots on and went around the back, intending to bring one of the bottles into the kitchen.

He went out into a blizzard, some of which blew into the house in the second it took him to get out of the door. Doggie whined to go out with him, but she kept a grip of him, telling him not to be so damn stupid. They had been allowing him out to do his business, but apart from that he didn't leave the house any more than they did.

Marcus was back without the bottle less than a minute later, looking in pain and stomping snow off his boots. His coat was covered in snow and even his beard was iced up. Doggie jumped about him but, for once, he was ignored. He pulled off his gloves and chafed his hands together, wincing.

"Fuck, that's so cold it hurts. I need my pistol."

"What for?"

"The lock on the cage has frozen solid."

"You're going to shoot it off?"

"That was the plan, yea."

"You think that's a smart idea? Shooting the cage holding gas bottles that could blow the whole house to shit."

He gave her a flat look. "What would you suggest?"

"I don't know. Stick a wrecking bar in there. Belt it with the axe, but don't shoot it."

Marcus stood for a long time, just staring at her, and for the first time it occurred to her that it was just the two of them. And she didn't know all of what was inside his head, who he could be.

In the end, he turned on his heel and marched out without another word, leaving the door ajar so that she had to catch Doggie, then hurry to close it. Even doing that, standing for a second in the icy, cutting gust, hurt her skin. She hurried to the other side of the house to see him, hunched against the wind, struggling through a white out and knee-deep snow towards the old town store, where they kept their tools. Only five or six steps away, he became invisible. Beside her, Doggie whined high in his throat and turned to look at her, like she should be doing something about it.

She chewed her lips, staring into the white that blew sideways across her vision, having to close her eyes from time to time and look away because it made her sick and dizzy. Fifteen minutes later, he still hadn't returned and she was beginning to panic, wondering had he fallen, or gotten lost.

It would be so easy to get lost; visibility out there could only be a few yards at best. She thought about getting her own coat, going to search for him. Would shouting work? She didn't think so. You'd probably need to be right by someone, scream into their ear just to be heard.

Maybe Doggie could find him. Maybe not.

Time ticked by, with nothing but the sound of the wind, and horizontal snow. She ran from window to window, getting frantic. He had been gone for well over half an hour. Then, almost an hour.

Finding she needed to be doing something, she hurried back into living room and stoked up the fire, putting more logs on. Got old towels and knelt to wipe up the thaw water on the floor, jumping back when the door burst open, and she kneeling in front of it.

Marcus was making a weird, keening noise, and his face was stretched out like someone in agony. He was holding the tall bottle and she jumped up to take it from her, but he all but screamed at her.

"No! Don't touch the metal."

Apart from the initial no, the words were stuttered and stretched out. He settled the bottle and she grabbed him, pushing Doggie away. Even touching his clothes hurt, but she dragged him to the fire, hauling them off as she went. Every layer felt as cold as the top one, as though all of his body heat had bled away. Finally, she got him down to his underwear and laid him down in front of the fire, as he shook and whimpered. She'd never heard a grown man whimper before.

She ran upstairs and grabbed the covers from the bed, hurrying down to lie beside him, cocooning herself in and pulling Doggie in tight. It made her shake almost as much as him, but she held him and rubbed his skin until he quietened, beyond a low level tremble.

"My fingers. Feel like they're going to burst open."

She laced her own with his, chafing them, getting him to work them out.

"How long was I out there for?"

"An hour maybe. I thought you'd got lost."

"I did. Eventually walked slap into the wall of the mill, which I figure saved my life. Had to track back, keeping the line of buildings. Every time I didn't have something to hold onto I was getting lost again."

She rubbed his skin and kissed him, and rubbed him some more. "I'm going to heat up some soup. You hug that stupid dog and stay in front of the fire."

Once he had some hot food in him, he seemed better, physically. But his eyes were staring, strangely faraway, like he was in shock.

He said, "We thought we were prepared for this, but we were kidding ourselves. We're not."

"This is surely about the worst it can get."

He nodded, but didn't look certain.

"Ok. Then we don't go out when it's like this. No matter what."

He picked up his glove and looked at it.

"This is a ski glove. And it just didn't cut it. Not even close."

She took it from him, wanting to say something to make him feel better, he looked so lost. Took his bearded chin and made him look her in the eye.

"Just as well your wife is a famous designer, then. I'm going to cut up that sheepskin rug. Make mitts to fit over our gloves. You got anything you can wear underneath?"

He shrugged. "Wool gloves, I guess."

She slapped the table. "Ok, maybe if I cut up my silk…"

He held up his hand, looking away. "Can we leave it for now?"

"Marcus, I…"

"Leave it. Can't you just leave it alone?"

She had to press her lips tight to stop herself. He wanted to leave it, she wanted to sort it.

***

The house was seldom warm, that winter, even with the log burner going constantly, burning through what they'd thought of as a huge stock of logs at a scary rate. Marcus moved their bedding down to the living room, which was pretty much where the three of them lived for almost three months. In the first few days after getting lost and nearly frozen, he was quiet and withdrawn, even more than when he was in the depths of what she thought of as his weed period. He just sat there, hour after hour, staring into the fire and rubbing Doggie's neck. Muttering good dog, over and over.

The fucking dog was just sitting there, looking up at him, being a dog.

One day, maybe a week after his experience of getting lost in a white-out, they opened the curtains to a bright and clear morning, with no wind. Marcus seemed to brighten with it and they put their warmest clothes on, with extra layers underneath and the bulky mitts she'd made.

The quiet and stillness and beauty of the lake and the forest stunned them into joining the silence. They walked around the snow-covered town and into the forest, the only sounds their own laboured breathing and the crump of their feet through snow. Doggie panting and scampering around.

Marcus hauled off his mitts and grinned. "I'm hotter than I've been since summer."

Nina, who was equally over-warm inside her many layers, laughed in something like relief, and threw her arms around him.

"This is the most beautiful thing I've ever seen. It keeps taking my breath away."

They kissed and moved on, having to shed clothes as they went, because the effort of walking was producing too much heat inside all those layers. They came to the pond, which was frozen over.

Doggie sniffed it, but when Marcus tested a foot on there, she pulled him back. "Think now."

"Looks a foot thick, honey."

He almost stepped on there again, but didn't, clearly imagining what it would be like if he went through, and moved away.

He pointed. "Tracks, look. Maybe a deer? Things are still moving around in this."

They went back to the house and pulled everything off, making love in front of the fire, something they hadn't done for weeks.

Afterwards, he said, "You know, we're barely going upstairs just now. Hardly ever up there."

She didn't want to think about that. Waved a languid hand. "We'll use it again in the Spring. We're hibernating."

"What I was thinking, I should fit the shutters. Cut down the wind chill on those windows up there."

"Won't be easy. Using a ladder in the snow."

"Still. It'll be worth it."

It stayed sunny for a couple of days, and Marcus did fit the shutters. It made it kind of miserable up there, gloomy, but he was right. She only ever went there to fetch things like spare clothes.

After that, it grew grey and overcast, and Marcus returned to sitting with Doggie, staring at the fire. It grew colder, and he surprised her by fetching shutters from the store and fitting them over the French doors.

Even though there were other windows, they were small, so it was immediately gloomy, but he didn't seem to notice. Just hurried back in front of the fire. Sat there staring into it.

She found she didn't want to talk to him about it, but had to.

153

"You shoulda asked."

"What?"

"Before putting those damn shutters on, you shoulda asked."

He shrugged. "You would've said no."

She opened her mouth to answer but for a moment couldn't, thinking about what that meant.

"Marcus."

He didn't answer.

"Marcus."

Finally, he turned. "Damn right I woulda said no. We got to survive the cold. But we need to avoid going batshit crazy as well."

His eyes snapped wide open. For a moment, he *looked* crazy. "What do you mean?"

"Cool it, man. What I mean, I got to live in this dark for all of winter, I'll lose my fucking mind."

He took a long breath, and turned away, back to the fire.

"So, if you don't take 'em off again, I'll do it myself. Then, I'll whack them with the axe till they can't ever be used again."

He still didn't look at her, but a minute later, he stood and pulled his clothes on. Stomped outside and took the shutters down.

***

Nina ventured out to hunt as often as she could throughout the winter and was never less than overwhelmed by the silence and beauty. Doggie invariably came with her. Not so annoying now that he was no longer a puppy, he stuck close to her as they went, and was always the first to know if there was any game around. She got so that she could read his expression and the signs, the way he stopped dead

154

in his tracks, staring until she caught on to whatever he was pointing at.

She made a point of never calling him a good dog, but it wasn't always easy.

Despite the extreme cold, she found she had to get out every day it was possible to, and sometimes just walked with Doggie, or went to one of her favourite places to look out across the lake.

She needed that, partly to be out of the damn house, partly to get away from Marcus. He seldom spoke now, didn't wash unless she nagged him into it, telling him he stunk. He spent most of his days and much of the nights sitting before the fire, his dog against his leg. Fetching logs and tending the fire was pretty much the only thing he did, but he did that obsessively.

It was almost as if the fire and Doggie were the only things anchoring him to the world.

Chapter

20

Alice

Alice's knuckles were white on the handle of her guitar case as she walked up the darkened stairs to the first floor of a low-grade apartment building. Grit crunched underfoot and there was a strong smell of stale water, overlain by pine cleaner. There was almost no light on the landing, so she had to bend close to the nameplate and squint hard to read. One word, on a scrap of card in shaky blue ink. Waters.

She blew out a long breath and knocked. Deep inside, there was a thud, like something falling over, and an old man's voice raised in anger, though she couldn't catch the words.

She stepped back as there were more noises, bumps and thumps from inside the apartment, someone talking, not sounding happy.

Finally the door opened a crack to show a skinny old man, black, with wattled neck and yellowed eyes, squinting in the gloom. She wasn't looking at the man, though. She was looking at the muzzle of his shotgun.

"Mr Waters? I'm Alice Simeon. Mrs Twining…"

He was searching the landing behind her. "You a boy or a girl?"

That set her back. "A girl."

"Sound like a boy. Too big for a girl."

"I'm definitely a girl."

156

"My eyesight aint so good, you standin' out there in the goddam dark. Could be anybody."

The shotgun muzzle was still pointing at her. Moving slowly, she raised the guitar case.

"I've brought my guitar. Mrs Twining…"

"You alone?"

"I'm alone."

The man's yellowed eyes were narrow and watery. His teeth were largely missing, and those that had survived looked like roasted peanuts. "You aint alone, I'll shoot! Don't think I won't."

"I'm alone. Honest, Mister."

"Won't be the first time. I'll shoot the fuck out of any *intruders*. Tell you that."

She stepped slowly aside to show the rest of the landing, still staring at the gun. "Look."

He was looking. He was looking at her chest. "Yea. You a girl. Thought you was some boy, pretendin'. Best come in."

The door closed and the chain rattled before it opened all the way. Waters was already walking down the hall, using a cane and limping hard. He had clearly once been a tall man, but now he was severely bent and walked with a twist. The shotgun was left propped against the wall by the door.

"Shut the door when you come. Make sure it's locked. Don't want any damn intruders."

She walked into a house that smelled of old grease and sweat. Fried onions and tobacco smoke. The walls were wallpapered, something ancient from Before, with vines and faded roses.

She followed him into a room where the smells were even stronger. It was a largish room, but ram-packed. A kitchen off in one corner, a bed in the other, a couch and a couple of sagging easy chairs.

157

There had been other doors off the hallway, but it seemed to Alice that the man probably lived all his life in this one room, eating, sleeping and listening to music.

Because the room was also home to a full wall of vinyl, racked top to bottom. It was, she thought, a wonder the floor could take the weight of all those records. There was also a pair of big speakers and a turntable.

The room was on a corner, so there were two windows, both of which were uncovered to let in as much light as possible. It was a lightsome room and, despite the smell of old food, clean enough.

Waters sat heavily on one of the easy chairs, against which lay a guitar that had been played so much most of the lacquer had been worn away. He squinted at her. "Couldn't see for shit when you was lurkin' in the dark out on that damn landin'. I can see you fine now. Nina Simeon, that your momma?"

"Yea."

"I recall her. Damn fine lookin' woman. You got a look of her awright."

He pointed , not to the other easy chair, but a hard-backed chair. "Set, then. Let's see what you got inside that case."

Alice, wanting to be anywhere other than here, did as she was told, unclipping with rubbery hands and pulling the guitar out.

The man's eyes widened. "A Martin."

"Yea."

His hands stretched forward, as though they wanted to hold it, but then dropped back to sit on his knees. "D18 Dreadnought, 'less I miss my guess."

"I dunno."

The man was looking more at the guitar than at her, his eyes slits. "Been played some, by the looks."

"Yea, sorry, it's real old."

"No, it's good for a guitar to be played. Gives it its voice. So…"

He had been sitting forward, but now he eased back in his chair. "Liz Twining says you want to learn how to play. Can sing some. Got some idea how to play the keys."

Alice was stung. "I can play the guitar too."

"Teached yourself?"

"Yup."

"Ok then, let's hear you."

Alice tried to get herself settled, wishing now she hadn't claimed to be able to play, coming out with it like that. She flicked the strings in turn to check the tuning, turning the pegs till she was satisfied. Then played a single chord, A minor. Waters shook his head.

"You're holding it wrong. Won't get no clean sound if you hold it like a damn washboard."

Alice blinked in surprise, but he wasn't finished.

"Fingers not coming down right on the strings, fouling the ones you ain't holding. All cause you aint holding the damn thing right."

"Nobody's ever showed me."

"Well somebody should. Lookit, sit straighter. Straighter! Can't you sit straight, Jesus?"

He picked up his own guitar and pushed to the edge of his chair. "Pull it right into your body, like this, angle the headstock like this, and bend that wrist round, so's your fingers come down *clean*. They gotta come down clean or it sound like shit."

Alice tried. Shook her head. "My wrist won't do that."

"Don't give me none of that whiny shit. Young girl like you. You just got to unlearn what you think you learnt. All that damn buzzin' you was gettin'. Jesus."

Whilst Alice was trying to contort her wrist, he said, "But you got the ear, that's plain."

"I do?"

"Tuned those strings perfect without hardly thinking. Didn't even check one against the other. Got a tunin' fork in your head. Shit, girl, can't you hold it better than that? You look like a goddam prayin' mantis."

As she struggled, he sighed, looking despondent. "Ok. Better play me somethin', I guess."

Alice launched into "May the Circle Be Unbroken' proud of the bassline beneath the chords, but he stopped her within a few bars.

"Stop! Stop! Play something else, Jesus. I can't be listenin' to that red-neck shit.

Play me some blues. Anything."

"Blues?"

He paused at that, frowned and looked out of the window, muttering, then he came back to her. "You know the blues. You just don' know you know it. John Lee Hooker, you play me something by John Lee?"

The man spent a few minutes listing names she'd never heard of before he gave up, and went back to staring out of his window. His lips shook, ever so slightly.

"A lot has been lost. Important stuff."

"Shall I go?"

He sighed. Then picked up his guitar and started to play. Up to that point, Alice had heard chords, and finger picking arpeggios, but that wasn't what he was

160

doing. He was pulling at the strings, holding onto notes somehow, sometimes with vibrato, sometimes not. Telling a story.

She sat wide-eyed, watching him. She wasn't sure if she liked it or not, but it was weirdly exciting. Then, he switched to chords, odd, sad sounding chords, and started singing. The first words out of his mouth, in his ragged old voice, *The thrill is gone.*

The song progressed, and it was like nothing she had heard before. Between verses and sometimes even between lines, his guitar would suddenly no longer be playing chords or keeping the beat. It would be wailing or muttering, like it wanted to speak.

Finally, he stopped. "I ain't no BB King, but that was as close as I can git. That there's the blues, girl."

He pointed. "Ok, let me see you hold that damn Martin like it should be held. Not like no broomstick, Jesus."

Chapter
21
Nina

Nina counted the years by the seasons, but still struggled to keep the tally. Some winters were less harsh than others and those were the best years, the ones when Marcus might leave the house to hunt.

She grew to dread the coming of the snow, when Marcus' mood grew bleak and black, every year a little worse. At first it lifted as Spring arrived, melting with the snow, but as the years slid by, it seemed what she thought of as his winter mood took longer to shift, if it ever did.

They were in their eleventh year at Tilly Whim, by Nina's erratic count, when the second group of intruders came. It was hard not to drop their guard, in a world where they seemed to be the only people left, but, whatever else they were doing, they kept their guns to hand. Over the years, Marcus had built timber barricades at points around the house, packing the far side with sharp stakes and razor wire so they were only usable from inside out.

It had rained steadily for six days straight, and the morning the intruders came was the heaviest yet, turning everything to mud and the sky to leaden water. Even though it was summer, it chilled to the bone.

Nina pulled her coat over her head and ran, splashing through the puddles to the polythene greenhouse to collect tomatoes. Even then she got soaked. That, she thought later, was why she didn't bring the rifle with her.

It was noisy under the plastic, the rain hammering hard. She wiped water from her face and shivered, then gave herself a shake and got on with collecting tomatoes, stepping wide to avoid the drips and worse that trickled through the increasingly holed polythene.

She focussed on her task, cocking an ear when she heard Doggie barking, but that's all she did. An older dog now, he still liked to kick up a row.

She paused, listening closer. Doggie's voice had grown familiar over the years, and there was a definite urgent tone to it. Going on and on, this was some serious barking.

She put her basket aside and hurried to the entrance in time to hear a man's voice, muffled but just audible in the downpour. It wasn't Marcus. She didn't catch what the guy was shouting, because that was when the shooting started.

The first shot had to be Marcus – she knew that Weatherby – but the next was different, a shotgun maybe, and then the distinctive rattle of semi-automatic fire. A series of visceral cracks, high-pitched and deep at the same time and so close together they mixed with their own echoes.

She sprinted through the rain to where she'd left her gun by the front door. The semi-automatic fire was ongoing, more than one rifle now, so loud she could feel it in her bones. She snatched up the Ruger, fingers clumsy as she sprinted through the house and burst outside. Into a firefight.

She cut right, throwing herself flat. Bullets smacked around her, shattering glass and knocking splinters from the deck. She slithered behind a pile of logs, squealing as more bullets hit, trying to make herself small. Rain smacked into her like pellets, hard enough to hurt.

To her left, Marcus crouched behind a barricade. Water flattened his hair and poured down his face. He caught her eye and grimaced, then straightened to take aim into the field beyond. Ducking quickly away as bullets raked the barricade, splinters flying around his head. Doggie was down by his feet, barking and making splashy runs, just a few stupid yards one side then the other.

Nina snatched a quick glance and saw three people, two men and a woman, crouching low amongst the corn. A youngish guy with an AK loosed off another burst at Marcus, forcing him down. The other man fired at Nina, making her curl into the mud.

Marcus stared at her, wide-eyed and terrified. Despite all their plans, they had been caught unawares, trapped behind their shelters by three – at least three – people with heavier armaments. All those folk had to do was get one of their number around the side until they had a shot. The rain probably made that easier for them.

Doggie kept up his din. Marcus tried to grab him, but a slug almost caught his arm and he jumped back. Doggie made a crazy run, straight into the field, barking.

When Nina snatched a peek this time, a man was lurching to his feet, stumbling backwards and shooting into the corn. She forced herself into the firing line and brought her rifle quickly up, two quick shots.

Her second bullet splashed his head open, throwing him back.

The woman turned towards Nina, racked her shotgun and let loose. A few pellets scattered nearby, but the range was too great. As Nina watched, a gout of blood spurted from the woman's shoulder. Marcus was already taking aim again.

Then he was falling away, a spray of bullets from the other man catching him somewhere. Nina snapped a shot at him, but missed. He twisted towards her, and she felt a round zing past her ear before she pulled away. The Weatherby bellowed, and when Nina risked a look the man was down and Marcus was back on his feet.

Marcus had blood on his face and the rain was already washing it across his chest.

She shouted. "You hit?"

He touched the side of his head, and looked at his bloodied hand. "Chip of wood, I think. I'm not shot."

Nina got to her feet and sprinted to join him, hugging him hard. In the cold and wet, he felt hot.

"Are they all dead?"

"Don't know. I don't think so."

He stood at his full height, eyelids flickering in the rain, and called out. "You guys alive, or dead, or what?"

When there was no answer, he shouted, "We can see where you are, pretty much. I guess we'll keep shooting, make sure of it."

The woman raised a hand. "Don't shoot. I'm hurt. Jonty is dead, for sure."

"Jonty?"

"My husband."

165

"The guy with the AK?"

There was a definite cry in her voice. "Yea."

"What about the other guy?"

The woman got slowly to her knees, only one hand in the air and drenched in water and blood. The other was dead at her side and, after a moment, she grabbed her damaged arm with her good hand, supporting it. Her clothes were ragged, too light for this weather and, of course, drenched. Her hair was on the long side, and plastered to her body. She cast around, as Nina centred her in the scope, finger tightening on the trigger.

"Paw?"

There was a noise, somewhere to her right, but it didn't sound like words. The woman got to her feet, slowly and painfully. It cost her a lot to get there.

Marcus tightened on his trigger. "Careful now."

She ignored him, taking a few unsteady steps to the side. "Paw?"

Her face twisted as she fell to her knees in the mud. Turned to look at where Nina and Marcus were still behind their barricade, aiming at her.

"Will you help us?"

Nina looked at Marcus, shocked. The woman had barely spoken loudly enough to be heard the first time, now she shouted. "Will you help us?"

Marcus called back. "You came here with guns. Fixing to…what?"

"Find something to eat. We're starving, isn't that obvious?"

Now that it was said, it was. These people were skin and bone.

"We could've snuck up on you, but we didn't. We shouted out. Wanted your *help*."

166

Ignoring Marcus' hissed warning, Nina left her shelter, but kept a bead on the woman, who kept talking as she got closer.

"Jonty's gone, and Paw's in a bad way. Will you help us?"

Nina dropped the rifle to her hip as she walked through the hissing rain. The older man lay on his back, watching her come. Marcus fanned out to the side, moving fast, getting into a position where he could shoot either of them.

She stopped a few feet away, seeing the sodden mess of the man's chest, the blood staining the water where he lay in. She shook her head. "I could get a pad for his chest. Sorry, it won't do a bit of good."

The woman bent at the waist and let out a long, keening note. Nina hopped back, never having heard such grief and desperation.

"I'm sorry. We can't help him."

Everybody stayed like that, as the light went out of the man on the ground.

The woman nodded to herself. "It's ok. It'll be ok."

"What are you saying?"

Desperate now. "They'll come back to me. Give them an hour, they'll be back."

Marcus shook his head. "No way. We're burning them."

The woman tore her hair. "You leave them alone."

"We're burning them. Not having zombies coming up around here."

"Leave them alone!"

Marcus lifted the gun. "You better git, or we'll burn all three of you."

167

The woman did a strange almost-dance, turning on the spot, and holding her arm up. Then, she wasn't holding it up because she was shooting a small pistol at Marcus, pop-pop-pop.

Marcus ducked and dodged and the woman launched into a stumbling run, putting distance between them but looking like she would fall over any second. Marcus sighted on her, then lowered the rifle.

They just watched the woman run through the rain. Watched her reach the trees, disappearing, before Nina asked, "Where's Doggie?"

He was lying in the corn, soaked, his breathing fast and shallow. His flank was covered in blood. Nina knelt down beside him and stroked his head.

"Good dog. You're such a good dog, Doggie. Saved us. That's twice you done it."

He licked both their hands, closed his eyes and stopped breathing. Just as if he'd been waiting for them to say goodbye. Marcus pressed his face into the thick fur at his neck, holding tight, but there wasn't time to grieve. They both knew that.

Nina glanced at the pile of drenched logs she had hidden behind, then up into the sky, closing her eyes against the downpour. Clenched her fists to try to stop herself shaking.

"How are we going to get a fire going in this?"

She looked at Marcus, but he just shook his head, stunned. He blinked the water away and made a visible attempt to make himself attend, but couldn't get there.

She stepped in front of him and hugged him hard, then took his face in her fingers. "Marcus. Think."

He looked away from her, avoiding eye contact. She shook him hard. "Marcus!"

He squeezed his eyes shut, opened them and said, "Joe's Cottage."

Nina turned to peer at the little cottage, just visible through the rain.

"Okay. Okay, then."

She walked quickly to the where the younger man lay in the corn, the one she had killed. Made herself look at what she had done, splitting his head open, then stepped away and bent over to vomit. Even when she was empty, she could barely imagine looking at the corpse again.

The second person she had killed.

When she finally stopped shaking enough to think she might be able to move him, she found Marcus in the same position she'd left him, his arms dangling down by his sides.

She wiped her mouth.

"Marcus."

He turned to her, still looking vacant, and she found herself getting angry. "Go get the barrow."

"What?"

"How long since we shot them? Get the barrow."

That seemed to get through, and he hurried off, coming back minutes later, pulling the barrow behind him because pushing it made the wheel stick in the sodden mud.

Together, they picked up the younger man and dropped him in, his arms and legs trailing outside. It was harder hauling the laden barrow through the mud, but they kept at it and finally dragged him inside the old cottage.

Marcus blew out a long breath, and when he spoke he sounded like Marcus again.

"You go get kindling. And gas."

"What about the other one?"

169

"I figure it's easier throwing him over my shoulder. Carrying him out of there."

She straightened her back, which was hurting from dragging the barrow.

"You sure?"

"Get the gas."

She watched him walking away through the rain, by no means convinced, but shook it away. It had been a long time since either of them had worn a watch, and Nina struggled to know how much time had elapsed. Maybe twenty minutes. Maybe twice that.

She splashed through the mud to the store, coming back with a can of gas and an armload of kindling. Peering through the rain, she could see Marcus had gotten the guy onto his shoulder and was threading through the corn. She'd gotten so used to it being just him around that she'd forgotten how big he was, and strong now with all the labour.

She ran back to the store, this time pushing the barrow. By the time she got back with it filled with logs, Marcus was there, gasping under the weight of the guy.

She followed him in and they quickly made a pile of logs and kindling, dragged the bodies on top and poured the gas over everything.

Nina flicked a match with her thumb and tossed it, both of them running for the door when it caught with a whoosh that seemed to drag the old walls inwards.

Outside, they stood in the rain and watched as the old building burned. They watched for a long time. Only when there was almost nothing left of Joe's cottage did they go to fetch Doggie. Dug a hole at the side of the house and buried him.

It was a week later that Marcus straightened from his hoeing, peering into the distance. He pointed to the trees.

"That's her isn't it?"

Nina, lifted her rifle and sighted through the scope, but struggled to find the woman because she was standing very still. Eventually, though, she caught a glimpse of dirty white. Her shirt, the blood darkened to near black. "Yea. It's her."

Marcus looked perplexed. "How about that? She survived."

Nina feathered the focus on her scope. "No. She didn't."

Marcus shaded his eyes, frowning at this new problem.

"Maybe we should shoot her legs out, so she can't get far. Easier to find her."

"Why would we want to find her?"

He looked at her, head cocked to one side. "You want one of those things creeping about the place?"

Nina focussed again through her scope. "She's not creeping anywhere. She's just standing there."

Chapter
22
James

"Have you considered engineering?"

"Engineering?"

"You're a natural with math. And you like to make things, see how they fit together. After all these years of slow decay, it seems we're finally mending things, even building again. Telecoms! After all these years with little radio and no television, very few telephones."

He shook his head. "Some of it is just fixing the old infrastructure up, but a lot has gone beyond the point of no return so…"

Bertillon shrugged, looking suddenly shy, and old.

"There was a time when I thought you were one of the ones who wouldn't make it. I can't tell you how glad I am you did."

James thought for one horrible moment the man was going to hug him, or maybe even cry. He did neither. Instead, he put out his hand to be shaken.

"You are my longest-serving boy. You came to us when you were less than 12 months old."

Bertillon searched his face. "If you ever want to know, well, we have records."

James shook, then sat back and put one hand on top of the other. "I won't."

Bertillon nodded gravely. "That's what you think now. It might not be what you think in two years' time, or ten. I have the ledger, and you will always be welcome. In fact..." Bertillon hesitated.

"In fact I would be delighted to see you any time you cared to visit. You're family."

He did cry then, although it was a controlled, manly sort of thing. Tears down his cheeks that required dabbing. James nodded, stiffly. "Thank you Doctor."

"Charles, please."

James doubted her would ever call the man anything other than Dr Bertillon.

"Thank you. For everything."

The entire population of the foundling home was waiting in the hall when he walked down with his packed case, dressed, not in mustard, but in black, the suit a present from Bertillon, one of his older ones that had been shortened in cuff and leg by Nina Simeon herself, so that it very nearly fitted.

There were thirty-two orphans, Ana-Maria, Frieda and Nicolette, plus the Doctor. They clapped as he came down, singing 'For he's a jolly good fellow.' The same send-off he had seen for several other foundlings, but there seemed to be more tears this time. A lot of kids crying. James didn't cry.

That done, the carers turned and walked away. He watched Ana-Maria disappear into the classroom to clean or prepare or whatever task she had to perform. She didn't glance back.

Last of all, he hugged Karen. Nobody knew what they had been to each other, these last few years, nobody but them.

He held on long enough for the murmuring to start, a few giggles starting up, before whispering, "I'll see you again one day. Back here in Manchester."

She stepped away and shook her head, didn't respond beyond a smile that struggled around her lips. He nodded, took one last look around the place that had been home to him for as long as he could remember, and walked.

Just like Ana-Maria, he didn't glance back.

***

James had a ticket that Bertillon had bought for him, one that would take him to Boston. His first time on a Greyhound, first time outside of Manchester. He walked to the bus depot and climbed aboard and shuffled uncertainly towards the rear, where people were standing. There weren't seats in the back section of the bus, which surprised him. The red-faced driver shouted at him, "Hell are you going? Can't you read, buster?"

James was offended, but kept his face quiet. "I can read."

The man pointed. "That's for deaders back there, look."

The sign the man was indicating said, "Returned Only."

"What's the difference?"

"You one of them liberal types? What's the difference? No seats for one thing. Don't need 'em, do they?"

James was surprised that he hadn't noticed that every one of the people standing back there were Returned. They were simply standing there, not moving, not doing anything. Not one of them was even looking outside.

As he went to sit, the driver called out again. "You come back in five years."

James turned to see the man, shouting, looking angry but somehow still managing to say exactly what had been in his own mind. He did intend to come back, and five years was probably about right. The man wasn't finished. "Hell, come back in two, one of them zombie bastards'll be doing my job."

It shocked him, hearing someone in authority bellowing the Z-word out like that.

Right in front of a busload of The Returned, too. He glanced quickly at the rear, but they stood just as before. If any of them heard, and they must have, it was of no more interest to them than anything else.

Chapter
23
Alice

Alice had only just turned eighteen on the day she took a huge and shaky breath before pushing through the scarred and chipped door of Rickman's bar on Concord Street. This was early one Monday in June, a little after five. There were a couple of guys already in there, hunched over glasses but turning to look as she came in, carrying her guitar case. A Returned woman wearing a long smock was polishing tables.

The smell in there was a shock, like decades of beer and tobacco smoke had saturated every fibre of the place. The barman, a tall, white-haired man with an impressive gut, lifted his chin as she approached. She saw him looking her over, not being subtle about it, and taking in the guitar.

"Help you?"

"Mr Rickman? I saw your sign outside."

"You a musician? Singer?"

She nodded. All three men were regarding her openly now. The only one not staring was the Returned cleaner.

The man lifted a cigarette from an ashtray on the bar and took a long drag, taking his time and leaving his eyes on her.

"Let's get this straight. I'm only interested in acts that fit the feel of the place. Don't want no girly ballads, none of that whiny soul searchin' shit."

Alice had to take a moment to recover herself, surprised at the feeling of being somehow in trouble. "I don't whine."

"You don't sound whiny, it's true. But you don't sound up-beat neither. Up-beat. That's what we're after."

"Up-beat?"

"Something that rocks along, without getting in people's faces." He indicated the unsmiling men at the bar. "Gets in the way of my fine clientele focussin' on buying product with some kinda enthusiasm."

One man muttered, "Maybe if your beer wasn't so far to the shit end of the scale, might sell some more, Rick."

"I got premium beer right here on tap, all you have to do is ask, Jonas Miles."

The man called Jonas did answer, but it was too low for Alice to catch. It made the other patron laugh, a little puffed out thing that didn't involve smiling.

She said, "I sing mainly blues, if that works."

Rick frowned uncertainly. "Blues, that don't sound…"

Jonas straightened, taking more interest. "There's a blast from the past. Back in the day I was all about the blues, me."

The other man grunted something unintelligible, but Jonas nodded. "Damn straight. Here's another for you. BB King. Remember BB?"

Another grunt, but one that Jonas took exception too. "That asshole? He wasn't no blues singer. Shit, man, don't you know better than that? He was rock."

Grunt.

177

"Blues rock my ass. He was a friggin Pop star. What? Ok, now you're talkin'. Alvin Lee! Didn't expect you to even know one thing about him, man. He's a Brit for Chrissakes."

Rick shook his head. "I never even heard of one of these people. Nobody since The Change wants to listen to that old-styley crap."

Jonas was looking into the corner, clearly going back in his memory. "Alvin Lee, man, I haven't thought about that guy in decades. The Bluest Blues. What I'd give to hear that again, you with me Bobby?"

Bobby, almost certainly, was with him. It was a kind of gift, Alice reckoned. When she played the Bluest Blues for Mr Waters, he had to wipe away a tear. Waters normally had a lot to say about white guys playing the blues, not much of it good, but made an exception for the Brit Lee who, he said, had the feel.

She cleared her throat. "I could give that a try, if you want to hear it."

The two men at the bar turned all the way around, giving her their full attention now. Rickman shrugged and stretched out a hand towards the stage. Trying not to look as scared as she felt, Alice crossed the room.

The stage was in the corner, and low, but there was plenty of room. Amplifiers and microphone stands and other equipment had been pushed to the side. Photographs up around it showed four-piece bands in full flow, the place packed and rocking. Energetic dancing going on at the little square of floor set aside for it. It gave her a thrill, seeing those shots, but it frightened her too. No way would she have people singing along, or dancing. She didn't play that kind of music, so maybe Rickman was right. She didn't fit what he wanted.

She pulled a high stool to the front of the stage, took out her guitar and tuned it. She looked up, taking a deep breath before starting in. The Returned woman kept cleaning, but otherwise she had the attention of the room.

Encouraged by Mr Waters, she'd largely moved on from trying to copy the guitar work on records, inventing her own pieces to accompany songs. But there was something about what Alvin did on The Bluest Blues that she liked just the way it was. She played it as close as she could get.

She heard a low, "Whoa." as she started on the intro, she thought from Jonas, and a responding grunt. Then, she closed her eyes, and sang.

It wasn't until the last chord faded that she looked back towards the men again. There was a fourth now, a bulky long-haired guy of around thirty, standing just inside the door.

For a few seconds, nobody spoke, then Jonas said, "Shit, girl, you got the bluest voice I heard since Before."

An enthusiastic grunt seemed to back it up.

"Damn right, she can play. Rick, that's good guitar work, right there."

Rickman nodded. "You can play. And your voice, I think your singing voice is deeper than mine."

Bobby was smiling when he said whatever he said next, making all three men laugh, but it was clear that it wasn't a joke at her expense. It was at Rickman's. The long-haired guy had come all the way to the bar now and Rickman poured him a shot glass of something without asking. He was, she saw, older than she first thought, late-thirties, something like

179

that, possibly even older. Deeply tanned, strong featured and heavy shouldered, like maybe he lifted weights, wearing a denim shirt, jeans and scuffed engineer boots. He nodded to her and raised his hands above his head in a silent applause and, yea, look at those arms. He lifted something a lot heavier than that shot glass.

"You want me to play anything else?"

Jonas, "Hell, yea."

Rickman shook his head. "That'll do 'er for now. Look, I gotta tell you, these guys here today seem to go for that stuff, but I don't know if it'll fly with most of the customers. Nothing up-beat about it, not one bit. You come here, Thursday next at eight. Play a two hour set and we'll see."

Alice tapped a cigarette from her packet, and bent to light it from Jonas' Zippo lighter when he offered, using the little routine to calm her jangling nerves. Blew out a long stream of smoke, and cocked her wrist back. "How does it pay?"

Rickman held up a hand. "This is just a try-out. I'm giving you a chance."

All three men had something to say about this, with Bobby sounding the most outraged. Alice found that she understood what he was saying this time. Something like, "Girl ain't no zombie, man. Pay 'er up."

Rickman shook his head. "I'm givin' the girl a *chance*. Opportunity don't just come a-knockin' for a girl young as that."

The long-hair stopped with his bourbon half way to his lips. His voice was surprisingly deep. "Bullshit. Pay the girl."

Rickman rolled his eyes. "Tell you what. You come Thursday, try out. They like you, I'll pay you a hundred dollars. They don't, you cut your losses and pack up soon as you like. Deal?"

The last thing he said, before she left, "An' wear a dress. So we can see some of those long legs a'your'n."

That, finally, was something everybody in the bar seemed to agree with.

Chapter
24
Nina

The switch to winter was sudden, and brutal. One day the sun was hot enough to work outside in a tee, the next the wind was so pure and cold it cut through many layers of clothing and hurt any bit of skin left exposed. They set to, surprised by the suddenness of the change, getting on with what needed to be done to batten down.

Soon enough, Nina knew, it would snow. And Marcus would have to face his first winter without Doggie.

As had become her daily habit, she focussed her scope on the dead woman, who stood the same as always, no change in stance or position. Her clothes were rags now, blowing in the wind. Her hair was gone. Her skin had darkened to slate.

Marcus watched her for a moment, and said what he always said. "We should go out there with a can of gasoline."

"She hasn't moved. She must've frozen solid. Like a chunk of meat. Maybe it will even kill her."

"Maybe."

"I keep thinking one of those high winds will just blow her over, and she'll be covered in snow."

"Maybe if we shoot her now, she'll shatter, like porcelain."

In the end, they did neither.

That was a bad winter, the worst yet. Long periods where it was too cold to venture out for more than the time it took to fetch another load of logs, following the guide rope. It was dark, and the snow was deep. One morning it occurred to Nina that she and Marcus had gone days without speaking, at least to each other. Now that she was thinking about it, she realised that wasn't confined to winter. Somewhere along the way, locked in together as they were, they had gotten out of the habit.

The dead woman preyed on Nina's mind, the thought of her standing, frozen in place. Surely the sub-zero temperatures would have burst every dead cell in her body, turned her old meat to something like wood. Nothing that had ever been flesh could survive months of those temperatures.

One bright morning, she woke up early. Shivered into her thermals and then her outer layers. Got her boots and coat and mittens. She worked her sore fingers before putting her gloves on. There had been too many days where her hands had gotten so cold it was agony returning to the house. She was, she knew, flirting with frostbite.

The gun she hefted over her shoulder was the assault rifle they took from the woman's own father.

On a walk like this, through the frozen silence, it would have been good to have Doggie bounding through the snow by her side. She had to remind herself that good boy had been getting older, and bounding through three feet of snow hadn't been on the cards for at least the last two winters.

Still, he was gone, and she could recall him however she liked.

The snow had an icy crust, frozen over, and was so bright in the morning sun that it hurt her eyes, tiring them quickly, even behind the Raybans. Every step was a grunting effort, and she grew warm despite the temperature. Her noise was the only sound in all the world. After ten minutes, she could see the woman clearly. She stopped for a few hard-breathing seconds, getting a good look.

She was still upright, thigh-deep in snow, looking like she'd been there almost as long as the trees around her. Her shirt was gone, so her upper body was bare. Every last strand of hair was gone too. The side facing the wind was snow spattered, the rest would be dirty grey, were it not for the milky layers of ice overlaying it.

Nina took her mittens off, so was only wearing two thin pairs of gloves, lambswool over silk. She dropped the mitts onto the crispy snow, the only dark things for hundreds of yards around, and unslung the rifle.

She approached cautiously, at an angle and one step at a time, waiting to check before the next step. The thing that had once been a woman was frozen as solid as anything could ever be. It was difficult to be sure under the sheath of ice, but it looked like her eyes might have been open, when she froze. They were frozen open.

Ten feet away, the gun at her hip and finger on the trigger, Nina called out.

"You still in there?"

Nothing. A darkened lump of old meat, left too long in the freezer and welded to the frost.

Nina looked back the way she'd come, her tracks not the only ones in the snow, but by far the biggest. There were still a few animals out and moving, something she invariably found comforting. She took comfort in different things these days.

The house was also comforting to look at, with the usual haze of smoke rising from the chimney. She imagined Marcus, maybe still in their winter bed, the one in the living room without Doggie in it. Maybe up and thinking, that crazy bitch has gone to see if she can speak to the zombie. Probably doing nothing beyond staring at the fire.

She turned back to the dead woman. "Are you properly, all the way dead, this time? Is that what you're telling me?"

The silence was profound.

"Ok, then. You won't mind if I shoot you with your Daddy's rifle. Marcus thinks, frozen as you are, you'll shatter into a hundred pieces."

Her finger tightened on the trigger. "What do you think? Shall we try?"

The woman didn't reply and didn't move. Nina sighed and lowered the gun. Took another couple of steps forward, so she could speak without raising her voice. It made as much sense as anything else she was doing.

"Look. I'm sorry. We couldn't have helped your Daddy, he was beyond it. Maybe we couldn't have helped you either, but we ought to have tried, Marcus and me."

She took a step closer, took another, close enough to be able to use the muzzle to tap the ice, covering the woman. She nearly did that, but couldn't go through with it.

"No offence, Missy, but I can't relax entirely with you here. I think I'm going to tell Marcus to go ahead. He's been talking about coming out here and burn you down since August."

Up close, the ice that covered the thing was ridged and many layered. Under it, the skin was the colour of dirty slate, interspersed with bands of lighter grey. Her eyes were definitely open. So was her mouth, just a little, the glint of teeth showing yellow.

The woman had been short, and skinny. If she'd ever had a bosom, malnutrition had taken it. She might have once been pretty. Not like she could have been a clothes hanger for Versace or McCartney. But definitely pretty. Nina had noticed that, just before she'd pulled the little pop gun and shot the air around Marcus.

Thinking about that, she checked the woman's hands. No sign of that little pistol. Her pants hung so ragged, it couldn't be tucked in there either.

Making her mind up to move, Nina dared herself and reached slowly out. Let the muzzle of the gun hover over the woman's head. She tapped it, a gentle double-click. It sounded like a serving spoon hitting a plate.

Nothing.

She exhaled. "Ok then."

It was when she turned away that she heard the creak, so that it came from behind her. It was only a small sound, but there was no mistaking it or where it came from. She spun so quickly that the snow trapped her legs and she fell on her ass. The rifle was socked into her shoulder, though.

The woman stood pretty much exactly as she had before, sheathed in almost an inch of ice. Except for her neck, which had turned, so her face was towards Nina. The ice below her jaw had cracked.

Nina shuffled backwards, trying to get back on her feet and keep the gun aimed at the same time.

The icy shell was coming off the woman's face now, fracturing and falling as she opened her mouth to expose a line of yellowed teeth and blackened tongue. She lifted a hand, ice splintering and cracking, and side fisted her own brow.

Nina gained her feet, breathing loud and fast. It was painful, hauling in lungfuls of that air. The muffling layers of clothing seemed to accentuate her heartbeat. Every rapid hammer blow was trapped inside.

The dead woman scraped at her eyes, mostly uncovering them. Her voice was nothing like human.

"Nina."

"Don't you move! Don't you take a *step*."

Then, quieter. "How do you know my name?"

The woman didn't answer straight away, so there was nothing to fill Nina's head but the horror of what she was looking at. The bald head of a once-pretty woman, still partly ice-encrusted, the flesh darkly petrified.

She regarded Nina steadily through frozen eyes.

"You were famous."

Nina didn't think much of that as an answer, but it seemed that was all she was going to get. The gun was heavy, but she pointed it deliberately at the thing's face.

"If you take a step, I'm going to unload on you. Things don't seem to work like they should, but I'm still willing to bet a full clip at this range, hitting something as froze up as your head…"

She didn't finish the sentence, and they stood there, staring at each other. Eventually, the weight of the gun was too much, and she dropped it to her hip.

"How come you were in the mountains? You and your family."

Making small-talk.

"We'd survived for years, hunting and scavenging. Moving on."

"I'm sorry we didn't help you. Maybe we could have saved you. Who knows?"

"That doesn't matter."

"It doesn't?"

"It's better this way."

Nina didn't think it possible that she could laugh, in a situation like this. A shot-up, froze-up, dead woman, a horror story just to look at, had told her it was better this way.

She puffed out a short laugh, then took the scene in again and had to drop the muzzle of her gun into the snow so she could double up. It seemed she couldn't make herself stop laughing. It hurt her face and it hurt her sides and it hurt her lungs.

She managed to point at the woman, her grey face impassive.

"It's better this way, hahahah!"

She fell to her knees, eyes screwed tight, tears freezing on her cheeks but still laughing. She had to put her face into the snow before she could find a way to turn it into sobbing.

Then she sat back, gasping for breath. "Were you this funny when you were alive?"

The woman just stared and, after a while, Nina had to climb to her feet.

"I'm going back. Some of us struggle in these sorts of temperatures. What are we going to do with you?"

"Just leave me be."

"Will you leave us be?"

"Yes. Unless you need me."

"Unless I *need* you? Jesus Christ."

She worked her hands, aware that she'd already been out too long. She was losing her body heat fast, and her fingers were hurting again. She'd pay a painful price, when they warmed.

"I'm not sure I can believe that. Marcus wants to burn you."

"You said."

Nina blinked in surprise. "You heard that? I thought you were asleep."

"I don't sleep."

***

Marcus was waiting for her at the first barricade, now just a rise in the snow. The first time he had been further than the store for weeks. He stepped to the side as she was approaching it.

"You went."

"I went."

"And."

"She's alive. Kind of."

"I'm going to burn her. Should've done that months ago."

"She said she won't come near us."

"She sign a paper on that?"

"You're crap at sarcasm. She said she won't come near, unless we need her."

He was shaking his head, sides of his mouth pulled down so far it was almost funny.

"Do you hear yourself?"

"I don't want you to burn her. Leave her alone."

"You're crazy."

"You think? Crazy means nothing now. Normal means nothing. We're just how we are. I want you to let her be."

He squinted into the distance, and she knew he was thinking about gasoline.

189

Chapter
25
James

It wasn't Karen Gill that brought James back to Manchester, and it certainly wasn't Alice Simeon. He was sure of that. It was the offer of a job. A good job someplace that didn't resound to gunfire and carry a constant sense of threat, like Boston, one of the few large cities to survive from Before. Manchester was a small city, one he already knew, and it was thriving.

He saw the advert in the Herald – Municipal Engineer, with the City Council – and at first dismissed it, knowing that he would make much more working for private firms in and around Boston, where there was no end of new building taking place, repairing the damage of the last decades.

It couldn't be dismissed that easy. Over the period of a week, he kept coming back to it, wondering about differential costs and whether his quality of life might not be a whole lot better in New Hampshire.

So, he posted his CV and had almost given up when, almost a month later, an invitation to interview arrived. He had a single suit, which he took to the cleaners just before the trip, and bought himself a new shirt and tie. Splashed out on a new pair of shoes, going for wing-tips from Godley's in Manchester. It felt like that might be a lucky thing to do, Godley's shoes walking him back home.

It was strange, arriving in Manchester on a freezing November afternoon, but not as strange as he had braced himself for. He disembarked at almost the same spot he had climbed aboard that Greyhound, eight years earlier. The depot looked unchanged, and the driver was a different guy, but just as alive. Jesus, but it was cold. He buttoned his coat and wrapped his muffler tight, picked up his bag, and walked.

It was only a mile to the hotel he had booked in Bridge Street, so he passed the taxi waiting hopefully outside the station, and picked up the pace, pushing into the wind.

Granite Street looked the same as it ever did, a lot of multi-level parking that nobody would ever use, now home to storage units. Across the lanes were a series of low factories, most of them looking busy, which he took as a good sign. The air was sweet with smoke.

Left onto Elm, and most of the stores he knew from before were still there and open, people congregating at this time of day, but James put his head down and hurried past, coming to the wide open space at Memorial Park. He and Karen had snuck off once to Memorial, got in trouble but it had been worth it.

He passed Merrimack to where the red brick really started, a lot of tap-rooms and bars here, the Italian restaurant Gino's smelling as good as ever. He'd always wanted to go in there.

Elm was always his favourite street, less so when the trees weren't in leaf, but he was coming up on City Hall now, the place he would go tomorrow for an interview with a Mr Teed. He kept his eyes on it as he walked, feeling chilled now and wanting to get to his hotel.

Bridge wasn't so attractive as Elm, until he reached Boufford Hotel, a pristine white colonial-style building. It had, he knew, once been a funeral home. He had only the haziest notion of what that might be.

He pushed through the doors into a warm and brightly lit hall, to be met by a short, round woman with a wide smile. "You must be Mr Spears!"

***

James could recall walking past City Hall when he was a kid. It had an age to it, and a solid kind of grandeur, even dwarfed as it was by the more modern Plaza building. Three stories of red brick and granite, in what he could now identify as Gothic Revival style. A central clock tower that doubled the height of the building, and hugely tall and narrow windows.

He took a moment to slow his breathing before pushing through the door. Inside, it smelled strongly of waxed wood, and was just as grand and old-world as he expected. The heels of his new Godley's shoes clicked as he made his way to the gleaming counter.

A stern receptionist looked at him over her spectacles, apparently unimpressed with his suit and tie. She was flanked by a City Constable, who stared at him impassively from behind mirrored sunglasses, assault rifle cradled and ready.

Her voice was as sharp as her features. "Yes?"

"I have an appointment with Mr Teed. James…"

Her voice grew sharper, cutting across him. "Interviews? All you had to say was interviews. Name?"

"James Spears."

She made a production of inspecting a bound ledger, running her pen down, lips pursed. "You are ten minutes early, young man. Go up those stairs and turn left. You will find a line of chairs, where you must sit. You may have to wait for quite some time."

James didn't respond. Instead, he twisted to follow her pointed finger for a moment, before turning back.

He noticed the woman blink, some surprise in there, and suspected that she was used to intimidating people into thanking her for nothing better than brusque treatment. In the moment before he turned on his heel, his eye fell on the page still open before her, his name the only one on there.

He found the line of cushioned chairs at the top of the stairs, but didn't have a chance to sit. A man in a stiff, three-piece suit – the word *portly* crossed James's mind, for the first time in his life – came striding out of a tall door on the right, his hand held out as he came.

"James Spears, is it? Mr Teed."

Moustachioed, definitely portly, high collared and shiny haired Mr Teed was grinning as he came. James made a point of smiling back, finding it easy. The man had mutton chop whiskers.

Chapter
26
Alice

Nina did not want her to play the gig, even though they could use the money.

"You think it's goin' to be something fine up there, playing your guitar while guys get blind drunk and want to fight each other? You'll hardly be able to hear your own self. Nobody even be *listenin'*"

"I think they'll listen. Why else would they have music?"

Her mother was the one not listening. Nothing new there, thought Alice.

"They be ogling up your legs, askin' to see your titties. All they interested in."

"If it's horrible, I won't go back. I thought you'd be pleased for me."

Even as Alice said it, she knew that wasn't so. Rather, she thought her mother ought to be pleased for her. Same as she ought to be proud of what she could do on the piano, and the guitar. Ought to be bursting with pride to hear her singing, encouraging her, rather than ignoring it.

"You goin' to be there?"

"You crazy? I wouldn't be seen grey in a dive like Rickman's. You want to, that's your look out."

Alice had known that perfectly well. Still, she had to turn her face for a moment.

She didn't walk into that fine establishment alone, however. This was the first time she'd ever seen Mr Waters outside of his little apartment, and was shocked by how bad his movement was. Limping around the little house, she'd got used to how it looked but, heading down the sidewalk, it was plain that every step was a trial. Even with the stick, he leaned heavily on Mrs Twining and panted hard. His face was sheened with sweat.

She shared more than one worried look with her old schoolteacher.

"Mr Waters, are you ok? I'm not sure you should be…"

He snapped at her, angry. "Don't fuss, girl. I can't stand fussin'."

"But…"

"Don't!"

They shuffled along, Alice wondering if the guy was even going to make it. He made it.

The bar wasn't so busy when they arrived, which was a relief. Maybe a dozen people in there, including Jonas, Bobby and the guy she thought of as Mr Long-Hair. The air, though, was already blue with smoke. The beery smell struck her anew.

Rick was behind the bar serving, along with an attractive blonde girl with spectacular boobs, most of which were on display.

Jonas and Bobby greeted her like a long-lost friend, and she could see they were more than half in the bag already, maybe having been there since opening time. Maybe that was their daily routine.

Rickman nodded at her but didn't smile, concentrating on taking money from a heavily bearded man in exchange for a tall glass of beer.

Long-Hair did smile, a grin full of white teeth, lighting up his broad face.

He pushed off from the bar, coming across to meet them and she thought again he really did have some size on him, this guy. Not just tall, but broad in the chest and shoulder. There was an awful lot of him.

He indicated Mr Waters and Mrs Twining. "This your folks, Alice?"

She shook her head, about to say, these are my tutors, changing it to, "My friends."

She glanced down at Mr Waters, who had collapsed into a chair. He was looking exhausted, slick with sweat, but getting his breath back.

Long-hair stared at him for a moment, his brows pulling together, but didn't ask if he was okay. Instead he turned and then his eyes flew open. "Mrs Twining, that you?"

"Eugene Vincelette! I've not seen you for years. How are you these days? You're looking well."

The man, so big and hard-looking, was suddenly embarrassed, like he didn't know what to do with his limbs. He even reddened slightly. "Shucks, Mrs T, nobody's called me Eugene since I left school."

He caught himself. "And I've not said shucks since I left school neither. Jeez."

"So, what you doing with yourself, Gene?"

"I work at the steel plant, in the Androscoggin Mill there." Again, he seemed to catch himself. "It's my plant, me and my brother. Vincelette Steel."

"That's just great. This is my friend, Mr Waters."

Gene, the steelman, shook hands with Mrs Twining, then bent to shake with Waters. "I guess you must be the guy teached Alice the Blues. No offence Mrs T."

"Call me *Eu*gene, Gene. I don't mind it." Waters narrowed his eyes, still holding the man's big hand whilst searching his face. "What are you? Crow or something?"

"Abenaki. Most folks can't tell."

Waters tapped his temple. "I got a good eye."

He turned to Alice, who he first mistook for a boy, and shrugged.

Then Rickman was there, not looking happy. "That your idea of a dress?"

She looked down at herself. "It's a dress."

"Yea. Maybe somebody'll catch sight of your shinbone, if you sit high on the stool. Get the clientele over-excited."

Nobody spoke for a moment, although she saw the expression on Mr Waters' face. How he managed to stay quiet was a mystery. Mr Vincelette – Gene – stared at Rickman with such a flat expression that it was as well he wasn't looking that way, or he might have been scared. There was a definite feeling of threat hanging around that guy.

Rickman led her to the stage and this time there was a microphone waiting for her.

"How do you set up your guitar?"

Alice came to a stop, having no idea how to answer this. Behind her, Mr Waters, who must have hauled himself to his feet and hurried to follow, said, "You got you a decent guitar amp?"

"Sure."

Waters leaned heavily on his stick and narrowed his eyes at the odds and ends of equipment lining the wall. "I mean a acoustic guitar amp? Acoustics sound shit through a 'lectric amp."

Rickman glared. "Then, no."

"She'll play through your PA. Best we can do."

197

When Rickman turned away, Alice bent to whisper to Waters, her voice very nearly squeaky. "There's no place on this guitar to plug anything in!"

He rolled his eyes. "You've an internal pick-up fitted. Jack is in the end pin."

When she just looked at him, he pointed. "Where your strap goes on, the ass-end of the damn guitar."

It was a night of firsts. The first time she had heard her own voice or the already full sound of the Martin through an amplifier. The first time she forgot the words to a song she knew perfectly well. Her fingers didn't forget what to play, though, not at any point. It felt almost as though they were operating all on their own.

Waters had suggested she start with something upbeat, like Rickman wanted, get the attention. They had worked out a set and he had made her write it on a sheet of legal paper in big blocky writing, which he taped to the floor in front of her. Once she got up there and started, she could see why. She was so nervous, she would have forgotten everything. Could have played the same song twice in a row and not noticed.

Mrs Twining took a seat at a table immediately in front of the stage, but Waters climbed up on there with her, waving her hand away when she tried to help him, showing her how to set up. She eased onto the high stool and glanced towards him, but he was staring out at the crowd, lost in his own head. His eyes had misted and for a moment his lower lip quivered.

Maybe feeling her looking, maybe reacting to a sudden cat-call from somewhere in the crowd, he jerked and stepped closer, patting her on the back, a tiny little double touch. It was, she thought, the only

198

time he had ever touched her. She watched as he climbed off the stage, only a foot high but it gave him trouble. She watched as he got settled beside Mrs Twining, worrying about him. He looked sick.

The bar had been filling, and was getting noisy, people leaning at the bar or sitting at tables, talking and laughing. A card game was going strong in the corner and the haze of smoke hung heavy at around head height. Jonas and Bobby were pointed her way, as was Gene Vincelette. She caught his eye and he nodded, raising his shot glass.

She took a big breath and held it, closed her eyes and then launched into Mustang Sally, a chunky, driving rhythm, more so through the speakers. Heads came up or turned her way as she kicked in, but mostly they turned right back to their beer and conversation.

Thrown slightly by the volume of the noise in there – people simply talked louder, so they could be heard over her – she put a bit more into her singing, which she could hear didn't improve it. She got through the song somehow, having to repeat a verse because the words deserted her, and paused for a smattering of applause.

Next was John Lee Hooker's Boom Boom, which she was sure would get them turning from their drink, but didn't. She caught Mr Waters' eye. He nodded encouragement, but made a flat sign with his hand, like he was pushing back a clock hand. Telling her she was rushing. Mess Around followed Boom Boom, then Tell Mama.

In a pause while she retuned, somebody shouted. "Play *Feel Like a Woman*."

Across the bar, somebody else shouted back, "I don' think she does feel like a woman. She sure don't sound like one."

The place had been loud enough before, now it was in an uproar of shouting and laughing. Somebody called out, wanting to see what was under her dress, a pussy or a cock. Wanting to be anywhere but here in this moment, Alice stared wide-eyed at Mrs Twining, who made a fist, and an uncharacteristically fierce face, go on. Mr Waters called out. "Fuck 'em. Give 'em Smokestack, honey."

That was the last song on her list, but Alice nodded. She slipped off her stool and stood, moved the mic up so that it was the right height. Her hands were hot and felt like they didn't belong to her. Her legs were shaking, but whether from nerves now, or frustration or outright anger, she didn't know. In that moment, she couldn't tell a thing about herself.

Mr Waters had told her, Howlin' Wolf, he used to scare the shit out of audiences. A massive man, imposing, and he used that. He howled at them.

She started the riff, playing it over and over as she swayed, and for the first time she heard a few people pick it up, tapping their feet or clapping. Gene was cracking the base of his shot glass on the bar, keeping time.

Keeping the groove going, she bent to the mic, but didn't sing. She *howled*, seeing faces turning in surprise as she turned it into, "A-Smokestack Lightning!"

It wasn't the cleanest she ever sang that song, but it was the loudest, and it was the angriest she'd ever sang anything. She hadn't even known she could sing angry. She was singing at all those faces in the crowd, spitting out the words, howling in between.

When she finished, some clapped with real enthusiasm, but others just stared and muttered as she unslung her guitar. The last thing Mr Waters said, before she left him in there. "The Wolf woulda been proud, honey."

Chapter
27
Nina

"Can we make a pact?"

"What sort of pact?"

"Can't you guess?"

Nina searched his face, and found the desperation there. Took a long step away. "I want to live, Marcus."

He shook his head. "That's not it."

"What then?"

"If one of us dies, the other has to burn them."

She exhaled noisily, nodding before he even got to the end of the sentence, thinking this was understood and wondering why he even bothered saying it. It was like he had read her mind when he said, "There was a time I thought that was a given. It's just what would have happened."

"What's going on in your head? Course that's what's goin' to happen."

"I've been thinking that if I die, you might just sit and wait for me to come back. I don't want to."

She shook her head. "Why would I do that?"

"Why don't you let me burn that zombie out there? All it does is stand there, year after year, watching us."

"She isn't somebody I *love*. She isn't anything. Burn her if you want."

"You call it she. Like it's a person."

"Marcus. Listen to me. If you die, I'll pile logs all over you and pour on the gas and burn you till there's nothing left. If I die…"

"If you die, I'm done. I'm going to burn us both."

Her eyes came wide. She had to put her hand on her breastbone for a second and then she wanted to slap him, but she'd only ever done that once and wasn't going to repeat it. "Don't say that, you stupid…"

"I'm serious. If you go…"

He had tears in his eyes and she had to take his shoulders in her hands, thinner now than they were, and shake them.

"Neither of us are going to die, Jesus Christ! Where is this shit coming from? We're young, still. I'm not even forty."

She took his hand and put it on her stomach. "We've more reason to live than ever we did. Don't you get that?"

He cupped the growing bulge there, and managed a smile that hurt her more than anything.

"I can't believe it happened. I don't know how it happened."

"I thought everybody knew that."

"No, but." He stepped behind her, and put an arm across her chest, still cupping her stomach.

"But I didn't think it would happen to me. Not to me."

"That's…" she almost said crazy, but stopped herself, knowing that was a word that held weight with him. "…bullshit."

"In fact, if we were still living in Manhattan, I'd think it was somebody else's."

"Seriously?"

203

He stared hard into her eyes. "I want to go, honey. I'm done. I've been done for years."

"Don't say that! Don't you fucking…don't just say it."

"Nina."

"Leave me alone." She cupped her stomach. "Leave us alone. Don't you fucking say it."

***

Nina hadn't gone near the dead woman since that first day, three years ago, but she was the first thing she looked at when she got up in the morning. Sighting along her scope or using the binoculars. Sometimes she wondered would Marcus just go out there one day, with a can of gas. Sometimes he talked nasty, saying how he could use her as target practice. Shoot out her knees and then just keep going, till she was a bag of broken bones, not able to move.

One hot day in mid-summer, Nina dropped her spade and eased out her back and just started walking, only pausing to sling her rifle. She struggled to know how far along she was, but the bulge was noticeably bigger now.

The woman watched her come, but didn't move. The underbrush was starting to claim her, Nina saw, weeds growing up her legs and tendrils of ivy reaching her from the nearest tree.

Coming close enough to talk, she paused.

"Hello."

"Hello Nina."

"You're looking well. Not many people can get away with undergrowth, but you're rockin' it."

No reply.

"Do you know something? You're the only other person I've spoken to in fifteen years."

"You consider me a person then?"

Nina frowned. "I'm not sure how else to think of you. I'm worried about Marcus."

"About him setting fire to me?"

"About him setting fire to me." She touched her belly. "These past few weeks, it's like a trip got thrown in his head, the things he's saying."

"That wouldn't be good."

"No."

"If you kill him, he'd see things differently."

Nina narrowed her eyes. "I think he *wants* me to kill him. Then burn him. I'm not doing it."

"He'd see things how they really were, when he returned. Killing him would be a kindness."

Nina took a step back, another. The rifle was still held casually, but both hands were on it now, ready.

"Should I be worried about you?"

"I told you. I won't come near you, unless you need me."

"Yea, but your idea of what we need might not be the same as mine."

"I won't hurt either of you."

Nina rubbed her blunted fingers against her lip. She had finally lost the tips of three fingers on her left hand during the last winter, having to cut them off herself with a carving knife. Slicing them like carrots.

"I'm worried he's going to kill hisself. But I see him looking at me, this considering look on his face. I want to say something out loud, get it out there."

The zombie didn't react.

"Marcus is mentally ill. Depressed. Probably has been, off and on, all the time I've known him. And here's the thing."

She chewed her lip. "I know I should be sympathetic. Like if he had a broken leg or cancer. But I'm not. I'm angry. I see him sitting there staring at his feet for hours on end and all I want to do is hit him. I could give into it too, let myself be dragged down, but I don't. I won't. Why does he?"

Those last few words were all but shouted.

"You could go back."

That surprised her. She looked all around herself, as if that would help. "Back where?"

"Civilisation. It's taking hold."

"Is it?"

"Things are changing out there. Things aren't so crazy."

"And you know this, how?"

The woman pointed at her bump, and Nina found she didn't want that ragged black finger pointed at her baby. She covered it, protectively.

"Your baby. You have to take care of it. Make sure it grows."

"Marcus didn't think this would happen. What I didn't tell him, neither did I. After all these years, I get pregnant now?"

"These things happen in their own time."

"Ok, Nannie MacPhee. What I'm saying, I'm not entirely happy about it."

"You have to take care of it."

A lot of replies went through her head, mainly along the lines of, what the fuck has that to do with you? She didn't answer. Instead, she took a long step backwards, then walked away from there.

Back at the house, she walked straight into the study and, for the first time in years, used the bulldog clips to attach the Land Rover radio to its battery. Feathered the dial, hearing nothing but static as usual.

Until somebody, a woman, said, "…a new pair of Godley's shoes. Godley's. The pride of Manchester."

A funny, tinny little jingle of bells and a man said, "Ok now folks, we have Shania Twain for all those fans out there. She feels like a woman!"

Half-way through the song, Marcus looked in, frowning. "What's going on?"

"This is Manchester."

It was a long moment before he said anything else. He turned his head, so he was looking roughly towards the little city. "They've got radio up?"

They listened most of that evening. Manchester FM played mainly country songs, but on the hour there was news. Local news talking about new businesses in Manchester, the repairs being carried out by the City Council. Some guy called Mayor Little talking in a drawl Nina associated with further South.

Then he said, "And, for those who thought it would never happen, it's getting close, friends. Maybe not this year, maybe not next, but pretty soon we're going to have us a President of the Reunited States. It's happening! Come to City Hall to find out more."

They searched for more stations, but Manchester FM was all they could get. Finally, they had to turn it off.

She reached for his hand. "We can leave Tilly Whim."

He searched her face. "You want to?"

"Don't you? That's civilisation talking."

"You call it that. But what's it like?"

"Like the world used to be."

"A world full of zombies."

"You don't know that. They weren't once mentioned."

He pulled his hand away, shaking his head. "I want no part of it. No part, Nina."

***

Marcus spent the next two days, building a new pyre. He chose an open spot on a slight rise, well away from trees and overlooking the lake. As if a person might enjoy the view whilst being immolated.

The first day was spent cutting wood, a mixture of long dried logs and kindling from the store, and longer limbs. Fresh wood he cut from the forest. Nina watched him in silence, one hand on her bulge, not wanting to miss any of the kicks inside there. Marcus happier than she'd seen him for a long time – industrious. He was even singing as he worked, some song she had never heard, but somehow knew was his own. The first new song in years.

That evening, they sat on the veranda and ate pasta with the nickel-plated Smith and Wesson on the table between them. Nina had opened one of the few jars of sauce they had left, so it was a proper Bolognese, with their very last bottle of wine. Finished, she stared at him. He smiled to himself as he watched the sun set over the lake.

"You're a fucking coward, Marcus Cole."

He took his time answering but didn't move his eyes from the sunset. "I guess."

She put both hands on her bump. "You're leaving us, to face what's next."

He turned then, his face lighting up. "Come with me, then."

She pressed her lips hard together. "How would that work?"

He picked up the pistol. "I could…"

She was suddenly panicked, seeing his expression. He wasn't looking depressed or over-excited any longer. He seemed so much at peace, like it would seem like the right thing to shoot his pregnant wife. Shoot her, put her on the pyre and then soak everything with gasoline from his stars and stripes can, climb on beside her with his Zippo, and the gun.

She licked her lips and made sure her voice was calm. "I'd like it if you put that down."

He didn't. Instead, he leaned over and took her hand. "Think about this, honey."

He dropped his eyes to her stomach, making her cover it protectively. "Do you honestly want to bring a kid, a baby, into this? What if he dies in childbirth? What will you do then?"

Her voice wasn't calm anymore. She jumped up and slapped the gun away, then, when it came back, grabbed it and wrestled it out of his hand. Pointed it at him, so angry suddenly that the muzzle was shaking all over the place.

"Don't you fucking say that!"

He didn't look worried. "What if, though? I'm serious. These are the questions we got to ask ourselves. Or what if he only lived for a few years? Our tiny little Zombie."

"What if he lived his whole life, had kids? Your grandchildren."

"They'd all end up the same, every single one. Part of the plague. You too, Nina."

She wiped her face, and took another gulp of wine. Sat again, but didn't give up the gun.

"I'll burn myself first, you know I will."

"If you want, I'll build another pyre."

She took her time, then nodded. "Build it then. I guess I'll need it eventually."

***

Nina woke up and Marcus wasn't in bed. Grunting, she got her feet to the floor and heaved herself up, absently looking for Doggie, three years dead. Jesus, she was big now.

209

He wasn't on the veranda, or on the dock. The skiff was still there.

Unlike the Smith and Wesson.

She walked around the back, not expecting him to be in the field, and he wasn't. He was further back, standing beside the pyre – the one he saw as his own – with the pistol down by his side.

The grass was wet with dew, so her legs and the hem of her nightshirt were soaked by the time she reached him. The stink of gasoline was strong in the air.

He turned, hearing her come. Lifted the nickel-plated Smith and Wesson, not pointing it, just showing her. His cheeks were wet, like he'd been crying for a long time.

"Can't bring myself to put the trigger. Been trying all morning."

She took his hand. "I love you so, so much. Come back to bed. Let's make love and…"

"I'm sorry to do this to you."

He was looking at her so intensely, it scared her. She wrung at his fingers. "Don't. Whatever it is that you're thinking. Just don't."

He kissed her then, a deep kiss and long, making her realise how long it had been, putting the gun in her hand in the same moment. She threw it down beside the pyre.

"If you think I'm going to shoot you. The person I love more than anything, you're a pure fool."

He smiled at her, such a sad smile, a ghost of the one he gave her at that fashion show in Paris. He kissed her again, this time on the forehead. A kiss goodbye.

"Remember that guy, the finance guy you burned out the back of our apartment? Turned out he wasn't dead."

"What about him?"

"I'm just sayin'."

Turning, he clambered onto the gasoline stinking pyre, his long, long legs getting him up there so easily. Got into the middle and laid himself down on the bracken there, like it was comfortable.

"Get out of there! I mean it."

She skipped foot to foot, screaming at him when he pulled his Zippo from his pocket.

"Don't you do it! Don't you fucking do it."

"Best get back, it might catch pretty hard. And best get that gun, unless you want to watch me burn alive."

"You can't do this to me! Marcus."

When he flipped the lighter open, and flicked the wheel, she jumped back. Somehow, she had convinced herself that he wouldn't really go through with it. That this wouldn't actually happen. Now, here it was, right in front of her and there wasn't a thing she could do to stop it.

She scampered back, screaming. "I won't shoot you! I won't."

Marcus was right, the flames caught with a gassed-up whoof that knocked her from her feet. She scrambled up and it was searing hot already. He'd built it a lot better than the one out back of their apartment block. Jesus, the second time she'd been in this position, but this time that was Marcus in there and he was alive and all the way conscious.

He shrieked, and curled up into a ball. She took a few stumbling steps back, clapping her hands over her ears. He shrieked again, a sound that was barely human, and writhed, then sat up. He was, she saw, trying to climb out of there.

She scrambled, desperate, screaming herself as she searched for the gun in the smouldering grass, feeling her hair sizzle and burn.

***

Nina's hands were blistered from picking up the pistol, which she had dropped the first time she grabbed for it, thinking there was no way she could keep hold of something so hot.

Her nightshirt was singed, too. And something had hit her in the head, she could feel that scorch worst of all. It zinged with pain.

It was all she could do to get back into the house, that was what was in her mind. Just get back inside and fall down anywhere. Take care of the burns when you wake.

That's what she thought until the water started down her legs.

Chapter
28
Alice

Alice's guitar stunk of smoke. Her dress stunk of smoke so that she could smell it right across the room. Even though she smoked herself, and Nina chain-smoked, she had to wash her hair just to be able to sleep that night.

Her mother didn't ask one question about the gig.

The next day, they walked in silence to their shop on the corner of Elm and Pearl, a walk of forty minutes, three cigarettes for Nina and one for Alice. Barely spoke all morning, just got on with cutting and sewing and serving customers. She was in the back shop in the late afternoon, running the sewing machine, when Nina stepped though the strip curtain from the front.

"You got a visitor."

She looked up, frowning. Whoever this visitor was, her mother didn't approve them one bit. Avoiding saying, "A visitor?" she stood and followed her mother through.

Rickman stood in the shop, blinking in the sun streaming through the window. Out of the bar, he seemed different, ill at ease.

"Alice."

"Mr Rickman."

"Call me Rick."

This caused Nina to fold her arms and breathe out loudly, through her nose.

"Ok. Rick."

"That didn't go so well, last night."

"Not so well, no. You told me, I guess."

"I guess I did, but look. There's interest."

"I'm not with you."

"I've had people calling me up, asking about the Blues Girl."

"What?"

He glanced at Nina, who stood silently, glaring at him.

"I think there's a market, is what I'm sayin'. People want to hear that shit, no offence."

"They do?"

"I don't guess it will last, once the novelty's worn off. But what I'm hearing, folks are willing to travel, come to Manchester from aways away, just to hear blues. Turns out some people like it."

"Ok."

"Look. Tuesday night, that's my dead night. Here's what I propose. You do a set once a month on Tuesday evening. Play your blues. I'll advertise. We'll see how it goes."

"Ok."

"But, one thing, I gotta be clear about this."

"Wear something shows my legs."

"That'd be good, but that's not it. It's don't ever play anything like that howlin' song again."

***

Alice fairly skipped up the worn steps, knocking on the door with the special code, so he would know she wasn't no damn intruder.

She listened for him clumping up the hall, her ear attuned to that, but didn't hear it. Didn't hear a thing

214

until the door suddenly opened wide. He didn't have his shotgun.

"Rickman called back! Came right to the shop. People want a blues night, they do. An advertised night when people who want to hear the blues will come along. A lot of folks have been askin' about it."

"That's good."

Alice frowned. "You don't look too sure. Really, Rick says it won't be like last time. The folks that come will come special, wantin' to hear the blues."

"That sounds just fine."

They stared at each other for a few seconds, then a few seconds more. Finally, she had to ask, "Did you die?"

"I've had a heart condition for years now. Been in constant pain from my hips."

She put her hands over her face. "Oh, Mr Waters."

"It's better this way. I've been in constant pain from my hips."

Alice dropped her eyes to his hands. No shotgun, and no stick either.

"Are you here for a lesson?"

She wasn't. Still, she asked, "You can still teach me?"

"Sure. Why the hell not?"

It was the words he might have said, and the accent was in there, but there was almost no inflection. He turned without another word and Alice followed him into the house, watching him walk stiffly but without that lurching, rolling gait. It looked just as it always had, and smelled the same, until she reached the living room.

"I lost control of my bowels when I died. Cleaned up, but a smell like that will linger."

215

"That's ok. Look, I don't have my guitar."

"I'm teaching you 'bout tension and resolution, remember. Can show you, then you go and think about it."

"I guess."

They sat in their familiar places and he picked up his guitar. Everything just the same, although he was sitting differently. He started talking about the elements that built tension in music and every bit of it made sense, she found herself agreeing with him, surprised that she hadn't thought of it that way before. He talked about going through the gears, using volume and rhythm and harmonic structure, saying stuff he'd said before.

Then, he started to play, showing what he'd just explained in words.

It was ironic, she thought. This lesson was about how to connect the music with the emotions of the listener, how to make them feel, and that was the only thing that was missing. His fingers were as dexterous as ever, like they knew exactly what to do, every beat where it should be. But there was something missing – the essential spark, the feel of the music.

That was gone.

<u>Chapter</u>

29

James

James arrived in Manchester three days before he was due to start work. Mr Teed had suggested Semple's Room and Board on Putnam Street in Notre Dame, describing it as inexpensive but immaculately clean. Telling him Mrs Semple was a highly respectable lady, mother of Councillor Semple, whom he would know doubt meet in due course. A good friend of Mayor Little. Giving him that last line like a warning.

James checked the map and found it ran right off Notre Dame Avenue. Probably only a ten minute brisk walk from Bertillon's Home for Foundling Children.

On his second day there, he sauntered slowly towards his childhood home, even though it was far too cold for sauntering. He slowed even further as he caught his first sight of its dramatically peaked roof. A white-painted Victorian pile, not exactly out of place in this avenue, but of a larger scale than any of the nearby properties. Even from a distance, he could see it had fared poorly in the intervening years. The paint was no longer white, and largely peeling or stained. One or two windows had been boarded, rather than re-glazed. It made him wonder if the slide had started before he left, as this had the look of years of long, slow erosion.

Still, there was the attic window from which George had his accident, stepping into the sky to join The Returned. Coming closer, and slowing to a stop, he could hear a child's voice, calling out, another responding. Laughter.

The main thing that made Bertillon's stand out on this street wasn't its size, he now saw, it was the high fence that surrounded it. It hadn't occurred to James when he lived here, because that was simply how it was.

Looking around now, the garden of every other property wasn't only smaller, it was also completely open, barely a picket fence to be seen. Bertillon's was fenced in by six feet of solid larch-lap, now leaning and dilapidated, but still too tall to see over. At least for him.

He walked closer, eyes running over the familiar architecture of the place. A tree had been cut down here and the stump gave him a place to stand, so that he could put his hands on the fence and look over.

Bertillon's Home for Foundling Children.

He watched as kids climbed on the bars of the jungle gym, the same game of side to side he and his friends had played. Any of them could have been him, or Karen, or Martin, but there was nobody he recognised. Maybe one or two of the older ones might have been pre-school when he was here, but he didn't remember them and, he was sure, they wouldn't remember him.

He stood very still and watched, noticing the same rhythms and currents flow around the grounds that he grew up with. Froze when a figure walked stiffly from the house, carrying a basket. Ana-Maria, looking exactly the same as she always did. Her head turned, so that she must be able to see him where he stood, his head poking above the fence, but she didn't break stride. He lifted a hand and, after a moment, she lifted hers in return and then was gone, into the gardening outhouse.

He was trembling, thinking how very close he had come to taking that step out of the attic window, so he could be with her always. This was where he had spent fifteen years of his life and look at it; the same, just a little more faded and worn down.

After a few minutes another familiar figure walked across the yard, and he took a step back, almost slipping from his stump. Dapper in his midnight blue suit, Dr Bertillon walked without seeing him. All he had to do was call out.

He didn't call out.

Bertillon's clothes were the same, but nothing else was. He had lost his hair, his beard too, the thing that framed and shaped his face. His skin was grey, only beginning to darken, and not yet drawn into deep, vertical wrinkles.

James stepped down from the stump, relieved to be hidden, and no longer in sight of the gardens. He turned and hurried away, head down against the wind, moving a lot faster than he had walked here.

He kept going, wandering around West Side for a while before braving the Notre Dame bridge. Even though the wind was bitter, cutting through his coat, he stopped half-way, looking down into the Merrimack, brown today, and sluggish. On either side, the long red-brick factory buildings, old mills that worked just fine for the new industries. One of the reasons why Manchester was doing just fine when so many similar small cities were wasting away, according to Mr Teed. The other was the Mayor.

He continued towards Downtown, stopping for a beer and a burger at a little joint on Spring Street. The burger was surprisingly good, the fries crispy, and the beer went down just fine.

SimeonStyle was still where he remembered it, on the corner of Elm and Pearl. It had seemed such a significant place to the younger James Spears, in the days when he had never seen anything beyond this little town.

The first time he walked past it, he did it slowly, taking in the place that had been home to so many of his fantasies, seeing what could be seen in what he hoped was a casual stroll past.

The window was still vibrant enough, he supposed, in a small town sort of way. The same mannequins as before, but he no longer thought them risky and sophisticated. Not challenging, after all. They were, he thought, a little sad. Sun-yellowed hold overs from Before, their surfaces beginning to craze and crack. Not all of them in possession of a full set of fingers.

The clothes were smart enough, but little different from any tailors. Maybe a bit brighter, but perhaps they had to be. Perhaps, like the horrible bolt of mustard cloth, they got what they got and beggars couldn't choose.

He paused, trying to see into the dim-lit interior, wondering if there was still a Simeon involved in SimeonStyle. But soon enough, he had to move on.

<u>Chapter</u>
30
Nina

The baby had been there, entirely and astonishingly all the way *there*, on her breast, and she'd been lying in a pool of her own sticky blood. That's what she remembered, when she came to herself.

The baby on her breast. A girl, so tiny and beautiful. The most beautiful thing she could imagine, appearing so new and perfect in an ugly world.

She blinked and forced herself into full consciousness and there was no baby. She flailed around, searching, desperate, but there was no baby. She forced herself into a half-sitting position, gasping aloud but she wasn't thinking about pain.

She searched the messy rug on either side, behind herself, but there was nothing there. Sitting up fully brought a proper cry out of her, but she did it, casting around the room.

She was, she saw, under a blanket, and that didn't make a bit of sense. From the doorway, five, six yards away, she heard a whimper and her head snapped around.

The zombie was standing there, completely naked now, holding her baby. The child looked so tiny and frail against her crusty grey chest, that Nina gritted her teeth and somehow made herself stand.

Her head swam wildly as she took a step, feet feeling miles distant. She could hear herself growling, like an animal. Then, it occurred to her that the child was wrapped. Swaddled, in fact, in a clean bath towel.

She paused, swaying, and held out her hands. "My baby."

The woman didn't move. She said, "Sit. You may fall over."

"Give me my baby."

"Sit."

She could see that the creature was making sense. Her legs weren't to be trusted, just staying upright was a trial. She slumped onto the couch, stretching her hands out.

There was nothing for it, when the woman brought the baby, but to take it from her hands, finger brushing finger on the transfer. She shivered, but was mainly focussed on her child. Helping her to her breast.

The zombie stepped back and watched as the baby sought the nipple, knowing what to do even though she was so tiny, so brand new, and began to suckle. Despite herself, Nina began to cry, but knew she was smiling too. Smiling even though she had shot and killed her husband only, what, an hour before? Hours, maybe.

The woman stood as minutes past, just staring. She said, "You should eat and drink. You should cleanse yourself."

Nina looked around at the mess of the room and shook her head.

The minutes spun out again, until she asked, "What's your name? I need to call you something."

"My name is Alison."

The woman, Alison, turned on her heel, saying. "I will fetch food and water. And run a bath."

Chapter
31
James

On Monday, James dressed for work. Mrs Semple made him a special breakfast that included eggs and smoked fish, both promoted as being excellent for the brain. Before he left, she stood before him in the kitchen and cast a critical eye, straightening his tie and rearranging the shoulders of his suit.

"I believe you will do, Mr Spears. You're a very presentable young man."

The sour receptionist was no less sour, now that he was an employee of the City Council. She looked up sharply as he walked in, and made a point of looking at the clock, for reasons best known to herself, given that he was five minutes early for his nine o'clock meeting with Mr Teed and Mayor Little.

"Mr Spears."

She didn't smile, and neither did he. It hadn't sounded like a question, so he didn't say anything and, after a long moment, she had to fill the silence.

"Mr Teed is expecting you."

When James still didn't respond, she pointed at the stairs he had gone up before.

As before, Teed came out of his office with his hand held out, smiling broadly, and with real warmth. James made a point of smiling back.

"James! Congratulations! So pleased to have you join us and not a minute too soon. A lot to do, you know. A lot to do."

"I'm looking forward to it."

"Come and meet the Mayor. But first."

With the stately air of conferring a great benefit, Teed held up two keys, hanging from a leather fob.

"This is the key to your office, which I'll show you shortly. Guard it well. And this…"

He fingered the second key, holding James's eye before handing them over. "Will permit access to the executive men's room. I had to pull some strings to get you that one, so don't let me down."

Mayor Little wasn't little. He was James's idea of an old-time farmer, or cowboy, but wearing a suit. He was in his late fifties, his face looking burned from wind and sun and bourbon. Everything about him was long and sort of articulated, even his nose. His hand was big and bony and hard. He got up from behind his massive desk to shake, and James noticed he was wearing gleaming, hand-tooled cowboy boots.

"Glad to have you on board, Jim. Boy, do we need a guy like you! We needed you years ago. Sit down, sit down. Coffee?"

While they were waiting for their coffee, the guy talked about Manchester, how it had been built to be a factory-city, way back in the 1800's. "Engineers like you built this place, the canals and factories. Did you know the Amoskeag was once the biggest cotton mill in the entire world?"

Everybody who went to school in Manchester knew that, but James said. "Really?"

"Really."

The mayor stood in front of his desk, feet crossed, leaning against it, and pointed to old photographs that decorated his walls. Talking about Manchester's past and his hopes for the future.

"We're gonna have a new President soon. Mark my words, I feel it in my water. Maybe even next year, think of that! America rising from the ashes of its old, burned self, and we got to be ready. Take our chance to be the manufacturing heart of the new country."

That seemed a bit melodramatic, but the guy's enthusiasm was enviable. He held up a finger. "We have a problem brewing with the Notre-Dame Bridge. Got to keep that in good order. Essential. And the television signal here…"

He rolled his eyes at Teed, who had remained silent so far, apart from the occasional chuckle at a joke, or a murmur of emphasis. "It's not worth watching. Am I right, Hector?"

Teed put his hands up and turned to James. "The mayor isn't exaggerating. It's unwatchable, most of the time. We got tall buildings here but, so far, haven't managed to catch a decent picture. Need to rebuild some of what got torn down back in the twenties."

James, who knew not a thing about how television was broadcast, nodded. "Let's look into that."

Mayor Little frowned. "If the president gets inaugurated and we can't see it, well."

He sighed, and put his hands on his hips, definitely more cowboy than farmer. "Well, now that would just be a goddamned shame, don't you think?"

"I do think."

When coffee came, the mayor kept listing things he was hoping for, things that James was expected to help with. Road infrastructure, bridges. Water, power, telephone lines. Sewage. Even a streetcar system in town, which seemed a bit far-fetched.

226

Walking from his office, Teed said, "You never did tell me why you chose this out of the way place. A young man from Boston." He held a hand up. "I'm aware that I didn't ask at interview, remiss of me."

James had hoped that this question wouldn't come up at the interview, and was no less comfortable about it now, thinking where it might lead.

"I studied in Boston, but I come from here. It's my home town."

Teed's expression was very nearly astonished, but also pleased. "I had no idea! Did you go to Central? Memorial?"

He shook his head and managed a smile.

"Bertillon's."

Now Teed was properly astonished, the little smile dying, though he hurried to cover it.

"Bertillon's! I see. I see."

James wasn't sure whether to speak or not, or what to say if he did speak. He felt his face heating, an automatic reaction that he had never found a means to control.

Teed recovered. "I knew Charles rather well, actually. We go way back."

"Charles?"

"Dr Bertillon. I knew him when he was alive. You could say we were buddies, actually, back in the twenties, when we were a pair of rather wild kids. Playing Grand Theft Auto and listening to Marcus Cole."

James had no idea what any of that was, but the man shook his head, obviously going back in his memory. "I bet you can't imagine that now, the tearaways we were. What a house that was! And those grounds."

It was James's turn to be surprised. "The foundling home used to be his actual home?"

"Indeed it was! His parents were very wealthy, going way back, old money you see. Textiles, naturally. Later, pharmaceuticals."

He waved a hand in the air. "Medicine, I mean. Big money in those days."

"I only knew him as the guy who ran the place. Didn't know he'd opened his actual house."

"You wouldn't have had him down for doing something like that when we were kids. He was a bit of a wild card, Charlie Bertillon, didn't give two hoots about anything."

"I struggle to imagine that."

"The child of the richest family in town. He blotted his copybook once or twice, I can tell you!"

Teed had been almost laughing, but glanced at James, and ground to a halt, reddening. He coughed and pointed at a tall door of glossy wood.

"This is your office."

The salary for this job wasn't anything to make a noise about, but the room stunned him into silence. It was larger than any office he could imagine himself occupying, set on the corner with tall windows overlooking the plaza.

The ceiling was high, giving an even greater feeling of space. A large desk was set in the corner, with a heavy office chair behind it and two lesser chairs facing. Across the other side of the room stood a drafting table and slim drawered map cabinet.

Teed, perhaps misunderstanding the reason for his stopping, was quick to say, "It's chilly, I know. These offices can get pretty cold in the winter, but you have a reasonable amount of space to get on with your work. Plus, excellent access to the executive men's room. It's just across the way!"

***

For the first couple of days, James sat in his huge office with virtually nothing to do. Teed wasn't wrong when he said it could be chilly. By the end of the second week, though, he was beginning to feel like there should be two of him, if not three. The list of tasks sent the way of the new Municipal Engineer just kept growing.

He met with Teed on a daily basis, sometimes having several discussions with him on any day, but seldom saw Mayor Little, who seemed to spend as much time as possible out and about, meeting voters. Having his picture taken.

In those photographs, he was always smiling, usually wearing a Stetson, and sometimes standing with a hand on his hip to show his pearl handled pistol.

Teed impressed on him that what the mayor asked to get done, well, that's what had to happen. You didn't debate it and you didn't drag your heels. The mayor was a nice guy, real nice, but he had expectations.

It wouldn't do to fail to meet those expectations.

What James didn't say, yet, was that the man had too many expectations. Even this early, he could see that he was going to have to ask for his tasks to be prioritised.

James got to know most of the other senior staff, all of whom seemed friendly enough – Caleb Jones, the town planner, Gabriel Lamont, the chief of Police who was often in tandem with the gigantic Gus Rheinhart, his sheriff. A man everyone called Rhino.

Mrs Clarke, the receptionist, remained just as frosty.

Ten days in, Lamont came into his office, handing over a list of the worst road maintenance problems his officers had collated before flopping into the chair opposite the desk.

"We coulda done with you here 'bout five years ago."

James took the list. "That gets further back every time somebody says it. I don't have my budget yet, so I guess I got to just get myself around these first. Put them in some order of priority, and do some indicative costing."

Gabriel pulled on his moustache. "You want, I can drive you around them. Show you around the place some."

James looked up, surprised. "That would be great, thanks."

The man eased his Sam Brown, pulling it away from his considerable belly before giving James a close sort of look.

"Although, I hear you already know the place some."

James had wondered if Teed would talk about that. It was, he supposed, only natural and it wasn't as if he had asked the man to keep it in confidence. It wasn't a secret. Still, he was disappointed.

"I know it a bit."

"You was a yeller jacket?"

"We got called that."

"Still are. Went to Memorial, me. Back then, we didn't have any deaders as teachers. Not a one."

He smiled. "My Pa wouldn't a stood for it. There was a nun, now. Sister Mary-Rose. She was my

230

teacher, hard as nails she was. You wouldn't cross her."

Jamie sat back, waiting to hear where this was going.

"She passed away, oh, fifteen, sixteen years back. Something like that. But, here's the thing. She just turned up for work the next day, like nothing had happened."

"So there was a Returned teacher there, fifteen years ago."

He shook his head. "It caused a real uproar, man, did it ever? In the end, she was taken off staff, as they called it, but kept on as a teaching assistant."

"She still there?"

"She is. Not the only one, either."

"Things change."

"That they do. My Sammy starts at Memorial next term and we already met his teacher."

James caught the man's expression of disapproval, the close way he was looking at him, and figured he was being sounded out. Good.

"Returned?"

The guy's expression became warier, hearing the expression. "Yea. Mrs Waterston."

"All the staff at Bertillon's were Returned."

The police chief leaned forward, belt creaking. "You didn't mind that? Honest, now."

He looked as though he really wanted to know.

"It was what I was used to."

"Still."

"They showed us nothing but kindness. Patient as the day is long. You want one word to describe them it's patient."

"Yea, I heard exactly that. Also, they work for next to nothing."

"That they do."

"Putting living folks out of a job."

"The way I understood it, Bertillon's survived on a wing and a prayer. Always one step from closing. The only way the orphans around here were kept off the streets was because of The Returned."

"That's maybe the way you heard it. What I heard, Bertillon was rollin' in it but just wanted more. Like those guys always do."

"If he wanted more money, he would have done something other than run a Foundling home."

Gabriel's eyes opened wide, apparently giving that some thought. "I guess he might at that. I'll tell you what I think, though, cause it's best that way. I don't hold with dead folks teachin' my kids, nor takin' up jobs the livin' should get."

"You put in a complaint? To the school."

"Deaders been teachin' at Memorial for three years now. Was a fuss at the start, but, like you say, things change. How you fixed for Friday? We could make a day of it, touring the slowly disintegrating roads of Manchester."

"Friday would be perfect. Thanks, Gabriel, I appreciate it."

Just before the man left, a question occurred to James. "When the school started to use The Returned?"

"Yea?"

"Did anything happen, out of order?"

"Out of order?"

"You know. Broken windows. Arson. Maybe even worse."

"You're thinking about that priest, the one got burned as a heretic? That was in the bad old days, we

232

moved on quite a ways since then. Law and fucking Order, man."

He had seemed annoyed for a moment, but shrugged and said, "There was some paint put up. A couple of windows got broke."

He narrowed his eyes, going back in his memory. "I was just a grunt back then. Rhino was *my* boss. We cracked a few heads, arrested a couple of those MALA guys. But that's about it."

He stepped out of the office, almost closing the door, then stepped back in again. "Shit. I keep meaning to ask you, do you have a preference for a handgun?"

"What?"

"We got Browning Hi-Power or Colt 1911. You want something else, we'd have to order it special."

"I'm being issued with a gun?"

"A-course! Should've done it already. Manchester downtown is safe enough, usually, but get out in the sticks…"

"Does Mr Teed carry a gun?"

"The Browning. He loves it."

"What's the smallest you got?"

The police chief looked disappointed. "Some of the guys carry a Kimber Micro as a back up…"

"Kimber Micro. That sounds perfect."

"Well, shit son. I wouldn't want to be caught in a fire fight with just a Micro."

"Me neither. Hoping to avoid them altogether."

The man rubbed his face. "I guess you could have a shoulder holster, carry it right under that suit, it wouldn't hardly show. That might be an advantage, 'specially for a cool kinda customer, like yourself."

He winked. "Don't give much away, do you?"

James had heard that exact phrase more than once. "Apparently not."

Chapter
32
Alice

It was a different walk to Rickman's Bar that Tuesday. Alice had hoped that Mr Waters wouldn't come, but he did. He made it plain he was coming so the three met at his apartment block, just like they did three weeks ago.

This time, they didn't have to climb to his house and help him down the steps. He was already waiting, with an amplifier in his hand.

"This'll be better than that PA in Rickman's. It's an old amp, for acoustic guitars."

It didn't look light, but he was holding it without apparent effort. Mrs Twining frowned at it. "Why didn't we bring this last time?"

"Forgot I damn had it. You can keep the damn thing, Alice. Got no damn use for it now."

It sounded to Alice's ear like someone doing an impression of Mr Waters, but not a good one. The words were too flat. She said, "Thanks. I'll pay you for it."

"I've little use for money. There's also a half-way decent semi-acoustic in my back room, been lying untouched for more than a decade."

"I can't take your stuff!"

"I can't keep it. The Returned can't hold leases, so I'll be out of there shortly."

235

Alice thought about the hundreds, standing in the forest doing nothing, even standing under the surface of the lake. Like Gabriel Lamont said, when Nina told him; they got to be somewhere.

"Well, thank you."

"If you give me your damn guitar case, I'll carry that too. I won't be able to be in Rickman's as a customer, but I can attend as your damn assistant."

Alice sought Mrs Twining's eye, hoping to exchange a horrified look, the strangeness of this dead version of Waters getting to her, but Twining didn't look her way. Instead, she nodded. "That sounds very sensible, Eugene. Alice?"

She couldn't answer. Her throat had clogged, and her eyes were hot and wet, but she let him take the guitar from her hand and watched him walk away. Twining reached out and took hold of her arm.

"You might not know, my husband is one of The Returned. You get used to the change, in time."

"I'm not sure I will."

"You probably won't have to. Not yet, anyway. He has no family, so nowhere to be. I doubt he'll hang around long."

This time, it was Mrs Twining who had to work to keep pace with Waters. He walked stiffly, but that was all, carrying both the guitar and the amp without strain.

In the week running up to this, hand-written flyers had begun to appear around town. They were poorly made, some with spelling mistakes, but all said the same thing – Blues Night at Rickman's, Tuesday 14th starting at 20:00 hours.

Meaning she had around thirty minutes to set up, stop shaking, and get the kinks out of her head.

They walked into the bar, Waters leading. It was busier than before, at least fifty people sitting at tables. An older crowd, she noticed, laughing and talking, but less raucous than last time. Nobody playing cards, and more women in there.

Rickman and the barwoman were working hard, serving drinks. The Returned woman she had noticed before was touring the room, picking up empties. Jonas and Bobby were there at the bar, and she felt a surprising jolt of disappointment when she couldn't spot Gene Vincelette.

But there he was, at a table with a big guy who had to be his brother, and two women. She was surprised at herself, how quickly she slid from disappointment to jealousy.

Why, she wondered, did she feel jealous? This was an old guy, thirties, maybe even forty. Not even good looking, but it scratched at her. A dissatisfaction she wasn't used to, and another distraction.

She raised her hand in response to Bobby and Jonas, and managed a smile. Heads were turning as she threaded through the tables towards the stage, following Waters. Gene had stood as she approached, smiling, but the smile slipped some as he turned to watch the old man.

Still, it was back by the time she came level with his table. "Alice! Lookin' forward to this."

He half turned, like he was showing the table. "Brought my brother Isaac and his Joanne. My wife Peg."

The woman who had to be Peg was holding a hand out to be shaken, smiling. "We just had to come, see what all the fuss was about. He hasn't stopped talkin' about you since your gig."

237

She shook hands around the table, and Gene leaned in, close enough so that she could smell the bourbon on his breath.

"Sorry to see your friend passed. He seemed like a right nice old gentleman."

"He was."

"I'm sure he still is. Anybody could see his time was near."

"I guess."

"We woulda brought my Mom along, she was a real big blues fan back in the day. But The Returned aint welcome in a bar, less they workin'."

Mrs Twining, at her shoulder, put in, "That's changing, I believe."

"I reckon so, Mrs T. Things are changing fast now."

Mrs Twining put her hand to her mouth. "Why Peggy Seger. Is that you?"

Alice made her escape, hurrying onto the stage where Mr Waters had lost no time in setting up the amplifier, and was already picking the guitar from its case.

He handed it to her. "Part of what I lost when I died was my good ear. I can't tune a guitar no more."

"Sorry to hear that."

"There's bound to be changes."

He bent then, stiff but somehow limber, and taped the set list to the floor in front of the mic stand. Then stood. "I'll go to the other side of the room. You can play some chords and do some one-two's. So we can get the levels right."

She remembered how he had almost wept, the last time they had stood on this stage, and how painful it was for him to climb off it. Now she watched him step off like it was nothing and walk to the back of the room, turn to look at her.

Chapter
33
Nina

The Silverado simply wouldn't start – a problem that couldn't easily be fixed, according to Alison. She said they'd have more chance with the Land Rover, because it was a simple engine with no fancy electronics.

Nina unclipped the battery from the charger, but it was heavy and her fingers still hadn't regained their full strength. Without a word, Alison picked it up, like it weighed nothing, and walked out of the garage.

Nina bounced the baby as the zombie went to work under the hood, looking like she knew what she was doing. Climbed into the roasting cab with the baby still on her lap and, when Alison stepped away, twisted the key.

The motor turned over fast, but didn't catch. After several attempts, Alison asked, "Where are the tools?"

Watching her change and clean spark plugs, clear old gasoline from the lines, and other stuff that Nina didn't recognise, she asked, "You know about mechanics?"

"I do."

An hour later, when Nina tried it again, the engine burst into life. She let it idle while she packed everything she wanted to take from Tilly Whim.

Including Marcus' favourite guitar and all the firearms, keeping them ready to hand.

Also the chainsaw, she didn't imagine it would be easy, getting out of there.

She looked at Alison, who was standing still now, staring at her. "You coming, or what?"

"Yes."

"Then you need to put clothes on."

The woman didn't nod, or even look down at herself, so Nina added, "I've got some things that shrunk, so might fit you. Kind of."

Nina Simeon left Tilly Whim for the first time in fifteen years, taking tiny glances in the rear-view mirror as she went. She had gone there with a man she loved and an annoying puppy she didn't know she would come to love. She was leaving with a dead woman and her baby.

In no time at all, it was out of sight and she was rumbling up a road that was much rougher than when she had driven it last, and it took all her attention just to stay on it. When they encountered a tree limb, and they encountered many, Alison got out and lifted it away.

The tree Marcus had dropped on the incline was still there, and it took a half-hour with the chainsaw to clear it. It scared Nina, being out of her refuge after all this time. Alone in all the huge world it felt like.

The first town they got to was Dorchester but it seemed deserted. Nina got in the back seat with the baby at her side, holding the Ruger, as Alison drove slowly through the little town. Nina could recall this place from before, and it gave her a scary feeling, seeing it so abandoned.

"You sure things have gotten better?"

"I'm sure."

"Don't look like it. Jesus."

Alison drove for a while, taking the familiar route to Manchester. They kept to the highway all the way, seeing burned out towns and some that looked half-way okay from a distance, but not going into any. The road was mainly clear of wrecks, but they sometimes had to change lanes.

They passed their first truck, coming the other way, near Plymouth. It honked its horn and Nina waved, turning in her seat to watch it sail pass, like some mythical beast out of a dream. It wasn't until the outskirts of Manchester, though, that she found inhabited houses and other buildings at the sides of the road, at first sporadic, but soon massing, hemming them in. More vehicles too, now, and people walking about, some armed, but some not. Actual people, going about their business, most of them alive. She held her baby close, and tried to keep her breathing quiet.

Alison drove past shops and houses and diners and churches, getting further into the centre of town, driving now onto Bridge Street. Took a left at Elm and pulled the Land Rover to a halt against the kerb.

Nina kissed her baby, a little girl still to be named, and looked around.

"This is pretty much the city centre. I remember Marcus and me ate in that exact restaurant. The Italian. It's still there, how about that?"

People were taking some notice, looking them over, living people, but only slight interest in there. The dead – there were a few of them – paid them no mind at all.

Nina sat and stared around herself, wide-eyed. All these people. Nothing like it used to be, not crowds of them, but after so long with only Marcus, Jeez. They hemmed her in, took her breath, all of them busy, going someplace. She shook her head, like to clear it.

"Look at them all."

They were dressed plainly, in the main; roughly. It had the feel of a frontier town from a hundred years back, except for the buildings, which were stone and red brick, some of them many levels high.

The engine ticked as it cooled. She blew a long breath out, and said. "Ok. What now?"

Alison hadn't replied to anything she'd said since they stopped, and she didn't reply now. She didn't look her way. Instead, she opened the door, stepped out, and walked away, until she was out of sight.

Nina never saw her again, as long as she lived.

Chapter
34
Alice

The third time Alice played at Rickman's Mr Waters was there to see her play the sunburst Gibson semi-acoustic he had gifted her, but Gene Vincelette wasn't. The following month, though, it was the other way around. Waters was missing, not just from the gig, but from town. As Mrs Twining had told her, dead men can't hold leases.

Gene was belly up to the bar when she walked in, carrying her guitar case. He turned and raised a hand.

"Hey. No minders tonight?"

"Mrs T can't make it, and Mr Waters…"

She shrugged, with the shoulder not carrying a guitar.

"Yea, that's how it is with dead folks. Sometimes they stick around, sometimes they don't."

"Peg not here tonight?"

"She don't much hold with bars, truth be told."

He grinned, and patted his chest. "So, you're stuck with lonesome ol' me."

Alice smiled a quick and tiny smile and moved on, thinking that this exchange was being watched by others with unusual closeness, Rick positively frowning at her. Gene was trying to hold her eye a little too long for comfort, using that lopsided grin that he probably thought was a killer.

She took her time setting up, getting everything just right. She was wearing a skirt tonight that was a bit shorter, stopping just above the knee, and a halter top, leaving her arms and shoulders bare.

As she taped her set list to the floor before the microphone, Rick sidled up. "Get you something? On the house, one drink that is."

"A soda, thanks."

"You sure? One beer won't hurt."

She shrugged. "A beer then."

"Coming up." He leaned closer. "Like the dress, honey. So will my clientele."

Instantly wishing she hadn't worn it and having to resist the urge to tug down the hem, she looked beyond him to where the bar was filling up. Some of the patrons who had been there last time were back, but most, she was sure, were new. She lit a cigarette, and watched her smoke spiral to join the haze already spreading across the room.

***

Alice kept some of the songs from the previous list, starting as usual with Mustang Sally, but this set was mainly new stuff. The strings on the semi-acoustic were lighter gauge than the Martin, and it was easier to play licks and riffs, easier to bend and hold notes.

She ended on Boom-Boom by John Lee Hooker, going on an extended improvised solo, buoyed up by the audience clapping along and cheering.

That's where she intended to end, but Gene shouted across the bar, "Do the Howlin' Song."

She had only played it that first time, when she was angry and Rick had told her never to sing it again. She glanced at him now as a few others took up the call. Bobby called out, "Smokestack Lightnin'! Yea."

245

Rick was serving, but looked across and shook his head, a quick side to side. Alice thought, the place has been full all night, Rick and the barmaid selling drink as fast as she could pour on an evening he himself described as his dead night.

She met Gene's eye, seeing a bit of devil in there, and couldn't help but grin.

The intro riff was met with a cheer, and she made a point of not even glancing at Rick. This time, she did a mellower version, the howling less a screech of pain, more hanging onto a blues note. As she came to the end, and received an even bigger applause than earlier, she couldn't help but wonder if The Wolf would've been proud of her this time. And if old Mr Waters would know one way or the other.

Gene was grinning ear to ear, lifting a glass in her direction, and she couldn't help but grin back. Rick gave her a smile she thought might be described as rueful, and patted his hands together twice, which was a relief.

***

As she was packing up, people kept coming forward to tell her how much they enjoyed it, and make requests for next month, some of which she wrote down. In that moment, it occurred to her that she'd never been so happy.

When she finally stepped outside, Gene was standing on the sidewalk, smoking a cigarette in the dark. He pulled hard on it, lighting his face up orange, then said, "You want a lift home?"

"You have a car?"

"Sure. And I don't like the idea of a beautiful young girl like you walkin' home at this kinda time."

He took a couple of steps towards her and, even though they were still feet apart she could smell the

246

bourbon on his breath. She imagined she could feel the warmth from his skin and her own skin was suddenly strangely hot. Her throat was hot. Her lower belly was hot.

She patted her bag. "I'll be ok. Anybody messes with me, they'll wake up grey."

"That's my girl. Still."

"Can you drive, all the liquor you had?"

"Bourbon don't slow me down none."

"Maybe it should." She thought that but didn't say it. She thought, don't get into a car with this big, liquored up man.

But the problem with that was a very simple one. She wanted to.

Gene's car was a Ford pickup – no surprise there – but fancy. Metallic paint and chrome, every bit of it polished to a high sheen. She felt almost out of touch with her own limbs as she slid her guitar case into the back seat and climbed into the passenger side. Leather. Expensive.

He swung into the seat opposite and turned the ignition, bringing a low rumble from a very big engine, and then sat there grinning at her.

"Well?"

She shrugged. "Well, what?"

"Where do you live?"

"Oak Hill Avenue. You know it?"

"Overlookin' the park there. Sure. I know it."

He put the car in gear and eased away from the curb. She had expected him to be a careless driver but, maybe cognizant of the amount of drink he'd taken on board, he drove slowly. It occurred to her that he was going slow to increase the time they had together, closed in this cab.

247

Her head was tingling, and she shifted in her seat, struggling to be comfortable. A crazy thought came into her mind – to say, just conversationally, "Would you like to fuck me?"

Had to press her lips together, to make sure that didn't come out, even though she absolutely did not want anything to happen with this man.

He wasn't even attractive, and he was old.

He drove slowly out of town, not speaking, eventually coming to Reservoir Avenue, but then, coming onto Oak Hill he rolled to a stop opposite the lane that led right into the trees.

"That's where the old Observatory used to be, right?"

"It's still there. All locked up now, but people say it's just the same inside."

"Want to take a look? Or you in a hurry to get home?"

Her throat felt tight, but her voice sounded ok. "I'm in no hurry."

He put the car in gear again and she dug her nails into her leg, struggling to believe she'd just said that. The guy about to take her right into the deep dark woods, asking before he did it, gentleman-like.

They didn't make it to the observatory. Once the road opened up into what was once a park, he slid the car under the trees and killed the engine.

"This is nice."

"I guess."

"You're nice."

"You think?"

"You're beyond nice. You're stunning. You stunned me, first time I saw you. I'm stunned yet, can't seem to get up over it."

"No?"

He was leaning towards her. A very large man with bourbon on his breath. Long, almost black hair. She liked that hair.

"Can I kiss you?"

"You're married."

"Can I kiss you?"

She licked her own lips, and found her tongue was dry. Her mouth was dry. She wasn't looking at him.

"You can kiss me."

He took the point of her chin between his fingers and the touch shook her right to her toes. Turned her face to him and leaned in to kiss her. There was nothing dry about his mouth. The bourbon fumes almost choked her, but she swallowed them into herself, and let his tongue into her mouth.

She heard herself groan and thought, was that me? Why did I do that?

His hands were on her waist, then, pulling her to him. His mouth slid sideways onto her neck.

She thought, ok, it's time to stop this. Time to stop.

She took his hand from her waist, having to put some effort to tug it away, and put it between her legs. Waited, eyes closed, while he touched her there, pressing his fingers into the fabric, pushing it into her.

Then, she pulled the dress up around her and he clambered over onto her side, clumsy. She scrabbled at his jeans, unbuttoning them, bursting out in shocked laughter when his erect cock sprang into view.

He stalled. "What? What is it?"

"Shut up," she told him, and her voice didn't even sound like hers. It was too rough. "Shut up and fuck me."

He was panting, leaning over her. "I don't have a rubber."

She shook her head. "It's ok. I can't get pregnant."

"What?"

"You can come inside me. I want you to. I won't get pregnant. I can't."

Chapter
35
James

James had walked past SimeonStyle probably a couple of dozen times since coming back to Manchester. He had once spotted Nina in the distance, could hardly miss her in a pant suit that was the reddest colour a person could imagine. A six-foot something black woman in a town that was mainly white, at least when living, and wore clothes best described as plain. She stood out.

He never caught sight of Alice, until the day Gabriel Lamont persuaded him to come with him and Rhino, to Rickman's Blues Night.

Gabriel asked, "You ever heard blues?"

"That's old-time music, right?"

"You got it. There's a girl been playin' at Rickman's for the last couple-three years, Alice Simeon. Other acts come too, mostly bands, but it's Simeon you want to see. She's something."

They were in the police chief's car, having just returned from visiting a collapsed roadway up route 101. James took a moment before answering.

"Alice Simeon. From SimeonStyle?"

"That's her. She's..." Gabriel made shapes in the air above the steering wheel, looking like he wanted to squeeze those shapes.

"She's a lot of woman. And that voice, Jesus."

James stayed quiet and Gabriel, as people often did, felt the need to fill the gap. "The Mayor saved her hide, years back, her and her mom both."

"He did?"

"Yip. They were in a bad ways, living in the wrong part of town back when that could get you killed. He kinda took them under his wing."

He winked lasciviously. "Course, it wasn't as simple as that. Never is with the mayor. Her momma was something back then, the way I heard it."

"So, the shop?"

"Yea, that shop they got, he owns it. Rents it to the mom."

"Nina."

"Nina, that's it. So, what do you say? You're so damn quiet normally, I want to see if a few bourbons loosens you off some."

***

James could tell he was a disappointment to the policemen, making his one beer last while Rhino probably downed ten, and became an alarming shade of red.

He surprised himself by enjoying the music, though. First on was a small band, a man singing and playing guitar, backed by a bassist and drummer. It was noisy, but not so bad. He found he recognised some of the songs, from records that his ex in Boston used to play. Irina had a large collection of music of different styles and played them all the time.

She just never bothered to tell him this stuff was called blues. Maybe she didn't know herself.

When the band left, to a smattering of applause, he turned to Gabriel. "That was great."

"Just the warm up act, man. Next up is Alice, she'll blow your mind."

Rhino grinned, and grabbed at his crotch. "Blow your cock too. Man, I get my rocks off just watching her."

Gabriel laughed, like this was hilarious. "Want another beer, James? You can't just drink one all night."

Rhino pointed with his empty glass. "Yea. It's against the law!"

The two policemen were finding themselves funnier as their beer count increased. James agreed to a second beer, even though he could feel the first one working in him.

"Now you're talkin', man. We might get you up and dancin' yet!"

Some people had gotten up on the tiny dance floor, it was true, but the thought of the massive Rhino up there was just bizarre. Twenty minutes later, people's heads were turning and James craned with them to see Alice Simeon walking towards the stage.

She was wearing a glittery blue dress, sheath-like and almost floor length, scoop necked so that most of her was at the same time covered up and accentuated. She wore heels, and her hair was high, so that she seemed like she had to be the tallest person in the room, certainly the longest. She held a guitar case in one hand, and trailed cigarette smoke from the other. Her wrist was cocked backwards, making it look cool. It looked cool to James.

James tracked her as she walked. In his ear, Rhino was saying something, probably something crude, but the sense of it didn't reach James. He watched as she climbed onto the stage, watched as she shifted around, her focussed expression as she plugged her guitar in, adjusted something on the amplifiers and then straightened to smile at the crowd. Her eyes

253

swept over him but didn't catch, and then she leaned into the microphone. The depth of her voice was a shock; a cello string, plucked hard so that it buzzed. He put a hand to his stomach, because that's where he felt it.

She said, simply. "Welcome to Rickman's Bar, ladies and gentleman. I'm Alice Simeon, and this is the blues."

No, not a cello. It was too dense, almost muddy. James once knew someone who played an instrument called a bass clarinet, a deep, reedy sound to it.

That was as close as he could get.

She started playing a driving riff that James had never heard before, but most of the audience seemed to know it. As soon as she started the rocking rhythm on her guitar, there were claps and whistles. Somebody at the bar shouted, Smokestack! Drawing even more whistles.

Then, she didn't exactly start singing. She *howled*.

A sound from a deep, and deeply sad well.

Chapter
36
Nina

Nina came to herself in stages, and none of it was good. The inside of her head was hot and messy and noisy, a metallic ringing noise sounding in there. She barely had the strength to move, but opened her mouth to call out for Marcus.

That couldn't be right. Tilly Whim was four years ago, and Marcus had been dead that whole time. Finally, she squinted an eye open to find that she was still on the floor of the derelict shop. She could smell blood, and shit and gun smoke, and recalled the men that came in the night. She winced as she recalled the fight, recalling how Alice had leaped on the guy's back, getting thrown across the room but maybe saving her life.

Her eye had closed again, so she cracked the other. A man was standing over her.

Somewhere nearby, Alice said, "Mommy?"

That got both eyes open. Alice's voice was hoarse and shaky and scared and a huge man had his hand on her shoulder. Two men were standing there, but not the ones she had fought. A massive guy held her daughter and the other guy looked like some kind of cowboy. Nina instinctively knew the cowboy was the boss, the relaxed way he was leaning against the counter.

Two men standing, two lying dead.

She licked her lips but there was no moisture on her tongue, so it did no good. Alice, again, sounding more panicky, "Mommy!"

From somewhere, she found the strength to sit up, having to put her hand on the guy she had stabbed to do it. That, she realised, was where the shit smell was coming from. She hadn't so much stabbed him as opened him up.

She put her hand out to Alice, who tried to step forward but the big man's hand tightened on her shoulder. Cowboy, watching this like it was an entertainment, said, "Miss Nina Simeon. That's you under all that blood, ain't it?"

Speaking her name like he was enjoying saying it, more syllables in there that was needed.

Nina didn't answer. She wiped her face with a sticky hand, surreptitiously looking around for her handgun.

"Nina Simeon. You were famous, Before. I was just a kid, but I remember you all right. Do I ever? You were the one for the teenage me. A supermodel, by Christ."

He looked around. "What a fuckin' mess."

"They attacked me. Burst in to my shop."

"Oh, I don't doubt. They have the look of real desperados."

Nina had closed one eye again, but kept the other open, trying to figure if this guy was having some kind of joke. He'd said desperados as though he enjoyed that word too, the syllables spaced out again. She looked from him to the huge guy, Jesus, he was massive. She and Alice locked eyes and she could see her daughter wanted her to fix it. But she was weak and the inside of her head was fuzzed up.

256

The cowboy picked up a piece of cloth, in the process of being made into a blouse. "You're a seamstress now? That it?"

Nina's eyes flicked from him to the big man to Alice, and back again. "I'm a clothes designer."

He sighed, like she was being difficult. "But you make clothes, yes? With your own hands."

"Sure."

The man nodded. "See, that's good. That's *good*, Nina. My own wife came home, happier than she's been in years and with a new dress, one you made. You got a skill we need, here in Manchester. One I need."

He looked around at the wreckage and shook his head. "You're in the wrong part of town, woman. Won't be law here for another four, five years, I guess."

"It's what I could get."

"It's free, that's true." He grinned. She was lying in a pool of congealed blood, shit and God knew what else, two dead guys down here with her and he was grinning, like he thought he was being charming.

"Name's Bruce Little. Mayor Little. I call myself that because others call me that, but I've not been voted in, quite yet. This here's Rhino." He caught himself, "Sheriff Rheinhart, I should say."

Little patted Alice's shoulder, the one Sheriff Rhino didn't have a tight grip on. Left his hand there. "This your daughter?"

Nina nodded, dropping her eyes again and sweeping her gaze around the floor, trying to catch sight of her gun. He surprised her, lifting it from the counter, muzzle to the ceiling. "This what you're looking for?"

257

He pointed it at her, grinning as he pressed the trigger, click.

"You shot it empty, Nina. You're a feisty one. Shot the fuck out of these guys, these *desperados*, then got to ripping their guts open with your Bowie knife."

Nina tried to moisten her lips, but her mouth was too dry. The man was still pointing the gun at her, seeming to find it funny. Playing with her.

"They attacked me."

"So you said. But they're dead, you're not."

"They broke in, where I was sleeping with my girl."

He put the gun back down. "You bad hurt, you think?"

"I don't know."

"Well, put a bit of effort in. See if you can stand."

Nina locked eyes again with Alice, then squeezed them tight shut and blew out a shuddering breath as she forced herself to her feet. The main pain was inside her head and the side of her face and, when she touched it, her hand came away bloody.

She blinked, refocussing. Then put her hands out to Alice. The big sheriff saw that and clamped down, but Alice surprised him by dropping suddenly to her haunches and out of his grip. He lunged forward to catch her again but she was quick. Scampering across the messy floor and into Nina's arms.

Nina squeezed her hard, and looked harder at Reinhart – she wasn't about to think of him as Rhino. "Why you holding my girl from me, man? That ain't right."

He opened his mouth, but seemed too surprised to respond.

Little smiled benevolently. "Feisty. I like it. Now…"

He held up a finger. "I don't want us to be getting off on the wrong foot here, Nina. I got a place not far from town, Oak Hill Drive. Would be perfect for you. You provide a service to our growing community here, one our lovely ladies need, and in return you get a proper level of custom. You could make a decent living, here in Manchester. Your girl here could go to school. Think on that."

She squinted her eyes at him, trying to make him out, where he was coming from with this offer. "What do you get out of it?"

Little smiled. "I'm the fuckin Mayor. I want Manchester to grow to what it was, even before The Change. Also, you can pay me rent."

"You think? I couldn't afford it."

"I reckon you'll make more than you think. In the meantime…"

He let his gaze run her up and down, as his big Sheriff sniggered.

"We can work something out, I guess."

Then his eyes slid beyond her, his eyebrows hopping. "Here we go."

The man Grace shot was stirring.

Little said, "Don't worry. He won't be lookin' for payback."

Nina clamped her lips shut on, "I know."

The man had been shot through the chest, and the neck. He opened his eyes, and sat up. Looked at the Mayor and Reinhart. Then at Nina and Alice. Finally, at the dead man still on the floor.

Little said, "What's your name, son?"

"Bernard Wilson."

"And your partner in crime?"

"Kenneth Wilson."

"You were brothers?"

259

"That's right."

The sheriff, pointed at Nina. "What were you doing here, with this here woman and her child?"

"We thought there might be food."

Nina shook her head. "Not hardly."

"Plus, we'd seen her. What she looked like."

Little barked out a laugh. "I hear you, boy. Here's your brother coming."

It wasn't so simple for Kenneth, getting back on his feet, as his belly had been opened and ropes of intestine wanted to fall out.

Little grimaced and guffawed at the same time, slapped his thigh.

"Look, now, ain't you a sight? You get rid of all those ropes hanging out of you – you don't need em for nothin' now – wipe all that shit off and we'd be happy for you to stay here. Working on the roads or picking up garbage. Plenty to do in Manchester."

The two Returned didn't answer. Instead, they gathered up their parts and walked out of there, into the growing light.

Little watched them go. "Might come back, might not. Don't hardly matter either way. Not like we need another couple of deaders."

Nina was thinking she needed to sit down. A wavy line of grey had started at the top of her vision, and she thought it would soon start to descend. Also, she thought she might be sick.

"Mommy, you're cut."

She put her hand again to the side of her face, finding it bloody again.

Little squinted at her. "Maybe you do need to see the Doc. Would be a criminal shame if you go scarred up. Or grey."

"I can't afford medical."

260

Little smiled. "I'll see you ok."

Nina narrowed her eyes at him, trying for a hard stare, but he just gave her an infuriating grin, like he held all the cards.

"What about this shop? Where is it?"

"Corner of Elm and Pearl."

"How come you own it?"

He didn't quite shrug. "Somebody has to own it."

"And the Doctor?"

He pushed off from the counter. "I own him as well. You want, we'll leave you here. Rhino and I will walk away, maybe never see you again. Or, you can make your mind up now, and come with. That Land Rover yours?"

"Yep."

"That's a good vehicle, and I might let you keep it, but I don't reckon you can drive right now, so you go in the Sheriff's car. Try not to bleed all over it. I'll follow in that Rover."

The line of grey was descending, her vision getting hazy. Even though he hadn't formed it as a question, she nodded. "Okay."

Chapter
37
Alice

Every time Alice was about to walk into the bar she had to take a second to ground herself, tell herself not to let her eyes go straight to him, like they wanted to. Most times, he was there, and mostly in his usual spot by the bar, a shot glass of good bourbon in front of him and an aromatic shop-bought cigarette smoking between his fingers. He'd told her he only smoked Virginia and drank the best brands, no rot gut for Gene Vincelette and Rick better not try to pass that shit off, he knew what was good for him.

Sometimes, quite often, he wasn't there when she started, and she had to hide her feelings about that. Not disappointment, or not just disappointment, but anxiety, a worm in her chest that said he'd had enough of what she had to offer. That he was done with her.

Once, he didn't turn up at all and she found that she couldn't wait till the next blues night – a whole month – to see him, make sure everything was okay between them.

She made an excuse to drop into the bar the very next night, saying she'd left her guitar strap. It was a thin excuse, and she caught the heavy look in Rick's eyes before he turned away, the amusement on the face of the barmaid, Charleze.

But Gene was there, and he was smiling at her and that made it alright. She walked up onto the stage and made a show of searching around before showing the strap she'd brought in her handbag.

Coming back, she made to walk past, waving her strap, but Gene called out. "Have a beer with us, Alice. Just the one."

He let his eyes run over her, a slow up then down.

"You can rock jeans and a tee, Simeon."

Rick's eyes stayed on her as he poured the beer, not smiling.

***

It was almost a year later, when she arrived to find Rick alone in the bar. He looked around, like he was checking, then said, "Listen, you can tell me to mind my business."

"Mind your business."

"I didn't finish. You can tell me that, but I'm going to have my say anyway."

"Seriously?"

"Yea, seriously."

"Jeez. You and my mom."

She took a seat at the bar, lighting a cigarette, Virginia Full-Strength, and blowing out a long plume of smoke before nodding at him.

"Gene Vincelette…"

Alice held a hand up. "Stop there. I don't know why you think there's something going on with us."

He ignored that. "What I have to tell you, Gene is at heart one of the nicest guys you could ever meet. He has that in him, even now."

Alice blew out more smoke, then ground the rest of her cigarette into the ashtray and folded her arms, deciding to see where he was going with this.

"I've known him and his family a long time. He helped me, more than once. Including, he and his brother saved me turning grey, during some of the tough times. I wouldn't have this bar, nor this skin, were it not for them."

"Really?"

"Yea, really. That's why I've put up with so much of his shit, when near every other place in town has banned him. He's a drunk, Alice, and sometimes a mean one. And there's a lot of him, as I'm sure you know better than me."

"Fuck you."

"He had a kid, a little girl. He tell you that?"

She opened her mouth as if to speak but nothing came out.

"He doesn't talk about her. Can't talk about her. God, was there ever a man loved a kid more? I don't believe there was."

"She died?"

"Aged four, took the whooping cough. Yea, she died."

"Did she…"

"He wanted her to. But Peggy had other ideas. Tilly died when he was at work and she dragged her into the yard and burned her up. I think she was about half-crazy and when he came back…"

He shrugged. "As for him, he's been more than half-crazy ever since. Now…"

He raised a finger. "Now, don't be thinkin' you're the one to save him. You ain't the first and you won't be the last."

"He's going to leave Peg. Set us up together."

"I don't believe he will, but you best pray he doesn't. He hit you yet?"

"No! He wouldn't."

"Peg knows about you, of that I'm sure. She knew about the others."

"You sayin' he hits her?"

"Yea. I'm sayin' that. His own brother took him out back one day and beat the shit out of him for it, and he wouldn't raise a hand to defend himself. He's a different guy, when he's sober. I give you this advice once only, because you've come to be a friend o'mine. Find a way to end it, any way you can. He's broken, Alice. A drunk with a mean streak a mile wide."

Chapter

38

James

James had been wearing the same suit to the office every day for six weeks, except for when he was wearing coveralls for site visits. That wasn't unusual in itself, but all the other professional men had a second or even third suit, and kept them clean. Mayor Little was never less than perfectly turned out in clothes that were at once homey and expensive-looking, whilst Gabriel looked like he wore a clean uniform, freshly ironed every day.

There were only a couple of tailors in the town, but Mr Teed had made a point of mentioning Mattheo's, saying he would never go anywhere else. Mattheo is a gentleman's tailor, James, an Italian, operating a highly respectable establishment.

He dropped his voice. "Mayor Little uses Mattheo."

What James was learning – Little would use Mattheo alright, and pay not a cent. He would have some kind of hold over the tailor, that's how it worked in this town.

Even given the mayor's patronage, and after those years of having to wear the horrible uniforms that earned him the nickname Yeller Jacket, there was no decision to be made. James wore his best shirt, freshly starched and ironed, and his silk tie. Got himself a haircut and combed it till it gleamed. His Godley wingtips gleamed too.

He paused for a moment outside SimeonStyle, pretending to take in the male mannequin in the window, who happened to be sporting a formal suit. The cut might be a little rakish for City Hall, but he wasn't looking at it anyway.

He was trying to see who was in the interior of the shop. Nobody, seemed to be the answer – it appeared to be empty.

He stepped through the door and Alice immediately pushed through a strip curtain from the rear. She smiled, with no sign of recognition. "Can I help you?"

He was surprised all over again at the quality of her voice. She might have grown since the last time they saw each other, she was certainly well over six feet, but so had he, so the gap was down to about a foot. Maybe.

"I need a suit."

Her eyes immediately focussed, running along his shoulders and legs before coming back to his face.

"Do you have any particular style in mind?"

"I'm the new Municipal Engineer, working for the City. So, it needs to formal."

Her smile widened. "Don't worry, Sir. We can do formal just as well as Danny Mattheo, and at a lower price. Is it something similar to what you're wearing? In terms of style and material?"

"Exactly the same would be ideal."

A frown line appeared between her eyes, but only momentarily. "Oh, we can do better than that, if you don't mind me saying."

She walked out from behind the counter – he quickly checked, seeing flat shoes, legs bare from the knees down – and circled him, touching him lightly on the shoulder then the waist. She smelled of some sort of perfume, but not strongly. He inhaled deeply as she spoke.

"Your current suit-coat is slightly overlong in the body, and baggy around the middle."

"Is it?"

"Yes it is. Now, as you are short, that accentuates the lack of height. Also, you are quite broad in the shoulder, and narrow in the hip. If you're lucky enough to be built like that, you want to make the best of it. The material…"

James had been casually smacked down and pulled up in the space of twenty words.

"The material isn't wool. It's a wool mix. If this is something for daily wear I fear it will grow shiny wherever it rubs."

James managed not to say, at least it's not mustard. "How long will it take, and how much are we talking about?"

"That depends on a number of factors, Mr. em…"

"Spears. James Spears."

"Pleased to meet you Mr. Spears." She put her long hand out to be shaken, which took him by surprise. "I'm Miss Simeon."

James nodded briefly, and shook. That out of the way, she got back down to business. "The cost and time taken depend on a few decisions. The material being the main one. What sort of lining were you thinking of?"

Alice fetched a pad, just like at Bertillon's, but this time he was asked to make choices. She showed him several bolts of dark cloth, and he tried to attend, but didn't want to look at them. He wanted to look at her.

As he'd noticed at the blues night, she wasn't such a skinny thing as when she was twelve, but was still slim. Today she wore a light summer type dress, buttoned up the front and v-necked. Her arms were bare. Her hair was up, piled and pinned high above her head, showing the long scoop of her neck.

Her arms were strong and her hands so long it drew the eye, the clever fingers moving quickly as she effortlessly slid out bolts of cloth. She was, he thought, stronger than him, maybe by some way.

They agreed on a cloth – dark blue wool in a fine weave that she herself was most enthusiastic about, with a lighter blue lining.

She showed him several photographs of men wearing suits, and he quickly chose one of the least adventurous.

She clapped her hands, "Excellent! That's the main choices made. Now to the cost…"

She mentioned a number that was to the higher end of what he had been prepared to pay, and he quickly agreed.

Alice looked pointedly at the clock above the door, and James could see she was trying to figure something out. Thinking to make it easy on her, he asked, "Are you tight for time?"

She made an apologetic face. "Just a bit. Got a lady coming in for a fitting in a few minutes, and I don't want to rush your measurements."

James didn't want that either. "I could come back tomorrow, about the same time?"

She looked relieved. "Perfect. I'll see you tomorrow Mr Spears. Lovely to meet you."

Chapter

39

Alice

The little blonde guy was striking, in his way. Alice had noticed him more than once, walking around the city in the last few weeks. He was striking for a few reasons; very blonde, well-dressed and undoubtedly handsome in a sharp featured sort of way. He was also really short. Always going someplace, a man in a suit with a destination, not hurrying, exactly, but purposeful. A serious man, there was something unusually self-contained about him. That was a lot to notice, but it was only in passing, and he invariably slid from her mind soon after he moved out of sight.

He'd been at the blues night, sitting at a table with other men, including the Police Chief and the leering giant, Sheriff Rhino. She'd tried not to look that way, because Rhino was part of her first, worst, memory. And sometimes nightmares, where he held her tight so she couldn't run to her mom. Couldn't save her from Bruce Little.

When the little guy came to the shop, asking about a new suit, she was happy to oblige and even happier to have some solid information on him. This was a good commission all on its own and, when she heard he was working for the Council, one of the professional officers, it became something else. It

270

became a real opportunity, one she told her mom about first chance she got.

Most of the men who worked for the Council went to Mattheo's, following Bruce Little like sheep. Bobby Mattheo had the gentleman's tailor market pretty much sewn up, literally, SimeonStyle being seen as more of a woman's wear kind of place.

There was something about the way the guy, Spears, looked at her, when he came into the shop. She was used to looks, often along with comments and insults and invitations of all sorts. But this was different. His eyes had been simply on her, calm and blue and unblinking. It made her nervous, that flat uninflected attention, but he didn't pick up on that and didn't look away, except to stare at material or the pattern book.

It wasn't like he seemed to be ogling, wondering what she looked like with no clothes on, he was quite simply looking. His expression was so blank, it was creepy. It creeped her out so much that she made a big performance out of looking at the wall clock, pleased when he eventually caught on and asked did she have another appointment, so that she didn't have to flat out lie. They agreed a time for him to come back, one when her mom was sure to be around.

"Not," she said to her that evening, "that he was doing anything wrong."

"He was looking at you, though, right? Staring."

Alice tried again to get to what she felt about it. "Not in a dirty way. Not perving, trying to peek down inside my blouse."

Nina blew out a long stream of smoke. "From what you say, sounds like he'd be better employed looking up your skirt."

271

Alice had to laugh at that. "Yea, he's a real short ass."

"Short and creepy. Nice."

Alice winced, thinking she had done the guy a disservice. There was something seriously strange about him, that was for sure, the flat way he looked at you, his lack of expression, but that was all.

She measured him for his suit the next day and it went without a hitch. Nina hung around, said hello, let him know she was there. Afterwards, she said, "I think he's just a very serious man, that's all. Contained. Not everybody has to be grinning like a damn fool all the time."

"I guess."

The third time Spears came into the shop, this for the fitting, she had been really happy with how the suit hung on him, accentuating his athletic build. She'd cut it just a tad nicer than the photograph, taking a chance, and it looked great. She knew that he was pleased too, not because he looked pleased, not a bit of it, but because he told her so.

Although he was only a few inches above five feet, he was nicely put together and, if she said so herself, he looked fine in that suit. He checked himself in the full-length mirror, moved around so he could see himself from the side.

"Delighted. You've done a fantastic job."

He didn't smile. There was that stillness to him.

It was when the horrible-looking Returned woman came in for Mrs Rickman's order – a dress that had had to be taken out for the second time to accommodate the woman's swelling girth – that things got weird.

The woman had been shot in the head, some fool thinking that would kill her, and she was a sight. Her face bulged every which way, bits of bone and tooth sticking out everywhere you looked. Alice didn't know her name, but Spears did.

He turned towards her, staring openly in that way he did. Kept staring for a long time before asking, "Frieda. Is that you?"

Turned out the guy wasn't from Boston after all, he had been brought up right here in Manchester. In Bertillon's, no less.

Once that had been established, Alice went back in her memory and made the connection, recalling the little blonde kid. Remembered measuring him, and how there was a point when she looked up and found those faded blue eyes on her, just as now. He'd looked at her in exactly the same way, even then.

The conversation between Spears and Mrs Fred's dogsbody was ongoing as she thought this through, which was a sight too horrible to look at. It was horrible to hear too, but Alice couldn't tune out the sound. What was left of the woman's face clicked and scraped as she talked, teeth grating against bone.

"My face is too frightening for the children."

She had that right. The man seemed concerned, talking just as if he was fond of her. When she left, Alice made a mistake, saying something like, you're not from Boston then?

Showing that there had been some gossip about him. Maybe that's what moved him to ask her to call him by his first name. James. She shut that down quick smart, but it shook her for the rest of the day, the serious way he said it, making like they could be friends.

Chapter
40
James

James's new suit, when it was finally made, was a much better fit than his other one. It fitted everywhere, and felt…he shifted his shoulders and looked at himself in the long shop mirror. It felt great. He looked as well as he had ever looked.

He stepped out of the changing room, feeling good about himself. Alice grinned as she caught sight of him.

"Excellent! Step into the light here, please, Mr Spears."

She walked around him, touching a shoulder and tweaking the fabric around his back, pulling the hem down, very nearly touching his butt. She was still smiling when she came back around the front.

Just like that very time when she first measured him, their eyes seemed to catch.

"I really am happy with this, Mr Spears. Even though I do say so myself, I've done a good job."

"You have, actually."

"You're happy with it?"

He checked his reflection. "Delighted. You've done a fantastic job."

During the time he had been in here, maybe fifteen minutes, nobody had come into the shop, but now a small Returned woman entered. Unusually for one of The Returned, she wore something like a turban, a black cloth wound around her head. In Boston, James had sometimes seen something similar, in both men and women. It was usually to hide a particularly messy death that had involved a head trauma, something that would be upsetting for the living to look at.

Alice turned, her smile switching off.

"Mrs. Rickman's order?"

The woman nodded, but did not otherwise reply. James could see that there was something badly wrong with her face. It seemed to bulge out, like a blackened and burst tomato, a line of teeth and pieces of shattered bone showing through her cheek. It took him some time to recognise her, but even then he wasn't sure.

"Freida? Is that you?"

"Hello, James. How are you?"

Frieda Jannis, one of his old carers. He took a breath, resetting, and put his hand to his own face. When Frieda spoke, the mess of bone, teeth and ragged flesh was forced into unsettling motion.

"What happened?"

"Someone shot me in the head."

"That still happens?"

"It does. A superstition."

The woman turned to Alice and collected her parcel, signing in a ledger before turning to go. James stopped her at the door with a final question.

"Don't you work at Bertillon's now?"

The woman paused, but only briefly. "My face is too frightening for the children."

When she left, James turned back to Alice to see her frowning at him.

275

"You were at Bertillion's? Jeez, I thought you'd come from Boston."

"I did live in Boston. For a while."

He saw her eyes narrowing in thought. She twisted her mouth to the side, before saying, "I think I remember you. The little blonde boy."

"Yea. That was me."

She gave herself a shake. "I was going to say what a coincidence, but I don't suppose it is, really."

When he didn't reply, she focussed again on the suit. "Well, if you are happy, how would you like to pay the balance?"

"Cash."

"Excellent. Always happy to see green, Mr Spears."

"Please. Call me James. We've known each other since we were kids, after all."

Her face underwent a strange transformation, a grimace very nearly sliding across it. The smile was gone.

"I prefer to call clients by their proper names, Mr Spears."

James had said it without thinking, it had just tripped off his tongue all by itself, but he simply nodded, stiffly, almost a bow, and fetched his wallet from the jacket still hanging in the dressing rooms.

***

Later, when he thought about it, he couldn't see anything wrong with asking her to use his first name. It wasn't much of a thing to say. He guessed though, a girl like her, such a striking and beautiful woman, would have trouble in a town like this, especially singing in that smoky bar. Guys hitting on her all the time.

276

Maybe it happened that paying customers would oftentimes chance their hand. James could see how that might be awkward, one minute you are in the position of serving some guy, the next he's hitting on you.

"I wasn't hitting on her."

He wasn't, but had to admit he wanted to. He also had to admit that what Martin told him all those years ago was as true now as it was then.

A squirt like him had no chance.

James had been lounging on the bed in his little room – there was only the bed and a saggy armchair available if lounging was in the offing – and now rolled to the side to search amongst the shoes and bags stuffed under there, coming out with a stiff cardboard box. His memento box.

Leaning back with a cigarette in his mouth, he flicked the top off and rummaged through the stuff in there – there wasn't much – picking up a paper envelope full of neatly stacked photographs.

There were only three from Bertillon's. One from the day he left, a stiff formal pose with the Doctor, both of them shaking hands. Another, even older, showing a group of smiling boys, including Martin and George. He tutted to see how tiny he looked, even though he was barely younger than the much larger Martin. Unlike Martin, he wasn't smiling, he noticed now. Neither was George.

The last one was of him, side by side with Karen. Nobody knew at the time that they were an item, what Karen described as sweethearts. He shook his head, re-evaluating, thinking, of course they knew. How could they not?

All that sneaking off to different rooms and kissing. Quite a bit of touching too, walking purposefully away from each other if anybody entered. In hindsight, come on, it was probably a joke that only they weren't in on.

That wasn't why he had searched the photo out. He'd done that to have a clear view of how they looked together. He was fourteen at that time, and she was a year younger, almost. She didn't tower over him, exactly, but there was a good four or five inches in it.

The next photograph was of his girlfriend at College, Irina. He knew perfectly well that she was taller than he was, because she was tall for a girl, and he a short man. It had caused great amusement amongst their friends and even strangers would comment when they were out and about.

Once, in a bar, a drunk guy came up and asked, "How does this work? She's gorgeous, and near on a level with me, and she's with this shrimp."

James didn't think that was what broke them up. In fact, they might have stayed together longer than either of them really wanted to, because of the judgement of others. Irina, who cussed, was prone to say, "They don't like it, fuck 'em."

She was also prone to say, "You're a really good-looking guy, James Spears."

Looking at those photos, there were a lot of them, he could kind of see it. They made a handsome, if lopsided couple.

Near the end, she said, "You're a good-looking guy, but you're so closed off. I give in, Jamie. I'll never get near."

"You're already near."

"Your smile."

"What about it?"

"It ought to be nice, but it isn't. It makes me sad, because it's an act."

He brought out another photograph and stared at it for a long time. So often laughing, what a laugh that girl had. So often laughing, so often sad.

She'd once told him, "This is me."

That comment was issued just before a high-pitched 'beep-beep-beep-beep', crazy eyed and jazz handed. He smiled, recognising her description of herself in that tiny mime.

"And this is you."

She followed that with a deep and doomy drone. A constant bass note, unwavering for as long as her breath held.

"That's me?"

"Yea."

"Is that good or bad?"

"Both, I suppose."

"It sounds dull."

When she finally gave him his ring back, he didn't say a word, simply took it then watched her walk away. Back at the apartment he shared with three others, he searched through the toolbox to find a hammer, took the ring into the street and smashed it again and again, until it was a thousand tiny fragments.

He tidied his photograph box and put it away, having made up his mind to go to Mattheo's for his clothes in future.

279

Chapter
41
Alice

Alice tried to keep her eyes from flicking towards Gene Vincelette but couldn't seem to do that simple thing. It was as if she always had to know where he was, what he was doing. If he was looking at her.

Coming to the end of I'd Rather Go Blind, she noticed him knock back another shot in one, and straight away wave to Charleze, impatient for another. Charleze frowned but leaned over and poured, giving him a good view of her impressive cleavage, which he goggled at candidly. He must have said something because she laughed and put a hand over her chest.

Even before Alice could start in with Mojo Working, he'd downed that as well. A single, straight down the throat throw, before waving his finger irritably over his glass. Come on, move it. Fill me up.

She turned away, not wanting to see. In the more than two years since they had been seeing each other, whatever that meant, she'd witnessed him in this state on a handful of occasions, but this might be the worst yet. He looked as though he wasn't entirely in his right mind.

She concentrated on singing, but before the end of the song he was there, not on the dance floor exactly, but standing immediately in front of the stage.

He wasn't looking at her. He was looking down, almost at his feet, which stumped in brutal time with the music. He wasn't smiling. His face was sweaty, even his hair hung damp and lank. Like it was wet.

He stamped harder, head rocking, eyes closed. Some people at nearby tables eyed him warily but others were laughing. Alice stumbled over her words and had to turn away, going deep inside herself to keep the groove going.

Someone shouted, "That a raindance, chief?"

Gene whirled in fury, hair swinging, dropping at the knee as his hands came way out, looking for someone to use them on. There had been a burst of laughter but now people were shouting. A thrown glass shattered. Gene ran into a crowd of men, fists swinging, as Alice stumbled to a stop.

Rick was shouting louder than anybody else, so loud it shocked most into a stall. Then, he was in front of Gene. Gene was taller and much stronger, but Rick had a baseball bat.

Charleze, Alice noticed with a shock, was still behind the bar, holding a pistol. Pointing it for the moment at the ceiling, but staring hard at Gene.

Rick held the bat high and yelled, "Gene Vincelette, you quit it now!"

Gene didn't look like he was about to quit anything. He moved in on Rick, who shuffled back, bat at the ready.

"Hear me. You go home. Come at me now you're barred for good. That what you want? Another bar you can't go to."

Gene wasn't listening. He stepped forward and tried to grab the bat, getting a crack on his arm, but just moved forward again, swinging a fist that missed. Charleze had gone from pointing the pistol at the

281

ceiling to pointing it at him. There was a commotion as people dived and ran to get out of the line of fire.

Alice shouted into the mic. "Gene! Please!"

He turned her way and his eyes were wet, but they were also wild. His lips were drawn back over his teeth, like he had given into the animal. Then, all the fight went out of him. She saw it happen. He looked suddenly drunk and confused, but mostly just sad.

Behind him, Rick said, "Go home, Gene. Don't come back in here for a month, hear me? This your last warning. Last time and we're done."

Everything stopped for a moment. Gene looked at Alice, his expression seeming to ask her to help, save him somehow. Then, he closed his eyes and all but ran for the door.

Rick shouted, "Show's over folks. Alice, give us something cheerful for once, for Gawd's sake."

***

Alice blinked as she stepped cautiously into the street, trying to adjust to the darkness. She paused, not sure what might be waiting for her, if anything. Her hand rested on her handbag, which was open, so that her fingertips touched the butt of the gun. Gene's pickup, she saw, was in its usual spot but it was too dark to see if there was anybody inside it. Seconds ticked by before he leaned out of the window.

"Hey."

She gave him a long stare, barely able to make him out. "You're smashed."

"Not now, I'm not."

"Just git, Gene."

He beckoned with his hand, the little double flick of movement visible enough. "C'mere."

She shook her head. "I'm telling you. Go home."

"Alice…"

"Go home, Gene. We're done."

He had been speaking calmly, his voice soft, but now he shouted, pointing a shaking finger. "You get across here right now, girl!"

When she shook her head he threw his door open, on his way to climbing out until a set of high-beams further up the street came on, illuminating his pick-up. Alice squinted, trying to see, eyes widening as a figure emerged from the darkness, resolving into Nina, holding her pump-action. She walked in the line of her own headlamps, all the way to where Gene sat, his hand shielding his eyes from the glare. She stopped with the muzzle pointed, only inches from his face.

Her voice was low and dangerous. "You be surprised at the number of people I kilt, Mr Luva-Luva. I'm pretty damn close to addin' to my tally."

Alice ran forward. "Mom! Stop."

"So this is him. I wondered who he be. What age are you, man, to be hanging round my daughter?"

Gene stared at the muzzle.

"An' I bet my last dollar you a married man. A married, drunken asshole."

She stepped back, "Git going."

"Get that fucking gun out my face."

Nina took another long step back and fired. Alice screamed, even though she could see that her mother had unloaded on the rear door, shattering the window.

Gene had thrown himself to the side, but now he hauled back into the car and screeched away, burning rubber, his driver door still wide open.

Nina watched him go, then turned to her daughter.

"*Mister* Rickman was kind enough to call me. Tell me it might be best if I come pick you up."

She looked around. "I guess we better git going, before I get myself arrested."

They climbed into the Land Rover, speeding through empty streets. The pickup was waiting a couple of hundred yards on, tucked into a side street. Alice gasped as they came up on it, locking eyes with Gene as he sat in his car, his arm hanging down the outside of the door, holding a large handgun.

"Mom!"

"I see him. Get that shotgun ready."

"I'm not shooting him."

They drove past, inches from the big Ford's grill, and it roared out behind them. Nina floored the pedal, but the Land Rover wasn't fast.

"Get that gun!"

The Ford moved closer, till it was inches away, brights on, blinding this close. It seemed huge, so much bigger than the little green Rover. Alice picked up the shotgun.

Gene stayed on their tail, sometimes drawing back and then accelerating till it seemed he must surely hit them. He followed them to Reservoir Avenue, slowing only when they turned onto Oak Hill Drive.

"Be ready with that gun, girl. He's crazy, that one."

"It was you who shot out his fucking door."

"Wish I'd aimed different now"

Alice had turned around all the way in her seat, holding the shotgun as she watched the pickup stop at the junction. Nina drove slowly now, easing up to the front of their little house, staring into the rear view. Her voice was no louder than a whisper.

"What's he doing?"

"He's drunk, and you shot out his car door. I don't think he knows what he's doing."

The Ford performed a messy turn in the narrow road, giving up and crashing straight through the Willison's nice picket fence and across their lawn, then roared away.

The women sat and stared at the empty street for a while. Nina said, "You can pick 'em, girl."

She pushed open the door. "You'n me both."

Chapter
42
James

A year after starting with Manchester City Council, James Spears could honestly say he was happy at work. Maybe content was a better word. The town Councillors seemed to like him and trusted his judgement. More importantly, the mayor seemed to trust his judgement. Little, he understood now, had an interest, financial, practical, and all things in between, in almost everything that happened in the town. He seemed to own great tracts of housing and much of the industrial buildings and lived in a big house with actual servants. Living ones.

James' first major project – an urgent repair to the steel stringer Granite Street bridge, a near fatal corroded substructure beam he himself had discovered – had gone better than even he had anticipated. It was brought in under budget and within time.

Mayor Little's view on that particular matter – you saved the Council's bacon there, fella.

Mr Teed had relaxed somewhat and, if anything, had taken to treating him like some sort of nephew. They had dropped their meetings to weekly but stuck to that religiously, ostensibly so that James could report on progress against his many targets, but it invariably turned into a general chat session. With Teed doing all the chatting.

Today, James was showing his design for a high television mast, to be constructed on the roof on the Town Hall Plaza, the tallest building in the city, one that loomed high over the city hall.

Teed pointed dreamily at the ceiling. "They're still up there, you know."

James was getting used to his boss, and the way his attention hopped from subject to subject, so took a moment to consider, still coming up blank. "What are?"

"Those satellites."

He made a big slow circle in the air with his finger. "Orbiting, around and around. But they might as well be on Mars."

James raised his eyes from the blueprint he had spent many hours designing. "Maybe they've fallen by now."

"Maybe they have! Probably ran out of gas years ago. It hardly matters, anyway. So, your mast. What progress?"

"The base plate is in."

"Excellent!"

"There's been another delay with delivery of the steel, but the suppliers have promised, again, that we should get it by the middle of next week. Thursday at the latest."

"Damn it. Vincelette's are going to hell in a handbasket these days. I hear one of the brothers…"

Teed finished the sentence by pretending to tip a whisky glass down his throat, shaking his head sternly. "I wouldn't want to be in their shoes, for all the tea in China. The mayor is losing patience."

"I want to be there for delivery, check every section myself."

"Wise. Very wise."

"Then, I estimate twelve weeks construction."

"Let's say fourteen. We don't want to raise the population's expectations, only to end up with egg on our face."

"After that, there's a final week for commissioning. Maybe two."

"You're confident in that? It's not like any of us have ever done anything like this before."

James thought. "Not entirely confident, no. But it looks straightforward enough."

He lifted his schematics. "On paper."

"The mayor has a lot riding on this one. You understand me?"

James took a deep breath.

"It would be fantastic if we could switch on in time for the President's inauguration ceremony."

"Nine weeks! That's beyond your most optimistic forecast. Way beyond."

"I could make it if we used The Returned. They're stronger, and they never get tired."

Teed sat back, his expression dropping. "I'm aware of that."

"And they can't be killed, if they fall. We could really press on."

The two men stared at each other for a long time. James could see the calculation going on in the other man's mind, what a coup it would be to televise the inauguration of the first ever President of the Reunited States of America. In something that could be seen beyond snowy static.

"This isn't a decision that either of us can make."

"No."

"The mayor…"

Teed frowned as he thought, pulling at his bottom lip, a habit he had when anxious.

"This is a door, once walked through, cannot be walked back. If the Council uses The Returned for construction. Even once…"

James thought it best not to respond, not to push. This might come off, and it might not, but he struggled to put away the excitement growing in his belly. He'd been imagining this for weeks now.

Finally, Teed nodded, and interlaced his fingers on the desk. "Very well. I will put it to Mayor Little, but I want *figures* James. Figures that we can both have confidence in and will stand up to scrutiny. Make no mistake."

He held up a finger. "Make no mistake. If the mayor agrees, you will be asked to make your report to Full Council. You will be putting your career on the line. And mine too. More than that, maybe. Are you sure that is what you want?"

"I think it's the right thing to do. It's important enough."

Teed held his chin courageously high, his expression one of extreme nobility. "It is indeed."

"And time is a-wasting, boss."

Teed sighed, collected his papers, and stood. "I hope we don't come to regret this, young man."

Chapter

43

Alice

Spears was often in the newspaper, and Alice would spot him regularly around Elm Street, always with that air he had about him – a serious man with things to do.

This was the guy fixing roads, the main man behind getting the town watchable television, managing to push that through in double time, so it was ready for the President's big day. The inauguration.

There was a real controversy about that, not everybody happy. Not the inauguration, or the television signal, everybody seemed delighted with that. But, to get it done on time the Council had used a construction workforce entirely of The Returned.

Personally, Alice didn't see the problem. One of her teachers – teaching *assistants*, she corrected herself, dead folk couldn't teach back in those, less enlightened days – had Returned. But it crossed some barely understandable line in the sand, using a team of them for construction. It made not a bit of sense to her, even when her mom tried to explain it.

This was just before the mast was built, and her mom was vehemently against using The Returned.

"Get them working in factories and building sites, soon there would be no jobs for live folks. Deaders don't need rest. Don't need to eat. It'll be the same old story as before the Change."

That's what her mom said, sounding none too pleased about it. "The rich guys doing every damn thing they can to get richer, and devil take the hindmost. Mark my words, factories like Godleys, in a few years the *only* workers will be dead ones."

Then she said, "We were meant to be the post-every damn thing generation. Post digital. Post productivity."

Alice hadn't heard that, she asked, "You mean the post-life generation?"

Her mom sat up, like a dog scenting something it didn't care for. "The post what now?"

"Sister Mary Rose called herself one of the post-life generation. You've never heard that before?"

Her mom took her time, thinking about it, before saying, very slowly, "The post-life generation. Don't that beat all."

She put her hand up. "Anyway. I'm glad we'll be getting a decent TV signal – so they say, I'll believe that when I see it – but I reckon there's going to be trouble."

There was trouble. The Make America Live Again red caps staged a whole bunch of demonstrations and twice tried to break into the plaza building to blow up the mast. A couple of people got shot and killed, including Sheriff Rhino, who had seemed too big to die. The next day he turned up to work on the mast, instead of guarding it, so it got built and if anybody went through with their threat to boycott the Inauguration, Alice didn't hear about it.

She and her mom wandered down to Derryfield on that most auspicious of days, where they were showing it on the drive-in cinema screen. The red caps were out in force there too, this time clapping and cheering along with everybody else, when Woody Moore was finally sworn in.

President #1, of the Reunited States of America. The New Stars and Stripes behind him, and the massed ranks of the marines, deafening folks by shooting the air up.

Before that, in the park, there was another, much smaller and more home-grown ceremony, where Spears and some overstuffed guy called Teed were given silly pretend keys by Mayor Little. Described as the guys who made this possible.

Of The Returned who built the mast, neither hide (which they had) nor hair (which they hadn't) was seen.

After the ceremony, she found herself face to face with Spears, an accident on both their parts, she was sure.

Still holding his silver-foil key, he inclined his head to both women. "Miss Simeon. And Miss Simeon."

Nina had been drinking something called punch, which must have been more alcoholic than it tasted, because she looked for a moment as if she was going pat him, like he was a little doggie.

"Hey, yea. Well done, man. Done a good job there."

They had a stilted conversation, before her mother wandered off, holding her empty cup like she intended to fill it again.

She smiled at him, feeling uncomfortable. Took a moment to tap a cigarette from her pack and light it with her Zippo. She offered him one, but he shook his head.

"I don't, thanks."

She blew an aromatic plume of smoke into the air, way above his head.

"I've not seen you back at Rickman's."

"I don't go out much."

"Oh. Okay."

"I might come, though."

"Okay."

"I liked it"

"Maybe see you there, then."

She gave him a tight smile and got out of there, hurrying after her mother.

***

It seems that she would spot Spears more frequently, after that. He came twice to the blues night, each time in company with a tall, Asian looking man. He clapped and even congratulated her at the end of each performance, but didn't drink much and certainly didn't climb onto the dance floor. She noticed that a lot of folks seemed to recognise him, and wanted to shake his hand.

The second time, he offered to buy her a drink, but she had learned not to accept drinks from men in the bar. She saw him after that in the vicinity of SimeonStyle, sometimes sitting in the diner on the corner of Manchester Street. There was nothing strange about that. None of it seemed strange until the day he followed her almost all the way home.

She'd been walking her usual route, deep in thought about nothing very much, when some distant warning bell rang in her head. A feeling that something wasn't right. She lifted her head, because she'd learned the hard way to attend to that distant bell, and thought, somebody is watching me. That was followed in short order by, somebody is *following* me.

It was still daylight, and she was walking along Pearl Street, a mainly residential area. There were a few people about at this time – the street was far from deserted – but she became more and more convinced someone was dogging her heels.

She knew who too, that wasn't hard.

Gene had stopped coming to Rickman's after Nina unloaded on his car, not having to be banned, but she still saw him around. He made damn sure she did.

More than once, when she was delivering orders, he had coasted along on the other side of the street in his pickup. Still shiny and expensive looking, with the glass replaced. But he'd left the holes Nina had made, the ragged metal silvery against the deep blue of the paintwork.

That had to be deliberate.

She could never see him behind the smoky glass, but he was there. Sometimes he stopped, sometimes he didn't, but it wasn't lost on her that he was around. It wasn't meant to be lost on her and the only way that could be was if he had been watching her. Maybe following her.

It occurred to her more than once to walk across and rap on the window of his shot up Ford. Ask him what he thought he was doing. But that gave her a shivery feeling in her stomach, and she didn't know what she would do if he opened with that lopsided smile and said, "Hop in. I've missed you."

Because, she missed him too. She missed the sex.

Now, trying to be casual about it, she shifted the bag slung over her shoulder and slid her hand inside, closing over the handle of the nickel-plated handgun. Hanging a left, she glanced quickly to the side and caught a glimpse of the man who was behind her, surprised to see Spears.

She frowned, and picked up the pace slightly. This couldn't be right, maybe he wasn't following her. This, after all, was a normal city street and he was the Municipal Engineer, the guy with the tinfoil key to the city. A quick right, another left and she checked again. He was still there.

At the next intersection, she walked a dozen paces and spun, her hand still inside her bag.

Afterwards, she couldn't recall what she'd said to him, but it amounted to, what the fuck you think you doin' man? Walk on. She remembered how it felt, though, the two of them standing there.

She showed him the gun but didn't bring it out and point it at him. She thought that, with him being a big-wig official, sharing a stage with the damn chief of police, it wouldn't do to outright threaten to shoot him.

As it was, he dropped his eyes to the handgun, left them there for a few beats, no expression at all, before coming back to her face. And that's how they stood, as the seconds ticked by. He opened his mouth to speak, but she wouldn't let him. That might have happened twice.

He just stared at her, after that, even then not looking upset or angry. *Nothing*, man. Whereas before his contained quietness was intriguing, here and now it was so unsettling she very nearly pulled back the hammer and pointed. Then, with the pistol in her hand and a guy who had followed her for the best part of a mile standing in front of her, anything might happen.

As if he caught that thought, he turned on his heel, and walked away.

Chapter

44

James

Sunday morning. James walked along Pearl, following the same steps he had taken just over a week ago, the day Alice Simeon threatened to shoot him. He turned at Belmont, and again at Harrison, but this time didn't stop. He followed High Ridge, overlooking Derryfield and the Weston Observatory, making his way to Oak Hill Drive and checking the numbers off to a small but neat house. He turned into the driveway and knocked, standing back to straighten his already straight clothes.

It was Alice who opened the door, her eyes going wide to find him standing there, the flowers in his hand.

He handed them towards her. "Please don't shoot me."

She didn't take the flowers. Instead, she took a long step back. "What the *hell?*"

"Look, please, hear me out."

"Hell, man. What you thinking?"

"I want to ask you out. On a date. I want you to give me the chance to ask that."

Now Nina arrived, a cigarette in her hand and a frown on her face. She was holding an automatic pistol down by her side, where he would see it straight away. "Fuck's happening here, honey?"

In response, Alice blew out a breath and indicated him with her hand, still standing there holding out his flowers. Nina glared.

"What you want, coming roun' here, Mr Spears?"

"I want to give your daughter these flowers. I want to ask her out."

Nina went from glaring to laughing in the space of a second, turning back into the hall and bending over to do it, slapping her leg with the flat of the pistol. She turned again, and looked one to the other.

"You want to ask Alice out?"

"Yes. On a date. To Gino's restaurant, if she'll come."

Nina was still laughing, smokily, pointing one to the other with her cigarette. "*You*. Want to ask my daughter out?"

James could feel how red he had gone. He was still standing there, with the stupid flowers out in front of him. Alice's hands hadn't dropped from her mouth, but her expression was no longer exactly stunned.

She looked at her mother, who couldn't seem to get words out, kept making her way partly through one before the laughter took her.

"What's so funny, Mom?"

"You really have to ask that?"

She dropped her hands, but they seemed to want to play with each other. "Yes. I do."

"Well, okay then. You must be the tallest girl in this God-forsaken little burgh. And he, sorry Mr Spears, but you are one short-assed fuckin guy. How would it look, the two of you steppin' out together?"

Of course, James knew that. He extended his arm, holding the flowers out. "Please. Just take these and I'll go. I apologise if I embarrassed you."

At first, he didn't think she would accept the flowers. Then, she stepped closer and took them from him. "Thank you Mr Spears. I appreciate the gift."

James nodded, a quick up-down, turned on his heel and got out of there. His last image of both women was of them looking...the word disbelieving was what seemed to fit best. They couldn't believe he thought he had a chance.

***

Two days after the incident at Alice's house, an incident that he was sure would make him wince for the rest of his life, Mrs Clarke herself came up from reception to knock on his door, the first time she had ever done that, opening it before he had a chance to say anything.

"You have a visitor."

With a real nasty twist of lemon on the word visitor. For a few seconds they stared at each other.

Clearly irritated at having to repeat herself, she told him, "I said you have a visitor. A woman."

"Who is it?"

Clarke made a point of looking at her notebook, her expression twisted even further into disapproval. "Her name is Miss Simeon."

James sat back. "Show her in."

Mrs Clarke took a moment so that James could benefit from her opinion on that, then turned without a word.

Alice looked different today. She dressed differently, in a floaty sort of dress, that accentuated. It accentuated quite a lot, in James's view. Her hair was down. She held a clutch bag in front of her that was surely too small for any kind of firearm.

She wasn't looking at him as he walked towards her, she was looking around his office, the blueprints and schematics on the walls. There was a half-drawn plan on the angled table.

"Miss Simeon. This is a surprise."

She turned, her eyes moved beyond him. "That's your desk? It's huge."

"I'm the Municipal Engineer. It needs to be."

"And you got a damn big, fancy office."

He shrugged. "It's a nice place to work. I'm lucky. Not so much in the winter."

He wasn't sure if he should shake her hand, or what. Her perfume was stronger today.

"Please, have a seat."

She sat, and he could see her knees. He made himself focus on her face, thinking it wouldn't do to stare at a lady's knees, but was perhaps a little late.

"What can I do for you?"

"Can't you guess?"

He was guessing alright but, after the meeting at her house, was scared to guess out loud.

"Well…"

"I appreciated the flowers. Thank you, that's something that's never happened before."

She straightened, looking closely at him. "I have a question I need to ask."

"Shoot."

She fixed him with a close stare, wanting to catch his reaction, he guessed.

"Why?"

"Why did I ask you out?"

"Yes."

He almost let his eyes drop again, but didn't. "Are you serious?"

It seemed that something changed behind her eyes her expression hardening. "It's a serious question, yes."

"Well, why does any man want to get together with a woman?"

"You can maybe answer that, while you're about it."

He had to check, see if she was messing with him, but there was nothing playful in her attitude.

"I can only answer for me."

"Okay."

"Okay, then."

He squared his shoulders and took a breath, took another.

"You aren't answering."

"It's harder than you'd think."

He had been about to talk about that first time he set eyes on her, all those years ago in Bertillon's. You were the most extraordinary and beautiful creature I've ever clapped eyes on and you stunned me into silence when you were just a girl. I've fantasised about you ever since. No, that wouldn't do, and she was looking at him, waiting but not exactly patiently. He searched for something original to say, something profound to help her understand the depth of his feelings.

"I really fancy you."

For a moment her eyes widened, then she closed her eyes and cackled. Cackled was the word for it. He had to wait it out.

"You fancy me?"

"I really do, yea. I think you're just great."

She puffed out another laugh, shook her head and looked around the room again. "This is really a very large office. Such a lot of space to work in. Is it a bet?"

James opened his mouth, but didn't want to repeat something she had just said, suspecting he'd being doing a lot of that since she came in here. "How can you think that?"

"That's Mom's current theory. The guys down at the Council, daring the little blonde guy to ask the big black chick out. So they can take photographs."

"You see me doing that?"

She took a moment then shook her head, no. Seeming definite about it, as though confirming something to herself. "If we were to go on a date, where would we go?"

"Do you like Italian food?"

"Uh-huh."

"I'd thought Gino's, corner of Manchester Street. Friday at eight."

She nodded slowly. "I walk past there all the time. Never been in."

Then she said, "Okay."

He had leaned back, crossing his arms over his chest so that he was half sitting in his desk, but now he pushed off and stood. He knew he was smiling, probably foolishly, but there was no help for that.

"That's great. That's just, that's great. I'm delighted. Really."

"You're smiling. I wasn't sure if you could."

"Yea, I can."

She was smiling too. She held up a hand in front of her, maybe thinking he was about to pounce or something, which he wasn't.

"But, think now. Mom was right about one thing. We got to go into this with our eyes wide open. James."

She called him James, he noticed. He liked the sound of it, liked hearing her say it.

"Yea, mine are."

"People won't be kind to us. They aren't always kind to me at the best of times. We'll look *odd*. They'll say stuff, if they see us together, and it won't be nice. You know that, don't you?"

"I know it. I don't care."

"Well, maybe you should. So, what happens now?"

***

James walked Alice down the stairs from his office to the double doors of City Hall. He thought about kissing her there and then, just a peck on the cheek, but could see how something like that could easily go wrong, and in front of eyes that were surely on him.

In the end, he put his hand out to be shaken and she took it, smiling properly. Beaming. The first time he had seen her smile like that. She closed both hands over his and then leaned in, offering that soft cheek and he did kiss it, brushing his lips against her skin for just a second longer than a person might with their aunt. She was on the sidewalk and he was one step up, so it worked just fine.

Then she turned and walked away, her light dress swishing, bouncing slightly with each step to offer tiny above-the-knee glimpses. If he wasn't mistaken, her head wasn't pulled down quite so far into her shoulders as was normal with her.

He told himself to go, not watch her, but he couldn't seem to persuade himself to do that. Maybe fifty yards away, she turned to look and he was pleased he hadn't, because she smiled and waved, and he waved back.

He couldn't have done that if he had gone.

Chapter
45
James

James Spears arrived for his date with Alice Simeon in a taxi, wanting to make an impression. The driver, who was maybe even shorter than him, smiled in the rear view when he picked him up.

"Somethin' nice tonight, pal?"

James thought about it, and shrugged, finding he wanted to tell someone. "First date."

The guy winked. "Knew that really, the way you're all gussied up."

"I look nervous or something?"

The driver took a moment to look at him. "Cool as a cucumber. Where we going?"

James gave the driver the address and he pulled out from the kerb.

"Don't mind me askin', you're the engineerin' fella aintcha? Guy who got us the television. Fixed the sewer on West Side so my wife don't have to close our windows for the stink."

"I'm the engineer, yea."

"Thought so. Saw your picture in the journal, 'longside the mayor and that stuffed shirt fella."

"Mr Teed. He's alright."

"Looks like a fart would kill him. Anyways, glad to meetcha, and tell you most of us are right glad you did what you did. Don't listen to them MALA assholes. Make America Live Again. Jesus."

"Yea, there was trouble."

"That Sheriff Rhino got shot. I'd say it was a damn shame, but…"

He trailed off, as though he realised he was getting into something he'd be better off staying out of. Started again. "It should be Make America *Alive* Again, by rights. MAAA. Sounds like a sheep, don't it?"

The guy talked about the roads for a while, telling James he was grateful but, man, they needed to sort out some of those out the way routes. The route towards Plymouth and Dorchester. "You take your life in your hands, heading up that way, man."

James nodded, aware of what the man was talking about. "It's on the list."

"What I hear. On the fuckin' list."

They pulled in at Alice's house and James hopped out the moment the car stopped. Curtains twitched in a neighbour's house.

The door burst open and Alice was out before he'd taken another step. She was dressed in something long and jade-green and split-skirted and shiny like silk. Her hair was piled atop her head. She was wearing heels, but not high ones. The beam, the same one she had given him earlier, was on full power, then it slipped away, gone completely.

"What's wrong?"

She looked down at herself, and back to his face. "What is it?"

He had to shake himself. "Wrong? Nothing's wrong."

She seemed far from convinced, and he had the feeling he had already made a mistake, ruined something. He stepped forward and put his hand out for hers, only hoping she would give it.

"You took my breath away, that's all."

She looked at him sidelong and he added, "I'm not even joking."

His hand was still out and now she stepped forward and took it and blew out something that was half-way between a laugh and a gasp, but brought the smile back to her face.

Now that she was standing by him, over him, she said, "I wore heels."

"I noticed."

"You don't mind?"

"They look great. You look great. And it's not as if nobody will notice that you're taller than me."

James squeezed and she squeezed back. Over her shoulder, Nina Simeon stood behind the curtains, maybe thinking she was invisible in the gloom. She wasn't, and she wasn't smiling.

***

The chatty driver wasn't smiling either as they reached the car, but he did open the rear door for them before climbing into the front. "Where to?"

"Gino's, please."

James sat, his thigh inches away from Alice's in her incredible sheath-like dress, the leg of which showed such a stretch of thigh his insides tingled. Some of his outsides too.

She was looking at him intently, like she was searching for something.

He smiled, and she smiled back, but it didn't stay long. Struggling for something to say, he tried, "That dress. I've never seen anything like it."

He caught the taxi driver's eyes, which had widened all the way they could.

She pulled the split somewhat closed. "It's Chinese. Chinese style, anyway. My Mom made it years ago. I never thought I'd find a time to wear it."

As the cab made its way into the town centre, they sat mainly in silence, just looking at each other. Struggling for something to say, he pointed. "I like your eyebrows."

That seemed to go down well, but he wasn't exactly sure if she thought it was funny or just pleased to have her eyebrows admired.

"I like yours too. I like a man with a nice eyebrow."

The drive downtown wasn't a long one, which was both a relief and a disappointment. Sitting so close to her, inhaling her scent, all on its own was intoxicating. But neither of them seemed able to think of anything to say and the cabbie, so friendly before, kept his eyes facing front, except for the occasional flick in the mirror.

Still, he hopped out quick enough after pulling into the curb outside the restaurant, opening the door on Alice's side. James gave him a generous tip but the man just pulled down the peak of his cap and muttered, "Much obliged."

He pulled away, leaving them standing outside the fancy double doors of the restaurant. The doors were glass, and it was getting dark, so it showed their reflection as they stood together.

Alice smiled a tight, letterbox sort of smile and widened her eyes till they looked crazy. Gave out a nervy, puffed-out *hah-hah-hah-hah-hah* laugh. He took her hand.

"It's ok."

"I'm really nervous."

"You look fantastic. Stunning."

306

"You know, I meant it about your eyebrows. You're a very handsome man."

She reached out and flicked his hair, "I love this."

He squeezed her fingers. "Well then, let's knock 'em dead. Head up."

"You sound like my mom."

She did raise her head, though. They both did, and pushed through the doors.

Inside, the lighting was low and there were maybe twenty tables, all with white cloths and candles flickering inside little red holders. A piano player was tinkling away in the corner, James recognised what he was playing as Blackbird, by The Beatles who, he was fairly sure, weren't Italian.

The restaurant at this time was maybe half-full, a few couples in there but also some families, and one group of men, laughing in that over-loud way that demanded attention. James had been in here twice before, once with Mr Teed and the mayor, so knew he had to wait to be called forward and seated.

Alice leaned down to whisper, "This is nice. Smells yum."

"It tastes yum too."

A few heads were turning their way, mainly just snatched glances, but one or two looked more openly before turning back to their friends, leaning over to talk or snigger. The table of four men, business-types with suits and ties, bellies pushing against their waistbands, took more notice than most, all four of them turning.

As one, they burst out laughing, leaning in to each other to blurt out asides that were none too quiet. Alice shuffled away to the side. James could feel his face beginning to burn. Alice, maybe for something to do, opened her pack and tapped out a cigarette. Made a show of lighting it and blew smoke high into the air.

Then the waiter was there, a short Italian man, smiling, his eyes flicking back and forward as though he didn't know what to do with them. "Mr Spears! Good to see you again. Madam. Your table is this way, please."

James was hoping that they wouldn't be sitting close to the four business men, who were looking over with obvious amusement, but that's where the waiter was headed.

Alice surprised him by stopping. "Excuse me?"

The waiter turned, stepping closer and lowering his voice. Everybody in the place was looking at them now, even the piano player.

"Yes, Miss."

She leaned down and whispered. "You know, it might be best if our table isn't beside those guys."

The waiter nodded, his eyes widening. "You know." He looked up at her. "You know I think exactly the same thing. No point giving ourselves a problem, is there?"

He looked around, smiled and turned away, bringing them to a table against the window. Behind them, one of the men wolf-whistled and another called across the room.

"What you thinking, man? Her ass is higher than your head!"

Chapter
46
Alice

"Can you walk all the way in those heels?"

Alice didn't answer.

"I can hail a cab."

She shook her head and bent, annoyed with the sheath-like dress now, slipping off her shoes. Walked bare foot, deliberately fast so that he had to hurry to catch her up. She didn't turn back to speak.

"I'm sorry. You're nice. But this isn't not going to work."

"Because of those guys?"

"There will always be more like them."

She walked even faster and he bobbed at the edge of her vision, close to having to trot. He was trotting.

"So. Because of other people?"

"You can't ignore other people. Pretend they don't exist."

"No, but you can say…"

He didn't finish his sentence and she stopped in her tracks, turning to look at him, hands – still holding a sling-back each – on her hips.

He raised his eyebrows. Nice eyebrows. "You can say fuck 'em."

She turned to walk again, but slower.

"You sound like my mom. Again."

"She cusses?"

"It was common enough, Before. She cusses more than anybody I know. And one of her most common is, fuck 'em. She means it, too."

"So do I. Fuck 'em. They'll get used to seeing us together, after a while."

She almost stopped again, looking down at him, surprised at this certainty. "Oh they will?"

"Maybe it'll take a few months, or years. But they'll get used to it."

She wasn't moving fast now. She watched her feet, long and bare, on the sidewalk.

"That was very nearly a lovely night, thanks."

He reached out and took her hand and she had to either stop, or pull it away. She stopped.

It was a lovely night, warm but not sticky, no moon, but the spray of stars offered good light. Wagner park stretched away to their right, and the houses across the way were either dark or had their shades drawn.

He put his hands on her arms bringing her closer. They stayed like that for a long time, searching each other's faces in the dark. His was quiet as always, but his eyes shone. She hadn't been blowing smoke earlier, he was a very handsome man, with lovely eyebrows. And there was something about him, an inner kind of certainty about his place in the world.

On an impulse that surprised her, she bent her neck to him, slid the edge of her cheek against the side of his face. He placed his fingers on the tender spot at her temple, just grazing it for a moment before he went on tiptoe, stretching up so that they kissed.

That first kiss. Oftentimes, first kisses are clumsy, or disappointing, or somehow wrong. That wasn't the way with James Spears and Alice Simeon. Their first kiss just went on and on, getting deeper and deeper.

310

His hands slid across her back, down to the swell of her ass, but went no further.

When finally they broke, she pushed her fingers through his hair, smiling. "You know what?"

"What?"

"Fuck 'em."

He kissed her again, and then asked, "Why did you change your mind?"

She started to ask, what about, but it was obvious. Alice had brought out the scene at her house more than once, the one where her mother had near bust a gut laughing at the idea.

She had been shocked to find him standing there, holding a bouquet of roses. A real nice spray of flowers, the likes of which she hadn't ever had, not from anybody.

Then, her mom laughed at him. Or maybe at them. Scorned the idea that she could be seen stepping out with someone who was, let's face it, only short.

His face had been quiet as he watched Nina bend right over to laugh, slapping her leg, but his skin heated up till it was bright red.

Now she touched the side of his face. "Because I fancy you, why else?"

***

The next day, Nina didn't ask about the date and Alice wasn't about to tell her. She struggled to know how it had gone herself. She went to bed feeling fine, but woke up with the feeling she'd done something really dumb.

They had kissed. It was different than with Gene, almost as though it wasn't the same thing at all. As soon as Gene crossed her mind, she winced. She even put her face in her hands.

311

If he found out. Jesus. That thought was followed by one that chilled – maybe he has. Maybe he was parked at the end of the street and watched her climb into the cab, followed it to Gino's.

She wished that felt more far-fetched. All the times she had been walking downtown and there was his pickup, the big engine rumbling and somehow just there, as if by accident.

If he found out, he could do *anything*.

That led to another question, what was there to find out? She shook her head, not ready to answer that one.

She and her mother busied about their morning routine, and Nina never was much of a talker in the mornings. They had coffee and eggs on toasted muffins, dressed for the day and then walked out together.

Alice was more careful than usual locking the place up, made sure her gun was handy, and scanned the street before she left the house. Kept scanning as they walked. Last night, James had walked her home over this same ground, stopping to kiss every hundred yards or so. Holding hands, like teenagers.

She hadn't let him come all the way to the house, stalling him at the junction of Oak Hill Avenue. The last thing he'd said, "I want to see you again."

Her response, "We'll see."

She'd been smiling when she said that, her palm cupping his little face.

He had kissed her one last time, then turned and walked away. She remembered watching him, such a steady, self-contained man. Even when he was kissing her, he was in control. Unlike Gene, who had no interest in control.

Coming to the spot where they parted, she stared at the sidewalk, as if it held something of them yet. He'd walked away but, if Gene had been watching, he wouldn't have walked far.

"What's up with you?"

Her mother was staring at her, because she had stopped dead in her tracks.

She shook her head quickly and dropped her gaze, catching up.

But, now she was thinking about it, it was all too easy to imagine Gene parked here at night, watching as she and James kissed, then waiting till he walked past before idling the big car up beside him.

Nina tutted. "First you stop, now you're damn near runnin'. Slow *down*."

She had other things to say, but they were muttered, and she grumbled to herself non-stop as they made their way into town.

Alice tried telling herself she was crazy, but it wasn't catching hold. There was no sign of Gene on the way into town, and no pickup in sight as they opened the shop. She had an order to work on and she threw herself into it, anything to distract herself.

Still, she was almost at the point of making an excuse to leave, walking to City Hall and braving the sour faced old bat on reception so she could see if he was ok, when a Returned delivery man came in with something for her.

A small bunch of roses, five perfect red blooms, and a card. It read, *Thank you for last night, I'd like to see you again. If you want to see me again, join me in Arrow's bar Monday at eight.*

Alice blew out a long shaky breath, but she was smiling. She turned to see her mother standing in the door to the back shop, looking faintly disgusted.

313

Gene was waiting for her when she locked up the shop and began the walk home. Or rather, his car was, the pickup idling in the lot in Manchester Street he knew she would cross.

She stared hard at it, giving it a wide berth before thinking, fuck this. Doubling back on herself and walking straight up to the driver side window. She'd imagined he would lower it as she approached, but no.

Irritated, she yanked on the shiny chrome handle, but it was locked. He waited till she took a long step back, probably not knowing it was a step back in order to kick the door panel, before dropping the window.

For a few seconds, they stared at each other.

She spoke first. "What are you doing?"

"What do you mean?"

"Don't act dumb. Every time I walk anywhere you're sitting there, idling your car."

"This is a parking lot. I'm parked."

"So, no 'sorry'? No, 'I don't know what I was thinking about.'"

He jerked his head towards the rear of his pickup, the holes there. "You think I should say sorry? Your nutjob mom unloaded a shotgun on me."

"You been drinkin'?"

He didn't answer that. "I miss you, honey. It's driving me crazy."

"Yea?"

"Pegn'me broke up. We can be together now, if you wanted that."

She took another step back and shook her head. "What?"

"Think about it. Think about how it could be."

314

All she did was stand and stare, as he put the car in gear and slid out of there.

***

Nina had ignored her for most of the day in the shop, leaving early without even saying she would. It wasn't unusual for her to knock off early on Saturday, but she would always say.

Alice didn't want to go home, be in the house with her mother's silent presence hanging like judgement. She took a longer route, deliberately circuitous and out of the way, crossing Derryfield Park, walking right by the pavilion. It still looked, and smelled the same as the day the Bertillon kid had grabbed her and thrown her in there. She paused and stepped all the way inside, breathing in the smell of damp concrete and piss.

She whispered, "You stink of piss. You do."

And waited to see, but it was just a draughty and run-down pavilion, no ghosts for her here, no matter how hard she sought them.

She turned on her heel and got out of there, continuing to Padden Field, where a softball match was going on, and skirting Stevens Pond. She wandered the quiet, out of the way spots and didn't look behind herself once, daring the fates to bring what they could bring. Eventually, she had to admit that she wanted something to happen, anything, but that nothing would.

Chapter
47
Alice

Nina probably heard the cab bringing her home, but the last thing Alice wanted was a conversation. She went straight to bed, and stayed there. Told her mom she was sick the following morning, and didn't get up all day, except to pee and have a drink of water. Even then she hurried, desperate to get back under her covers.

Nina arrived home earlier than usual and walked straight into her room, not even knocking.

"You're back with him."

Alice just stared at her, so she added. "That fucking drunk Vincelette. Middle-aged, married asshole."

Alice told herself not to respond, just stay quiet, but she said, "He's broken up with his wife."

Her mom rolled her eyes. "Did I raise you to be so goddamned dumb? I don't think I did."

"Anyway. No. I'm not back with him."

Even as she said it, she wondered how true that was. The day after they had spoken in the parking lot, she had searched everywhere for him, whenever she was outside, always expecting to spot his pickup. She even made excuses for getting out, special trips she didn't really need to make.

It was the day after that he was waiting in the same spot as before. This time, she walked straight to the passenger side, opened the door and climbed in.

"You and Peg still split up?"

"Course."

"Does that mean your house is empty?"

They had sex in the hall, she didn't even take her coat off. Then, she pulled away from him and dragged him into the kitchen. Pulled everything off, the first time she had ever been completely naked with him, and made him fuck her over the table, knocking a plate and cup to shatter on the floor.

They fucked in the living room and the dining room. She said, "Where's your bedroom?"

"Upstairs."

"All these ornaments. These little things. They Peg's?"

"What do you think?"

"The furniture?"

"She chose it."

"Come and fuck me in her bed then."

They fucked until they were both exhausted.

He said, "Damn. I needed that."

Then he sat on the edge of the bed and opened the cabinet, pouring himself a small glass of bourbon. Took a healthy swallow and refilled it, offering it across. She shook her head.

"You keep liquor by the bed?"

"For a nightcap."

"Peggy doesn't mind that?"

The way he looked away, she knew that it hadn't been there while she was.

"Where is she?"

He shook his head. "You think I want to talk about her?"

317

"So. What happens now?"

"You want to just…move in?"

"Live here? In Peg's house. No, I don't."

"What then?"

She shook her head. She didn't know.

"Your mom will try to shoot me again, probably."

"If she'd tried to shoot you, you'd be shot."

"You sound angry."

Alice hadn't known how angry she was until he said it, but she was mad as hell. She just didn't know why, or who at. She crawled out of bed and had to run around the house, searching for her clothes. He followed her, trying to speak, but she slapped at his hands, sobbing hard as she hauled her clothes on, and ran.

Chapter
48
James

Two weeks had gone by since the disastrous date, and those horrible hours alone in the bar, where the acceptance that she wasn't coming grew by painful minutes. Since then, James had done his best to put Alice Simeon out of his mind. He was able to work, which was a relief, and often continued in his office until it grew dark.

Then he would walk home to his little apartment in Piscataquog, make himself something to eat and maybe watch whatever was showing on television. He liked to catch the national news, which often as not had President Moore or someone in his cabinet making some kind of speech or talking to an interviewer. He found that reassuring, even though he often couldn't remember what had been said, and would often as not be unable to recall even the subject.

It had been another late night at work, and he was walking head-down over Granite Street Bridge when he became aware that somebody was just behind him.

The bridge was sometimes busy with traffic, both vehicles or pedestrians, but getting on for nine o'clock and with the light failing, he expected to be pretty much alone out here.

Whoever it was, they were catching up. Since the television mast was erected, James was more careful. It had been a while since he'd received a death threat, but Gabriel had warned him, be on your guard man, those mad bastards might not have forgotten, or forgiven. He put his hand under his coat as he turned, closing on his gun butt.

Alice looked surprised, staring at his hand.

"You as well?"

"Are you following me?"

She looked behind her, shivering extravagantly even though it wasn't cold.

"It seemed like that would be fair, seein' as you followed me."

"You didn't show."

She breathed loudly through her nose.

"Can we get off this bridge? It feels kind of…exposed."

He let her catch up and they continued, side by side. It seemed that she wanted to walk fast, so he had to match her.

"I have an apartment in Walker Street, if you want to come back for a coffee."

"Maybe." She frowned, then nodded, the frown still in there. "Yea. That would be good."

After that, he couldn't think of anything to say to her, nor she to him, so they walked in silence until they reached his address, a distance of about two feet between them. The stairs were wooden, and on the outside of the building. She climbed behind him, keeping her head low, and slid quickly inside when he opened the door.

In the living room, she looked around. "It's very…neat."

He followed her eyes. "I don't like mess."

She stalked around the room, looking stiff and tight. Then she stepped suddenly to the side, lifting the Perspex lid on the music system. It played, he knew, old-style vinyl discs.

"What you got?"

"Sorry?"

She looked around, searching. "Your records. Where are they?"

"I don't have any."

Her hand was still holding the lid, a question in her eyes.

"The system came with the house."

"It's not a system. It's a record player. Jesus. Is any of this stuff even yours?"

"The apartment came furnished."

"From Bruce Little, I bet. Is there anything here that's personal? Anything at all."

He shrugged, feeling he had been judged and somehow come up short. "I'm not much interested in stuff. Coffee?"

"Sure. Sugar and cream."

He thought she would sit down, and take off her coat, but she did neither. Still looking cold, hands in pockets and shoulders high, she followed him into the tiny kitchen and watched as he made coffee.

He took his time, for a reason he couldn't pin down wanting to give her a really good cup. The beans he used were one of his few luxuries, the most expensive he could get.

She watched in silence.

"You're very efficient."

"Why does that sound like a criticism?"

She looked surprised. "Does it? It isn't meant to be."

"Why don't you sit down? Make yourself comfortable."

She nodded. "Make myself comfortable." Sounding like it was an alien concept.

When he came through with the coffee, she was on the edge of the only easy chair, still with her coat on.

He had both coffees on a tray and handed her one.

"I felt sure you were going to ask, don't you want something a bit stronger."

"It's strong coffee."

She blew out a laugh.

"See, I can never tell if you're joking or not. You've got such a poker face on you."

"I don't have anything stronger."

"You don't keep a bottle of bourbon?"

"No."

She sipped the coffee and her eyebrows raised. "This is really nice. It's nice coffee."

She wasn't looking at him when she said, "I could stay the night, if you wanted."

And started crying. Not just a few tears running decorously down her cheek. She put her head in her hands and sobbed, her whole body racked and shaking.

Chapter
49
Alice

Alice picked up on the familiar rhythms of Nina's speech, talking to a woman in the front shop about clothes. Moving her around to what she, Nina, thought would work best.

She tuned it out, or very nearly, focussing on cutting Mayor Little's new coat. A wool mix with a lot of cashmere in it, this would be a beautiful garment and, for anyone else, extremely expensive.

This time, the expense was all on their side.

She very nearly lost herself in the task before hearing her mother call her name. Tutting, she stood, easing the stiffness from her back before stepping through the strip curtain, with her professional smile firmly in place. It died all on its own when she saw who was standing beside her mother.

Peggy saw that, she couldn't miss it, and smiled brilliantly. "Ah Alice, there you are."

It was obvious that Nina could see something was off, but she just narrowed her eyes and muttered, "I'll leave you two to it."

Peggy kept the brilliant grin in place, not quite switching it off when Nina disappeared into the back shop.

"In my house. That's a first."

Alice couldn't get a word past her throat. She didn't know what word to use anyway. Peggy picked up a piece of fabric and rolled it between her fingers. "Yea, that is certainly a first, and a tough one, but you aren't. Not the second, the third, or even the fourth."

"I don't know…"

The woman talking right over her. "But, it always ends the same. He sobers up and drags his sorry ass back to me, begging my forgiveness."

"He's done that?"

"Yesterday. Crying like a little baby. So, stupid me, I'm back. Leave him alone."

"It's not me who has to leave him alone."

"Was it you unloaded a shotgun on the car?"

"No."

Peggy sighed, and put her head on the side.

"What did you think was going to happen? You and he were going to set up together? Happy ever after."

Alice was done talking, but shook her head. She was thinking about the nice china cup that had been shattered, when she knocked it off the woman's kitchen table.

"So. At some point, his desperation or need for approval or just so he can prove he can, whatever shit it is that drives him. That will bring him back to you. He really is that weak, and predictable. There's a path that this follows, but it won't do either you or him a bit of good. It won't be good."

"Why do you put up with it?"

The woman had kept the strange, brittle smile in place, but now it slid away to show the anger beneath. "What the fuck's that to do with you?"

Alice looked down at her hands, and found that she had curled her notebook up tight. She didn't raise her eyes again as she said, "Ok. I've heard what you had to say."

"Is that, go? You're telling me to get out."

Alice raised her eyes. "Get out."

"You were in my house, you filthy slut. In my *bed*."

Alice dropped the notebook on the floor and took a step towards her, seeing the surprise on her face. "You git."

Afterwards, she didn't know what she would have done if the woman hadn't backed up quickly, calling her more names but keeping out of reach before getting herself out of there.

Chapter
50
James

Alice Simeon wasn't the person James Spears had fantasised about all those years. She was somebody else altogether, a stranger, by turns tough, vulnerable, off-hand and over-emotional to the verge of being crazy. He had been shocked when she'd suggested staying the night, just blurted it out, and more shocked when she followed that by a crying jag that lasted long enough for his shirt to become wet.

At first, he hadn't moved across to comfort her. That hadn't even crossed his mind. He simply sat there, staring in horror. It was she who put her arms out to him, asking him to come to her, face puffy and streaked with anguish and tears and suddenly not pretty at all.

In truth, the last thing he wanted was to go to her. The crazy woman in his house. He was thinking that she had a strong streak of crazy running through her.

Still, it wouldn't do to refuse, when someone was asking to be comforted.

He knelt down, and she engulfed him in her arms, pulling him tight and crying against his chest. He had seen people cry before, but not often, and nothing even remotely approaching this. This was loud, it was vocal. It involved a lot of squeezing and pulling. A lot of pressing her face and head into his chest.

James was concerned his neighbour, Mrs Manners, would hear. Then maybe the mayor would hear about it.

After what felt like twenty minutes, she subsided, levelling out to a series of shaky breaths. She eased her grip on him, so that they were arms' length, looking at each other. Her face was raw, and soft looking, and he struggled to decipher her expression.

She would, he thought, still stay the night if he wanted that. He didn't want that.

"I'll call you a cab."

She blinked and looked around the room, pulling in a shaky breath.

"You have a phone in here?"

"I had it installed. I guess that's the one thing that's mine."

She nodded looking down and away.

"Made a fool of myself."

"No."

She nodded, like someone had asked her a question. Did that again.

"You best call your cab."

***

Waiting for the taxi to come was painful. Neither of them spoke, they just waited in silence. His relief when it drew up outside was huge as, he could see, was hers. He watched her walk out to the waiting car, head down.

She looked defeated. Or perhaps lost.

Chapter
51
Alice

Alice hadn't seen Gene for over a year, not since the visit from Peggy. She hadn't seen James Spears either, not close up. She played the blues night in Rickman's once a month, and sometimes men would hit on her, but she never let anything happen with them. Sometimes women did that too, and once or twice she let that happen.

Occasionally she would catch sight of Gene's pickup, still same one, with the bodywork now repaired, but it was always going somewhere, not hanging in wait. It never stopped and she couldn't see past the darkened screens.

She thought about James whenever she was in the vicinity of City Hall, wondering if she would see him coming out of there, but never did until literally almost bumping into him on the corner of the plaza as she was carrying an order to a customer. He was coming the other way, and they both had to stop.

She dropped her eyes to his suit, charcoal wool with a fine pin-stripe.

"You got that from Danny Mattheo?"

He looked down at himself, as though checking this was true.

"Didn't think I should come to your shop."

"Why not?"

328

She held up a hand. *Don't answer.*

They did no more than incline their heads at each other, then, and walk on by. Five paces on, James turned. "You want to catch a coffee?"

She lifted the parcel. "I've got to deliver this. To Notre Dame."

He nodded, a brisk up and down, then continued on his way, and was another ten steps away before she said, having to raise her voice, "Want to tag along?"

He stood looking at her, with the air of someone waiting patiently.

She did a big, overdone shrug. "What?"

He checked his watch, taking his time. "Ok."

The summer had all but ended, and the late afternoon was warm but not overly hot. Clouds scudded across the sky and trees were in full leaf, with only the slightest hint of the reds and golds to come. Fall was just around the corner, she could feel it.

They walked in silence for some minutes, all the way to Memorial Park. Finally, she thought of something to say. "You done for the day? Work, I mean."

"Yea. Could be, if I wanted."

"Okay."

They turned right at Granite Street, and the smell from the bar and grill reached her. She hadn't eaten lunch and was starving, having only pretended to eat breakfast, something she'd done often lately. James walked by her side, apparently comfortable with the silence.

She wasn't comfortable with it.

"Last time we saw each other…"

"It's okay."

"I'm not asking if it's okay. I'm saying, I was going through some stuff. Was in a mess. We're going left here, onto Second Street."

"Where's your client?"

"Not far. Corner of Second and School, you know it?"

"I know it. If you want, we could head up to the diner just by there. Grab something to eat."

She glanced at him. He was staring straight ahead, but must have felt her looking, and turned his head. She managed a smile, although her face felt stiff. "That would be nice."

***

This time, other diners glanced up as they entered, had a look and then went back to their plates. Because, Alice thought, they didn't look like they were on a date. There might be any number of reasons why they were eating together.

He ordered steak and fries and, after a moment, so did she. He asked, "You want something to drink? A beer?"

She lit her cigarette and drew in a deep lungful, blowing the smoke away from him. "A beer sounds good."

He smiled, a sudden full-on grin, and it changed his face so much that she couldn't help but grin back.

Chapter
52
James

Alice left around two in the morning, telling James to stay where he was, not bother getting out of bed. He did as he was bid, lay and listened to her moving around his apartment, imagining what she was doing and waiting for the thud of the front door.

In the end, she closed it so quietly that he wasn't entirely sure she had gone. Had to wait it out for almost fifteen minutes before he could be certain he was on his own.

He was relieved to be alone. He put his hand under the covers and held himself, his cock and balls felt wet, and a bit raw. If he drew in a long breath, he could smell her. The perfume she had worn and the perfume that was all her own.

He closed his eyes, sending out his feelings, asking himself how he felt. The truth was, he didn't know. Stunned, was the word that got closest.

He posed himself the question out loud. "What just happened?"

The better question, he thought, was, *what does it mean?*

He drifted into sleep, waking sometime after eight. It was Saturday, so he hauled himself to his feet and stood staring at his rumpled bed for a while. Then, he wandered into the kitchen and made himself coffee.

Realising he was ravenously hungry, he made eggs and bacon, eating them at the counter.

After his second cup of coffee, he showered, even though he regretted the loss of her smell on him.

***

James went through the rest of the weekend on autopilot. He'd heard that inexplicable expression more than once, something to do with Before, but now felt he knew what it meant. Monday was a kind of relief, getting back to work, but the relief didn't last long. He struggled to concentrate, wondering if he would hear from her. Every call might be a call from Alice, every knock on his door Mrs Carr's disapproving, sucked-in face telling him he had a visitor. The day dragged by, every second clinging to the one before.

He thought about going to see her, walking into her shop, but that just didn't feel right. He thought she wouldn't want that, but struggled to answer if he asked himself why.

At the end of his working day he stood for a long time in front of the plaza, more than half expecting to see her in the distance. It was dark, and frigid rain was blowing through the night, like Fall had landed all at once. He pulled his coat closer and walked by her shop, but it was closed, no lights inside. The mannequins looked miserable, posing in the dark.

He hurried home, head down against the bitter wind, turning to see if she was there every few minutes. At home he stared at his telephone, but it didn't ring.

The week dragged by with the feeling of waiting, something about to happen, but nothing did. There was no knock on the door on Saturday or Sunday. No call on his phone.

On Monday, he got up knowing that he was going to have to do something about it. Instead of going to work, he went straight to SimeonStyle. Nina was in the front shop as he came through the door.

"Mr Spears."

"Miss Simeon."

"How can I help you?"

The way the woman was standing, it was obvious that she didn't want to help him with anything.

"I'm looking for Alice."

"She isn't here."

He waited, to see if she would eventually add anything, as people so often did. She didn't.

"When will she be back?"

"I don't know."

He waited a long beat. Another. She crossed her arms.

He wondered, should he ask her to pass on the message, tell Alice he'd been here and would she please call him, but that was putting himself in her hands. He turned on his heel and left.

It was a brighter day today, but cold. He paused for a few seconds outside the shop, looking upwards to feel the sun on his face so didn't see Alice until she was standing right in front of him.

She didn't look exactly happy to see him.

"You here lookin' for me?"

"Isn't that ok?"

She looked over his shoulder, squinting into the shop.

"She's staring."

He looked over his shoulder. "I don't think she likes me."

"No, I don't believe she does."

"Do you like me?"

Her eyes opened wide at that. She looked away, patting her hair.

"I guess. I must do"

"Can we see one another again?"

Looking directly at him now. "What are you thinking?"

It was such an obvious question, asked sharply, but he hadn't thought about it. He considered but discarded another restaurant date-night.

"What do you like to eat? I could cook, and you could come around any evening that suits."

"What? So you can get me back in your bed?"

He shook his head. "That wasn't what I was thinking."

She looked at him sidelong. "No?"

"Well…" he felt flustered, wrong footed. There was nothing straightforward about her, it seemed. He always felt like he was stepping on sinking sand.

He put his hands out to the side. "What would you like?"

She twisted her mouth and narrowed her eyes. "*Can* you cook?"

"A bit."

"I can cook. I even like doing it. But I've never cooked for anybody but my mom."

"So?"

She nodded, like something had just clicked into place. "So, I'll come to your house Friday, and I'll cook for us. I'd like that."

She leaned to the side and stared hard at the shop window. "She's still standing there, watching us."

James said, "I'll buy the stuff in, if you tell me what to get."

She glared at her mother, then turned back to him. "I don't know what I'm making yet. You like chicken?"

"Sure."

"Ok. I'll drop you a letter, at City Hall. Give you a list."

"I like lists."

"Why doesn't that surprise me?"

She said it with a smile, the first she'd given him that morning. "I got to go."

"Okay."

"You think you might want to kiss me?"

She was always surprising him.

"In front of your mom?"

In reply, she bent and they kissed. Not a full-on passionate kiss, but a bit more than a friendly smack. She stepped back and moved away, again with that half-smile.

"See you Friday."

***

As promised, she left a letter for him with a list of ingredients, including wine, stating two bottles. Even underlined it.

On Friday she arrived at his door buttoned up in a long, thick coat, with only a few inches of slim leg showing between that and her boots. Under her arm was a hessian bag, very flat and square.

They stood awkwardly for a moment, then he moved aside.

"Come in, out of the cold."

She stepped inside and immediately kicked off her boots, put the bag down and unbuttoned her coat. James had briefly fantasised about what she was wearing under it, but it was a dark blue cotton dress

335

that stretched from neck to below her knee, stylish, but demure.

Only when she stepped past him did he see that most of her back was bare, almost to her waist.

She picked up the bag and advanced on the record player. "Does this thing even work?"

"I don't know."

"You like Jazz?"

"I don't know that either."

She gave him a look as flat as the disc she slid from the bag, something obviously very old. The sleeve showed a man playing a trumpet, blue on black.

"This is Kind of Blue. Miles Davis."

The apartment felt like a different place, she made it different. He stood, leaning against the doorway to the little kitchen and sipping wine as he watched Alice busy around. The air was full of music and the smells of frying and herbs and the sounds of chopping and cooking.

Without slowing, she asked, "You like this?"

He grinned. "I really do. I like it."

Then she did stop, putting her head on one side to look at him. "I mean the music?"

"Oh, that. Yea, I like it. I've heard it before."

"You have?"

He didn't mention that it was one of his ex-girlfriend's favourites, or that he hadn't known it was jazz.

"Yea."

"Well, turn it over then, play the other side. You know how to do that?"

"I can figure it out."

She pointed the carving knife at him. "Do *not* scratch it! It's fragile. And irreplaceable."

The ate at the little table, and she was right, she could really cook.

Afterwards, they sat on the couch and listened to more of the records that she'd brought, and spent a long time kissing.

She pulled away from him. "If we go to bed, I want to spend the night."

"I want that too."

"I mean the whole night. Get up tomorrow and have breakfast, like I belong here. You can cook breakfast."

He kissed her, a long and deep kiss. "I can definitely cook breakfast."

***

Weeks became months and the line of albums beside the record player grew until it took up a whole wall – Alice had been gifted a huge cache of vinyl from some old guy – and James took to playing music even when she wasn't around. Kind of Blue became his favourite and he surprised himself by discovering he positively liked Jazz.

He also liked The Beatles, and Prince.

She spent every Saturday and most Fridays at his house and he learned to cook, partly by working alongside Alice, augmented by reading an old cookbook he bought. As Fall merged into Winter, they spent most of their evenings indoors, but sometimes went out, mainly walking, but occasionally dropping into diners or bars, where they tended to attract attention. There seemed to be no help for that.

Time didn't run on time around Alice. They spent long hours in bed, no need for rubbers because she was unable to get pregnant. They spent other hours listening to music while she smoked and sometimes sang along. Those, he thought, were his favourite times.

A strange notion occurred to him, one evening. He thought, I am happy.

It wasn't a thought he shared with Alice. It didn't occur to him to.

Chapter
53
Alice

Four months after they drank a few too many beers in the diner and ended up in James' bed, Alice climbed the stairs to his little apartment. She took the steps much slower than usual, not wanting to reach the top.

It was a grey day, frigid, and she pulled her coat tight but that didn't stop her shaking. It wasn't the cold that was making her shake.

She used her key to open the door and found the little table already set for two. She stared at it, seeing how much effort he'd put in, even flowers in a vase between the plates. An open bottle of wine with two glasses waiting.

She could smell something delicious coming from the kitchen and, even though she felt nauseous, still her stomach growled. He'd gotten to be such a good cook, coming all the way from hardly being able to fry an egg without making a crispy mess of it.

He came from the kitchen holding a dishtowel.

"You're just in time. I've made…"

He didn't get to the end of the sentence. Something in her face stopped him.

"Has something happened?"

"I've been thinking."

He looked like he was going to come to her and maybe take her in his arms. Thankfully, he didn't. Instead, he sat down.

She hauled in a huge, shaky breath. "I'm sorry. I just don't think it's going to work out with us. I like you, but…"

She couldn't think of a way to go on, so dropped into the other chair.

"You must've seen this coming."

She had an unlit cigarette in her hand, with no recollection of tapping it out, and she started to shred it, paper and tobacco falling unheeded to the floor.

James waited a few beats before replying, as she knew he would. She'd grown used to the odd beat and rhythms of his conversation.

"I didn't see it coming. Is it the height thing?"

"No."

"The colour thing?"

"Not that either. James, you're…" She shredded the last of the paper from the cigarette and flicked it all away, making a mess on the spotless carpet.

"You're not all the way *present*. Nothing touches you. I think you enjoy my company. I think you enjoy looking at me, get turned on for sure. But otherwise, there's something missing."

He shook his head. "No. There isn't."

"Yes. Sorry, but yes."

"What are you saying?"

She pressed her fingers hard against her breastbone, and didn't answer.

"You're saying we're done?"

She didn't want to say it, the words trembled as they came out. "I am, yea."

He shook his head again, harder this time. "No."

Alice stood up, thinking she had to get out of this apartment before she started to cry.

He hurried forward, getting in front of her. "No."

She knew her cheeks were wet, and could feel her whole face shaking. He stood there, blocking her way, his expression as mild as ever, only the slightest frown denting his forehead. She started to brush past him.

"Nothing *touches* you, James!"

He jerked and hopped, and was in front of her again. "You touch me. You do."

"Let me past."

"No."

"James…"

He came at her then and from the sudden, shocking change in his expression she thought he was going to hit her. Instead, he threw his arms around her and slid, as though his legs folded beneath him, falling all the way to his knees. His head pressed against her thighs and it was a few moments before she realised that he was crying. Not just crying. Sobbing.

She put a hand to his hair, so blonde it was nearly white, but couldn't speak.

His voice was so hoarse and tight, it sounded like someone else. "Please. Please!"

He looked up and the expression of anguish on his face shocked her into snatching her hands away, all the way up to her chest.

"Don't leave me. Don't. You're the only person I've ever loved."

She tried to get him to stand, but couldn't, no matter how hard she tried. Instead, she dropped down herself, where she was only slightly higher than him. Held him tight and they stayed like until his sobs began to subside.

He was still crying, just about, but managed to say, "See. You're not taller than me. You've just got really long legs."

She wiped his face. "Do you mean it?"

"What?"

"Come on!"

"I mean it. I love you."

His face was red and blotchy and wet, puffy from crying. She kissed his eyes, his cheeks, then his mouth. They clung closer as they kissed, and he moved his hands up over her ribs, pausing before cupping her breasts.

She heard his breathing change, and her own with it.

***

Later, in the tangled sheets of the bed, she said, "So. The only way to get you to show any emotion is to threaten to leave you?"

"Don't do it again."

"No? What should I do?"

"Marry me."

"What?"

She sat up, the sheet falling from her breasts. Then she stood up.

He knelt on the mattress and moved quickly, taking her hand. "I mean it. Marry me."

"You're crazy."

"That's what love is, I think. Marry me."

"You keep saying that."

"I know. I'm about to say it again."

"Don't. I got to think."

"What is there to think about? Let's just do it. Tie our lives together. I've got a good job."

"I know all about your job."

"We can buy a house outright. Do that together. Do everything together."

"You're serious."

"I'm serious."

"What about…"

"Fuck 'em. Whoever they are."

The only other time he had cussed in front of her was the night of their first date, and maybe that was why it made her laugh. And maybe it was the laugh that led her to say, "Yes".

Then she said, "Well, we'll better let people know, then."

Chapter
54
James

Early evening in the square outside City Hall, the light failing fast. It had been raining without stop for two days, and it was raining now. Everything – the buildings, the paving and the massed people – looked so wet James could hardly imagine them ever being dry again.

He watched as drips formed on the flap of the awning he and the dignitaries were sheltering under, dripping into the stage to form puddles. The PA system was dry, though, he had to keep checking that.

As if reading his mind, Mayor Little leaned in to whisper.

"There's no chance now, when we turn this whole thing on, that half these fine folks will get electrocuted."

He sought Alice out at the front of the crowd, locking eyes for a moment, then shook his head. "No."

"They better not, hear me? I better not feel so much as a tingle."

"I hear you."

"Okay, then. Let's go, people aren't relishing this soaking."

In truth, the hundred or so people who had braved the weather on this momentous day seemed patient enough. Most looked excited.

Little stepped forward and tapped the microphone. "Let's get this show on the road. It's getting dark and no point keeping you good people waiting in the rain any longer."

A ragged cheer at that, one or two people even bounced up and down and clapped.

"Some of us old uns will remember what it was like – the streets being lit at night. We took that for granted. This is something that I've been workin' towards and prayin' would happen for more years than I can count."

He held up a hand. "We're starting small, Downtown only, and there won't be as many lights as there was Before. But, we're starting! Right now!"

He put his hand onto the big, overdone handle-like switch, getting a bigger cheer, more clapping. Despite the rain and now the gloom, people did seem positively energised, a lot of smiles out there. James shared another look with Alice, who widened her eyes and clasped her hands tightly before her, grinning stiffly, like a letterbox.

"There are a lot of people to thank for this. A lot of the people you see standing up here have bust a gut to make it happen. But none more so than our own little Einstein, our Engineer, James Spears."

The cheer at that was the biggest yet, surprising James.

"You all know what this guy has done since coming here. Sometimes it seems there's nothing he can't do. So…"

Little raised his hand from the big lever, calling for quiet. "So. I'd like him to have the honour, the

345

great honour, of throwing the switch that brings light to Manchester. That vital spark that says, we're back, and stronger than ever."

Although this was rehearsed, James did his best to mime surprise and delight. Alice had coached him on that, as it didn't come easy.

He stepped forwards, Teed and others patting his shoulders, to join Little at the microphone. The switch didn't need to be so big – there didn't need to be one here at all – but Little wanted it to work like that. Dramatic.

"Well, thank you Mayor, this is quite a surprise. Surely you should be the guy pulls that switch? All I did was what you asked me to, none of this woulda happened without you!"

The way Teed explained it, this way you get your spot in the limelight, and the mayor looks like the man of the moment, and magnanimous into the bargain.

Little threw back his head and laughed, patting his back.

"Throw the switch, son, you earned it."

At that he stepped back indicating the oversized lever. So far, everything had been choreographed, but now James diverged.

He gripped the handle in both hands and pretended to pull and strain. Mock wiped his brow and grabbed on again. It was such an obvious pantomime, that everybody got it. they were laughing. A few were clapping.

"Pull that thing, shorty!"

Behind him, Little muttered, "Good so far, but don't milk it, Spears."

James spoke into the mic. "This is an awful big switch for a little guy, Mayor. I wonder, could my fiancée come up and help me?"

Little was immediately by his side, his eyes lit up and fatherly hand on his shoulder. "Well, Ladies and Gentlemen. How about this! I didn't even know my man here was engaged. Where is the little lady?"

The audience were enjoying the show, smiling and playing along, but there was a palpable pause when Alice walked forward, and climbed the stairs.

Little paused too, but not for long. "Why, it's Alice Simeon! How about that, folks? Our very own singing beauty."

He clapped vigorously, and the crowd followed on.

Then Alice was beside them and he dropped back again. James kissed her briefly on the cheek and then they both grasped the red handle and leaned into the microphone, counting together.

"Three-two-one. Go!"

All across downtown, the lights came on, dim at first but getting brighter. The crowd made a hushed 'oh' sound, then cheered.

Alice ducked her head and whispered into James ear. "Well, they know now."

Chapter
55
Alice

Alice only had one wedding photograph on her wall and it was of her and James, on the steps of the chapel. She had wanted to stand one step down but he wouldn't hear of it. It was a good photograph because they were beaming, both of them. Nothing fake or put on about those smiles, especially the one almost breaking James' face.

That guy looked so damned happy.

She had more photographs, of course, every one featuring her mother showed her glaring stone faced at the camera, like she was fixing to walk across there and punch the photographer.

When they came back from the developer, Alice was horrified, but James surprised her by laughing. He kept pointing to Nina's face and giggling and pretty soon Alice got with it as well and they were both laughing.

The woman's over-done glare was so determinedly in place in photo after photo that it was downright funny.

Mr Teed, Hector, attended, as James' best man, and gave a speech so boring that it was the highlight of the day. Mayor Little was there too, acting graciously and talking loud, which didn't help Nina's mood any.

They got out of there as soon as they could reasonably leave, and jumped the bus for Hampton Beach, two glorious weeks away from everything either of them knew, before returning to the house they had bought in Rimmon Heights. The Heights were about as far away as they could go from Oak Hill and still be in Manchester. That wasn't talked about out loud, but the location worked for both of them.

They returned also to reality, James working long hours at the Council while Alice went back to dressmaking in SimeonStyle.

Months turned into a year, and then into two and found Alice on a day, when the line of her sewing skewed all the way off the edge of the fabric, the machine chattering to a stop sewing nothing at all, and she found herself crying. Crying so that she couldn't stop.

Nina stood behind her, arms folded.

Her cigarette was smouldering in its ashtray and she took a drag, blowing out a shaky plume of smoke. "I don't know what's wrong with me."

"No?"

"I'm just so…"

"You're just so pregnant, is what you are."

Alice stared for a second, then shook her head. But her hand went to her stomach. Slid up to her breasts, which she had recently had to tell James to stop touching, because they were sore.

Still, she shook her head again. "How could that be?"

Nina regarded her coolly, and didn't reply.

"But." She looked down at herself, cupping that belly again. "I don't think I can."

James looked bushed when he came home that evening, talking about Mayor Little expecting miracles. It took him a minute to get most of what he needed out of his system and let his eyes fall on her properly and the words dried in his mouth.

For a few seconds, they just stared at each other. This was in the kitchen. Her back was to the worksurface, she was leaning on it, and he stood a couple of paces away, the glass of water he had just poured stalled half way to his mouth.

He put the glass down and came to her, hands coming out to take her arms.

"What's wrong?"

Her lips shook as she tried to speak, and his eyes widened further, looking properly scared now. She cupped her belly. Put her other hand to her breasts.

"I think."

She was looking at him intently, so saw the light going on. He hopped in place, stood back and stared at her stomach, her hand still spread protectively over there. Came back to her face.

Then he was down on his knees, his head pressed into her, but lightly. She drew her fingers through his hair, such beautiful hair he had.

"I think I might be pregnant."

Chapter
56
James

Throughout her pregnancy, and even afterwards, James Spears was haunted by a worry that became a kind of obsession. It had seemed a lot more than likely that he wouldn't simply wouldn't feel anything for the baby.

It was the thing that was there in his mind when he woke in the morning, and dogged him through the day, never further than just out of sight. He didn't mention it to Alice. So, it was a surprise the first night they put her down in her crib, on her own, this when she was about a month old and they were no longer terrified that she would pass away if not constantly under their eye, and Alice said, "I'd been scared I wouldn't love her."

He looked at her, blinking his surprise. She grinned. "I know how crazy that sounds. And how wrong I was."

He nodded, vehement. "Yea."

"Doesn't stop me being scared though."

"That will pass."

"Will it? How do you know?"

"I don't. It's all so brand new."

"I love that about her. She's so new. Everything ahead of her."

He nodded again, feeling surprising tears come into his eyes despite the fact there was no reason for them. "Yea."

Alice lit a cigarette, stifling the inevitable few coughs, then grinned. "I love her smell."

"Me too."

"I love it when she feeds from me."

"I can't say *me too* to that. But I like to watch."

Alice was looking away, out of the window to where it was still just light, so he could watch her now. She blew out a long stream of smoke and smiled to herself, like something kept tugging the corners of her mouth. He had always enjoyed doing that – watching her from the side, taking in her high cheekbones and those so-full lips – but now it seemed to fill him up.

She turned, letting the corners of her mouth be tugged all the way up, showing a lot of teeth. She put her hand on his.

"I love her *colour*. The colour of her skin. I like to put my hand across her little belly to see how much darker I am. We'll have sex again soon, don't worry."

"I'm not in a hurry."

"Liar. Even Mom loves her. You see it in her face every time she looks at her."

James, not sure he was seeing the same thing as his wife, just nodded at that.

"And you. Mr Poker Face."

He smiled, knowing what was coming.

"What?"

She poked him in the ribs, and not just once, making his squirm and laugh, move his arms protectively.

"Nothing poker faced about you around that little girl."

He caught her hand, to stop her trying to tickle him. "Things are okay, aren't they? Right now, in our life, things are fine."

She drew on her cigarette, and blew it away. Coughed once. "Easy for you to say, sneaking off to work every day. I'm more tired than I've ever been in my whole life. But yea, everything's pretty damned okay." Her head jerked up, hearing something, sensing something. "That's Kirstin."

The next moment there was a squall he couldn't miss. Alice waggled her eyebrows at him. "Your turn."

***

James turned around and Kirstin was walking, saying her first words. Turned again and she could run. Boy, did that girl ever run! She never seemed to want to stop. More than two years had slid mysteriously by, and things were still pretty damned okay.

James had hoped for another child – a boy – but kept that quiet. As well as this private hope, he'd harboured a new fear to replace his worry about not loving her – that Kirstin would present a face to the world devoid of emotion. That she would feel there was a shell between herself and what passed for real life.

That fear was put to rest quickly and with no room for doubt.

As he said to Alice, "Can you imagine if adults acted like that? Screaming and throwing themselves on the floor when the tiniest thing didn't go their way? It would make Council meetings interesting."

"Running around the house, like she's never going to stop. Where does that girl get all the energy?"

Kirstin could be serious sometimes too. Whenever she became engaged in a task – and she could become very engaged indeed – she became deeply serious. In James' view that was when she was funniest.

Alice would whack James on the arm and bug her eyes when he sniggered at her, but he couldn't help it. Crazy black ringlets framing a face so solemn as resolute as she painted her own feet purple. Alice was right, his poker face didn't work around her, not one little bit. She blew it away with hardly a glance.

Turn around again and he was helping her into the lowest branch of the Sugar Maple in the garden, catching her as she jumped shrieking into his arms. "Again, again! Again, again!"

Again, again – Kirstin's litany for life.

Turn once more and he and Alice were getting ready to walk her to school. This a terror and torment for his wife, whose own school days were just that. She was struggling with her expression, trying and failing not to look terrified as Kirstin bounced around the house. Their daughter had put her uniform on as soon as she got out of bed, and wore her satchel all through breakfast.

Alice leaned in to whisper to James. "Maybe you should take her. I'll stay home."

"Don't be scared, hon. She'll be fine."

She held his eyes. Held his hand. "I think she's got a better chance of being fine if we don't take her together."

He took that quietly, even though it surprised him. But, giving it some thought, she was spot on. Even after all this time, they got looks when they were out together. Less comments and insults now, but sometimes those too.

To most eyes, they looked odd. And it was all very well saying fuck 'em, when it was on their own behalf.

Such a striking visible mismatch in her parents, Kirstin didn't need such a gift for the bullies.

He squeezed her fingers and put his other hand over hers. "Why don't you take her?"

***

James had taken the day off work to take his daughter to school, but now watched from the window to see her walk down the street, hand in hand with Alice. Walk wasn't a word that fit. Alice was smoking as she went, but her other arm was tugged and flapped around in time with the daughter's hopping and bouncing. Nothing unusual, this was typical Kirstin, but this morning it was turbo-charged.

James, as he often did, puffed out a laugh to see her, surprised when it ended in something that had nothing to do with laughing.

Not a praying man since watching old Father Michael burn, he closed his eyes now and sent a plea wherever it might reach. "Please make it ok for her."

***

It was ok for her, at least at first. She burst into the house just after lunchtime, trailing her mother in her wake. Desperate to get to her room, and her toys.

James called after her as she ran upstairs, all knees and elbows. "Wait. What was it like?"

She called back over her shoulder, sounding irritated. "Fine."

"Do you know anybody in your class."

James already knew this, he just wanted her to speak to him about it. Make sure she was okay.

"Cheryl and Brittney. Little Bo."

"What's your teacher like?"

"Daaaad!"

"Just tell me."

"Fine."

"A man or a woman?"

"No."

"What? What is…how can that be?"

Kirstin had been jiggling at the top of the stairs. Now she stopped and gave it some thought. It occurred to James that she'd never looked so beautiful.

"She's a sister."

"A sister! You mean a nun."

"That's it. A nun."

Then she was gone, hurrying to her room, maybe just needing to spend some time alone, James thought. She sent one last comment over her shoulder. "Her name's Sister Mary-Rose."

Chapter
57
Alice

Kirstin positively enjoyed school. Looked forward to going every day that she didn't fall out with Little Bo, her on-again off-again best friend. At the mid-term parents' night Sister Mary-Rose told Alice and James that she was doing well in all her subjects, but had to work harder than most at math.

She was particularly smart at English and her Art skills were many years ahead of her actual age.

It was strange for Alice, speaking to her old assistant teacher, now an actual teacher once more. She looked exactly the same as when she'd taught Alice, and didn't acknowledge their previous relationship.

With no emotion, and barely any movement beyond her mouth, the nun told her. "She has many friends, but has a tendency to climb things that shouldn't be climbed and get into fights."

The climbing was no surprise, but the fighting was. "What, physical fights?"

"Yes."

The nun sat quietly, and Alice had to ask, "How does that happen?"

"She becomes excited if someone disagrees with her and may push them over."

"Oh no!"

"If it becomes more significant than that, we'll contact you."

Alice crushed her cigarette into the ashtray and leaned forward. "Is she being bullied, maybe?"

"No."

"Are you sure?"

"Quite certain. Even older children are intimidated by her."

***

That evening, they sat Kirstin down at the kitchen table. She looked solemnly from one to the other, her face still, her hands quiet on the table before her. Nothing else was still, however, she wagged her hips side to side on the chair, and tapped her feet together.

Not a sign of nervousness, Alice knew, just standard Kirstin.

James said, "Is there anything you want to tell us about school, hon? Anything upsetting you?"

She frowned. "No."

"Any*one* upsetting you?"

"Little Bo says she's getting a dolphin for Christmas, but that's a big fat lie! She's a big fat liar!"

It was true that Little Bo made daily claims about everything from her father's job to her extraordinary successes. Last week she had claimed to be able to hold her breath underwater for over an hour.

"Nobody else?"

"No."

"We hear you've been pushing people."

Her wiggling stopped. "No. I never!"

"Sister Mary-Rose said you pushed Izzie Sloan right over, and made her cry."

"She started it! She said Nana looked like..." Her eyes went even wider. "She used the z-word."

"Did she?"

"Said she was a big old Z. I said she is not. She said she is."

"So you pushed her?"

Kirstin nodded, her face solemn. "And I pinched her on the leg."

Alice could feel James shaking beside her, trying not to laugh. She turned and gave him a fake smile, pinching his leg under the table.

"I wonder if you could get me a drink of water, honey. For my cough."

Chapter
58
Nina

Nina probably wouldn't have gone visiting Alice and that short-ass blondie, if it wasn't for Kirstin. She had never said that out loud to her daughter, but she was sure that she knew that was so.

She could hardly bear to be in the same room as James. The guy would just look at her with that face she would never get tired punching. It was a face asking to be punched.

And he could never say anything without there being a criticism wrapped up in there somewhere. About her drinking, her language. Her clothes.

Kirstin, though, she was simply too much of a draw. Alice had been a bit on the quiet side when she was a little kid, maybe not surprising, the things she'd witnessed. There was nothing quiet about her granddaughter. The girl was sometimes, often, too much. Too noisy, too demanding, too opinionated, too much of every damn thing.

She could tire you out, but boy, could she make you laugh. Nina didn't think she'd laughed as much in her whole life as she had these past few years.

She was scary too, a jumping daredevil. The last time Nina had been left alone with her, the girl had called from the hallway, "Gramma, watch this!"

That particular phrase was always a cause for concern coming from Kirstin, so Nina hurried out of the room.

She was more than half-way up the stairs, maybe ten steps up, wearing swim-goggles and her soccer shin-pads. She said again, "Watch this!"

Nina had no more than opened her mouth when she launched herself, basing her style very loosely on that of a ski-jumper. She cleared the last step with inches to spare, landing hard on both feet, but her momentum threw her forwards, her head colliding hard with the wall opposite.

Nina ran faster than she had for years, reaching Kirstin and rolling her onto her front. She was shouting, angry but mostly terrified. Kirstin wasn't exactly conscious and was covered in plaster, having knocked a hole in the board.

She blinked, coughed and groaned.

"Are you okay?"

She shook her head and bawled loudly for a few seconds, quickly stopping to say, "That didn't happen last time."

"Can you stand?"

She could. She stood shakily and dusted herself down, rubbing her forehead, which was scraped and bleeding slightly. Then, she caught sight of the hole in the plasterboard. Her eyes widened.

"Whoa! Look what I did."

"I'm looking."

"Right through!"

"Yea, I know."

"I'm going to be in so much trouble."

"I think it's me that's in for the trouble. I'm supposed to be minding you."

Kirstin rubbed her head some more but didn't take her eyes of the hole. She didn't look particularly unhappy, especially now she had been told it would be her grandmother who was going to cop for this.

"I put my head right through it, see?"

"I can see."

"I'm going to tell Little Bo, Gramma."

She nodded sagely. "She'll be impressed."

***

Later, she and Alice sat out on the sun deck, smoking and sipping lemonade, Nina's only slightly fortified. Kirstin swung on a tyre, hung from the sugar maple, trying to get high enough to catch twigs from the lower branches. Alice watched her daughter, then closed her eyes and turned her face to the sun, so Nina had a chance to look properly at her.

It was a passing strange thing, seeing your own child age. Alice had been nothing short of stunning as a teenager, and so beautiful it could take your breath away as a young woman. Now, approaching forty, her face had become lean and lined to the point of being gaunt.

Nina was ashamed of the thought, but she believed that her daughter was no longer truly beautiful. She looked old. She looked haggard. When had that happened?

Maybe feeling her mother's scrutiny, Alice cracked her eyes and looked sideways, frowning.

"What?"

"You getting enough to eat?"

"Not this again."

"I don't think I ever said that to you. Not since you went through that dumb starvin' yourself shit."

"James keeps saying it."

Nina took a deep draw on her cigarette, and started coughing. Alice took a pull on hers and got into her own coughing bout. The two women started laughing then, both of them with wheezy smokers laughs, broken up by the occasional cough.

Chapter
59
James

James knew there was something up as soon as he got home, but Alice plainly wasn't going to discuss it until Kirstin was in bed. Still, he felt sure he knew what was wrong. The last time Nina had been here, she had winced every time she moved, holding her side like something in there hurt.

Like he had told Alice, on more than one occasion, "It's coming, love, and soon. She's one of the oldest people in Manchester. I'm sorry, but you best get used to the idea."

Alice almost never drank liquor, but when he came back from another marathon bed-time story session, she had a glass of bourbon for herself and one already poured for him.

He hugged her tight, sitting on the couch beside her, and could feel how wired she was. Could see she'd been crying. He thought, here it comes.

"James…"

He put his hand, so it was cupping her face. "I know. She's not been well this last year, hon."

Alice blinked, surprised, and he saw realisation flit briefly across her face. His brave, supportive expression dropped away, along with his heart. He could hardly breathe.

"I got some tests back from the hospital."

"You did?"

She frowned, searching his face, and placed her hand flat against her breastbone. "I mean for me."

He jerked upright, eyes blinking rapidly as he tried to figure this. "What? What tests?"

"I didn't want to worry you."

James struggled to get his next words out. The room suddenly seemed far away, and the space between his ears filled with a strange, grey noise. He pulled himself back, shaking his head.

"You've had something wrong with you, and didn't say?"

"I didn't want to worry you. I know how you worry."

He took both her hands in his. "So…"

"You look really pale. Do you want a glass of water."

"Alice! Just…" he blew out a long breath, making himself take his volume down. "Just tell me."

"It's not good news."

"Is it the cough?"

He squeezed her fingers, massaged them. Heard the crack in his voice. "Just tell."

"It's the cough, yea. Or it started there. I've got cancer."

He closed his eyes for a moment, then opened them. "There's treatments. Things can be done."

But she was shaking her head, tears in her eyes now. "I left it too long, honey. Didn't think it was anything to worry about."

"Where?"

She put a hand again to her chest. "My lungs."

He pressed his lips together, feeling how much they wanted to shake. She moved her hand to her stomach.

"It's in my liver. My lymph nodes. It's everywhere."

"Can they operate?"

She wiped away tears. "The Doctor said, they couldn't have cured me, even Before. All they could have done was put it off, for maybe a year or so."

The room still felt far away. "A year."

"Before, when they had all those fancy treatments, I might have lived a year."

"What are you saying?"

"It will get worse really fast."

She put her arms around him and pulled him in as he cried. "It will go really fast, that's what I'm saying, darling."

Chapter
60
James

"When I was a girl, if a person died, they just died."

Lately that line had gotten to feel like fingernails on slate, and James didn't hide his irritation. Nina put a hand on his wrist. "I love her as well. She's my daughter."

James stared at the back of her hand, more veins than flesh these days, it seemed. She had kissed his cheek on the day of the wedding, reluctantly, but this might be the only other time she had touched him.

"I know that."

She leaned in to whisper, "It's not her who will come back, do you know that too?"

He went to yank his hand away, but she surprised him, tightening her grip, still surprisingly strong. Hissing, "She'll be a fuckin Zombie! That's what she'll be."

Seeing his expression she let go, almost threw his arm away. "Don't give me that Mr. Friggin' Virtuous look! I used the Z-word, boo-fucking-hoo."

James stood. "Maybe you were born a long time ago, when things were different, but I'm done making allowances. That's an offensive, disgusting word, and you know it. Or you should. Especially as it won't be long before." He stalled, started again, "Before Alice…"

No, he couldn't get to the end of that line. They were in the hospice, the only ones today in a brightly coloured room called the day-room. James had been drinking hot chocolate in a paper cup, but tossed it in the trash.

"You get to decide if you're coming back or not. So does she."

She narrowed her eyes. "Aren't you listening? That thing, the thing that comes back, won't be *her*."

"I'm going back in." He locked his eyes on hers. "You know what? You should go home."

The woman flinched, like she had been slapped, but James just turned and left her there.

Alice glanced up when he walked into the room, awake now, smiling despite the pain. Coming to her end, she had been moved out of the ward and into a private room. James made himself smile back, but he was angry, and not just at her mother. He quivered with a rage that had no outlet.

He bent over and kissed her forehead, not her lips. He couldn't say why, but he'd stopped doing that. He stayed with his head pressed to hers, inhaling the too-sweet smell he associated now with her illness. That wasn't her smell.

Finally, she pressed gently on his chest, wanting him to sit down, then searched his face.

"Where's Mom?"

"Gone home. Be back tomorrow"

Her eyes widened. "Tomorrow?" Like that was an alien notion. "I'm scared."

He squeezed her hand. "You'll be back before you know it."

"Will I though?" She put her hand on her breast. "Will it be me?"

"Of course it will."

"What if those MALA bozos are right, though?"

"Hush. Don't say that."

He glanced around, checking the door was closed, and almost as if his thought had summoned her, Nurse Grace entered the room. James thought of her as a girl – she had clearly been a teenager, when she died – but who knew how old she was now.

"How are you, Alice?"

"Comfortable enough."

She walked around the bed.

"I have to change your meds."

James had half stood, but she said, simply, "Stay."

Alice, James could see, was staring openly at the nurse. Her lips were trembling.

"What did you die of, Grace?"

James caught his breath. "Alice!"

Of course, the nurse showed no reaction, but her eyes turned to him. "We're used to those questions in here."

She surprised him, then, beginning to unbutton her tunic. Got to the third button and pulled it aside to show her crispy chest and two black, dried-up holes, right about where her heart would be, in the days when one beat inside there.

"My father shot me. Shot my mom too."

Grace was done, but Alice wasn't, not yet. She said, "We've all heard what it's like, but I've never asked one of The Returned, face to face."

Grace paused. "You mean, am I still Grace Dijkstra?"

Alice nodded.

"You don't have anybody you could ask that?"

"Didn't know my father. There's a Returned woman works at Rickman's. But I've never felt comfortable asking."

"I'm still me."

"But you're different. You act different."

Grace straightened, clearly ready to leave now. She stood stiffly, she moved stiffly, her desiccated skin was drawn into heavy vertical wrinkles, dark grey, especially over her hairless skull. She stared at Alice as seconds ticked past, finally asking, "You had a life changing experience?"

She glanced quickly at James. "Sure."

"Dying is bigger than anything life will throw at you. But you will still be you."

***

Twenty minutes later, Alice's eyes closed. That wasn't unusual, but shortly afterwards her breathing changed too, catching and rattling, the pauses between each breath getting longer. James held her hand as it cooled and stroked his fingers through her hair.

Her breath caught hard then, and James's eyes sparked open, wide and scared. When she breathed again, he hurried out to the payphone in the hall, and called Nina.

"I'm sorry. I'm really sorry for chasing you away, I'm just…"

On the other end, the old woman was crying. "I know. I know how much you love her."

"You've got to come. Get here quick. I think she's passing."

Nina began to speak, but her voice twisted, and stopped.

"Please come."

"I can't. I'm sorry, I just can't. The thing that will rise…"

370

"Nina, please…"

"No, listen. I love my daughter. But when she dies, she's gone forever. I believe that. I don't want to see something rise in her place."

Left alone with a dead telephone receiver and a dying wife, James didn't move for a while, like his systems had shut down. Then, he started, coming to himself, and hurried back inside the room.

Alice was unconscious but still breathing, thank God. He placed his hand on her rapidly cooling one, and stroked it.

"I'm here. I'm still here. You are loved, Alice Spears. You are loved."

He kept that up, stroking her hand and her forehead, both unsettlingly cool now, talking to her. Telling her the truth – how much he loved her and that he would never leave. Alice's breathing stopped.

He dropped his head to his chest and put his hands over his face. When he reached out blindly for her fingers, they were cold. Still, he held on, and waited.

Chapter
61
James

James Spears was good at waiting, that's what he'd always thought. An unusually patient man, was how he had been described by others. But the fifty-six minutes holding his wife's dead hand were the longest of his life. His back ached, his legs ached, he struggled to sit still.

He knew he could leave and come back, but that didn't seem like the right thing to do.

He was having a wake, and a vigil at the same time. It seemed important to see it through. It seemed right to avoid clock watching also. After she died, and he knew her to be dead, he checked his watch and didn't look at it again. Turned it around on his wrist so that it wasn't in easy view.

He had expected that the first he would know about the Return would be a twitch of her fingers. Surely those fingers would twitch.

That wasn't what happened. His eyelids had been closed for a while, concentrating on the feeling of time passing and her hand in his. He opened them to find her eyes on him.

It was a jolt, a surprising one. In the second he caught those eyes on him, he felt a visceral rush of fear so powerful that his testicles rolled inwards and his skin chilled and prickled. His hair stood literally on end. Her fingers lay still and unmoving in his, and the touch of it horrified him so much that he snatched his hand away, lurching to his feet and stumbling backwards.

She said, "James."

James' mouth was suddenly too dry to speak.

"James."

He licked his lips, and managed. "You're back."

"I'm back."

"Are you though?"

"I'm the same Alice Simeon who took your measurements for a yellow uniform, when you were twelve."

He rubbed his hands on his sides, rubbing the feel of her skin away, and glanced towards the door, but snapped his head back when she spoke again.

"The same Alice Spears who buried you in sand on Hampton Beach."

She sat up abruptly, without warning or struggle to sit, simply bending at the waist. James took another involuntary step backwards.

When she swung her legs to the floor, he was ready for it, but still felt another visceral rush of ice, trembling through his limbs and telling him to for God's sake, *run*. His voice sounded squeaky, a thread of panic running through it.

"You should stay in bed."

"I don't need to."

She stood. An IV line tore out of her arm without her noticing. The attached drip stand teetered and tottered but did not fall. Her eyes were on James.

"We should go home."

Chapter

62

Nina

It was the same damn woman on reception. Unless there was a school where they got taught that expression, Jesus, she must be ancient.

"Yes?"

"I'd like to speak to Mr Spears."

"Do you have an appointment?"

"No."

The receptionist raised both eyebrows, pretending shock at the mere idea of someone coming to see a City official without making an appointment.

"No? Then I suggest…"

"I suggest you pick up that phone at your elbow and call him. That's what I suggest."

"You can suggest all you wish, Madam, I can…"

"Look, cut the crap lady. You're just the woman on reception and you've never helped a soul this last twenty years. You also know who I am, so get my son-in-law on the phone and stop wasting my damn time."

"I'll thank you to keep a civil tongue in your head, Miss Simeon."

"And I'll thank you to call James. Give me one reason you can't reach out your hand and do that."

It was the first time Nina had been in this office, though Alice had described it to her. She sat on a chair in front of his huge, important-looking desk and looked around, taking it in.

He asked her, "Are you alright?"

"No, I'm not alright. You alright?"

"Not really."

"Kirstin?"

"Her mother died last week. I doubt any of us will be alright for a long, long time."

"Yea, her mother has died and she's walking about the place just as if she hasn't."

"Nina…"

Nina closed her eyes and put her hands in the air, palm out. "I'm not here for a fight. I'm tired of fighting."

"Ok."

"I'd like to see Kirstin. I miss her, like you wouldn't believe."

James looked at her in that direct, unsettling way he had, taking too long to do it. Finally, he said, "She'd like to see you too."

"Good."

"You can come to the house anytime you want. You know that."

Nina clenched her fists in irritation. How could the man be so dim-witted?

"I can't come 'round there. You know I can't."

"Why?"

She'd said that she was tired of fighting, but her head was prickling in that familiar way, and she had to work to stay calm.

"You *know* this. I can't be seeing that, whatever the hell it is, going around on my own daughter's bones. Looking out her eyes."

375

She held her face tight and shook her head. "Naw. Can't do that."

"You want me, what, to bring Kirstin to you?"

"Yea. That's what I want. I think Kirstin would want that too."

He looked off, thinking about it. "Maybe she would, for a while. You don't want it to turn into a chore for her, seeing her Granma. A duty."

Now he was just being awkward, a fucking prig, cut from the same damn cloth as the woman downstairs. "Kirstin and I get along just fine."

"Okay. I'll bring her around tonight, when I get home."

She blew out a long breath. "I'm obliged."

"I'm not doing it for you, Nina."

They stared at each other in silence for a while. He didn't mind the silence, why should she?

"I get that. One last thing before I go."

Predictably, he just waited, and she leaned forwards, urgent suddenly. "Don't trust it."

When his eyes widened, she added, "Do *not* trust it. Not around Kirstin. Don't leave them alone any more than you have to."

It took him a few seconds to answer. "I think it's time you left. But, hear this loud and clear, if I get even a whisper from Kirstin that you're poisoning her against her mother…"

"That's not her *mother*. You want to believe it's her, both of you but…"

"Even one whisper. The arrangement stops dead, and you stop being able to see your granddaughter. We clear?"

Nina put her hands up again, and had to look away. "We clear."

"Good. I don't think you'll get very far if you try. anyway. Kirstin loves her mom."

***

As she was leaving City Hall, Nina glanced across at the receptionist, catching the pursed lip imperious glare of the woman. She gave that look right back, stopping in her tracks to do it until it was the old bag who blinked and looked away.

Then she walked the short way along Elm to her shop. It wasn't far but, like her walk to and from work, it was no longer comfortable. Her back hurt, and her feet hurt. Her left hip hurt most of all. The weight of the gun in her bag dragged at her, making the ache in her back so much worse. Maybe it was time to stop carrying it.

The thought of sitting all day cutting and sewing made her want to stop altogether, just stand there in the street. She had been thinking about employing an assistant, an apprentice maybe, but didn't have the heart for it. After all these years, she'd finally paid that dirty, blood-sucking bastard Bruce Little off, and owned her little house outright. Maybe it was time to retire. She had enough money put by to get along, if she switched to hand rolled and cut down on her bourbon some.

She could sell the Land Rover, and her rifles.

She got herself moving again but stopped dead at the shop door. It was open. She looked around the street. It was around ten in the morning and people were going about their business, paying neither her nor the shop any mind.

She slipped her hand into her bag and came out with the gun, holding it down by her side. Her heart was hammering, fit to just burst in her chest, and she thought *I'm just too damn old for this kind of shit.*

377

She stepped inside, but quietly, as quiet as her papery lungs and shaky legs would allow.

"Whoever's in there, you best come out where I can see."

It wasn't really such a surprise when Alice stepped through from the back shop, but it was a hard, hard moment. She had to turn her head, not look at what had become of her beautiful, her *beautiful* daughter. She put the gun down on the counter, it was too heavy anyway and she was already feeling the after effects of the adrenaline.

Only a week after dying, the creature still looked like Alice had in her terrible last weeks. Cheeks sunken and fleshless, because the cancer had burned it all away. But she didn't stand like her. Nina kept her eyes averted, and her words burst from her chest like a sob.

"What d'you want here?"

"I work here."

Nina shook her head, put her face in her hands. "My *daughter* worked here."

"I'm your daughter."

Nina forced herself to look. Forced some strength into her voice, but it still came out thin and reedy.

"I don't know what you are, but you aint her."

"I can work long hours. Work overnight. Save your back, and your fingers, Mom."

"Don't you call me Mom! You just git."

"You need me."

"I'm closing the shop. I'm done with it. Git now."

"You aren't…"

Nina didn't know she was going to shout before she did it. "Just go! Go! Get out of here."

She doubled up, holding her middle, feeling tears streaming down her face.

378

"My beautiful girl's dead, and I got to see you goin' roun'. Using her. Go."

It was Nina who lurched and stumbled from the shop, just needing to get out from under the creature's eyes. Outside, a man stopped and came over, putting a hand on her shoulder and asking was she ok. She squeezed her eyes tight and spat out, "Leave me be."

She did *not* want that man to touch her. He had clearly died a long time ago.

Chapter
63
James

James no longer slept beside Alice. Alice no longer slept. She would lie down beside him if he wanted that, he knew that to be true, but the thought made his skin crawl. She remained downstairs at night, either doing chores or just standing. Quite possibly without moving.

There were people at work he could speak to about it, people with Returned relatives. There was even a local forum, *Prodigals*, where he could talk to others who had made the adjustments in the lives and in their heads to continue living with the Returned, and actively wanted to help and share their experiences.

James wasn't a talker.

Kirstin chatted to her mother like she always did, chattering ten to the dozen and bouncing around her. Just like Ana-Maria, Alice never got tired or bored, or said the game had to end. She would wait with incredible patience as Kirstin climbed into the limbs of the Sugar Maple, waiting to catch her.

The house was cleaner than it had ever been, the garden better kept. Food was tasty and produced on time, without fuss. Time slid by, and they fell into a routine.

One night, after she had taken Kirstin to bed, reading her God knows how many stories, Alice stood in the doorway and said, "I still love you, James."

He searched her face. She was hairless now, her natural colour faded to grey, vertical lines beginning to appear but not yet forming the deep wrinkles that would come later.

"Do you?"

"Just like I always did."

He couldn't say it back. It stuck in his throat.

She said, "We can have sex."

Somehow, he kept his horror off his face. "I don't think we should."

She accepted that calmly, with no sign it interested her one way or the other.

***

By September, when the colours of the maple were at their most vibrant, James came home to be told Kirstin had fallen out of it when her mother wasn't around. She'd climbed the highest she'd ever got, and slipped.

Alice was telling him this in the moment he walked through the door, with Kirstin standing quietly by his side. Kirstin, the girl who never stood quietly anywhere.

He looked one to the other, his blood stilling in his veins. "Are you ok, Honey? Were you hurt?"

He was asking this, even though he knew the answer. "I was hurt."

He licked his lips, took a moment but still his voice was a whisper. "You died?"

Alice answered. "She hit her head on a lower branch, when she fell."

James could see that was true, had seen it the moment he walked into the kitchen to see them standing there. Her forehead was sunken, ever so slightly, just above her left eye.

He couldn't speak. Couldn't move. Didn't want to move, or speak. Couldn't imagine himself doing either, ever again. It occurred to him that if he walked back outside, though, came back in, there would be a different scene in front of him. One with his daughter alive and well, without her head stove in.

Kirstin said, "I'm okay now, Daddy."

They both stood so still and calm. His eye refused to rest on his daughter; it was too much to bear. Before he knew he would or could do such a thing, he put his head back and screamed. He didn't just scream once.

He was aware of his wife and daughter taking hold of him, but dimly, his eyes were screwed shut and his ears were full of his own sobs. On some level, he knew he was being lifted and carried upstairs; put to bed.

At some point, he opened his eyes and knew he had been asleep, as it was dark. He felt hollowed out, ruined, his life at an end. Alice stood, framed against the window. They stared at each other in darkness and silence, until he said, "How do I know that's really what happened?"

"What else could have happened?"

"She was on her own with you. Now she's dead."

"There's more life flowing through her now than you can ever imagine. Not the fragile, solitary life you know."

James put his hands over his face. "I can't stand it. I can't live with it. It's too much."

"I understand."

"Do you? I'm not sure."

She stepped closer, and he saw the pistol in her hand, his own Kimber Micro. He froze, his eyes on it.

"You can join us."

"No."

"You can only understand once you pass. You can be one with us in a way you could never hope to before."

He shook his head, not moving his eyes from the gun.

"Your pain can end. You can be with Kirstin and me."

"No."

"There is a oneness that should be the human reality, but isn't."

She stepped closer, the gun coming up.

"Alice…"

He watched as she placed it on the bedside table.

"Join us, James."

***

Saturday, surprisingly warm for October. James had insisted on going with Alice and Kirstin to pick up some provisions. All for him, of course. He had been determined to come, even though she told him, we don't need help.

"I just want us to walk out together, like we used to."

What he didn't add, like a real family.

They walked in silence to Elm Street, but at least they were together. James told himself he was simply out for a stroll with his wife and daughter. What could be more normal? The sun was unseasonably warm, gleaming on Alice's scalp, which was only just beginning to show signs of drying into grey striations. Kirstin – you might see Kirstin and not know she had ever died, except for the quietness. Especially if you'd known her before, the girl who could not bear to keep still. Like electricity in her veins.

The first he knew about something happening, something bad, was when Alice and Kirstin stopped dead in their tracks. It wasn't just them who stopped – a street scene in busy movement had just frozen. Every one of The Returned had become very still, all of them turning their heads to look at something that wasn't in any way obvious, not to him.

Like every first-lifer there, James squinted, trying to see what had stalled them, and taken their attention. The apartments above Baldwin's Dry Goods, apparently, although there was nothing to see at the grimy window. A tall, skinny man lifted his gaze from a Returned who could only be his father and caught James' eye, a question in there.

James shrugged and had only just turned to speak to Alice, ask what was going on, when the acrid smell of burning gasoline caught in his throat. Seconds later, the deafening rattle of an automatic weapon, coming from the vicinity of the apartment so many eyes were staring at.

Then, just as suddenly as The Returned had hit pause, they were in movement, Alice and Kirstin included, walking quickly towards the entrance to the building. Seconds later, a second-floor window exploded and something came tumbling out, a body, fiercely aflame.

As James staggered back, Alice stepped forward, pulling her coat off to dowse the flame. James grabbed Kirstin by the shoulders and hauled her back. For a second, just one, she resisted hard, but then she allowed herself to be dragged, into his arms and away. Others joined and soon a huddle of The Returned were helping a horribly burned figure back to his feet.

James turned away, blocking Kirstin's view, disgusted by the sight and smell, but almost instantly threw himself flat as three men, living men, burst from a doorway, firing indiscriminately.

They screamed, "MALA". And "Death to Zombies". One had a bottle of something, with a flaming plug in it. He threw it hard and it shattered, spreading fire amongst a group of The Returned. The air was filled with gunfire and stink and smoke. Half the street was suddenly aflame.

James covered his ears, staying flat on the sidewalk, covering Kirstin as the men ran, spraying bullets and throwing Molotov cocktails. A small Returned woman not three feet away was hit by a series of slugs, knocking her backwards and off her feet. Bits of dust and desiccated flesh flew from her, some landing on James.

As he watched, half-deafened and shaking, she rolled, got stiffly to her feet and walked. Towards the shooters, not back.

James had never felt so frightened, didn't know it was possible to feel this frightened, with the screams of the living and the rattle of heavy guns and the strike of shells, some of them hitting inches away from where he lay. Cracking stone and smashing glass.

Amongst all this mayhem, Kirstin kept trying to get up and he was struggling to hold her. Alice was somewhere nearby, his wife, and he wasn't doing anything to help her. He pulled himself to his feet, throwing himself and Kirstin flat again as another deadly spray of bullets raked the street. Deadly to him, not Kirstin. Or Alice

The flames were deadly to them.

Kirsten wriggled out of his grasp, got up and walked towards the fight. He lurched to his feet again, hurrying after her.

The MALA guys were heavily armed and determined, laying down fire of both kinds as they moved sideways, the term rear-guard action occurred to James – that's what it looked like.

The Returned just kept coming, knocked about, knocked down, set afire, they kept coming. Alice was in there, in the middle of everything. He snatched at Kirstin's hand but missed. Had to hurry behind her, grabbing her shoulder about the same time as the men were overrun, and overwhelmed.

One man was lying on the ground, surrounded by The Returned, but there was no tearing and rending. No kicking him senseless.

Instead, they simply held on. As James watched, he screamed at them, calling them monsters, and struggled in their grip. He caught sight of James, the only first-lifer there and yelled, "It's the fuckin' apocalypse man! Can't you see?"

Then he saw whose shoulder James was holding. He wrenched his arm free and a pistol was suddenly in his hand, but he didn't have a chance to fire it. Kirstin moved surprisingly quickly, pulling away and taking the gun from him. In one swift movement, she pressed it to his chest, and pulled the trigger.

Chapter
64
James

"James! Come in, stranger."

Nina was surprisingly pleased to see him. Her expression changed. "What's happened? You look…"

"Yea, I know how I look. You see that shooting, on CNN?"

"The one near Baldwin's? Those crazy MALA assholes, shooting the place up."

"I was there."

Seeing the shock on her face, he added, "And admit it, you don't think they're one bit crazy."

She shrugged one shoulder. "You could use a drink."

Once they were sitting with their bourbons, James told his story. She listened, smoking and sipping her liquor. Her eyelids flickered in her own smoke.

"I was alone, when Alice was born. I ever tell you that?"

James shook his head, and watched her going back in her memory.

"Yea. All alone. Stinking of smoke. I hate the smell of burning gasoline to this day. Hate it."

"Gasoline?"

She opened her hands, showing old scars, raised weals on the inside of her fingers. "My hands were blistered, my nightshirt all scorched and burned away, when my waters broke."

She laughed then. "Wasn't the best of timings, that's what I thought at first. Like, come on! Really? You kiddin' me, God?"

James was trying to follow her, but couldn't. He asked, "What you thought at first?"

"Yea. But then, once it starts, you don't have no space in your head for nothin' else. And then, there I was, lying in my own mess on the bedroom floor, and I had my baby. Girl saved my life, see?"

"Gave you something to live for?"

"I needed something, in that moment. So bad."

James closed his eyes, just to give himself some respite. "She's still here."

"You believe that?"

He looked down at his own hands.

"Honestly? I don't know anymore. How can anybody know?"

Nina ran her fingers thoughtfully over the burn scars on the inside of her fingers. "I still smell it sometimes, like my sinuses have been impregnated, or something. It's the last thing in life I'm going to smell."

James was thinking that sounded a bit melodramatic, till she added. "That's my intention. My plan. It's nearly time."

He looked around the room, searching for a can of gasoline, but not seeing it.

"Yea, I got some. I don't have long to live, James, but I'm not leaving it to chance."

"I guess you've got tablets of some kind?"

She shook her head, and lifted her nickel-plated revolver, turned it in her hand, not quite smiling. "I've had this a long time. Longer than I've had anything else in the whole world."

"You ever…"

She nodded. "I've shot it. Is there going to be trouble? A man was murdered in plain sight."

"Murder, what's that? By the time Gabriel arrived he was on his feet again, they all were. Telling how they had a whole different perspective on things."

"Saw the error of their ways?"

James raised his glass. "The error of their ways. Guy was screaming about the apocalypse, happening right in front of us."

"It's what these guys think."

"You reckon The Returned can hear something, we can't? Like ultrasound? That's why they knew one of them was being set afire."

"Could be."

"But you don't think so."

Nina had finished her bourbon and poured herself another, not hurrying. Took a drink that was more than a sip.

"No, I think something altogether different."

Chapter

65

Nina

A month after James told her about Kirstin shooting the MALA guy, Nina woke early as usual and made her usual toast and peanut butter breakfast. The sky outside had that look of snow about it, that always put her in mind of Tilly Whim.

Her heart sank when the snow came up there in the mountains, and she never lost that feeling. She waited until the first flakes appeared and shooed herself away from the window. Wandered into the living room, turned the television on and let it wash over her. She drank coffee and when it was finished she simply sat there, barely moving. In truth, she wasn't really watching the television, it was simply on, a background of movement and sound in her otherwise empty house, but after a while something flickered at the corner of her eye, and made her attend. A red 'breaking news' screen had replaced *Friends Forever*.

Grunting, holding her side, which was paining her more and more lately, she got to her feet, stumped over and turned up the sound.

Soon a reporter appeared, some new guy she didn't recognise, looking sombre at his desk and reading from a paper in front of him.

"Good morning. CNN has, in the past few minutes, received a special report from the White House with some truly shocking news. I will give viewers a moment to brace themselves and stop what they are doing."

Nina pursed out her lips, and backed up till the sofa hit her in the back of her knees, and she sat.

The man shuffled his paper, dropping his eyes for a moment. Nina pushed backwards into the cushions, like she could get away, hands coming up to cover her mouth. She looked around the house, but of course was alone.

The reporter raised his head. "Yesterday evening, whilst The President was taking his morning walk in the Rose Garden, there was an incident. An assassin from the radical, terrorist group First Life, posing as a gardener, discharged a handgun at him at close range."

Nina gasped, fluttered her hands before her face.

"Before he himself was killed, he succeeded in shooting President Moore."

Nina started. If she had been able to, she would have hopped to her feet.

"Oh shit!"

"President Moore was struck by three .22 calibre rounds. One hit his neck, and the other two his chest, impacting his heart. He was pronounced dead at the scene."

The reporter was clearly allowing several seconds of respectful dead air to pass, underlining the solemnity of the moment. His eyes cut up and to the left, and he gave the briefest of nods.

"The President will now address the nation."

Nina lurched to her feet and snapped the consul off before hurrying to the telephone.

When James finally arrived, she greeted him at the door and asked, "Have you heard?"

"I've heard."

"That can't be right, can it? A zombie President."

She saw him wince at the word, but wasn't in the mood for any of that shit. He shook his head.

"No, it doesn't seem right, but the legal situation...I think he's still in office, for now. He'll step down, I'm sure. He'll have to."

Nina muttered and cursed. Shook her head. "Jesus, it's getting worse and worse all the time. There's so many of them now. More every day."

James nodded, his usual calm self, then his face shook, like the bones under there were jelly, and tears started in his eyes. He wiped himself with his sleeve, but they kept coming.

He said, "Kirstin."

"What about her?"

"She's not her."

"No, she isn't."

He surprised her, grabbing her wrist, his face contorted like she'd never seen it.

"I can't stand it, Nina. Can't...I just can't cope. It's bad enough with Alice, but Kirstin, my baby. I can't stand to see whatever that thing is, walking around in her body."

He was looking at her so intently, she would have taken a step back, had he not such a tight hold on her arm.

"What are you saying?"

"I'm saying..." He blew out a long shaky breath, "...I don't know what I'm saying."

He let go of her, but now she grabbed him, his expression crazy.

"But it can't stand. It can't go on."

"James. Think now!"

James rubbed his face, surely hard enough to hurt. When he stopped, he asked her, "Will you help me?"

Chapter
66
Nina

Nina was waiting at the window, so saw James and Kirstin as soon as they came into sight, which was almost at the end of the street. Everything was under a good foot of snow and the town plough hadn't made it here yet, so they were walking down the middle of the road. James was well wrapped up, layers under his heavy coat, and snow boots. Kirstin wore jeans and a tee, her feet bare.

James, she knew, probably hadn't bothered asking her to wear shoes. He was done with that.

She put her hand over her mouth to see him, the agony clear in his face as he stole glances at his daughter, none of which she noticed.

Nina limped to the door and opened it, before they got there. Christ, James looked even worse up close, like he might puke or start crying. He had aged these last months, years of pain etched deep into a face that had so recently seemed weirdly unlined.

"Come in, quick. Don't want to let all the heat out."

That was a strange thing to say, given that she herself was dressed in heavy boots and a padded coat. She knew it struck an off-note as soon as it was out of her mouth, but of course Kirstin didn't notice.

Once she had closed the door behind them, she stared hard at James, needing a sign. He nodded, and she closed her eyes. A very old woman now, she felt her years. Shaky on her pins. Shaky in the face.

James could no doubt smell the bourbon off her, and didn't refuse when she offered him a pull on, not a glass or even a flask, but an actual bottle. She doubted he'd ever drunk liquor from a bottle in his life, but he gulped down a healthy dose, wincing.

Kirstin didn't look one to the other. Didn't ask what the hell was going on. Didn't do anything.

After a moment, Nina said, "I guess you two will better come out the back. I guess you should do that."

James didn't seem able to trust his voice, so he simply nodded, and they followed her out of her kitchen door, waited while she struggled down the steps and then onto the snow-covered yard.

She pointed at the shed. "Something in there I need help with."

The snow around the shed was heavily tracked. They skirted Nina's personal pyre, the one James had built for her, and followed their own snowed-over tracks to the shed door. The stink of gasoline was strong in the air.

Nina withdrew the bolts and opened the door. Inside, the stink was even worse, almost choking. Logs and kindling were piled around the inner edge, a lawn mower and some other garden tools in there.

For a moment, they stopped there. The three of them, James, Nina and Kirstin, standing in a semi-circle in front of the open door, doing nothing.

James breathed hard through his nose, psyching himself up, it looked like.

He looked down at Kirstin, and blurted out. "I'm sorry."

He stepped back and pushed her, putting everything he had into it, knocking her off her feet and into the shed. The Returned are strong, but they aren't heavy. Nina immediately slammed the door closed and threw the bolt.

In the second before she sparked her lighter, the door shifted and the wood squealed and bulged, pushed hard from the inside. The gas-soaked timber caught with a whoosh, driving them both back.

James shouted, "I'm sorry! I'm sorry."

The door shuddered under a blow from the inside. Another. The fire was so hot that they were forced back, and back again. The whole structure was a sheet of flame. But the blows from inside kept coming, and suddenly some of the boards burst outwards, and James screamed as Kirstin's head and shoulders appeared, burning fiercely as she tried to force her way out of the gap. Her hair was gone, burned away already, and it looked as though her flesh was sizzling and bubbling on her skull. Her arm, when she drove it through the hole, searching for the bolt, was carbon-black.

James yelled and ducked when Nina fired her gun, only a foot to his left. The first bullet missed its mark, but the second hit Kirstin squarely in the face, knocking her down.

Only seconds later, she was back, her skull shattered and more badly burned than before, her hand crawling across the burning wood to find the bolt. This time, when Nina shot her, she jerked back, but didn't fall away.

Nina shot the gun empty, and still the girl fought to find that bolt. In something like horror, she watched her fingers finally close, and slide it aside.

The door, what was left of it, shuddered open, and the sudden roaring wave of heat pushed Nina back, singing her hair, even ten paces away. Kirstin stood in the open doorway, flaming, but didn't run out.

Instead, she stayed still for a second, before her left leg went from under her, and she went down on one knee. James fell to his knees too, wailing.

A group of people ran around the house now, Nina twisted to look, even through her tears taking in that they were all Returned, before turning back to Kirstin.

Kirstin rocked back and forth and then toppled, to lie face down, still burning. The Returned had been moving towards her, but now they halted. Stopped as one, simply watching her burn.

"That's right." Nina shouted at them. "You're too late. She's gone. What you going to do about it?"

They stayed there watching for no more than a few seconds before, without so much as glancing towards Nina and James, turning and walking back the way they came.

Nina might have passed out then, or maybe just had some kind of brain skip. The next thing she remembered was James trying to pull her to her feet, because she was on her knees in the snow. The fire was still smoking, it reeked horribly, but it had gone out. Kirstin's charred body lay where it had fallen in the doorway.

James pulled again on her arm. "Get up. You're starting to freeze."

She tried to get up, but at first couldn't. James was right, her knees felt like they had frozen solid, welded to the ground.

Chapter
67
James

Alice wasn't in the house when he got home, stinking of smoke and gasoline. He walked every room, calling her name, willing to take whatever was coming his way. The last room was Kirstin's, and he pushed it open expecting to find her there, but it was empty, except for the things that had once made it Kirstin's.

He stepped inside and looked around, tears burning his cheeks. All those things that she once loved, the clothes, the paints. Her paintings were still on the walls.

He sat on her bed, where she hadn't lain since she was properly alive, picked up her bedtime bear, and wept bitter tears.

But crying came to an end, and he sat up, looking out of the window. It was getting dark, but he could still make Alice out, standing in the garden, facing the house.

She could see him, standing in the window, he was sure of that. He raised his hand but she didn't respond. After a while, he walked heavily downstairs and out of the back door. Trudged through the freezing snow to where she stood in a light shift. Stopped in front of her. He was swaying, but she stood completely still, no expression whatsoever.

"Do you know what I did? You do, don't you?"

"I know."

Seconds stretched out, until they might have been minutes and his feet hurt from the cold.

"What are you going to do?"

"Nothing."

"Aren't you angry?"

"No."

It was suddenly him who was angry, for no reason he could explain, beyond the flaying of his mind. The loss of contact with reason.

"Why *not*? How can you not be?"

Not waiting on an answer, he pulled his fist back and hit her, a cumbersome roundhouse she could have easily avoided. She took it on the side of her face, and her expression remained the same.

"Why would I be?"

He sank to the ground, his hands searching for purchase on her legs as she began walking. "I killed her, Alice. I killed our girl. I watched while she burned."

"I know."

She stepped from his grip and left him there, on his hands and knees in the snow.

***

Less than a week later, James was sitting down to eat dinner when the call came in from Nina. Alice answered, and said simply, "Yes. I'll get him."

She handed over the receiver. He put a question in his face, for all the good that did. Even after all this time, he struggled to drop habits like that.

"Hi, James Spears."

"James."

Nina's voice was so weak and shaky it was barely recognisable as her.

"What's wrong?"

"It's time."

He flicked his eyes to Alice, who stood staring at him, not because she was interested, he thought, but because that's the direction her head was facing.

"Are you sure?"

"I'm sure. Come quick, son. Quick as you can."

He dropped his eyes and nodded. "I'll be there. Hold on."

He replaced the receiver and didn't glance her way.

"I have to go out."

She didn't say, to see my mother? Or, is my mom ok? She didn't say anything.

He hurried to the door and pulled his coat on. The temperature had risen slightly in the last week or so, so he could use his bike, although it would still be uncomfortably cold.

At the last minute, he glanced behind. She was still staring at him.

It was just starting to snow as he cycled through the dark to Nina's house, tiny flakes that blew through the air and weren't ready to lie yet. It would either blow clear later this evening or those flakes would grow fatter and tomorrow everything would be white.

The lights were on in her living room as he turned into her street and, when he got to her drive and hopped off his bike, he was surprised to find two people standing by the front door. The door was open, light from her hall pouring into the street, and cold from the street pouring into the hall.

He dropped the bike and ran, aware now that the man and women in the doorway were Returned. "What's happened? What are you…"

He had been hurrying into the house, but they put their hands out and caught him at the door. Stopped him and held him. He struggled and thrashed out of their grip and stepped back, heart suddenly hammering.

"What the hell do you think you're doing?"

The woman said, simply, "You can't go in."

"I've been invited! I've been invited by the owner of this house. Who are you to stop me?"

They didn't offer any response, and they didn't move.

He made another, more serious, attempt to barge past, but was pushed back, this time hard enough so that he stumbled and almost fell.

"You've no right to do this! Let me in."

Again, they didn't answer. He raised his voice and shouted. "Nina! Nina, can you hear me? They won't let me in."

He glared at the man and woman barring his way, then turned, pretending to walk away across the lawn before twisting and sprinting down the side of the house. The man followed him, but he wasn't running. He walked. James reached the back door, expecting it to be locked, but it wasn't. He hauled it open, immediately catching the odour of gasoline. Something Nina had done, he was sure.

There was a small Returned woman just inside the back door. She said, "You can't come in."

Behind her, in the kitchen, there was a scene in motion. She could see Nina in there, and it looked like she was being manhandled out of the room by two of The Returned.

"What the hell? Out of my way."

He tried to force his way past but, even though this woman was small, she caught hold of his arms and pinned them to his sides. It *hurt*. Her fingers dug into his biceps, crushing muscle into bone.

Then the other man was there, and he was thrown back out of the door, hitting the ground hard enough to made him suddenly nauseous. He made himself roll to his feet, seeing the man was still coming for him.

He rolled to his feet and dodged backwards as the man came on. Threw a punch, landing a good one on his jaw, for all the good that did. He skipped backwards again.

The man stopped. "You can't come in."

"What are you doing to Nina?"

When the man didn't answer, he pointed. "I'm leaving. But I'll be back with the cops."

As soon as that was out of his mouth, he wished he hadn't said it. Still, the man made no attempt to stop him as he dodged sideways, and ran back the way he came. He wondered if the woman would block his way at the front, but she hadn't moved from the door. He grabbed his bike and hopped on.

Before he left, he bellowed, as loud as he could. "Nina! Hold on, I'll get help."

It was around an hour later that he got back, this time in a Police cruiser, with another behind, their blues lighting the street up. There was nobody guarding the door, so the officers ran inside, with James and Gabriel Lamont in their wake.

Nina was in the living room, alone, and she was standing without a cane.

Gabriel, slightly out of breath, asked, "Ma'am. Are you ok?"

Nina didn't nod. She didn't blink.

"Everything's ok."

James stood as still as she did, for a while, just staring at her. He could have told her, I'm sorry. I'm sorry I didn't do it, like you asked. But he would have been wasting his breath.

Gabriel put a hand on his arm. "Sorry, man."

He nodded, his eyes on Nina, who gazed calmly back.

Chapter
68
James

Derryfield Park was buzzing by the time James, Alice and Nina got there. The temporary bleachers were getting full, and James had to put away his underlying anxiety that he had gotten his calculations wrong, and they might collapse under the weight of hundreds of spectators.

Nothing would go wrong, he knew that really. He had made sure the bases were firm, and had checked the construction himself only last night. Everything was ok.

It was a sunny day, cloudless and if anything slightly too hot, although it seemed churlish to complain. The whole park smelled of roses and hot dogs and popcorn, and there was tinny music of one kind or another playing at some of the stalls, enthusiastic hawkers calling on people to step on up, have a try.

Mr Teed caught sight of him and waved him forward, into the enclosure for dignitaries and their friends. James hadn't seen his boss in sunshine for some time and was struck by how old he looked, his skin papery over his doughy face.

But his eyes glowed, the man excited. He even clapped his hands.

"The 1500 metres is about to start! You got here just in time."

He smiled over James's shoulder, at the two women he was with. "So glad you came, Miss Simeon. Alice."

There were no Returned in the shorter races, because short fast bursts weren't what they were good at, but the 1500 was split evenly between the living and the dead. Mayor Little himself was playing master of ceremonies, introducing the races and the runners, clearly enjoying himself.

In fact many people were enjoying themselves, having fun, but James wasn't and, looking around, he wasn't the only one. Watching the runners line up, he thought, this is one of the weirdest sights in a world of weird sights. You just have to keep reminding yourself of its strangeness.

Three living runners were lined up, alongside three of The Returned, one of whom looked like they had been dead a long time.

He turned to Alice, honestly curious. "Why are they doing this?"

"They are taking part."

"Yes, but why?"

"The Returned take part. They take part in the activities of the town."

That was true, James could see it, but, for the first time, he found himself wondering why. They didn't need to eat, or drink. They didn't need shelter, even in winter.

"What's the motivation, though? You live in our old house, but you don't need to." He heard the word he'd just said. "I mean you *reside* in our old house. So does Nina. You both make clothes even though you don't need to wear them. Just like you used to."

Alice and Nina simply stared at him, their faces expressionless. Then, the mayor said, "On your marks, get set."

The starter's pistol launched the runners into motion.

This was a first for James too. Seeing The Returned running, getting a really good look at it. Their gait was stiff, much less bend in the legs than the living runners.

He turned to Hector Teed, not bothering to lower his voice. "That is so damn weird."

Teed leaned in, keeping his own voice quiet. "Eat up the ground, though, don't they?"

James nodded. All six runners were roughly keeping pace with each other, in a bunch. After the first lap, one of the living runners kicked on, and a gap started to open up. Within seconds, all three Returned increased their pace, so that now there was a group of four, with the two slower first-lifers trailing.

Teed leaned in, his voice even lower, "You can't help but think, if he goes faster, they'll just match whatever pace he sets."

James was thinking just that. People were cheering now, living people urging their man on. The dead stood quietly. The last lap now, and the strain was telling on him. Still, he kicked again, and a gap opened.

This time, it didn't close. This time, something very strange happened that James just couldn't understand. Not at first.

The Returned athletes stopped dead, all three in the same moment. In an instant, they went from running to standing. The chasing first lifers kicked, meaning to take the chance and sprint past, but they were prevented. The Returned simply put their hands out and grabbed them, stopping them dead.

Mayor Little had been commentating, trying to whip up the excitement, but now he dried, leaving dead air. James glanced around, seeing the same thing played out amongst the crowd, over and over. The Returned turning to first lifers, putting their hands on them. Taking hold.

He looked up as Alice gripped his upper arm, turned again and there was Nina, holding his elbow. They weren't holding so hard that it hurt, but it was a close thing. The two women loomed high over him, stepping uncomfortably close.

All around, over and again, the same thing. People were calling out in panicked, querulous voices. Somewhere, somebody screamed. A full throated and terrified sound.

He blinked up at his wife. "Alice?"

Both women answered. "It's time."

Not just Nina and Alice. All around him, he could hear the same line being said, the same two words exactly. He looked about, seeing the same tableau everywhere his eye fell. Baffled and frightened first-lifers, with the hands of The Returned on them, being told, *It's time*.

He swallowed hard. "Time for what?"

Every dead voice spoke in unison, all around the world for all he knew.

"We are enough."

"Enough for *what*?"

He jerked his arm away, intending to haul himself out of Alice's grip, but she didn't let go. Her fingers tightened, and now they did hurt. It felt like being caught in a machine.

407

Again, The Returned spoke as one. "We are enough."

He looked around, beginning to panic. A few people were fighting, trying to tussle themselves free, some shouts and punches being thrown. Somewhere nearby, shots were fired, but nobody was running.

The living were being held tight. The dead stood still as stone.

His heart was suddenly booming so hard it hurt. His arms hurt badly now, the flesh crushed hard into bone.

"Let go of me."

So many voices, speaking as one. "It's time."

"No! Let go of me. Alice!"

More shots were fired, sporadic pops from different areas of the field. More scuffles and shouts and full-on screams.

"There is a oneness. We are one."

"Let me go!"

Surprisingly, they did let go. All around, that same thing was happening. People who had been restrained being freed. He stepped away, holding his bruised arms, but bumped into another of The Returned, a very small woman standing behind him.

All of The Returned spoke at once, again. The words echoed around the park, like a prayer.

"We wait."

"Wait for what?"

"The burning is forbidden."

He crouched, fists coming up in a fighting stance. "You going to try to kill me, is that it? Kill us all?"

They didn't all talk together, then, it seemed that was done. Instead, Nina alone spoke to James, answering his question.

"We don't require your death. We are enough."

"What are you saying?"

Nina answered. "We need you to live. So, you will live."

James took that in, the icy deliberation and certainty of it. He looked around the field, at familiar faces with unfamiliar expressions, baffled and angry and terrified.

He licked his lips and kneaded his damaged arm and returned his gaze reluctantly to Nina. Who stood implacable.

"Why do you…"

"In time, these bodies will fail. In time, you will die. Your children will die."

He shook his head, no longer able to pretend he didn't understand. "No."

"There is a oneness. You will be part. Your children's children will be part, all down the ages."

"We won't have children! We won't do it, be your…what? Feedstock? You can't force us."

That was ignored. "The burning will cease. It is forbidden."

Without another word they began to disperse, heading in different directions but heading away. It looked to James as though Nina and Alice were quite simply heading home.

As they drifted away, they left a field of the living behind, and now James could see clearly how few there were. He glanced towards Mr Teed, who looked as though he was having trouble breathing. Mayor Little hung red-faced over the podium rail, hat off and hair dishevelled. He wiped his face, but left his hand over his eyes.

A man with crazed eyes raised a shaky pistol, and loosed off a few slugs at a departing Returned woman, knocking dust from her chest but not affecting her progress. Soon enough, the echo of gunshots fell to nothing.

Chapter
69
James

The dead are gone and the living stand abandoned. One or two fold to the grass. Some put arms around each other. Some weep. Nobody speaks, or if they do, nobody listens.

James Spears lifts watery eyes to the sky, the impossible, vast blue of it. Sunlight sears his skin. The world overflows. Trees are in full leaf and birds of all kinds vie to out-sing and out-wing each other. Roses and rhododendrons glow, their beauty an ache in his chest.

His arms ache too, from where greyed-out fingers crushed muscle to bone. He can feel his heart beating inside the bruised flesh, ticking away the seconds remaining in his life.

Certain and relentless, like the patience of the dead.

THE END

About the Author

Bill Davidson is a Scottish writer of mainly horror and speculative fiction. His debut novel 'The Orangerie' was released the year prior to this novel by Close to the Bone Publishing and his second 'The King of Crows' was published in September 2022 by AM Ink, including in audiobook form. His debut collection 'New Gods, Old Monsters' was published by Dark Lane Books in 2020 and around 100 of his short stories have appeared in quality anthologies and magazines around the world including Ellen Datlow's prestigious Best Horror of the Year.

Look for us wherever books are sold.

Printed in Great Britain
by Amazon